WILD CAT

"Danger, desire, and sizzling-hot action! *Wild Cat* is a wild ride. Jennifer Ashley walks the razor's edge of primal passion as human and Shifter fight for their lives, their families, and a love that breaks all the rules. This is one for the keeper shelf!"   —Alyssa Day, *New York Times* bestselling author

"*Wild Cat* is a riveting read, with intriguing characters, page-turning action, and danger lurking around every turn. Ashley's Shifter world is exciting, sexy, and magical."
     —Yasmine Galenorn, *New York Times* bestselling author

PRIMAL BONDS

"[A] sexually charged and imaginative tale . . . [A] quick pace and smart, skilled writing."   —*Publishers Weekly*

"Humor and passion abound in this excellent addition to this series."   —*Fresh Fiction*

PRIDE MATES

"With her usual gift for creating imaginative plots fueled by scorchingly sensual chemistry, RITA Award–winning Ashley begins a new sexy paranormal series that neatly combines high-adrenaline suspense with humor."   —*Booklist*

"A whole new way to look at shapeshifters . . . Rousing action and sensually charged, MapQuest me the directions for Shiftertown."   —*Publishers Weekly*, "Beyond Her Book"

continued . . .

"Absolutely fabulous! . . . I was blown away by this latest release. The action and romance were evenly matched and the flow of the book kept me glued until the last page . . . Paranormal fans will be raving over this one!"

—*The Romance Readers Connection*

"Ashley has created a riveting tale that . . . explores different interpretations of human and nonhuman interaction."

—*Fresh Fiction*

THE MANY SINS OF LORD CAMERON

"Big, arrogant, sexy highlanders—Jennifer Ashley writes the kinds of heroes I crave!"

—Elizabeth Hoyt, *New York Times* bestselling author

"A sexy, passion-filled romance that will keep you reading until dawn."

—Julianne MacLean, *USA Today* bestselling author

LADY ISABELLA'S SCANDALOUS MARRIAGE

"I adore this novel: It's heartrending, funny, honest, and true. I want to know the hero—no, I want to *marry* the hero!"

—Eloisa James, *New York Times* bestselling author

"Readers rejoice! The Mackenzie brothers return as Ashley works her magic to create a unique love story brimming over with depth of emotion, unforgettable characters, sizzling passion, mystery, and a story that reaches out and grabs your heart. Brava!"   —*RT Book Reviews* (Top Pick)

"A heartfelt, emotional historical romance with danger and intrigue around every corner . . . A great read!"

—*Fresh Fiction*

THE MADNESS OF LORD IAN MACKENZIE

"Ever-versatile Ashley begins her new Victorian Highland Pleasures series with a deliciously dark and delectably sexy story of love and romantic redemption that will captivate readers with its complex characters and suspenseful plot."
—*Booklist*

"Mysterious, heartfelt, sensitive, and sensual . . . Two big thumbs up." —*Publishers Weekly*, "Beyond Her Book"

"A story full of mystery and intrigue with two wonderful, bright characters . . . I look forward to more from Jennifer Ashley, an extremely gifted author." —*Fresh Fiction*

"Brimming with mystery, suspense, an intriguing plot, villains, romance, a tormented hero, and a feisty heroine, this book is a winner. I recommend *The Madness of Lord Ian Mackenzie* to anyone looking for a great read."
—*Romance Junkies*

"Wow! All I can say is *The Madness of Lord Ian Mackenzie* is one of the best books that I have ever read. [It] gets the highest recommendation that I can give. It is a truly wonderful book." —*Once Upon A Romance*

"When you're reading a book that is a step or two—or six or seven—above the norm, you know it almost immediately. Such is the case with *The Madness of Lord Ian Mackenzie*. The characters here are so complex and so real that I was fascinated by their journey . . . [and] this story is as flat-out romantic as any I've read in a while . . . This is a series I am certainly looking forward to following."
—*All About Romance*

Berkley Sensation Titles by Jennifer Ashley

PRIDE MATES
PRIMAL BONDS
WILD CAT

THE MADNESS OF LORD IAN MACKENZIE
LADY ISABELLA'S SCANDALOUS MARRIAGE
THE MANY SINS OF LORD CAMERON

WILD CAT

JENNIFER ASHLEY

BERKLEY SENSATION, NEW YORK

THE BERKLEY PUBLISHING GROUP
Published by the Penguin Group
Penguin Group (USA) Inc.
375 Hudson Street, New York, New York 10014, USA
Penguin Group (Canada), 90 Eglinton Avenue East, Suite 700, Toronto, Ontario M4P 2Y3, Canada
(a division of Pearson Penguin Canada Inc.)
Penguin Books Ltd., 80 Strand, London WC2R 0RL, England
Penguin Group Ireland, 25 St. Stephen's Green, Dublin 2, Ireland (a division of Penguin Books Ltd.)
Penguin Group (Australia), 250 Camberwell Road, Camberwell, Victoria 3124, Australia
(a division of Pearson Australia Group Pty. Ltd.)
Penguin Books India Pvt. Ltd., 11 Community Centre, Panchsheel Park, New Delhi—110 017, India
Penguin Group (NZ), 67 Apollo Drive, Rosedale, Auckland 0632, New Zealand
(a division of Pearson New Zealand Ltd.)
Penguin Books (South Africa) (Pty.) Ltd., 24 Sturdee Avenue, Rosebank, Johannesburg 2196,
South Africa

Penguin Books Ltd., Registered Offices: 80 Strand, London WC2R 0RL, England

This is a work of fiction. Names, characters, places, and incidents either are the product of the author's imagination or are used fictitiously, and any resemblance to actual persons, living or dead, business establishments, events, or locales is entirely coincidental. The publisher does not have any control over and does not assume any responsibility for author or third-party websites or their content.

WILD CAT

A Berkley Sensation Book / published by arrangement with the author

PRINTING HISTORY
Berkley Sensation mass-market edition / January 2012

Copyright © 2012 by Jennifer Ashley.
Excerpt from *Mate Claimed* by Jennifer Ashley copyright © by Jennifer Ashley.
Cover art by Franco Accornero.
Cover design by George Long.
Hand lettering by Ron Zinn.
Interior text design by Laura K. Corless.

ISBN: 978-0-425-24578-1

BERKLEY SENSATION®
Berkley Sensation Books are published by The Berkley Publishing Group,
a division of Penguin Group (USA) Inc.,
375 Hudson Street, New York, New York 10014.
BERKLEY SENSATION® is a registered trademark of Penguin Group (USA) Inc.
The "B" design is a trademark of Penguin Group (USA) Inc.

PRINTED IN THE UNITED STATES OF AMERICA

10 9 8 7 6 5 4 3 2 1

ACKNOWLEDGMENTS

Thanks go to my editor, Kate Seaver, and everyone at Berkley Publishing who puts so much hard work into editing and producing these books. I'd also like to thank the readers who love the Shifters and encourage me to write more about them. For more information about the Shifters and their world, visit the Shifter series site on the web page www.jennifersromances.com.

CHAPTER ONE

Heights. Damn it, why does it have to be heights?
Diego Escobar scanned the steel beams of the unfinished skyscraper against a gray morning sky, and acid seared his stomach.

Heights had never bothered him until two years ago, when five meth-heads had hung him over the penthouse balcony of a thirty-story hotel and threatened to drop him. His partner, Jobe, a damn good cop, had put his weapon on the balcony floor and raised his hands to save Diego's life. The men had pulled Diego to safety and then casually shot them both. Diego had survived; Jobe hadn't.

Diego's rage and grief had manifested into an obsessive fear of heights. Now, going up even three floors in a glass elevator could give him cold sweats.

"Way the hell up there?" he asked Rogers, the uniform cop.

"Yes, sir."

Shit.

"Hooper's pretty sure it's not human," Rogers said. "He says it moves too fast, jumps too far. But he hasn't got a visual yet."

Not human meant Shifter. This was getting better and better. "Hooper's up there alone?"

"Jemez is with him. They think they have the Shifter cornered on the fifty-first level."

The *fifty-first* level? "Tell me you're fucking kidding me."

"No, sir. There's an elevator. We got the electric company to turn on the power."

Diego looked at the rusty doors Rogers indicated, then up, up, and up through the grid of beams into empty space. He could see nothing but the gray dawn sky between the crisscross of girders. His mouth went dry.

This cluster of buildings in the middle of nowhere—which was to have been an apartment complex, hotel, office tower, and shopping center—had been under construction for years. The project had started to great fanfare, designed to draw tourists and locals away from the heavily trafficked Strip. But construction slowed, and so many investors pulled out that building had ground to a halt. Now the unfinished skyscraper sat like a rusting blot on the empty desert.

Tracking Shifters wasn't Diego's department. Diego was a detective in vice. He'd responded to the call for help with a trespasser because he'd been heading to work and his route took him right by the construction site. Diego figured he'd help Rogers chase down the miscreant and drive on in.

Now Rogers wanted Diego to jaunt to the fifty-first level, where there weren't any floors, for crying out loud, and chase a suspect who might be a Shifter. Shifters were dangerous—people who could become animals. Or, maybe animals who became people. The jury was still out. In any case, they'd been classified as too dangerous to live with humans, rounded up into Shiftertowns, and made to wear Collars that regulated their violent tendencies.

Diego had heard that regular guns didn't always bring them down, Shifters having amazing metabolisms. Shifter Division used tranquilizers when they needed to shoot a Shifter, but Diego was fresh out of those. Rogers, rotund and near retirement, watched Diego with a bland expression, making it clear he had no intention of going up after the Shifter himself.

A high-pitched scream rang down from on high. It was a

woman's scream—Maria Jemez—followed by a man's bellow of surprise and pain. Then, silence.

"Damn it." Diego ran for the elevator. "Stay down here, call Shifter Division, and get more backup. Tell them to bring tranqs." He got into the lift and shut the doors, blocking out Rogers' "Yes, sir."

The lift clanked its way up through the few completed finished floors, then onto floors that were nothing but beams and catwalks. The elevator was an open cage, so Diego got to watch the ground and Rogers recede, far too rapidly.

Fifty-first level. Damn.

Diego had been chasing criminals through towering hotels for years without thinking a thing about it. He and the sheriff's department even had followed one idiot high up onto a cable tower two hundred feet above Hoover Dam five years ago, and Diego hadn't flinched.

A bunch of cop-hating meth dealers hang him over a balcony, and he goes to pieces.

It stops now. This is where I get my own back.

Diego rolled back the gate on the fifty-first level. The sun was rising, the mountains west of town bathed in pink and orange splendor. The Las Vegas valley was a beautiful place, its stark white desert contrasting with the mountains that rose in a knifelike wall on the horizon. Visitors down in the city kept their eyes on the gaming tables and slot machines, uncaring of what went on outside the casinos, but the beauty of the valley always tugged at Diego.

Diego drew his Sig and stepped off the lift into eerie silence. Something flitted in his peripheral vision, something that moved too lightly to be Hooper, who was a big, muscular guy who liked big, muscular guns. Diego aimed, but the movement vanished.

He stepped softly across the board catwalk, moving into the deeper shadow of a beam. The catwalk groaned under his feet. There were no lights up here, just the faint flush of morning and the glow from the work lights down on the ground that the power company had turned on.

Diego saw the movement again to his left, and then, damned if he didn't see a similar flit to his right.

Son of a bitch—*two* of them?

A sound like the cross between a pop and a kiss came from down the catwalk the instant before something pinged above Diego's head. Diego hit the floor instinctively, trying not to panic as his feet slid over the catwalk's edge.

His heart pounded triple-time, his throat so dry it closed up tight.

What the hell was he doing? He should have confessed his secret fear of heights, gone to psychiatric evaluation, stayed behind a desk. But no, he'd been too determined to keep his job, too determined to beat it himself, too embarrassed to admit the weakness. Now he was endangering others because of his stupid fear.

Shut up and think.

Whatever had pinged hadn't been a bullet. Too soft. Diego got his feet back onto the catwalk and crawled to find what had fallen to the boards. A dart, he saw, the kind shot by a tranquilizer gun.

Uniforms didn't carry tranqs, and Shifter Division hadn't showed up yet. That meant that one of the Shifters he was chasing up here had a tranquilizer gun. Perfect. Put the nice cop to sleep, and then do anything you want with him, including pushing his body over the edge.

Diego moved in a crouch across the catwalk to the next set of shadows. The sun streaked across the valley to Mount Charleston in the west, light radiant on its snow-covered crown. More snow was predicted up there for the weekend. Diego had contemplated driving up on Saturday night to sip hot toddies in a snowbound cabin, maybe with something warm and female by his side.

On the other side of the next beam, Diego found Bud Hooper and Maria Jemez. Maria was fairly new, just out of the academy, too baby-faced to be up here chasing crazy Shifters. The two cops were slumped together in a heap, still warm, breathing slowly.

Diego heard footsteps, running fast—too fast to be human. He swung around as a shadow detached itself from the catwalk in front of him and rose in a graceful leap to the next level.

Diego stared, openmouthed. The thing wasn't human—it

had the long limbs of a cat, but its face was half human, like a cross between human and animal. Did Shifters look like that? He'd thought they were either animal or human, but as he watched, gun ready, he realized he was seeing one in midshift.

The Shifter landed on open beams on the next floor up, then its shape flowed, as it ran, into the lithe form of a big cat. Morning sunlight caught on white fur and the flash of green eyes. Snow leopard? It sprinted along the beam, never losing its balance, and vanished back into the shadows.

Diego heard a step behind him. He whipped around in time to see the flash of a rifle barrel in the sunlight, aiming directly at him. He heard the pop as his reflexes made him dive for the floor.

He came up on his elbows to return fire, but there was nothing to aim at. Whoever had the tranq rifle had vanished back into the shadows.

All was silence. Nothing but rising wind humming through the building.

Diego reassessed his situation. He had a Shifter running around up here, plus one asshole with a tranquilizer gun. Someone hunting a Shifter? Could be. The laws about humans hunting un-Collared Shifters—those Shifters who had refused to take the Collar and live in Shiftertowns—had loosened in the last couple years.

But this Shifter hunter had pegged Jemez and Hooper with tranqs, and was trying to shoot Diego too. Why, if the guy was hunting the Shifter legally?

Another pop had him rolling out of the way just before a dart struck the catwalk where Diego's head had been.

As he scrambled up again, the catwalk, loosened and dry-rotted from years under the desert sun, slid out from under his feet. Diego lunged at the nearest steel beam, the metal burning his skin as he tried and failed to grab it.

The catwalk's boards splintered and came away from the bolts. Diego's heart jammed in his throat as his body dropped. Splinters rained past him. At the last desperate moment, he got one arm hooked around a girder, and he hung there, stuck like a bug fifty-one stories up.

Son of a fucking—

He couldn't swing his feet around to get them back on the girder. His arm shook hard. He realized he still held his Sig in his other hand, but for some reason, he could not make himself open his fingers and let it go.

His arm was aching, and he was slipping. He was going to fall. Five hundred feet to the ground. Why the hell hadn't he asked to be put on desk duty?

Diego tried to swing his feet up again, but he missed the girder. The jolt of his feet swinging back down nearly jarred him loose. That's it, his hold was going. *Damn it, damn it, damn it . . .*

Two strong hands caught Diego under his shoulders; two very strong arms dragged him up and up, stomach grating on the beam, and onto the catwalk. Diego lay there, facedown on the relative solidity of a catwalk, drawing long, shuddering breaths.

When he could, he rolled onto his back and found himself looking up into the white green eyes and ferocious face of the Shifter, again in its half-shifted state. A female Shifter, from the hint of breasts under the fur and from the sheer, strange beauty of her. She had a wildcat's face, and the morning light glinted on silver links of a chain around her neck.

Before Diego could find his voice, the Shifter spun away in another gravity-defying leap. She landed on all fours, flowing back into the shape of a snow leopard. Diego sat up and watched her, stunned by the beauty of the long, powerful animal running with inhuman grace fifty stories above the ground.

Another pop of the tranq gun had him on the floor on his stomach again, this catwalk staying in place. Diego raised his head, finger on his trigger. He heard a snarl, the leopard's angry growl, and then running feet, both human and animal.

Diego pointed the gun through the shadows, but he could see nothing. The rising sun showed that he was on this floor alone, though the footsteps continued above him. Lights approached on the road below, Shifter Division finally arriving, bringing a couple patrol cars and an SUV.

A blinding flash lit up the floor above him. Diego squinted through the spaces in the catwalks, aiming, but the light vanished as suddenly as it had appeared. The running ceased, and all was silent except for the patrol cars' sirens wailing below.

Diego lowered his Sig and was about to sit up when two feet landed on the catwalk in front of his face.

Two human feet, female feet, naked feet. Diego lifted his head to find two strong female legs, skin tanned from the desert sun, right in front of him. He looked up those legs to two strong thighs, with an enticing thatch of dark blond between them.

Diego forced his gaze to continue upward, over her flat stomach with a small gold stud in her navel to firm human breasts tipped with dusky nipples. He made his gaze move past *them*—though he knew he'd dream about them for a long time coming—to be rewarded by a breathtaking face.

The Shifter woman's face was strong but contained the softness of beauty. Her eyes were light green, a shimmer of jade in the darkness. Sleek, pale hair fell past her shoulders, and a chain with a Celtic cross fused to it glinted around her slender throat.

Damn. And *damn*.

She was definitely all woman, not in any in-between state now. Diego had never seen a female Shifter before. His cases had never taken him to Shiftertown, which lay north of North Las Vegas, and he'd only ever seen the male Shiftertown leader, Eric Warden. He'd had no idea that their females were this tall or this crazy gorgeous.

Her breasts rose with her even breath, and she expressed no embarrassment at her nakedness, didn't even seem to notice it. "He's gone," she said. "You all right?"

"Alive," Diego croaked. He dragged himself to his feet, trying not to look at her delectable body or to imagine what that smooth, tanned skin would feel like under his hands. "Where'd he go? The guy with the tranq gun?"

"I don't know." The answer seemed to trouble her. The man hadn't fallen, the lift wasn't moving, and no one below was chasing him.

"At least I've got one of you," Diego said.

"Wha—?" She stared at him, stunned, then her light-colored eyes flicked to the beams above, calculated the distance. Diego brought up his pistol.

"Don't try it, sweetheart. Get facedown on the floor, hands behind your back."

"Why? I just saved your ass."

"You're trespassing on private property, that's why, and I have two cops down. On the floor."

He gestured with the gun. The Shifter woman drew an enraged breath, eyes flashing almost pure white. For a moment, Diego thought she'd leap at him, maybe change into the wildcat or half Shifter and try to shred him. He'd have to plug her, and he really didn't want to. It would be a shame to kill something so beautiful.

The Shifter woman let out her breath, gave him an angry glare, and then carefully lowered herself facedown on the catwalk. Diego unclipped his handcuffs.

"What's your name?" Diego asked.

Her jaw tightened. "Cassidy."

"Nice to meet you, Cassidy," Diego said. "You have the right to remain silent." He droned on through Miranda as he closed the handcuffs on her perfect wrists. The Shifter woman lay still and radiated rage.

Diego's hands were shaking by the time he finished. But that had less to do with his fear of heights than with the tall, beautiful naked woman on the floor in front of him, hands locked together on her sweet, tight ass. The best ass he'd ever seen in his life. He wanted nothing more than to stay up here and lick that beautiful backside, and maybe apply his tongue to the rest of her body.

Diego broke into a sweat, despite the cool wind wafting from below, and made himself haul her to her feet. The Shifter woman's look was still defiant, but he couldn't help himself imagining crushing her against him to kiss that wide, enticing mouth.

Diego made himself steer her to the lift.

Not until they were rapidly descending did Diego realize that since Cassidy in her human form had come into his view, he'd not once thought about how far he might have fallen had she not caught him, and the spectacular splat he'd have made when he hit the ground.

CHAPTER TWO

The hunter watched from his safe perch, tranq gun on the girder beside him. He seethed in frustration as Cassidy Warden was led off and stuffed into the back of the patrol car, the damn cops ruining what he needed to do. He'd been so close.

Nothing personal, Shifter bitch, but I need your blood. All of it. It's the only thing that's going to open the gate for me.

The hunter hated himself for what he'd become, someone who would hunt another for something more than basic survival.

It is survival! part of him screamed.

No, it was the perversion of what was natural. It was something *they* would do. They'd made him become like them—cruel, obsessive, ignoring the pain of others—and for that they'd pay.

He had to get Cassidy first. It was the spring equinox, a year after he'd first tried the spell, failing because the human hunters he'd hired made such a mess of it. Cassidy's mate had died for nothing. The Shifter male had been sacrificed needlessly, and the hunter hated that.

This time, he'd work alone, trusting no one. But he had to hurry. The spell had to be worked at the equinox or the few days on either side of it. Time was running out. Cassidy was the best candidate—she was strong, powerfully strong, and besides, she was still grieving her mate, and Shifters were barely alive when they grieved. He'd be doing her a favor, he'd convinced himself.

His self-loathing filled him again, but his need to work the spell overrode it. He needed to get home. He could taste it. Exile was bitter. This time, he'd succeed, no matter what.

They gave Cassidy a blue coverall to wear and made her sit alone in the interrogation room, her hands on the table. At least they'd let her out of the cuffs.

The room smelled like something rotten, the walls dirty yellow and puke green. Shifters liked warm colors, clean paint, and places that didn't stink of human sweat. Humans considered Shifters to be wild and dangerous, but Shifters had much better taste in décor.

The door opened, and Cassidy tensed. She'd been sitting in here for hours, no one coming to her, no one offering to let her call a lawyer, or even her brother. But that, she'd heard, was what they did with Shifters.

The man who came in was the cop she'd saved up in the building. Lieutenant Escobar, she'd heard the others call him.

He'd been the one to usher her into the back of the patrol car, after he'd draped a blanket around her naked body. His movements had been quick, efficient, his large hands warm.

She hadn't realized that humans could be so warm. His voice was dark, sliding around her in liquid syllables, though he hadn't spoken directly to her since telling Cassidy her rights.

Which he should have known wasn't required for Shifters. The man must not know much about Shifters or human laws for Shifters. So why had they sent him in here?

Lieutenant Escobar gave her a dark-eyed look as he shut the door. Without saying a word, he moved to the table and placed a file folder on it. He took off his suit coat—again, his movements economical—and draped the coat over the back of a chair.

His white button-down shirt hugged powerful muscles, his black holster and butt of his gun stark against his left side. If he removed the shirt, she knew she'd see an undershirt pasted against hard abs, muscles solid under dark skin.

Escobar's black hair was cut short, almost buzzed, which emphasized the sharp lines of his face and a scar that cut across his temple to his forehead. His dark, almost black eyes held intelligence and something even an alpha Shifter would acknowledge.

I'm not taking shit from you, those eyes told her. *If I like what you say, I might play square with you. Try to fuck with me, and you'll regret it.*

He sat down, smoothing his tie so it wouldn't be caught by the table's edge. Escobar opened the file folder and flicked a switch next to the small microphone on the table.

Without looking at her, he said, "Interview with Cassidy Warden, Shifter from the Southern Nevada Shiftertown, by Lieutenant Diego Escobar, arresting officer." Diego looked up at Cassidy with those bottomless eyes. "Tell me, Ms. Warden, what you were doing at a closed construction site forty miles west of your Shiftertown."

Cassidy felt a strange impulse to blurt out the whole story—*tell me everything, and it will be all right*, he seemed to say. But Escobar was human, and Cassidy had to be careful. Going out to make her peace with the place her mate had died was only half the story.

"Shiftertowns aren't prisons, Lieutenant," she said, pinning him with her gaze. "I'm allowed to come and go as I please."

He didn't seem impressed. Diego Escobar either didn't understand that her looking straight into his eyes was a challenge to his authority, or maybe he just didn't give a rat's ass.

"You broke into a fenced-off property on a shut-down, private construction site," he said. "Plus you endangered the lives of three police officers, one of which happened to be me. So, tell me what you were doing there."

Cassidy folded her arms. "None of your business."

Diego eyed her for a moment longer, then he flicked off the microphone, stood up, and came to her side of the table.

He was angry; she could scent that and tell from every tense line on his body. He'd shown deep rage at the construction site too, not necessarily at Cassidy. A man like him shouldn't fear anything, and yet, in the unfinished skyscraper, he'd been afraid, with a deep gut-wrenching fear, and that was before he'd fallen.

Diego looked at Cassidy for a while, then he leaned one hip on the table, arms folded across his chest. The movement made his muscles play, but it also let him keep his hand near his gun.

"Shifter Division had a cage in their SUV," he said in a flat voice. "They wanted to subdue you with shock sticks, lock you in that cage, and haul you back here. Without the blanket."

Cassidy flinched but she didn't break eye contact. "Typical human fear response," she said, trying to sound bored.

"You know why they didn't, *mi ja*?" He pinned her with eyes like pieces of night. "Because I told them not to. I'm the only reason you're not downstairs, naked in an animal cage, with the shits in Shifter Division walking around you deciding what they want to do to you."

How did he want her to respond? She didn't know how to react to humans, especially not to one like him. Humans she danced with at the clubs were different—but those were Shifter groupies who would do anything even to stand next to a Shifter. Diego Escobar was a human who didn't care that she responded to the warmth and scent of him, that she was a female Shifter without a mate.

Diego leaned to her. "You cooperate with me and tell me what I want to know, or by regulation, I have to let Shifter Division have you."

Cassidy looked right back at him. "Are you playing good cop, bad cop?" she asked tightly. "I've heard about that."

"I'm playing *you tell me what I want to know or I escort you downstairs*. There's no choice, no games. They only let me talk to you because I claimed you saved my life up there." Diego sat back, holding her with eyes so dark. "Why did you?"

Cassidy shrugged. She was still wound up from her run from the hunter who'd chased her up into the tower, the edge barely off her fighting instincts.

The hunter had been stalking her, she realized that now, and must have been waiting for her in the place Donovan had died. She'd picked up the hunter's scent before she'd gotten the candles lit, and she'd slipped into the woods to shift, but he'd found her before she could get away from him.

Cassidy had led the hunter back down into the desert, thinking she could lose a human in the giant, half-finished building on the outskirts of town, but damned if he hadn't followed her right up into it. His seeming defiance of gravity proved that he wasn't human, nor was he Shifter. He'd terrified her.

The chase, the cops' arrival, saving Diego from falling, and then the feel of Diego's hands as he cuffed her—all had Cassidy's Shifter adrenaline soaring. Sitting here waiting had increased her tension, not eased it. She needed the comfort of physical contact, to be held and stroked until she calmed down.

She looked up at Diego and wanted to touch him. No, she *needed* to touch him. To brush his skin, to feel the rough of whiskers on his face. He'd shaved—she smelled the faint odor of aftershave lotion—but his dark skin was already touched by new growth. A man who had to shave religiously or have a permanent five o'clock shadow.

Most humans seemed uncomfortable with their own bodies, but Diego Escobar leaned against the table with ease, knowing he controlled the room. His eyes were hard but had little crinkles in the corners, which meant he smiled sometimes.

Cassidy reached out her hand, slowly so she wouldn't startle him, and rested it, softly, on his thigh.

Steel hard muscles met her touch, and Cassidy closed her eyes. Diego's flesh was warm beneath the fabric of his pants, and oh, Goddess, wouldn't it be heaven to touch his bare skin? His skin would be hot and smooth, tight against the strength beneath it.

Cassidy's rising need surprised her, but she didn't move her hand. She hadn't touched a male since Donovan's death, hadn't had a sensual thought until Diego Escobar had looked at her with sin-dark eyes fifty stories above the ground.

Cassidy opened her eyes. Diego held himself so still, watching her, not making a move to touch her in return.

"You're supposed to keep your hands on the table," he said.

Cassidy curled her fingers into her palm and drew her hand away. A shudder of pain went through her. She was never going to calm down.

"Please," she said. Goddess, now she was begging. Second in command of Shiftertown, Cassidy Warden was begging a human for sympathy.

"All you have to do is tell me what you were doing up there."

"No, I mean. I need . . ."

She couldn't explain. Cassidy got out of the chair. Diego watched her come, not pulling his weapon, but not moving his hand from near it, as though curious to see what she'd do. Cassidy read in his eyes that he'd let her do only what he wanted her to, nothing more.

Cassidy put her hands on his folded arms. Diego remained still. She slid her palms up his arms, the female in her responding to the firm strength of biceps under the shirt. On up to his shoulders, which held even more power, while Diego simply watched her.

His warmth was calming, amazingly so. Cassidy had never touched a human before, not like this. She'd had no idea that touching one would be so comforting, so satisfying. It eased something in her that had been tight for a long time.

Diego still didn't move as Cassidy stroked her hands up his neck to his close-cut dark hair. She liked how the ends of his hair felt, soft yet prickly. Cassidy cupped his face, his whiskers like fine sandpaper against her fingertips. She read rigid anger in dark eyes, vast pain and guilt. Unhappiness she didn't understand.

Diego's voice, when he finally spoke, was completely steady. "You need to sit back down, Ms. Warden."

"Wait. Not yet."

Diego put one hand on her wrist. She noticed that he kept his other hand over his gun, snapped inside the holster, keeping her away from it.

"You need to obey the rules."

He wasn't afraid of her; he was stating facts. Cassidy's adrenaline wouldn't let her obey any rules but Shifter instinct. She twined her fingers through the backs of his and raised his hand to her face.

"Please, just a little while," she said. "I'm so scared."

Diego's eyes flickered, and Cassidy couldn't believe she'd said that. Admitting fear was the last thing she should do.

"You'll be all right," Diego said. "I've got you."

I've got you. Three simple words, but Cassidy felt a blanket of safety wrap around her. She knew damn well it was a false blanket and that she needed to get the hell out of here, but the basic need inside her responded to the firm strength of his voice.

Cassidy let go of Diego's hand, wrapped her arms around him, and pulled him close.

Diego found himself with his arms full of tall, beautiful Shifter woman, her naked body obvious beneath the baggy coverall. *Dios mio.*

He thanked all the saints that no one was in the observation room—at least that he knew of. Diego had spent two hours persuading Shifter Division and his captain to let him interrogate Cassidy Warden alone. Cassidy could have let Diego die up there in that tower, and she hadn't. Diego wanted to find out why.

But it was against all procedure—Shifter Division viewed Shifters as deadly, unstable animals, no matter what form they were in, no matter that their Collars were supposed to keep them tamed. Diego had won a few minutes alone with Cassidy only because his captain sided with him—reluctantly. Diego hadn't lied when he'd said that if he couldn't persuade Cassidy to talk, he'd have to give her to Shifter Division. He sure as hell didn't want to.

Now, Diego felt Cassidy Warden's long body against his, the sleek warmth of her hair on his cheek. He inhaled the scent of her, which, considering she'd been running around naked in the desert plus sitting in here for hours, was sweet and good.

Diego's body responded. He'd kept himself celibate too long, and this woman was beautiful.

No, she was damn *hot*. He remembered her fine ass when he'd locked the cuffs on her wrists, her beautiful breasts when she'd stood over him on the catwalk.

He felt those breasts now, still unfettered, against him, her strong thighs along the length of his. She had one sweet, gorgeous body, and her face was strong and lovely. A man would have to be dead not to respond to her.

More than that, Diego wanted to lean her back over the

interrogation table, open those coveralls, and explore everything he found inside the package. Beautiful, warm woman.
Sex with Cassidy would be . . . explosive.

But Diego also felt her fear. He'd heard truth ring when
she'd said, *I'm so scared.* It had cost this woman a lot to say
the words.

Cassidy wasn't afraid of Diego. Or of being arrested, he
sensed, as though she didn't truly believe the bad shit that
could happen to her here. Diego needed to figure out what the
hell was going on. It killed Diego to push her away, but he had
to do it. Spreading her across the interrogation table, as fulfill-
ing as that might be, would be the end of him.

"Sit down, Ms. Warden," he said into her ear, liking how
the softness of her hair tickled his lips. "And tell me about the
man with the tranquilizer gun."

Cassidy lifted her head. Her eyes were white green as
she stared into his, her breath coming fast. The silver Collar
around her throat was so damn sexy, though Diego knew it
was a controlling device, which would pump shocks and pain
into her if she turned violent.

Diego wanted to stroke her hair, to tell her that he'd take
care of her and she'd be all right. He wouldn't let anyone, or
anything, hurt her.

He deliberately did not touch her.

Cassidy looked at him for a moment longer, drew a breath,
and very slowly sat down again. Diego flicked on the microphone, looked at her, and waited.

"I don't know who the man up there was," Cassidy said.
"I never saw him before, and I didn't get a good look at him."

Diego nodded, encouraging her. "Why were you chasing
him?"

Fear flickered through her eyes again. "He was chasing
me. That's why I ran into the building. The two cops saw us
and came up, and he shot them."

"Why was he after you?"

"I don't know. Maybe he wanted a Shifter pelt to hang on
his wall. Hunters are allowed to shoot Collarless Shifters, you
know. Sometimes they don't bother to check whether they
have a Collar or not."

Her tone was bitter, grief and rage tainting it. Diego had

read the file on Cassidy Warden, so he thought he knew what she meant.

"Another reason you shouldn't have been running out there on your own," Diego said. "What happened to your clothes?"

Cassidy touched the top button of the coverall just below her Collar. Diego couldn't stop his gaze from going there, down into the shadow between her breasts. "I chucked my clothes. I needed to strip to shift."

And wouldn't Diego have loved to have seen that? "Leaving behind your money or any ID . . ."

"I hadn't brought it with me," Cassidy said quickly.

"Which is illegal for a Shifter. Why did you leave everything at home?"

Cassidy's gaze flicked sideways. She was trying to decide what to tell him. She was a bad liar, but Diego sensed that she lied out of fear, not cunning. He was very familiar with lies born of fear. He'd told them for years.

Cassidy wet her lips and shrugged again. "I wanted a run. I'd been cooped up too long. I needed to get away, out of Shiftertown, be somewhere else . . ."

Diego snapped off the microphone. "Stop."

She jumped. "What?"

Diego leaned his fists on the table to look into her face. Her green eyes were so near his own, and he could feel her breath on his face.

"Listen to me, *chiquita*. Trespassing isn't a misdemeanor for Shifters. It's a crime with a prison sentence attached. I know you didn't hurt Hooper and Jemez, because that guy with the gun shot at me too, and I watched you chase him off. But there's no evidence, only my word, and yours, and you have to know by now that the word of a Shifter isn't worth shit. If you admit you were running around in the desert for the hell of it, and some crazy Shifter hunter started chasing you, I can help you. You start talking about running away from your Shiftertown, and I can't help you anymore. They'll tranq you and lock you up. I'm your best shot at freedom, *mi ja*, so shut up."

No Shifter, besides her brother Eric, would look at Cassidy like this or get in her face and talk to her in that stern, *obey-me* voice. Not unless he wanted to be knocked across

the room or go up against her pissed-off brother. But Diego
Escobar wasn't asking for submission or fealty. He was trying
to get Cassidy to understand, to obey because it was necessary. To trust him, because he knew the rules of this place,
and Cassidy didn't.

Diego turned the microphone back on. Cassidy's heart beat
in slow, thick beats as she leaned toward it. "I needed a run for
the hell of it," she said carefully. "To let off steam."

Diego gave her a look that said she'd finally got it. "Good.
Now tell me why."

"Because I lost my mate. It's the anniversary of his death,
and I was going to the place he died to make my peace with it.
All right?" That part was the truth.

Cassidy blinked back angry tears. Diego was human—he'd
never understand. Donovan had been her mate. You didn't just
say a eulogy and get over it.

Diego looked at the file on the table but not because he
was conceding ground. He was giving her a moment to col-
lect herself.

"Donavan Grady," he read. "The Feline Shifter who was
living with you. Died a year ago."

"He was my *mate*, not just living with me. The union was
blessed under sun and moon. Not that humans understand
what that means."

One year ago, Donovan's mother and Cassidy had burned
photos and mementos of Donovan under the moonlight, while
their clans moved in solemn circles around them, easing Donovan into the Summerland. The Guardian—the Shifter whose
sword turned a Shifter's dead body to dust—had done his job,
and Eric had held Cassidy as she'd wept.

Donovan the fun-loving *any-excuse-for-a-party-baby* Shifter
had been killed, before his time and for nothing. Cassidy had
avoided the place of his passing for a long, long while, but tonight, something had drawn her there. Tomorrow, on the exact
night of his death, they'd have his remembrance ceremony at
home, but she'd wanted to burn an offering, alone, in the place
of his dying. But someone had been there, waiting for her . . .

"I'm sorry," Diego was saying. "I know it's rough, losing
someone."

Cassidy looked up to find his gaze on her again. He'd turned off the microphone, and understanding lingered behind his no-nonsense stare. He knew.

Because, Cassidy realized in shock, he'd lost someone too.

"Was it someone close to you?" she asked.

Diego gave her a surprised look, then he cleared his throat. "My partner. Jobe Sanderson. My best friend."

"I'm sorry," Cassidy said, heartfelt. "I'll say a blessing for you." A lit candle, a prayer to the Goddess for the human Jobe now in the Summerland.

Diego said nothing, but hurt and grief screamed for touch. Drawn to his pain, Cassidy slid her hand over his, giving him a touch to soothe and ease, like a cat might curl into another for comfort.

Diego's gaze flicked to their hands as Cassidy drew her fingers along the curve between his thumb and forefinger. He looked up at her, and they watched each other for a while, Cassidy's heart pounding like crazy, Diego never moving.

After a long time, Diego lifted her hand, placed it back on the table, and turned on the microphone.

"Cassidy Warden," he said. "Because you have no police record, and because I saw the third person with a tranquilizer gun fire at me, I'm not going to charge you for the trespassing. I'll record that I gave you a warning, and that you swear to stay out of restricted areas. Also, I'm confining you to your Shiftertown for a period of two weeks, so you'll have time to calm down and think about it. Interview ended at twenty-one hundred hours."

Cassidy opened her mouth in outrage, but Diego held up his hand, stopping her as he turned off the microphone again.

"I can't stay in Shiftertown for two *weeks*!"

Diego closed the file and lifted his coat, his movements brusque and no longer warm. "I can't let you go without some kind of punishment. I'll be checking up on you to make sure you do it. This is my call, Cassidy. I'm putting my ass on the line for you. Don't make me regret it."

She stared at him. Diego looked back at her, that same unfathomable gaze locking her in place.

"Why would you put your ass on the line for me?" Cassidy asked. *Your very fine ass.*

Diego slid his strong arms into his coat. "I don't know, *mi ja*. Maybe because you could have let me fall but you helped me instead; maybe because I like your face. Whatever reason, you got lucky. Now go. I called your brother before I came in here. He should be waiting for you downstairs."

Eric. The relief that her brother had come made Cassidy want to spring up and run to him, but she forced herself to rise calmly. She liked how tall Diego was when they stood toe-to-toe. He was almost the same height as Eric, and he smelled good, like dust and sunshine.

Diego opened the door of the interrogation room and gestured her to leave in front of him. The human-style courtesy betrayed how different their worlds were—a Shifter male would walk out first, checking the hall for danger before beckoning the female out the door. How humans had survived this long, Cassidy had no idea.

Cassidy passed Diego in the doorway, keeping her gaze on him. "You're a shithead, Lieutenant Escobar."

His answering smile erased every hard line on his face and made his eyes sparkle. His eyes were so dark, so deep, an entire world within them.

"I do my best, *mi ja*," he said. "Go home."

Diego walked away from her, leaving her to the uniformed policewoman who waited outside in the hall.

His backside moved nicely under his coat. Cassidy thought about the feel of his body against hers, and a shiver went through her as she continued to watch Diego walk away. No doubt about it—despite being human, despite him placing a curfew on her, Diego Escobar was *hot*.

Eric waited for Cassidy downstairs, all six and a half feet of him, his jade green eyes holding concern. Jace, Eric's full-grown son, waited with him, eyes just as green but holding more restlessness.

As the policewoman let her out through the locked door, Cassidy ran to her brother and nephew, and they closed arms around her in a strong, soul-healing hug.

Diego's captain grabbed him before Diego had the chance to return to his desk and start his report. Beckoning Diego to follow him into his office, Captain Maxwell went inside and snapped at Diego to close the door.

Captain John Maxwell stood five feet six and looked thin enough to be taken out in one blow. But the man could out-shoot every person in his command and pin a two-hundred-and-fifty-pound biker to the wall and cuff him in five seconds flat. A reminder that looks could be deceiving.

Captain Max now turned a look of fury on Diego. "You are damn lucky I was the only one in the observation room, Escobar. What the hell were you doing?"

"I didn't touch her," Diego said.

"No, you let her crawl all over you instead. I thought she was going to lick you."

Diego had thought so too, and the visual that came with the thought was hot and satisfying. "She stopped when I told her to."

Captain Max gave him a don't-bullshit-me-I'm-not-in-the-mood look. "Confining her to Shiftertown for all of two weeks? That's *it*? Shifter Division is going to shit a brick."

"If I charged her with trespassing, they'd lock her up," Diego said. "You know that. A judge can give her a death sentence for trespassing, if that judge is asshole enough to do it. Cassidy didn't do anything. Who cares about a building rusting in the desert?"

"And she's gorgeous," Captain Max said.

Diego couldn't stop his grin. "OK, so that didn't hurt."

"Damn you, Escobar. I thought your brother was the maverick. You're supposed to be the steady one, the responsible one." Captain Max shoved some file folders around his desk, which he did when trying to relieve his temper. "I'm holding you responsible for this Shifter woman, Escobar. I want you checking on her every day. *Every* day, do you understand? Whether you're on duty or off, weekdays and weekends. Got it?"

So much for the cabin on Charleston. "Yes, sir."

"She so much as sets her toe outside Shiftertown, Shifter Division gets her. If she screws up, I'm putting the blame entirely on you. It's your ass that will get kicked, not mine. Understand?"

Diego nodded. He knew that Captain Max would do his best to save Diego if things went wrong, as he had done before, but Diego didn't want to put Captain Max in that position ever again.

"Yes, sir," Diego said, and left the office, dismissed.

CHAPTER THREE

"Tell me again."

Eric didn't need to be told again, and Cassidy knew it. But she also knew that the story bothered him, especially the part about the hunter's sudden disappearance. He'd want to hear it again in case there had been some detail he'd missed.

Cassidy humored him and told him the story from beginning to end, while Eric stood at the barbeque in the backyard, fork in hand, muscles moving under his spiraling tattoo as he turned the steaks. Cassidy omitted that fact that, in the interrogation room, she'd had an uncontrollable need to touch Diego, to embrace him, and hadn't stopped herself. She also neglected to mention how much clinging to Diego had both comforted and confused her.

Eric went silent as he flipped a red piece of meat, the juices sizzling on the coals. He kept his gaze on the grill, but Cassidy knew that her brother was thinking through the story, reassessing it.

"This hunter wasn't Shifter?" he asked after a time.

"Couldn't have been. I would have scented Shifter." Cassidy rubbed her arms, cold despite the balmy March temperature. "I've never smelled anything like him, actually."

Eric looked at her, green eyes sharp. He didn't say anything, just stood still while one muscle moved in his jaw. Then he said, "Hmm."

"What?" Cassidy asked, worried. "What are you thinking?"

"I'm thinking the human cop is right, and you should stay close to home."

"I didn't finish making the offering."

"Finish it another time, Cass. Donovan would understand."

Cassidy felt the anger, which a year of grief had honed. "I'm going to find the bastards who killed him."

Eric's look softened. "I know you are." He pulled his sister into a one-armed embrace, the other hand still holding the barbeque fork. "You'll do it, Cass. But not tonight. Now, help me cook this mess of steaks. The trackers are going to help us eat them, and you know Brody's always hungry."

The next day after work, Diego drove his restored Thunderbird into Shiftertown and stopped in front of Eric Warden's house.

Shiftertown wasn't at all what Diego had thought it would be. This one had existed on the north edge of town for twenty years, but Diego had never been there. He'd expected a slum, as in the rougher neighborhoods of Las Vegas where he'd grown up. In his old neighborhood, prostitutes openly walked the streets and meth labs occupied every other house.

The streets of Shiftertown were completely different. Diego drove through an open chain-link gate to find small, well-kept houses and trimmed yards lining every street.

These houses had been built by the government twenty years ago, a housing project that had been turned into a Shiftertown once word came down that Shifters would be located here. The houses were crap, like any lowest-bid project houses, but they were painted, clean, and well repaired.

The yards were neat, either with tiny patches of grass or xeriscaped to conserve water. Water was a prized commodity in the Las Vegas valley. When strict conservation had to be enforced, Shifters were the first ones required to ration.

Eric Warden's house looked no different from others on the block. Diego had thought that, as Shiftertown leader, Eric would have commandeered one of the biggest ones. Would at least insist on having the most windows, or more plants in his yard, or *something*.

But the house—a one-story, long, plain building—looked the same as the houses to either side of it. A small front porch ran the length of the house, with thick posts holding the porch roof in place. The porch had been added on, Diego saw, and he noticed that many houses on the street had similar additions. Shifters must be handy with lumber.

Diego opened the screen door before knocking on the front door, which was jerked open almost immediately by Eric Warden himself.

Tall, green-eyed, brown hair buzzed short, Eric wore a muscle shirt that revealed a scrolled black tatt that cupped his shoulder and trailed down his arm. His Collar, a thick silver and black band, hugged his throat. He regarded Diego with an unwelcoming expression.

"I'm here to see Cassidy," Diego said.

Eric's glittering eyes were hard to meet, but Diego didn't let himself look away. Diego had faced deadly criminals— hard, hard men with no remorse, who would shoot a handful of people for the hell of it and go home for a good night's sleep. But, somehow, Diego thought, even those men would back down from Eric Warden's stare.

Diego pulled out his ID and held it up in front of Eric's face. "Lieutenant Escobar, LVPD. I warned Cassidy that I'd be checking up on her." Diego kept his voice calm but spoke in a way that told Eric he wasn't leaving until he saw her.

Eric's eyes flicked to Shifter white, his pupils becoming the long slits of a cat's. That looked weird in his human face, but Diego made himself not react.

"Cassidy told me what happened," Eric said. "I know you went easy on her." His eyes flicked back to human again, and he opened the door wider. "For that, you are welcome in my house."

Technically, Eric had no choice but to let him in. Diego was human and police, and no search warrants were needed for Shifters. Diego had the feeling, though, that if Eric hadn't wanted him in the house, Diego wouldn't be entering the house. This was a man who knew exactly how much he could do and how to maintain control while pretending to have none.

Diego gave Eric a little nod, meeting his eyes squarely, and stepped inside.

The interior of the house matched the exterior—neat, well kept, not luxurious. A sofa with faded upholstery looked comfortable, and tables held dog-eared paperbacks, videotapes, and inexpensive trinkets that were kept with care. Shifters weren't allowed the technology of TiVo, HD, DVDs, cable, streaming, high-speed Internet, Wi-Fi, or anything else that smacked of the latest technology. Videotape was allowed, but Shifters weren't going to be reading e-books anytime soon.

A second man came in from the kitchen in the back. His hair was the same color as Eric's but a bit shaggy, and his eyes were as jade green. He looked to be the same age as Eric, but Diego knew from the Wardens' files, which he'd read cover to cover, that this was Jace, Eric's son.

Shifters' life spans were about three hundred or so years, and cubs didn't come of age until they were nearly thirty. Jace was a little past that; Eric, pushing a hundred twenty.

Both father and son watched Diego slide his ID back into his coat. Diego realized that they were waiting for him to drop his gaze, to concede that they ruled here, that he was an outsider. It had been much the same in the neighborhood in which Diego had grown up, so he understood what was going on. But too damn bad. Diego had a job to do, and he wasn't Shifter. His gaze was staying put.

"Cassidy here?" he asked.

Eric didn't blink. He didn't look away, and neither did Jace, because that would be giving ground to Diego on their territory.

"Look, I'm not here to mess with you," Diego said. "The sooner I see Cassidy, the sooner I get out of your face."

"She's not here," Eric said.

Damn it. "Then where is she?"

Jace folded his arms. "She has a friend who lives behind us. Cassidy likes to visit her."

Diego, who'd lost count of how many hardened drug dealers he'd interviewed over the years, caught that Jace never actually said that Cassidy had gone to visit her friend.

Diego picked up some old car magazines from the sofa, set them on a table, and sat down in their place. "I'll wait."

Eric growled, a strange sound to come from a human-looking throat. His eyes flicked to wildcat white, and he gave Diego another long look. Diego tensed, feeling his gun heavy in his holster.

If Eric shifted to his wildcat, the only way Diego could fight him was with firepower. Diego's research since yesterday had told him that yes, bullets *would* hurt them, even kill them; you just had to get lucky or pump a lot of rounds into them. If Eric attacked, and his Collar didn't stop him, there would be nothing else Diego could do.

It lay between them. When Eric went for Diego, Diego's gun would be out. End of story.

Eric saw that. Jace, behind him, did too.

Eric's eyes finally changed back to human and green, and he relaxed his stance. "Jace," he said. "Get the man a beer."

Diego let out his breath, muscles unclenching. "Not for me. I'm on duty until I'm done here."

"Get him coffee, then."

Jace wordlessly strode back into the kitchen, and soon they heard water running in the sink. Jace was going to brew it from scratch.

Eric sat down on the coffee table, resting his arms on his blue-jeaned thighs. The enviable tattoo swirled around Eric's muscular shoulder and down the inside of his arm. Nice ink. When Diego had gotten the jagged chain tattoo across his shoulders at age sixteen, his mother had expressed displeasure. Loudly. For a long time.

Diego suddenly wondered what his mother would make of Eric—or Cassidy.

"Lieutenant Escobar, let me tell you a little bit about my sister," Eric said. "Cassidy has had a rough time of it. Really rough."

Diego thought through the files he'd read. "I know her boyfriend died last year."

"Donovan was her mate, not her boyfriend. Mating is like a marriage, in human terms, but much more powerful than that. When Donovan died, we thought Cassidy would die too. Cassidy has a lot of spirit, a lot of guts. Not afraid of anything. But she grieved for a long, long time. She still is grieving. It's been tough."

To Diego's surprise, he saw tears in Eric Warden's eyes. A big, bad Shifter, weeping for his little sister.

But then, Diego's brother, Xavier, had cried for Jobe when they'd buried him. Diego's thoughts flashed before he could stop them to the huge, loud-laughing black man—Jobe pouring drinks into Diego the first time Diego had brought down a suspect with deadly force; Jobe with his arm around his beautiful wife at one of his backyard parties; Jobe laughing as he lifted his daughter into his arms. Jobe, who'd gotten to his knees and begged for Diego's life, right before he'd been shot by a single bore, straight through the chest.

Diego dragged in a breath and blinked, finding his own chest tight.

"You all right?" Eric asked. He laid a hand on Diego's shoulder, a firm but soothing gesture.

Diego blinked some more. "Yeah. Fine."

"You were thinking about something pretty intense," Eric said. "What happened? You lose your mate too?"

Diego shook his head. "A cop. My partner. I was remembering my brother at his funeral, trying to hold it together. My brother's a cop too, and when one gets shot, it's like . . ." Diego's throat tightened, and the words wouldn't come.

"The worst thing imaginable."

"You got it."

Diego had no clue why he was saying this to Eric Warden, a Shifter he'd met five minutes ago. Diego hadn't talked about what had happened in more than a cursory way to anyone—not to his mother, not to Xavier, not to the other guys on the force, or even to the counselor they'd made Diego see.

"It was damn bad," Diego said. "Especially since Jobe died trying to save my life."

Eric pressed Diego's shoulder, the movement almost a caress. "I'm sorry, Diego Escobar. I will say a blessing for him, and for you."

Cassidy had said much the same thing. *I'll say a blessing for you.* She hadn't simply said it, as a stranger might politely say, *I'm sorry for your loss.* They understood, these Shifters. A loss for one person was a loss to everyone.

The phone rang in the kitchen, then stopped, followed by

Jace's low voice. Eric listened, head cocked, not letting go of Diego.

When Jace hung up, Eric called to him. "Jace, come on with that coffee."

Something clattered. "Don't get your pants in a twist, Dad. It only brews so fast."

"I don't need coffee," Diego said. "I just need to see Cassidy."

Eric's hand slid to Diego's neck and cupped it in a way that was a little more personal than Diego liked from another man, but he didn't pull away. Eric kept up the pressure for a few seconds before releasing it.

"Cassidy's not here," Eric repeated.

"So you said. Can you call her? I'll talk to her, make my captain happy, then I'll get out and leave you alone."

Eric rubbed his lip, a very human gesture. "Thing is, Escobar, I lied. Cassidy's not here. I mean not here in Shiftertown."

Diego got to his feet. "Then where the hell is she?"

Eric rose with him. "She's all right. She insisted she go make her offerings, and I had to let her. But I sent my trackers with her. They'll make sure she's safe to their last breath, or they'll answer to me. Trust me, they don't want to answer to me."

Diego glared at him. "Damn it, that's not the point. Cassidy isn't supposed to leave Shiftertown—*at all*. If she's seen out of it, she'll be arrested, Shifter Division will get her, and there won't be anything I can do."

"She won't be seen," Eric said in a hard voice.

"How the hell do you know that?"

Jace came out of the back carrying a mug of coffee. He looked from Eric to Diego, assessed the mood, then lifted the mug and drank the coffee himself.

"The phone call Jace just took was from one of my trackers," Eric said. "They're checking in every half hour. I heard what he said. Cassidy is fine."

Jace nodded confirmation and took another sip of coffee.

"Son of a *bitch*," Diego said. "It's not about how well she's guarded. The only reason she's not in a Shifter Division cage is because I vouched for her, promised that she'd stay home. You need to find her and get her back here. *Now*."

"I just told you what she's going through," Eric said in a hard voice. "Her mate was cut down by human hunters. Tonight is his remembrance blessing, and she's making her peace with where he died. She hasn't been able to make herself go there until now, which is a huge step forward for her. I couldn't tell her no." Eric's expression reflected anguish, but Diego couldn't let this go so easily. "I know what she's feeling," Eric went on, "because I went through it too. She needed to go, and I understood. I sent the trackers with her to make damn sure nothing happens to her. She's praying, and she's fine."

"I'm damn glad to hear she's fine, but you should have stopped her," Diego said heatedly. "Do you know what Shifter Division will do to her if they find her running around without a leash? Whatever the hell they want. They won't stop themselves. She's only a Shifter, a female Shifter. That's how they think."

All compassion vanished from Eric's eyes. "If they touch her, they're dead. I don't care about Collars, and I don't care about rules. Think about that." Eric flicked Diego's tie. "Without a leash. Yeah, that's funny."

Diego didn't move. "If you fight the cops, it's you that's dead. You, your son, your sister, and anyone else Shifter Division decides to put down. You think about *that* while you take me to her."

They faced each other, brown eyes staring into green. Diego saw anger congealed inside Eric, twenty long Shiftertown years of it.

The man had power, yes, and Diego saw that Eric hated dampening that power to obey the rules. But he'd do it, Diego also saw. Eric would do anything to keep those in his protection safe. Had done it, was doing it every day of his life. Diego understood, because he had the same instinct.

Eric raised his hands. The gesture might be conceding, but the look on Eric's face was anything but.

"I'll take you out to where she's gone, but only if you promise not to arrest her. We'll bring her back, you tell your Shifter Division she's doing fine, and you leave her the hell alone."

"No," Diego said. Eric's eyes widened a little, the blaze of rage startling, but Diego faced him down. "We find her, we bring her back here, and then *I* decide what to do with her."

Eric wanted to fight him; Diego read that in his face. The man wasn't just Collared and confined, he'd had every natural authority taken away from him, and he hated it. Eric had nothing left in his arsenal. But that didn't mean he still didn't have power. Diego knew that if he'd confronted Eric in Eric's true territory, with Eric's rules, before the Collar, Diego would already be a smear on the floor.

"Ready to go?" Diego asked softly.

Eric snarled, the sound low and laced with menace. He held Diego's gaze a little while longer, then he abruptly turned and yanked open the front door, just stopping himself from ripping it off the hinges. He strode out, and the door banged behind him, hard enough to bring plaster down from the ceiling.

Before Diego could follow, Jace stepped in front of him. "Bring her home," Jace said in a quiet voice. "You're right, human. Cassidy shouldn't have gone."

It wasn't anger that made Jace voice the thought. It was worry for Cassidy. But Diego didn't miss that Jace had waited until his father was out of the house before he'd expressed his disagreement.

"I'll get her back," Diego said, then he went out after Eric.

CHAPTER FOUR

Outside, Eric leaned against Diego's black T-Bird, waiting. To most observers he'd look relaxed, but Diego sensed the tension in him, a cat ready to spring.

As Diego made for the car, another Shifter came out of the house next door. This one was damn tall and hugely muscled, with a big, granitelike face. He wore a biker vest, which showed off tatts that ran down his arms. He was much bigger than Eric, much bigger than any human Diego had ever seen. Bear Shifter, maybe?

On the porch behind him stood a woman almost as tall as the man. They both wore Collars, which glinted in the late afternoon light. "Everything all right, Eric?" the woman called. "Who's the human?"

The bear man gave Diego a toothy smile. "Mama don't like humans. They worry her."

Dios mio, that woman was his *mother*?

"Everything's fine, Shane," Eric said. "This is Diego. I'm taking him to Cassidy."

Shane's smile faded. "What happened? Did Brody call? You need me?"

"No." Eric's voice was calm, even casual. Diego realized

he was deliberately downplaying his anger, perhaps so the bear wouldn't react to it. "Nothing's going on. I'm just going to round up Cass and bring her home."

Shane laughed suddenly, a loud, booming sound that reminded Diego of Jobe. "Round up Cass. Right. Call me if you need backup."

"You'll be the first." Eric opened the door of Diego's car and got inside.

Diego found himself once again the object of Shane's stare, plus mama bear's from the porch. A big male bear and his pissed-off mother, eyeing the pesky human in their midst. It might be funny if not for their uncanny resemblance to grizzlies.

Diego deliberately turned away from Shane and got into the driver's seat. Without looking at the bears, he started the car and pulled onto the street.

He saw Eric watching him.

"What?" Diego asked in irritation.

"Shane and Nell are some of the highest-ranking bears around," Eric said. "Nell is head of their clan. And you just turned your back on them like you didn't care."

"I'm armed," Diego said. "And they're Collared."

"Doesn't matter. You did the equivalent of flipping them off, or if you were a Shifter, spraying."

"Yeah, that's what I need. A pissing contest with bears." Diego knew though, from his childhood, how important pissing contests could be.

Eric leaned back in the seat and put his booted foot on the dashboard as Diego drove down the narrow street to the entrance of Shiftertown and out through the gates.

"You're right that I shouldn't have let Cass go out," Eric said as the dilapidated streets outside Shiftertown flowed by. "That's why I sent so many guards with her, including Shane's brother, Brody. One mean bear."

Diego glanced at him, but Eric was looking out the window. It must have cost Eric, leader of all Shiftertown, to admit he was wrong.

"Why did you?" Diego asked.

"Because it's the one-year anniversary of her mate's death. There are rituals we do for that. Cassidy will do one in the place her mate died, and then we'll have a family memorial, which these days includes everyone in our Shiftertown. Rituals are important for us, damned important. Important enough to risk danger for. Stay for the memorial—you'll understand."

Eric issued the invitation offhandedly, but Diego sensed that it was significant. First, though, they had to find Cassidy.

Shiftertown stood on the northern edge of North Las Vegas. As always, Diego marveled at how quickly city turned to open desert, developments and convenience stores soon falling behind. The street became a two-lane highway, running north.

Eric told Diego to take a turnoff to a smaller highway that went due west into the foothills of mountains north of Mount Charleston. After a few miles, the road started climbing, the dry, treeless landscape giving way to pines and scrub. The world was completely different up here, a damp and cool contrast to the desert floor. Pines soared, the clean smell of woods was in every breath, and the air became cold, even frigid.

Eric rode in silence, folding his arms with eyes closed, as though taking the opportunity for a nap. Just when Diego thought the man asleep, Eric opened his eyes, alert as anything, and told Diego to turn on the next dirt road to the right.

It was nearly dark now, and Diego had to look hard for the road. He found it after passing it once and having to back up to it, a faint strip winding into darkening woods.

The sun dove behind the trees and things got black fast. Diego drove slowly, taking care of his car on the washboard road. There was nothing out here, no cabins or ranger stations—just trees and sky, and a large Shifter saying nothing in his passenger seat.

Eric went from lounging to straight-up alert in a split second. "Stop. Here."

Diego stood on the breaks. The car slid sideways, catching on the soft, slippery dirt, then stopped. Diego could see nothing in his headlights but the bank of a hill and the trunks of aspens, leading off into darkness.

Eric opened his door and slid out into the night. Diego quickly got himself out, his gun comfortingly at his side.

Eric hadn't run off. He waited while Diego opened the trunk, got rid of his suit coat and tie, and pulled on a padded jacket against the cold. Diego lifted out a tranquilizer rifle he'd checked out from Shifter Division—just in case—loading a dart into it. He tucked a box of more darts into his pockets, plus extra ammo for the Sig in his shoulder holster.

When he looked up, Eric was giving the rifle a hard look. "You won't need that."

Diego slammed the trunk. "I'm out here, alone, with a Shifter who claims he's got other Shifter guards around. Yeah, I need it."

Eric growled in his throat again, a long, low sound. Which was exactly why Diego had brought the gun. He'd learned, in his ten years on the force, that while you didn't use firepower recklessly, you didn't hesitate to use it when the danger was real. Jobe had hesitated, and now he was dead.

"This won't kill her," Diego said. "Tranqs are strong enough to knock out a Shifter in its animal form but they don't do any permanent damage."

"I know," Eric said. "Who do you think they experimented on to find the right mix?"

Shifters themselves, Diego had learned. And not always willing volunteers.

Diego hadn't realized the extent of the research performed on Shifters until last night when he'd stayed up late to sift through files from Shifter Division. Some of the things he'd found out made him sick. "I'm sorry about that. Seriously. Experiments on Shifters are restricted now."

"Shifters died in those experiments." Eric's eyes were sharp. "Males, females, cubs. I know this, because I was one of the ones they experimented on."

Diego slung the rifle over one shoulder, his survival pack over the other. Eric was angry, and Diego didn't blame him, but he wasn't about to let Eric take out his rage at all humans on him.

"I'm sorry it happened," Diego said. "I didn't know about it until yesterday. I was only a kid at the time."

"So was my son. When they wanted to poke and jab him, I told them I'd go in his place."

Diego couldn't think of an answer to that. Would Diego have volunteered to let people stick chemicals in him or perform weird experiments on him in order to save Xavier? Or his mother? Or Jobe?

Hell, yes.

Eric seemed to sense Diego's understanding. He gave Diego a little nod, then turned around and started pulling off his shirt and boots.

"Whoa," Diego said as Eric unbuckled his jeans. "What are you doing?"

"I can move around better out here if I shift. Plus Cassidy and the other Shifters will scent me faster and won't attack."

Good to know. Diego looked away as Eric slid off his pants.

When he glanced back, Eric was stark naked, moonlight shining on a honed body and the tattoo that spread from his right shoulder down his arm and across his upper back. Diego looked quickly away again, and Eric huffed a laugh.

"Humans. Terrified of nudity."

"Not terror. Respecting space and privacy."

"Right. Humans are all about their space," Eric said, then he shifted.

He didn't roar or howl or make strange noises like were-wolves did in movies. The change was smooth, practiced, and fast.

Eric's face distorted first, his nose and mouth elongating, his slit-pupiled eyes going from deep jade to light green. His chest became the thick chest of a big cat, his legs bent into powerful back limbs, and his feet and hands sprouted claws and fur.

The whole process took about thirty seconds, but it was a very long thirty seconds. At the end of it, Diego found himself facing a huge, exotic wildcat.

Shifter cats were a combination of all the big cats, the files said, bred together long ago—by fairies, according to the Shifters, though Diego wasn't sure he believed that.

Shifter cats had different characteristics from family to family, clan to clan. Eric and Cassidy resembled snow leop-ards, but Eric was a hell of lot bigger than a usual snow leopard. He had black spots on a thick white coat, tufted ears, and a well-muscled chest, but he also had the powerhouse limbs of a lion.

Eric's family had lived in the ragged wilds of Scotland, Diego had learned, until the family turned themselves in as part of the Shifters coming out. How snow leopards had bred in the Highlands, Diego didn't know. But there was a lot about Shifters no one understood yet, and the Shifters didn't exactly volunteer information about themselves.

Eric studied Diego with an almost amused look on his cat face before he turned and loped off into the darkness.

Diego switched on a lantern flashlight and hiked after him. They were far from paved roads and civilization out here on the edge of the Sierras. Towns and farms were nonexistent, and the mountains were vast.

Eric could be leading Diego anywhere—into an ambush with other Shifters maybe—but Diego wasn't afraid. He was armed, he had his cell phone and radio, and he knew how to fight. Hand-to-hand combat was his specialty, and he was a more than decent marksman.

No, the only thing that terrified Diego Escobar was being held upside down off a balcony thirty stories up. If those drug runners had met Diego in the middle of a flat field, he'd have won the day. They'd be incarcerated now instead of running loose somewhere south of the border.

The leopard trotted along the cut of a dry wash and up a ridge on the other side of it. Eric was at least nice enough to let Diego keep him in sight.

At the top of the ridge, Eric stopped and sniffed the wind. To Diego, the chill breeze smelled like pine and dust, but Eric made a sudden, fierce growl and loped away, disappearing quickly beneath the trees.

Diego swore under his breath as he picked his way along the steep-sided hill after him. There was no path the way Eric had gone, and Diego's feet slipped and slid in the soft dirt and pine needles. The rifle and pack unbalanced him, but no way was he going to drop them and leave them behind.

Eric was nowhere in sight by the time Diego reached a clearing in the trees. Annoying, but Diego wasn't worried about getting lost. He had a powerful flashlight and a GPS device, and he'd noted the exact position in which he'd left the car.

No, getting back to civilization wasn't the problem. Falling, breaking a bone, being bitten by a snake or a rabid coyote—any of those could shut him down fast. People still died out here, and quickly. The Wild West wasn't so long ago.

Knowing Cassidy was in this wilderness somewhere kept Diego from walking to the car and leaving Eric to make his own way back. A Shifter had the advantage out here, not a human. But Cassidy . . .

In spite of Eric's reassurance about guards, Cassidy's story about being chased into the construction site by the hunter, not to mention the same hunter trying to take out Diego, worried him. A lot.

A couple of the more aggressive hunting groups had, a few of years ago, gotten the government to lift the ban on hunting un-Collared Shifters. The ban had been in place for a decade, but the hunters argued that Shifters who'd refused to take the Collar were still out there, still very dangerous.

Those Shifters could kill livestock, and worse, they said. Maybe even kidnap human women or children to do unspeakable things to them. Not that anything like this had ever been documented, but the hunters claimed anecdotal evidence.

Their arguments had finally been acknowledged, and the hunting of un-Collared Shifters again had become legal.

Cassidy was out here in the pitch dark. Would a hunter see—or care—that she wore a Collar?

Diego scanned for signs to tell him which way Eric had gone. The earth didn't show any paw prints, but a bush had been recently broken, a larger rock moved to expose its clean underside and the bugs hiding there.

Diego climbed around a stand of trees and started over another arm of hill. To his right, the ground sloped downward into darkness; to his left and ahead of him, the earth folded into treacherous grooves, deep washes that would flood during snowmelt later this spring.

About half a mile on, Diego was rewarded with a paw print in his beam of light, unmistakable in the mud. A wildcat, but a big one, much bigger than the elusive mountain lions that lived out here.

Diego followed the direction of the print, finding another in the drier dirt. He hiked on through the wash, eyes stinging with the dust he kicked up. He came out of the trees and found himself on a wide ridge, under an outcropping of black rock.

He heard a snarl—harsh, breathy, animal-like. He raised his flashlight and saw a mountain lion standing in the shadows of the rock. A real wildcat, not Eric, and this mountain lion was seriously pissed off.

The cat was so close that Diego could feel the hot *whuff* of its breath. Its ears were flat against its head, and it bared its teeth in a red-lipped snarl. Diego knew he'd never get the tranq rifle around in time or his pistol from its holster. Sometime tomorrow, rangers would find shredded Latino cop all over the bottom of the hill.

He heard a second snarl, this one louder. Another wildcat leapt down from the rocks above, a snow leopard, complete with Collar. Not Eric—this one was a smaller than Eric, and its eyes were a more vibrant green.

The leopard growled, long and low, throat vibrating with menace. The mountain lion's hackles rose, and it backed away. The snow leopard gave it a narrow-eyed stare, then jumped straight at it. The mountain lion let out one high-pitched yowl and took off up the hill, scattering dirt and gravel behind it.

The snow leopard landed and stopped, watching the mountain lion go with what Diego swore was a satisfied expression. The big cat then turned and looked at Diego with almost glowing green eyes, assessing him.

Diego put his hands around his rifle. If this wasn't Cassidy Warden, rangers still might find shredded Latino cop all over the hill.

"Cassidy?" he asked.

The wildcat gave him one slow blink, then moved toward him on graceful feet, step by step. Diego watched it come, tensing, but not raising the rifle. The leopard huffed a little, a more friendly sound than the mountain lion had made, then it butted Diego solidly in the stomach.

The push was hard but playful, almost affectionate. The leopard walked around Diego, twining close to his legs like a house cat before it bumped him in the backside.

"That is you, Cassidy, right?"

The wildcat rose, planted large front paws on Diego's shoulders. Diego overbalanced and went down on his ass, two hundred pounds of wildcat on top of him.

Reflexes made Diego toss aside his rifle and pack before he fell on them, then the leopard settled on his chest, nuzzling him with a soft, whiskered nose.

The wildcat was heavy, but in a warm-blanket way, not a crush-the-prey way. Diego's rifle had landed just out of reach, and he noticed she'd pinned him so that he couldn't go for his pistol.

"Good kitty." Diego put a hand on her shoulder. The cat's fur was incredibly soft. "What are you doing to me, *mi ja*?"

The leopard licked across his chin, tongue like very rough sandpaper. Diego couldn't help grinning. "You know this might be considered soliciting a police officer, don't you?"

She gave a grunt, heaved herself off Diego's chest, and started to walk off. Diego rolled and got the tranq rifle cocked and aimed so fast he should win a prize for it.

"Stop."

The leopard looked back at him with green cat's eyes. It snarled, then it shifted.

Limbs elongated, and the wildcat rose to the cross between cat and human that had saved Diego up in the construction site. The body continued to change and finally settled into the leggy, lush female who'd faced him right before he'd arrested her. Cassidy was as naked as she'd been then, her blond hair as unkempt and as lusciously beautiful.

Cassidy folded her arms, which lifted her breasts under the bright moonlight. The areolas were large and dusky, and Diego imagined how they'd feel filling his mouth, velvet against his tongue.

In the interrogation room, when Cassidy had wrapped her arms around him, it had been all Diego could do to remain immobile. The feel of her body bare through the coverall had made him want to rip open that ugly blue jail suit and have her right there, damn who might be watching. Now there was nothing between him and her but the darkness.

"Where are your bodyguards?" Diego managed to ask.

Cassidy gestured. "Out there."

Diego scanned the moonlit woods but could see nothing, hear no one. If the trackers were nearby, they were masters of stealth. But they would be, wouldn't they? Shifters were animals with human intelligence. Incredibly dangerous—hence the Collars.

"Eric called them his trackers," Diego said. "What does he mean by that?"

Cassidy shrugged, which did nice things to her body. "All

clan leaders have Shifters that help guard the clan, keep tabs on any problems that might come up, alert the clan leader to danger. Eric's Shiftertown leader now, so his trackers help him guard all Shiftertown."

Diego lowered the rifle but held on to it. "He's not supposed to have people working for him."

Cassidy gave him a half smile, which made her even more dangerously beautiful. "Eric doesn't care, Diego Escobar."

"So Eric sent the trackers to keep you safe? He shouldn't have let you come at all."

"I know. Don't blame my brother. He knew why I needed to come, and now I've finished my ritual. I can be very persuasive."

Diego just bet she could be. She'd look at a man with those green eyes, dark now in the moonlight, and he'd do anything for her. "Last time you came here, someone started hunting you. What makes you think it's safe here now?"

"I don't." Cassidy gave him a stubborn stare worthy of her brother. "But I refused to let him keep me from honoring Donovan. If I do that, the hunters will have won, won't they?"

Her words made Diego pause. He'd felt the same after Jobe died, when everyone had told him to take leave, transfer out of vice, and other such asinine suggestions. No. If Diego stopped hunting drug dealers—who caused a hell of a lot more damage to the world than people wanted to believe—the bad guys would have their victory. He couldn't let them stop him.

"I get that," Diego said. "But I'm still going to take you home to keep you safe."

"You're being protective of a Shifter?"

"You saved my life. That's nothing I take lightly, *querida*."

Cassidy took one more step toward Diego until she stood right inside his personal space. There must be half an inch between her breasts and his chest, but Diego couldn't trust himself to look down and check.

"What does that word mean?" Cassidy asked. Her voice was soft, sexy. Mind-blowing. "*Querida*, or whatever you said? I don't speak Spanish."

"It's a term of endearment. An Anglo might say *darling* or *honey*."

"What was that other one you used? Me ha?"

"*Mi ja.* Short for *mi hija.* It's what you say to someone you care about."

She smiled. "When you say that you sound—I don't know—affectionate."

"Maybe I like cats," Diego said.

Cassidy rested her hand on his chest, and her smile widened. "Meow."

Diego couldn't breathe. Her mouth was right there, red and moist, and he wanted to kiss her so much. He wanted to lock his arms around her, lift her against him, slide his hands down to her beautiful backside.

He *wanted* her. Right here, right now. Too damn bad about whoever was in the darkness watching.

Diego had rarely had to worry about female company in his lifetime, but this wasn't the same. This was Cassidy—exotic, beautiful, and brave. Anything he started with her would mean something.

That realization surprised him. Diego wanted to pause, to touch the feeling, to explore it. He'd been a walking mass of anger since Jobe's death, keeping others, including his own family, at arm's length.

This woman he definitely wanted *inside* his arms.

But Diego couldn't have her right now. She was in his custody, and violating that would break every rule he knew, not to mention his own principles. *Custody* meant taking care of someone as much as being in charge of them.

Even knowing all that, it was all he could do to take Cassidy's hand and lift it from his chest.

"Cass," he said with difficulty. "We need to go."

He didn't imagine her look of disappointment. Shifters weren't ones to hide their emotions. But Diego would be back to see her—often—and he hoped she never looked at him with that kind of disappointment again.

Cassidy kept hold of his hand, her fingers warm and strong. "I'll let you take me home," she said. "But can I show you something first?"

Diego's heart beat faster. He wanted to see anything she had to show him, though he knew he shouldn't let her lead him anywhere.

But what the hell? He'd already left procedure way behind. He might as well go for it.

"Show me," he said.

Cassidy released Diego's hand, stepped away, and shifted back to her snow leopard form.

She was beautiful, even as a wildcat. Cassidy stretched—front legs first, then back—and shook out each foot as she straightened up. She looked back at Diego with light jade eyes, then trotted away into the darkness.

CHAPTER FIVE

Cassidy heard Diego muttering behind her as she bounded up the path. He was slower than a Shifter, all humans were, but Diego was in good shape—admirably good shape. Diego had a honed, taut body and terrific reflexes, plus he moved with that fluidity she'd observed in him before. He'd make it.

He did make it, but he scowled at Cassidy as he crested the top of the hill and stopped next to her, breathing hard.

Cassidy wished he didn't smell so good. She didn't usually like human scents, but this man smelled of coffee, outdoors, soap, and a musk all his own.

She also scented his wanting. She'd have known Diego wanted her even if he hadn't given her that burning look when she'd stood against him. To Cassidy's shock and dismay, she'd been ready to let him take what he wanted.

Too soon. It's too soon. But her body had other ideas.

Diego had pulled back. Humans who craved sex with Shifters usually made complete idiots of themselves, as did the groupies in the Shifter clubs. Diego only looked at Cassidy and kept his thoughts to himself.

He watched her now with dark eyes that were all about control.

Diego might want her, but he wouldn't violate his own rules and go for her.

"What did you want to show me?" he asked.

He'd slung the rifle over his shoulder, but Cassidy knew damn well he could and would shoot her with it in a heartbeat. Control.

Cassidy led him between the granite boulders that studded the hill and down into a little depression filled with thorny bushes. The moon shone hard on the dark rocks of the clearing and tall trees that ringed it, giving the place a beauty all its own.

It was a place she'd never forget.

Cassidy shifted back to human form, ending up sitting with her arms around her knees on one of the flat, black rocks.

"It was here," she said. "One year ago tonight, this was where we found my mate's body, shot by hunters."

Diego crouched next to her, warmth in the darkness. "I know," he said. "I'm sorry."

Cassidy shivered, suddenly cold. "Donovan's Collar was off when the rangers found him. *We* know the hunters stripped it from him after he was dead, but the hunters claimed they didn't see a Collar and therefore thought Donovan fair game." The anger of that boiled inside her. "The hunters claimed that Donovan must have taken the Collar off himself, and so they weren't to blame. An innocent mistake, they said. Innocent, my ass."

Diego listened with quiet sympathy. "Donovan couldn't have taken his Collar off himself?"

"The Collars don't *come* off. If Donovan had tried to pull off his Collar, he could have died from it. They're programmed to shoot shocks and all kinds of crap through us when we're aggressive, which includes trying to take the damn things off."

"Shifter Division would have known that," Diego said. "What did they say?"

"They conveniently ignored that detail," she said, tasting bitterness.

"In other words, the humans got off, and nobody cared?"

"You got it, Lieutenant."

"Call me Diego." Diego sent a gaze down her body. "Seems like you should."

Fire licked through her. Usually it amused Cassidy how hung up humans were about clothes, but right now she was very aware of being bare in front of Diego.

Shifters *did* understand the eroticism of naked human bodies. Cassidy had first gained Donovan's interest when she'd flashed him in the dark parking lot outside Coolers. She'd pulled up her tight top, no bra beneath, and Donovan had decided right then to mate-claim her. They'd both been crazy, loving to dance and party and laugh. They'd laughed so much. The fact that, the night Donovan had gone out to die, he'd left in anger had haunted her to this day.

"It's a warm night," she said, forcing her tone to be light. "Maybe you'd be more comfortable if you shed some of *your* clothes."

Diego flashed her a sudden grin. "Not out here where I can get thorns up my ass."

"I'd make sure you didn't."

"You're a tease, woman."

She returned his grin. "Yeah, they all say that." She hadn't much felt like teasing anyone for a long time. "You know, Diego, you're not bad for a human."

"No? Damn, I'm flattered."

She stopped smiling and studied him. "There's a darkness in you, though. You told me that your partner, your best friend, died. I'm truly sorry about that."

Cassidy sounded truly sorry. Like she understood.

"He got shot," Diego said.

He'd never forget the horror of watching Jobe, a towering giant of a man, get to his knees and lay his pistol on the floor in front of ten guys armed with various pistols and shotguns. Then the greater horror of watching Jobe buckle as a bullet went into him, his blood bursting onto the white carpet of the hotel room.

"They shot me too," Diego said, the words stiff. "I lived. Jobe didn't. He was my closest friend, and I should have been taking care of him."

The counselors were supposed to help Diego deal with

his pain and guilt. They'd told him that he needed to see the shooting in a larger context, but Diego knew damn well that there was no larger context.

Diego hadn't thought there were more than two men in that hotel room, had thought that he and Jobe could bring them in without much trouble. An easy bust.

He hadn't known until he'd burst in, twenty steps ahead of Jobe, that the men who'd rented the penthouse had sneaked half a biker gang up there for a party. When Diego had entered by himself, one Sig to their arsenal, the bikers had decided to play the game of Hang the Stupid Cop off the Balcony.

Jobe had called for backup, but instead of waiting for them, he'd tried to rescue Diego himself, terrified for his partner. Jobe had paid the price.

Diego had expected to get dismissed from the force, but even after the department's investigation into what had happened, the police chief decided to turn Diego and Jobe into heroes. Jobe deserved it, yes, but Diego didn't. The counselors could placate Diego all they wanted to, but Jobe was dead because of Diego, and Diego knew it.

"It pains you," Cassidy said. "I know this pain. What happened to the ones who shot you?"

"They got away." Diego tasted bitterness. "They ran off while Jobe and me were bleeding to death in the hotel room."

"Did you try to go after them?"

Hell, yes. "By the time I was out of the hospital and could function again, they were long gone, to Mexico or Central America. I was taken off the case and ordered to stop looking."

Cassidy rested her head on her knees and looked at him. "But you didn't."

"No. I never will."

"Good for you."

Her approval ignited a spark in his heart. Diego had kept it to himself that he was still tracking the men who'd killed Jobe, because he'd get all kinds of hell for it. The department had told him firmly to leave it alone.

The fact that this Shifter woman approved of what Diego did made him feel strangely warm, but there wasn't much normal about Cassidy Warden.

No, *strange* was sitting next to a beautiful naked woman in the middle of the woods. She had amazing eyes, the green in them changing with her emotions. Her lashes were dark, but her hair held the light of sunshine.

Diego wanted to see her hair spread over his pillow, wanted to open his eyes in the morning and look into her green ones while she smiled at him. Maybe when her probation was over, he could take her to the Mount Charleston cabin a cop friend let him borrow from time to time, where they could drink hot toddies under blankets. He'd bet she'd look good snuggled up with him under a blanket.

Cassidy inhaled, and her eyes softened. "You want me."

Diego's heart beat faster. "It's that obvious?"

"You throw off pheromones like crazy." Cassidy touched his shoulder, the lightest brush. "You smell good."

So did she. Her hair was warm, so near his lips. Her body moved against his. Diego could lift her hair in his hands, feel the warmth of the back of her neck, kiss the lips that turned up to him so readily.

He touched her cheek . . .

Cassidy jerked away, but not because of Diego. She riveted her attention to the trees, her body completely still.

"What is it?" he whispered.

Cassidy noiselessly rose in front of him. Diego got a great view of her tapered back, fine ass, and long, strong legs as she scanned the night.

"Can you smell that?" she asked.

Diego sniffed, but all he caught was pine, damp earth, and Cassidy's warmth. "No."

She gestured, keeping her hand close to her body. "Something in those rocks down the hill. Not the trackers, not Eric."

Diego lifted his rifle. He had a starlight scope on it; nothing too high-tech, but there was enough moonlight out here to help him pick things out pretty clearly.

At the bottom of the hill and about twenty yards to the right was the outcropping of jagged rocks they'd climbed around to get up here. Diego trained his scope over it, picking up the movement of a rabbit, the flutter of an owl.

And something upright and human-shaped. "Got him," Diego said. "It's not a Shifter?"

At the same time Cassidy said, "No," Diego knew it wasn't.

The silhouette didn't have the bulk of any of the Shifters he'd seen so far, and it moved too smoothly. It also burned bright hot, showing vivid green through the scope. Something with a temperature warmer than a human's, maybe hotter even than a Shifter's.

The man rose, turned, and raised his arms in a stance Diego recognized.

"Down!" He grabbed Cassidy and was on top of her, both of them facedown, as a bullet pinged on the rock she'd been standing next to.

"Sharpshooter," he whispered into her ear. "He the same one from the construction site?"

"I don't know." Cassidy wriggled against him as she tried to raise her head to look.

Diego pinned her with his weight. "Stay down."

"Let me shift."

"He can shoot you in your animal form as fast as he can shoot your human form."

"Yes, but I move better as a cat. You shoot at him, keep him looking your way, and I'll get around behind him."

"Screw that, Cassidy. No way am I letting you get anywhere near him."

Cassidy turned her head to look at Diego. The rocks had scratched her cheek, and her face was smeared with dirt and blood. "Then what are we going to do? Lie here all night?"

"No, we're going to lie here while I call for backup."

Cassidy's look turned to a glare. She thought that *backup* meant police.

"Screw *you*, Diego."

She started to shift. It was bizarre being on top of her naked back as her body contorted into the lithe, furry one of the wildcat. Diego felt strength pour into Cassidy's limbs, then he toppled off her as Cassidy scrambled to her feet.

"Damn it, Cassidy. Stay here."

Cassidy snarled. Her ears went flat on her head, teeth bared—long, sharp, scary-looking teeth.

Another bullet pinged next to Diego's shoulder. Cassidy leapt on Diego, sending him down to the dirt. Now *she* was on top of *him*. Her snarl softened, sounding admonishing rather than angry.

Staying close to the ground, Cassidy stepped off Diego and flowed away from him. She slunk down the hill, moving rapidly, and was almost instantly lost to sight.

Diego lifted the tranq rifle. The rifle shot only one dart at a time, and its range wasn't great, but it had a scope. Otherwise, Diego couldn't see a damn thing out here.

Diego drew his Sig, keeping the rifle on his shoulder at the same time. He found the shooter through the scope, the man still holding whatever powerful weapon he had. Diego brought up his pistol over the rifle's barrel. He knew he didn't have a chance in hell at hitting his target with the Sig, but maybe the noise and flying bullets would keep the shooter distracted. He shot.

The report was loud, and the shooter ducked. Two seconds later, another bullet chipped rock somewhere above Diego's head.

He started to swear in Spanish, his preferred language for venting. No one could vent like Diego's mother, and she'd taught her sons well.

They needed backup, and Diego didn't have the faintest idea how to alert Eric and his trackers, or even where they were. The shooter had a hell of a silencer, good cover, and a decent rifle. The man could sit in those rocks all night and pick them off one by one.

Fuck that.

Diego lay down flat, pulled out his cell phone, hit number one on his speed dial, and hoped he wasn't out of range of every cell tower in the region.

He got a phone ringing, to his relief. *Come on, pick up. Pick up.*

"Hey, *hermano*," a deep voice said on the other end. "What's up?"

"Xavier," Diego croaked.

The ever-present cheerfulness left Xavier's voice. "Seriously, what's up?"

"I'm pinned down in the mountains by a sniper, and I need firepower."

Xavier knew Diego wasn't joking. "Shit. Did you call it in?"

"No. We're not calling it in. Just get here." He told Xavier exactly where he was, GPS coordinates and all.

"You got it," Xavier said. The phone clicked, and he was gone. Another thing Diego loved about his little brother was that Xavier acted first, asked questions later.

Diego calculated that it would take Xavier half an hour to load up and get out here, and that was if he hurried. Meanwhile . . .

The hunter was still in the rocks. Diego shot at him again, rewarded with another bullet whizzing by him. When Diego dared lift his head again, he used the rifle scope to scan the area.

He saw a slinking form of one wildcat approaching the rocks from the left, but he couldn't tell which wildcat it was. The scope picked up another slinking form, closing in on the hunter from the other side. This wildcat was larger—possibly Eric. Then a giant, hulking form of a bear. Damn, it was big.

A couple more wildcats and then a wolf crept out of the shadows to join them. The animals circled the outcropping in a perfect pincher move, coming at the shooter from all sides to pen him in. Diego let fly another shot to keep the hunter busy.

The wildcats, bear, and wolf moved in beautiful formation. The animals couldn't communicate in words, had nothing to go on but instinct and visual cues. Yet they maneuvered like a well-oiled team, exactly anticipating each other's moves. Diego could work like that with Xavier, had been able to work like that with Jobe.

Eric and the wolf slunk the last ten yards and lowered themselves, disappearing from Diego's sight. The bear moved slowly behind the rocks and it too disappeared. The cats moved in the other direction, hugging the ground, readying themselves to spring.

Diego trained the scope on the hunter again. The heat signature around the guy had grown larger, much larger. A second person? Diego saw no sign of anyone else, just the man with the rifle who suddenly seemed very hot.

The heat bubble exploded, flooding green through the scope. Diego jerked away, blinking. At the same time, the animals let out snarls—the bear roaring—and charged.

Diego gave up his cover and scrambled down the hill. He'd have to stop the Shifters from ripping the guy apart, though Diego would be happy to slap cuffs on whoever it was in there. He'd charge him with illegally hunting Collared Shifters, assault with a deadly weapon, shooting at a police officer, and—if this was the same hunter that had been at the construction site—tranqing Jemez and Hooper and nearly causing Diego's death. This would be fun.

The deep roar of the bear boomed up and down the mountain and vibrated the moonlit sky. His roar was answered by the deep growls of a wildcat and the howl of a wolf. Diego ran faster.

He reached the outcropping the hunter had been using as a blind, took cover behind a massive boulder, and trained his pistol on the interior. "Drop your weapon, and get on the ground. *Now.*"

Nothing happened.

The wildcats came out from behind the rocks, Cassidy with muzzle pressed to the ground, sniffing, sniffing. The bear shambled around from the side of the outcropping, the biggest damn grizzly Diego had ever seen.

Eric's head was up, his leopard eyes white with rage. Sparks chased around the Collar on his massive neck. The wolf sat on his haunches, looking angry.

Diego risked a look inside the rock shelter. It was empty, the mud inside smooth, no sign of anyone having been there.

CHAPTER SIX

Xavier came roaring up in his F-250 as Diego climbed down to the road. Dirt and gravel shot into the air as Xavier braked, then he leapt out of his truck. Xavier spied Diego flanked by two wildcats and a bear, and stopped, a shotgun resting loosely in his hands.

"All clear," Diego said as he hiked the last few feet to the road.

Xavier didn't raise the shotgun, but he kept it handy and looked hard at the Shifters.

"These are Cassidy and Eric Warden," Diego said, jerking his thumb at the wildcats. "And their neighbor, Brody. I need to give them a ride home."

Xavier warily eyed the bear. "That's a frigging grizzly, Diego."

"I know."

Xavier raised his brows, then caught what was in Diego's expression and shrugged. "OK."

Cassidy chose that moment to change into her tall, lithe, human form. Xavier's eyes widened, and Diego stepped protectively in front of her.

"Stop ogling and get her a blanket."

Xavier blinked at his older brother in surprise, then he grinned hard. Still carrying the shotgun, Xavier stepped to Diego's car and pulled out a blanket.

Cassidy wrapped the scratchy wool around her, not missing how Diego had tried to hide her from Xavier's gaze. Mates did that, instinctively, protecting their females from other male Shifters, but Cassidy knew Diego had not done it for any mate reason. He was thinking like a human, believing Cassidy would worry about Xavier seeing her without clothing.

Xavier was Diego's brother all right. He stood the same height as Diego, had the same square, handsome face, broad shoulders, and black hair—though Xavier wore his a little longer—and eyes so dark it was like looking at midnight. They had the same stance, the same way of moving.

What kept the younger man from being a twin of the older was that he smiled more readily, moved more rapidly. Diego had learned to hone his energy while Xavier was still being ruled by his.

Eric padded calmly to the pile of clothes he'd left in the dirt, shifted while Xavier's eyes widened again, and dressed himself. Brody, instead of shifting, turned and walked heavily back into the darkness.

"Where's he going?" Xavier asked.

"To meet up with the others and get home," Eric answered. "He's shy about shifting in front of people."

Xavier raised his brows but didn't comment on Eric's seeming *lack* of shyness. "And you're all out here because . . . ?" Xavier asked Diego.

"Doesn't matter now. I'll explain it later."

Xavier watched his brother another moment, then shrugged and nodded. Not happy, but trusting Diego.

Diego ordered Eric and Cassidy into his car and told Xavier to follow them back. Diego drove, hands firm on the wheel, Eric in the backseat, Cassidy in the front with Diego.

Cassidy liked watching Diego drive. She enjoyed the way the muscles in his arms moved, how his eyes flickered as he watched the road, how he could give attention to all things at the same time. He was a good hunter, she thought. He'd trained himself to be.

The butt of Diego's pistol peeped around his flat stomach,

within his easy reach but not Cassidy's. Eric drowsed against the door behind her, his legs across Diego's backseat. Eric often napped after an intense stalk, retrieving the energy he'd spent, and besides, his Collar had started to go off. He only rested like this when he thought himself safe, so he must feel safe with Diego.

The moon was bright tonight. Cassidy's neighbors were out, waiting for the ceremony for Donovan to start—on porches or in yards, a few already burning fires or lighting candles to the Goddess. Shane and Nell lounged on their porch next door, watching as Eric and Cassidy climbed out of Diego's car.

Jace slammed open the screen door and ran outside. "Dad, what the hell? Nell was about to have a clan roundup and go extract you."

"Shit happened," Eric said. He grabbed his son in a brief but hard embrace.

"You all right, Cass?" Jace took Cassidy's hand, his familiar warmth already easing her tension.

"I'm fine, sweetie."

Cassidy pulled him into a full hug. She'd held Jace when he was a tiny cub, when he'd been still in cat form. He'd liked to chew on her pant legs, insistently, until she picked him up and cuddled him, his true goal. That cute cub was a long way from Jace the man, but affection between nephew and aunt remained.

Xavier pulled up in his truck and drew more Shifter attention. Cassidy sensed all eyes on the brothers, noses taking in scents.

Eric didn't invite Diego and Xavier inside, but he didn't keep them out either. Which meant that Eric wanted to hear Diego's view of what had happened.

Diego and Xavier kept their weapons with them as they entered the house. Jace made more coffee, Eric yawning in the living room, as Cassidy ducked into her room and pulled on her clothes. For some reason she grabbed her cutest lace panties and bra before she covered them with jeans and a cropped top.

Her friend Lindsay had convinced her to buy the underwear at a time when Cassidy figured there was no point. She was glad now she'd listened even though she'd be the only one who knew she had them on.

Cassidy went back out to the living room as Jace was handing out coffee like a gracious host. Xavier gratefully accepted a cup; Diego declined his. The ritual was due to begin soon, but Eric yawned again as he collapsed to the sofa.

"Sorry," he said. "Hunting makes me sleepy."

It hadn't been just the hunting. Eric was fighting the effects of his Collar going off when he'd rushed the hunter. Eric had, not long ago, gone out to the Austin Shiftertown to learn a technique the father of the Shiftertown leader there had begun to use to override Collars. The override didn't last long, and the payback was hell, but Dylan Morrissey and his two sons could sustain a fight long enough to finish it, clean up, and then retreat to go through the delayed reaction.

Eric had returned and sent Jace back to learn the technique, which involved hours of meditation and mind exercises. Jace had been teaching Cassidy and Eric the exercises, but it was a slow process. It was also a secret process, known only, so far, to the Morrisseys and now Eric and his family, and possibly whatever other Shiftertown leaders the Morrisseys had decided they trusted. Neither Eric nor Cassidy had mastered it yet, though Jace was getting pretty good at it.

Cassidy's Collar hadn't gone off tonight, however, because she'd realized the moment she'd started her charge that the hunter was no longer there. She'd slowed in confusion, her Collar remaining dormant.

Xavier leaned his shotgun against the wall behind the chair he sat in, within easy reach, and she saw the bulge of its ammunition in his jacket pocket. Diego was the most formally dressed of all of them, having resumed his suit coat, though he hadn't put his tie back on. He looked damn good in a suit.

Cassidy found herself swaying her hips a bit as she leaned to grab the coffee from the table and sit with Eric on the sofa. Eric moved his legs for Cassidy as she sat down, then she lifted Eric's feet and rested them on her lap.

"So what the hell happened out there?" Diego demanded. "The guy was there, and then he wasn't. Tell me the truth. Did one of you kill him?"

Eric gave a short laugh. "You'd have found a torn-up corpse

if I had, and I'd look a hell of a lot worse than this. These Collars are a bitch."

"Then what happened to him?"

"Good question," Eric said.

Cassidy shivered. What she'd smelled among the rocks had been a whiff of acrid smoke with a bite of mint. Not good.

"Cassidy?"

She liked the way Diego said her name. He sounded the way a dusky wine tasted.

"I don't know," she said. "I guess he had an escape route."

"I was watching through the scope," Diego said. "He didn't run. His heat signature went off the scale and then he was gone. Like he'd exploded. Silently."

Cassidy did her best not to look at Eric. She felt his legs tense in her lap, though he lounged as negligently as ever, eyes half closed.

"I didn't see anything like that," Eric said. "Like Cassidy said, he must have had an escape route. Maybe he torched something in his way."

"Leaving no fire, smoke, or ash," Diego said. "There wasn't anything inside that rock cave, not even footprints."

"Neat trick," Xavier put in.

Eric let his eyes close all the way, as though he was going to nap no matter who was in his living room. "Yeah, well. He's gone."

"Cassidy." Diego got to his feet, his face unmoving. "Talk to me?"

Eric cracked his eyes open as Cassidy slipped from under his legs. There was warning in the look, but Cassidy didn't need to be told not to reveal to the human police what the hunter might have been.

Xavier remained in the living room, sipping coffee and looking nonchalant. He and Eric were going to compete in the who-can-look-like-he's-the-most-at-ease-when-he's-not contest.

Diego walked out through the kitchen door to the backyard like he owned the place. Cassidy followed him.

The yard wasn't fenced, as so many yards in Las Vegas were. Shifters didn't like fences, so all houses opened to a common strip of land where kids roamed and played, and where adults held informal cookouts or formal rituals. Shane and some others were building the bonfire that would be used in the public ritual to honor Donovan. Cassidy looked away, fighting pain, torn between the past and present.

Diego moved down the common, away from the activity. Nell lifted the curtain of her kitchen window and looked out at them as they walked by.

When they stopped, Diego took a small white business card out of his pocket. "Whenever you and Eric are ready to stop bullshitting me," he said, tucking the card into the neckline of Cassidy's shirt, "you call me."

Diego's fingers didn't touch Cassidy's skin, but the swift heat of his hand, the scrape of the thin card, made her mouth go dry.

"Diego, believe me when I say that I'm as confused about what's going on as you are."

"Maybe, but you're not telling me everything. I want to know what you know, and even more than that, I want you to stay the hell home and *don't leave again*. Finish your probation. Understand?"

The alpha tendencies in him stirred the dominant in her. Cassidy was second in command of Shiftertown, not only because she was in Eric's family, but because she was that high in the dominance order. Jace was plenty old enough to be Eric's second, but he was third, conceding second to Cassidy. Jace didn't seem to mind always letting Cassidy know that, as third, he had her back.

Cassidy poked a gentle finger at Diego's chest. "I don't take orders from anyone but Eric, policeman."

Diego's eyes got warmer, and she could feel the rise of his body heat. "Right now, you have to take a few orders from me," he said. "My price for not arresting your ass again."

His mouth was firm. Cassidy imagined it against hers, the hot pressure of his lips. Would he open her mouth right away, or would he linger at her lips? Kiss her softly or slant his mouth across hers, demanding access? Their bodies were nearly together now, except for a small sliver of space between them.

"Seriously, Cassidy, be careful." Diego's voice dropped to its velvet tones, and she thought of wine again.

"I will." She slid her arms around his waist, flowing to him.

Diego stiffened. "What are you doing?"

"Saying good-bye."

"This is *good-bye*?" He looked surprised. "I thought it was *come up to my place and see me sometime*."

Cassidy grinned. "You're already at my place. This is how Shifters take leave of each other. I won't hurt you, Lieutenant Escobar."

"You hurting me wasn't what I was afraid of. And anyway, I'm staying. Your brother asked me to watch whatever ritual you're going to do."

"He did?" Eric hadn't mentioned this. Shifter rituals were very private, meaning that humans weren't welcome.

Then again, perhaps Cassidy did want Diego there. She wanted him to see what losing a Shifter meant to them, and the things Shifters went through.

"All right, then," she said. She took both Diego's hands in hers and raised them to her lips. Then she skimmed her touch to his shoulders and put her arms all the way around him. "This means, *The blessing of the Goddess be with you*."

Diego came against her without resistance. His breath touched her face as he let her pull him close, and his unshaved whiskers brushed her cheek.

Diego drew back after a minute, but his eyes were darker than ever as he looked down at her. "Thank you. What am I supposed to say back?"

"You can say, *May the Father God watch over you*. Or you can say nothing and just nuzzle me."

Diego leaned down, brushing his nose across her hairline. Cassidy felt his breath, his warmth, which both confused and elated her. "I can see why Shifters like their religion."

"You're an unusual man, Diego. Humans don't always acknowledge that we have a religion. They say we follow primitive rituals without really knowing what they mean."

Diego's hands on her back were strong. "I'm Roman Catholic. We have a lot of rituals that people don't understand either. Some of them were borrowed from the Celtic pagans, which is where I bet you got yours too."

"You're saying we have something in common?"

"I'm saying doing a ritual makes sense to me. You can find a lot of comfort in it. Your life might be hell, but to stop for a quiet minute and light a candle for someone you cared about helps."

He did understand. Five minutes of simple prayer could calm the soul. "Maybe that's why Eric asked you to stay."

Diego shook his head. "I think your brother wants me to know exactly what I'm dealing with and wants to watch how I react to it. Your brother is pretty damn canny." He glanced at Cassidy's house and released her. "Looks like you're ready to start."

The Shifters were gathering around the bonfire. They formed the circles, close friends and family in the inner one, the rest of the Shifters in the outer.

Donovan's mother was there in the inner circle, with his three brothers. This Shiftertown's Guardian, Neal Ingram, who had stuck his broadsword into Donovan to render him dust, joined them. The sword stuck up behind his back, a silent symbol of death. Shifters believed that their souls would not be sent to the Summerland unless the Guardian slid his sword through the dead Shifter's heart—the Fae magic in the blade made the Shifter's body crumple to nothing. Guardians lived lonely lives, because very few females wanted to mate with a man who was a walking reminder of mortality.

Eric came out of the house, no longer looking tired and hurting. He was alert, rested, ready. Cassidy didn't miss how every unmated female turned her head his way. The females always watched Eric.

Diego faded back as Cassidy walked toward the bonfire and her family. He was giving her space to do what she needed to do. Cassidy felt a little warm spot in her heart for that understanding.

Eric put his arms around Cassidy, his strength comforting. Jace embraced her from her other side. Eric and Jace had been there for Cassidy every second. Goddess, she loved them.

The Shifters quieted as Cassidy approached the bonfire. Eric handed her the photograph she'd saved for the ceremony, the one of Donovan grinning at the camera in the dark of a bar, one hand around a beer bottle, the other giving a thumbs-up sign. *Donovan, I'm so sorry.*

Donovan's mother met her, also clutching a photo. The

circles of Shifters closed behind them. The Guardian started chanting a prayer in the ancient Shifter language, a cross between Celtic and Fae.

Cassidy pressed a light kiss to the photo, her lips touching Donovan's face. *Rest in peace, big guy.*

Donovan kept smiling as Cassidy dropped the picture to the flame. Donovan's mother, tears streaming down her face, took her photo, another of Donovan at a party—he'd loved a good party—and fed it into the fire.

Neal Ingram came forward, drawing his sword. He touched the blade to the fire, and the Fae runes on it lit up, seeming to chase up and down the metal. Eric put his hand on the hilt, over Neal's.

"From this side of the veil," Eric said, his voice deep and solemn, "we honor Donovan Grady."

There was a moment of pure silence, the only sound the crackling of the flames. Then someone yelled, "Donovan!"

The cry was echoed in every Shifter's throat. They screamed, they cheered, they toasted Donovan Grady, beloved friend, brother, son, cousin, and nephew—now partying in the Summerland.

Donovan's mother closed Cassidy in a crushing hug, then turned away to be comforted by Donovan's brothers.

Cassidy wiped tears from her eyes and found a cold bottle of beer pressed into her hands. Her friend Lindsay released the beer and dragged Cassidy into a hug. "Goddess be with you, honey."

Cassidy choked out her thanks. Music blared out, and lights strung through the trees twinkled in the darkness, the memorial segueing into the party. The dead were always celebrated with joy. The music was country, because that's what Donovan had loved.

Lindsay put her arm around Cassidy. "Drink up. Get plastered drunk, dance your feet off, and then find someone to shag. You'll feel much better."

Cassidy couldn't help the laugh. "Sure, Lindsay."

The music kept blaring. The Shifters started dancing, waving beer, shouting.

Lindsay favored clingy dresses of sunny colors, tonight's

white with big orange and yellow flowers. She was a Feline, her family's wildcats more lynxlike, small and wily.

Lindsay kept her arm wrapped around Cassidy's neck as she drank. "I saw those human hotties bring you home. Who are they?"

Cassidy felt a growl build in her throat. "They're cops. Diego Escobar is the one who arrested and interrogated me."

Lindsay looked over at Diego, and she swayed her hips. "*Rowr.* I wouldn't mind *him* putting me in handcuffs." Her eyes widened as Xavier joined Diego, handing his brother a bottle of beer. "Sun and moon, they aren't twins, are they? That would be too perfect."

"No, Xavier is the younger."

They watched Xavier clap Diego on the shoulder and the two men walk toward Eric, who'd set up his grill. Their moves echoed each other's, though Cassidy again noticed the restlessness in Xavier and the control in Diego.

"Diego and Xavier Escobar," Lindsay said. "Goddess, Latino men are hot."

Cassidy hadn't met all Latino men, but she agreed about Diego's heat level. The man was walking sensuality. She folded her arms tighter, stifling her growls.

Lindsay broke into laughter. "Look at you going all possessive because I'm licking my lips. Hey, if I provide the handcuffs, do you think his brother will do me the honor?"

Cassidy made herself relax, unclench, take a sip of beer. "You are one hormone-laden female, Lindsay."

"Hey, I'm mateless and ready. Just like you. The body clock is ticking, and it's telling me to have a good, good time before I mate for life. You can't tell me your body clock isn't telling you the same thing. Even if Diego Escobar is human."

Diego started talking to Brody, who was already unsteady on his feet. The bear brothers liked their beer. Diego laughed at something Brody said, dark eyes flashing over his wicked smile.

Yes! Cassidy's libido told her. *Why not?*

Careful, said her heart.

"No. Not yet. It's too soon."

Lindsay shook her head. "Honey, believe me, I'm torn apart for you. But you also know that Donovan, of all people, would never expect you to put on sackcloth and ashes and grieve the rest of your life. He understood that Shifters have to produce as many cubs as we can. He wouldn't be that selfish."

"I know that. I also know you're rationalizing to get me to go out catting with you."

Lindsay laughed and gave Cassidy a half hug. "Oh, come on, I gotta try. Let's go out after the party and dance until dawn. You can't tell me a night on the town wouldn't be a good thing."

"It would be." Cassidy felt restless and itchy, needing to work off some heat. "Can't. I got confined, remember?"

Lindsay rolled her eyes. "You aren't taking that seriously, are you?"

Cassidy glanced at Diego again. He wasn't looking at her, but she could feel the awareness stretching between himself and her.

She knew damn well she could avoid the cops and Diego and go about as she pleased. But for some reason, she wanted to keep to her probation, wanted to show Diego she could be trusted. "Yes. I think I am."

Lindsay sighed. "Ah, well, we have better celebrations right here in Shiftertown anyway. The night's still young, and as I said, Donovan always liked a good party."

"Yes," Cassidy said. "Go on, enjoy yourself."

Lindsay saluted Cassidy with her beer bottle. "Let me go see if I can land me some Latino cop." She laughed again as Cassidy's tension returned. "Don't worry, Cass. Xavier. I'm going for Xavier." She licked her lips. "Damn, what a great name."

Cassidy watched her go, feeling the tightness in her body. All over the common, Shifters celebrated the life of Donovan Grady, the Feline Shifter who'd made friends with everyone. He'd been funny, stubborn, impossible, wild, and well loved.

Maybe Lindsay was right. Donovan had always laughed at Cassidy whenever she moped. That had irritated her a little, as though Donovan couldn't acknowledge that sadness was important. But he'd tickle her or tease her, or take her out to Coolers and tell her to dance like a maniac until she felt better.

What the hell?

Cassidy upended her beer bottle and took a long draught. Then she ran back into the house, changed into her favorite dancing dress, and went out again. She'd push down her guilt about her fight with Donovan the last night she'd seen him alive, let loose, and party as hard as Donovan ever had. She'd been his mate, and she'd honor him.

She pretended not to acknowledge her little shiver when Diego's gaze went to her in her slinky blue tube dress. Looking away, she stepped into the middle of the dancing Shifters and let out a wild whoop.

"Cassidy, I swear to the gods, you have the best tail in town." Shane danced up behind Cassidy a few crazy hours later, beer bottle in one hand.

"You should know, Shane," Cassidy shouted over the noise. "You chase enough tails."

Music continued to blare through the trees, and Shifters were dancing, drinking, laughing, shouting. Diego was spending his time talking to Eric and Jace, though Lindsay had enticed Xavier into dancing. Cassidy drank beer after beer and danced with male after male, but Diego didn't seem to notice.

Shane laughed at her. "You put on a tight dress and shake it, sweetie, you gotta expect every male to come running."

Cassidy lifted her hands over her head and swayed to the music. She'd discarded her heels to dance. She could move better barefoot.

Shane wanted to mate, Cassidy scented. But Shane always wanted to mate, so that was nothing new.

Nature made female Shifters as horny as the males, more sometimes. Cubs were few and far between, so females in their fertile years had the drive to go for it as often as they could with as many males as were available, in order to search for the most viable seed. Mr. Viable Seed got to be the permanent mate, blessed under sun and moon.

At least, that's how it had been centuries ago in the wild. Now Shifters were more civilized. Right?

Biological urges didn't explain the mate bond, however; that almost magical twining of hearts. Mate-bonded mates would live and die for each other—literally.

Thoughts of mating—casual and otherwise—conjured the

dark eyes and handsome smile of Diego Escobar. How he'd looked at her out in the woods, how he'd felt against her body when she'd hugged him before the ritual started.

"Sorry, Shane," Cassidy said. "I just want to dance."

Shane moved in close behind her. "Oh, come on. You never heard of the horizontal bop?"

Cassidy burst out laughing. Shane was a shit and never changed. "You only like to do it as a bear. My wildcat's not letting a bear on her back. No way."

"I'd make an exception for you, Cass."

"Sure, for me. And for Lindsay. And Sadie, and Michelle . . ."

"Hey, I'm a bear in his prime."

"You're a bear whose mom is looking for him."

Shane jerked around. "She is? Where?"

Cassidy laughed harder. "Goddess, you're easy. Your mom's the sweetest woman alive."

"Shit, Cass, don't do that to me." Shane blew out his breath. "She might be sweet to you, but Mama can be one mean grizzly."

Cassidy laughed. She'd been baiting Shane for years, and he'd been teasing her back.

Lindsay came whirling in between Xavier, who looked like he was having a fine time, and Kyle, Eric's Lupine tracker. "Great party!" Lindsay shouted. She whooped as she let both men lift her and carry her back under the lights.

Cassidy looked back to where Eric stood, and she stopped. Diego was no longer with him. Where was he?

She scanned the crowd but nowhere saw the tall human with midnight hair. His brother was still dancing with Lindsay, his body moving with rhythmic grace, but no Diego.

Shane bumped into her. "What's up, Cass?"

Cassidy shrugged. "I don't feel like dancing anymore."

"Fine by me. My room's empty. Brody will be out all night, and that's good, because you know how he snores . . ."

"Sorry, Shane. I can't."

"I get it." Shane embraced her from behind, the gigantic man giving a gigantic hug. "Donovan was a great guy, Cass. We all miss him."

Cassidy's heartache came back. She wiped her eyes as Shane released her and gave her a quick kiss on the cheek.

"Good night, Shane," she said.

"See ya, Cass." Shane sounded downhearted, but let her go.

Cassidy walked away from him, unsteady after all the beer she'd had, and sought the house. She was drunk, she was sad, and she'd do nothing but make a fool of herself if she stayed outside and kept obviously searching for Diego.

She blundered into the lightless house, the music blasting away on the porch. It was pitch-black inside, but Shifters could see in the dark, right?

Cassidy ran smack into the tall, hard body of a man walking through their kitchen. His scent was all over her in an instant.

"Diego," she said, her breath gone.

Her emotions, her need, and way too much beer rocked through her. Staying pressed against Diego's chest, Cassidy twined her arms around him, rose on her tiptoes, and kissed him on his hot, smooth lips.

CHAPTER SEVEN

Diego found his arms full of luscious, beautiful Shifter. Cassidy's mouth opened his, and she swayed against him, arms tight around his neck.

The taste of her . . . He had to have more. He had to have more, *now*.

Diego cupped her head in his hands and pressed her up to him. *God help him.*

Her mouth was on fire. He devoured her, licking, tasting, sliding lips on hers. Her tongue met his in a rapid dance, her mouth strong.

He was hard, and Cass wriggling against his front wasn't helping. She smelled like beer and musk and Cassidy. And damn, he loved what she was wearing.

The dress under his hands hugged every inch of her. He felt her ass, her back, the curve of her waist, and he wasn't finding a line of any bra. When she'd walked out of the house in that, he'd forgotten how to breathe.

Cassidy kissed him hard, harder. Diego wrapped one arm around her buttocks, pulling her up against him, his hand finding bare thigh. Her skin was satin soft and hot, so hot.

Cassidy's fingers furrowed his hair, while Diego moved his hand upward . . .

"Whoa." The male voice boomed through the living room—not Eric, not Jace, not Xavier. "What the *hell*?"

Diego eased his mouth from Cassidy's. She made a little sound of protest and sought his kiss again.

Shane the bear stood in the doorway to the kitchen, empty beer bottle in hand. The man was nearly seven feet tall and radiated menace with a capital M. Grizzlies could be placid when content, but get them mad, and it was a different story.

"Listen, human cop," Shane said, a growl in his voice. "I get that you let Cassidy go when you didn't have to, but that don't give you the right to touch her. If you don't *stop* touching her, I'll pull your arms off. Understand?"

"If I let go of her, she's going to fall," Diego said. Cassidy was sagging in his arms, her eyes half closed. "She's drunk off her ass."

"Am not," Cassidy said in an indignant slur. "Shifters don't get drunk."

"This Shifter is." Diego scooped her into his arms. Cassidy smiled up at him, still holding on. She was so beautiful when she smiled. "Where's her bedroom?" Diego asked Shane.

"Aw, Diego," Cassidy purred. "I didn't know you felt that way about me."

Shane gestured, still looking unfriendly. "This way." He led Diego down a short hallway to a door at the end.

Diego carried Cassidy into a room that was painfully bare. A four-poster bed covered with quilts stood against one wall. A nightstand with a lamp and a pile of paperbacks reposed next to the bed, and a rocking chair with a cushion stood in the corner. Nothing more, no pictures, knickknacks, or electronics.

When Shane snapped on the lamp, the room glowed—Cassidy had painted the walls a soft yellow that made the barren room seem warm.

Shane stripped back the quilts, and Diego laid Cassidy on the sheets. Diego had to deliberately unclasp her hands from his neck to make her let go.

Cassidy was already barefoot, the soles of her feet dirty

from dancing outside. Well, she might have to wash the sheets
tomorrow. Diego turned Cassidy onto her side, in case she
decided to lose all that beer in her sleep, and pulled the quilts
up over her shoulders.

"Thanks, Diego," she murmured. "You kiss nice."

So did she. Damn, did she ever. "Glad you think so."

"You're not so bad, for a human. Stay with me, and keep
kissing me."

Shane rumbled. "She's really drunk if she wants to kiss
a human." He bent down and dropped a peck on her cheek.
"Sleep it off, Cass, honey."

Diego looked down at Cassidy with a hunger he'd not felt in
a long, long time. He pictured himself stripping off his clothes,
climbing in behind her, pulling her back against him. Holding
her all through the night. And in the morning, if she felt better,
rolling into her warm nest and making swift love to her.

Diego settled for squeezing her shoulder. "Good night,
Cassidy."

She didn't answer, already asleep. Diego turned off the
lamp and left the room.

And found himself against the hall wall with a half human,
half bear face an inch from his.

"I'm not kidding, human." Shane's voice was guttural,
his teeth sharp, his breath like . . . that of a bear who'd been
drinking a lot of beer. "Don't mess with Cassidy."

Diego had faced plenty of hard, conscienceless men in his
time. But he'd also faced desperate men, and he'd learned the
difference between anger born of arrogance and anger born of
worry. Shane had anger born of worry.

"You care about Cassidy," Diego said. "Are you in love
with her?"

Shane's eyes didn't soften. "I met Cass twenty years ago,
when we were shoved into this Shiftertown together. Brody and
me thought my mother would be leader, because she's naturally
alpha. But Nell conceded dominance to Eric. If something happens to Eric, Cassidy takes over, not my mother, not Jace. Do
you understand what I'm saying? Cassidy's next in line. That's
weird for a Feline, because Felines rarely let their females rule.
But no Shifter is able to touch Cassidy. The only things that can

hurt her are humans and human laws. That means you, human cop. So don't."

A hand that ended in sharp grizzly claws landed on Diego's chest, just below his throat. One swipe, and Diego would be dead. Shane's Collar wouldn't be quick enough to stop him.

"You didn't answer my question," Diego said calmly.

The bear snout receded and Diego looked again into Shane's human face, but the claws remained.

"Of course I love Cass. I have for years. But she's out of my reach, and I know it. When Donovan started chasing her, I faded in her eyes. Donovan, the charmer, charmed himself right into Cassidy's bed. The two of them didn't come out for days. Eric and Jace couldn't sleep inside the house, and me and Brody had to get earplugs."

And I'm standing outside the bedroom in question, while a half-drunk grizzly tells me about the sex life of the woman I'm seriously attracted to.

"Donovan passed a year ago," Diego said. "What's stopping you now?"

"Cass herself." The claws became blunt fingers again. "She's not interested in me. I'm fine with that." Shane gave a shrug, a man long used to the fact that he'd have to look elsewhere for happiness. "But I'm not going to let a *human* start confusing her and threatening his way into her pants."

The claws had receded, but Diego knew that Shane could easily crush his windpipe with his huge fingers.

"First, I've already seen her without her pants." A sight Diego would never forget, though that blue dress was damn sexy too. "Second, I want to keep her safe as much as you do. That's why I want her here in Shiftertown. If she gets caught out again by someone besides me, she'll be arrested and jailed, and I might not be able to protect her." Diego fixed Shane with a sharp stare, even though he had to look up to do it. "Do me a favor and watch her for me, Shane. If she tries to leave Shiftertown, you stop her. And if you can't stop her, call me. Me, and no one else. Can you do that? Help me out?"

Shane's eyes narrowed. "You should ask Eric to help you."

"Eric already let her go once."

"That's a point. Eric won't stop Cass doing what she thinks she needs to do." Shane drew a breath. "But I will."

For some reason, Diego wanted to pat Shane's shoulder and say, *Good bear*, but decided that might not be wise.

"I'll come by, but I can't be here all the time," Diego said. "Just keep her out of trouble."

"You got it, human cop."

"Call me Diego. And I'll tell you something." He leaned a little closer to Shane. "If you think your mom's tough, you should meet *my* mother."

Shane's face finally softened, and he chuckled. "Humans have a saying: *When Mama ain't happy . . .*"

". . . *ain't nobody happy*," they finished together.

Shane laughed a little harder and clapped Diego on the shoulders. Diego fought to keep to his feet.

"You're funny, human cop. I mean, Diego. I'll watch over Cass. I'm your bear. Time for you to leave now."

Diego let the man put a heavy arm around his shoulders and lead him to the front door and out of the house.

Diego wondered, as he watched the bear Shifter sway toward the house next door, whether Cassidy would remember in the morning what had been the most spectacular kiss of Diego's life.

Diego figured he'd get shit from Shifter Division for how he'd handled Cassidy's arrest, and sure enough, Lieutenant Reid, a man with ambitions in Shifter Division, accosted him the next day.

Diego was still reeling from the kiss he'd shared with Cassidy, still reveling in the scent and taste of her. He'd dreamed about her all night, thought about her while he showered, shaved, and readied himself for work. Imagining her being in the shower with him, smiling her red-lipped smile as she soaped his back, almost made him late.

Reid stopped him in the wide hall downstairs as Diego made for the elevator. "Anything to do with the Wardens is mine," Reid said without greeting him. "You overstepped, Escobar."

Diego eyed the man in dislike. Reid had a tall, lithe body—a runner's muscles rather than a bodybuilder's—and his eyes were so dark they were almost black.

"I made the arrest," Diego said. "It was my call."

"Two weeks' confinement to Shiftertown?" Reid stepped closer, his dark eyes narrowing. "That's *it*?"

"If you read my report, you'd know why I made the decision," Diego said.

"Yeah, I read it. She still broke the law."

Diego had no intention of explaining his motives. He'd learned as soon as he'd become a detective that people would question his every decision, especially those in his own rank in other divisions. Human nature, his captain told him.

"I've worked on Shifter cases a hell of a lot longer than you have," Reid said. "They can look human, and they try to act human, but if you don't treat them like the dangerous animals they are, you'll pay for it. Don't let the Collars fool you. You can't tame them, you can't trust them, and most of all, you can't be their friend."

Reid's eyes held conviction, but Diego gave him a neutral nod. "Thanks, Reid. I'll keep it in mind."

Reid gave him a disgusted look but turned and marched away down the hall.

Diego could almost feel sorry for him. Shifter Division was the crap assignment—to make sure Shifters obeyed rules and didn't go where they shouldn't. For the most part, it was an easy assignment, because Shifters seemed to be pretty anal about obeying strictures. Shifter Division cops sat around panting for a chance to arrest and harass Shifters. Reid obviously fit right in, maybe too well.

Diego went upstairs to his desk and greeted his brother, whose bloodshot eyes looked worse than Diego's. Xavier gave him a tired wave but a cocky grin. Xavier loved a good party.

Diego turned to his reports for a three-month-long case he'd concluded a couple of days before he'd met Cassidy. Now, the final bust, which had been such a victory, seemed to have happened in another lifetime. He'd met Cassidy and . . . everything changed.

Diego walked around that thought as he finished the report and e-mailed it to the captain. Then he got Xavier, who wasn't getting much paperwork done here, and took his brother with him to Shiftertown.

* * *

Cassidy lifted her aching head from the kitchen table when she heard the throb of the Thunderbird outside. "Oh, Goddess, it's Diego."

Shifters weren't supposed to have hangovers. Their metabolisms were strong enough to negate the dehydration of too much alcohol. Cassidy didn't remember drinking that much beer, but then, if she'd been able to remember all the beers, she probably wouldn't have this hangover.

What she did remember was the kiss, finding herself in Diego's arms, his mouth slanted over hers in the dark living room. His big hand on her thigh, the strength of him as he held her. He'd tasted of warmth and power, and she'd loved it. She'd flung her arms around him and kissed him with wild abandon.

How embarrassing.

Jace opened the front door and greeted Diego and Xavier. Eric was . . . Who the hell knew where Eric was? Cassidy struggled to her feet as Jace led the brothers into the kitchen and offered them coffee.

Did Diego look ashamed of the kiss, of the way he'd scooped her up to him with his arm under her buttocks? No. He flashed her a grin, his eyes dark and sparkling with teasing wickedness. He looked fresh and rested and not the least bit worried.

Cassidy felt her face heat. What was the matter with her? Shifter women weren't prudes. They enjoyed their love affairs and made no secret of the fact that they were after the best mate they could get. Cassidy hadn't pulled up her shirt to flash Donovan on accident.

She found herself wanting to look away from Diego, so she made sure she met his gaze. "Hey, Diego. I'm still in Shiftertown. I feel too crappy to run away anywhere today."

Diego's gaze roved her up and down. "Yeah, you look a little ragged."

Xavier took the steaming cup of fresh-brewed coffee from Jace. It smelled wonderful in the kitchen—the rich coffee scent overriding everything. Jace's brew was legendary. Cassidy reached for the cup Jace handed her and cradled it like a lover.

"Never tell a woman she doesn't look her absolute best," Xavier said. "Bad, bad idea." He took a sip of coffee and shot Cassidy a white-toothed grin. "You look great, *hermana*."

Diego shrugged as he sipped his coffee. "This is good." He gave Jace an admiring look. "Do you always make the coffee?"

Jace gestured to the old-fashioned coffeepot with the percolator on top. "Just call me coffee king."

Diego looked around. "Where's Eric? I'm going back out to that rock cave to look around, and he might want to come too."

Cassidy opened her mouth to say she'd join them, then she remembered that she was grounded. Damn humans and their stupid laws. Shifters had never worried about going everywhere they pleased before the Collar. She sat down, head pounding, and filled her mouth with beautiful coffee.

She sensed warmth next to her. Diego had sat down with her and now smiled into her face. "You all right, *mi ja*?"

Cassidy loved it when he called her that, the beautiful syllables rolling in his dark voice. She heard Xavier and Jace in the background, the two men walking out the back door, but she barely registered them.

"Headache," Cassidy said.

"I thought Shifters didn't get drunk."

Cassidy blushed again. "Hey, last night was rough for me."

Diego's arm rested across the back of her chair. His body heat touched her through her thin T-shirt, making her want to squirm. She inhaled his scent . . . and stopped.

What met her nose was Diego's usual musk and spice, but something touched it a tiny bit, a hint of acrid smoke and mint she'd smelled last night at the place where the hunter had hidden. Cassidy turned her head and sniffed his suit jacket. No, she hadn't mistaken it, though it was very faint.

Maybe something lingering from last night? Could be. Diego had showered—she smelled the soap, and he was wearing a different jacket today. Plus, she hadn't noticed the same kind of smell on Eric.

"What are you doing?"

Diego's low voice arrested her. Cassidy looked up at him so close, noting his face was clean-shaven again this morning.

She liked his dark skin, his hair as black as midnight, and his eyes nearly as dark.

"You smell . . . interesting," she said.

"Oh, great. Do I need more aftershave?"

"No." Cassidy inhaled the scent of his coat again while Diego sat very still. Eric had told her, when she'd limped out this morning, feeling like shit, what the smell up in the mountains had been.

Fae.

Cassidy had never met or seen a Fae in her long life. Fae hadn't lived in the human world for centuries, leaving finally for Faerie after the Fae-Shifter war. Shifters had elected to remain in the human world and live the best they could, while the Fae had gone. The Fae had already begun leaving when humans started using more and more iron. Fae hated iron.

Cassidy's head was too fuzzy to puzzle it all out this morning. Eric hadn't given her a long explanation. Cassidy had just sort of mumbled, "Fae, right," before sitting down and begging for coffee.

But now she wondered. The shooter had been using a rifle—which was made of steel. Plus he'd vanished in a bright light, just as he had up in the construction site. Did Fae do that? And why did Diego smell like one now?

"Cass."

Cassidy looked up at Diego, who was watching her with dark eyes. "Hmm?"

"I shouldn't have kissed you last night," he was saying. "Or let you kiss me. I was way out of line. But I haven't been doing anything right since I met you."

Cassidy could only look at him. She should think of something witty to say. She'd always been able to be witty with Donovan. Their mutual wisecracks had filled every room. Now, with Diego, Cassidy sat tongue-tied. She couldn't think of anything more witty to say than, "Oh?"

"But I don't regret it," Diego said. He drew his thumb along the back of Cassidy's neck. "I don't regret it at all."

Cassidy shook her head. "Me either."

Diego grinned down at her. Damn, he had a nice smile. "Good. But if I try anything like that again, you stop me, all right?"

Oh, sure, stop him. Cassidy had been the one pretty much climbing up him last night. "OK," she said. Could she carry on a brilliant conversation, or what?

"I'm supposed to be watching over you," Diego said. "I'm the arresting officer, and you're under probation. I don't have any business kissing you. Or wanting to kiss you."

Cassidy casually leaned back until her head rested on his shoulder. "What about after my probation is over?"

His smile widened, his dark eyes warming. "We'll see what happens after that."

Cassidy's heart started pounding off the scale. The promise in his smile sent hot things through her body, awakening a frenzy she thought had died the day Donovan had.

Oh, no.

Oh, yes. It was happening, the tingling in her fingers, the buzzing in her head, the hot need that flushed her body. She felt warm, open, needy. And it wasn't just the hangover. Crap.

Cassidy rubbed her head on Diego's arm again, and again, he sat unmoving. She didn't like the Fae-like scent, but if she nuzzled hers on him, she could cover it.

"*Mi ja,*" Diego said softly.

Her mating frenzy wanted to answer. It wanted Cassidy to turn around and straddle him in the chair, strip off his tie and open his shirt. She wanted to unbuckle his pants, open them, reach inside to find him hard for her.

She'd shed her own shirt and jeans, let him lick her bare skin, touch her all over. Some Shifters liked to have sex only in their animal forms, but Cassidy loved the feel of human skin against human skin, where she could make love face-to-face. Kissing was the best thing, mouths melding as male and female joined.

Diego's breath came faster. Cassidy looked up into his eyes, her heart thumping as she saw the naked need in them.

He wanted her. Whatever he was fantasizing right now, it was driving him as crazy as Cassidy's fantasies were driving her.

But Diego was holding himself back. He was a strong man, would be an alpha if he were Shifter. Diego had rules he had to follow, and by Goddess, he was following them.

Cassidy was about to throw the rules to the wind and let

her frenzy out when Eric walked in the back door. Her brother took in Cassidy and Diego sitting so close, and his nostrils widened.

Eric must have smelled the faint Fae scent, because he stopped, sniffed, and riveted his gaze to Cassidy. She shook her head the slightest bit.

Diego was definitely human, not Fae, not even half Fae. Though Cassidy had never seen a Fae, she knew what signs to look for; every Shifter did. Full-blood Fae had pointed ears, white blond hair, and cold, cold eyes. Half human, half Fae could look human, but their eyes were just as cold.

Eric didn't pursue it. "Your brother says you want to have a look at that outcropping where the shooter was," he said to Diego. "Good idea. You can drive."

Cassidy itched and burned. She wanted to go with them; she wanted to find out why this hunter was stalking her, and whether he had anything to do with Donovan's death. Despite her awakening frenzy, she wasn't letting go of her quest to bring down the hunters who'd killed Donovan. He'd been her mate and hadn't deserved to die.

She knew that if she told Diego she wanted to hunt and kill the men who'd shot Donovan, he'd do his best to stop her. Shifters were Collared, tamed. Supposed to be anyway. Diego would say it was his job to stop her.

Cassidy had things to do, anyway. She folded her arms as Diego stood up, his warmth going away. She had this hang-over to get rid of, for one, and people she had to take care of. Being Eric's second meant she helped Shifters with their troubles, keeping Eric from being overwhelmed with all but the direst problems. People came to Cassidy first.

"Just tell me everything," she said.

Eric came up behind her chair, leaned down, and folded his arms around her. He nuzzled her cheek, his warmth comforting her as it had since she'd been a tiny cub. Eric rubbed her arms, kissed the top of her head, and straightened up.

Diego was looking at them, as though he longed to give Cassidy a good-bye hug too. Cassidy stood up, arms slightly open at her sides, a signal that she was open to an embrace. Whether Diego understood the body language or not, he gave her a regretful look, turned away, and followed Eric out the door.

CHAPTER EIGHT

They took Xavier's truck back up the mountain, because he had four-wheel drive and Diego didn't want to abuse the T-Bird any more than he had to. He remembered the way—he was good at memorizing terrain—but let Eric point it out anyway.

The three of them went over the area for several hours but returned to Shiftertown without much to report.

Cassidy was in the backyard when they returned. Diego took one look at her bending over in her form-hugging jeans, her cropped top hanging a bit loose at her stomach, and started sweating. The woman was gorgeous. Her light hair swung over her shoulders as she played with the small wildcat at her feet.

Cassidy wasn't skinny—Diego had noted that most Shifter women were larger than human females—but she was well proportioned to her height. That meant the long, strong legs he'd seen nice and bare, full breasts, and curved hips. Luscious.

When she heard them come out, Cassidy scooped up the cub and greeted them. The cub looked like a white tiger, and it had the sweetest blue eyes Diego had ever seen.

"This is Torey," Cassidy said, holding up the cub, its over-sized paws batting the air. "He just lost his dad."

"Poor thing," Xavier said. He put a hand out to pet it, then jumped back when Torey growled and swatted at him. "OK, looking at the cute kitty from over here."

Cassidy grinned. The squirming cub had pulled Cassidy's shirt up a little, baring her navel with the little gold stud. Diego would have to ask her what happened to the stud when she shifted.

Jace walked out behind them and started handing out bottles of beer. He seemed to be the beverage dispenser of the family. "Torey doesn't trust full-grown males yet, for good reason."

"Why's that?" Diego asked. He politely took the beer but didn't open it.

Eric answered while Cassidy stroked the tiger's head and cooed at him. "Because he's an orphan, no father, mother, or pride leader to look after him now. The other males in the clan instinctively want to kill him."

"Shit," Diego said. "Why?" And just this morning he'd sneered at Lieutenant Reid for claiming Shifters were too violent.

Eric shrugged. "It's instinct. A male wants his own genetics passed on. When a male dies, other males move in to try to take the female, kill her cubs, and start their own prides or packs. That way they don't have to worry about those cubs—especially the male ones—growing up and pushing them out."

Xavier listened, openmouthed. He closed it again. "I was going to say that was barbaric, but you know, after our dad got killed, other men tried to put the moves on our mother. And they didn't much like me and Diego. She didn't have any money or anything, but she was good-looking. And alone."

Cassidy's compassion showed in her eyes as she looked at Diego. "I'm sorry. I didn't know you'd lost your father."

"Shot by a robber in his own store," Diego said flatly.

"And then Mamita lost the store," Xavier said, never shy about giving anyone who asked his life history. "Too many bills, taxes, and besides, the store wasn't doing good at all. She had to go scrub toilets to put food on the table. Bless her. Now we take care of her."

Jace listened, sipping his beer. "So did any of those men who put the moves on her succeed?"

Xavier laughed. "With Mamita? No way."

Diego thought about his mother and the fierce way she'd protected him and Xavier—at the time they hadn't always appreciated it. But she'd kept them safe and together, and for that he'd love her forever.

"So what did you find out there?" Cassidy asked. She put Torey down. The cub scampered off but didn't go far, as though an invisible tether tied him to Cassidy.

"Nothing," Eric said in disgust.

"Shell casings," Diego said. "From a rifle that shoots thirty-aught-six rounds, pretty common for a hunting weapon. I'll run licenses and see who owns one, but there are tons of *un*licensed weapons out there."

"Then we don't know anything more?" Cassidy looked from Diego to Eric, seeming to ask Eric a silent question. Eric shook his head, and Cassidy turned away to walk after Torey.

Eric, Jace, and Xavier watched the cub awhile, then drifted back into the house. Diego handed his unopened beer to Xavier but stayed put, lingering to be alone with Cassidy.

He followed her around some tall mesquite trees to the middle of the common. "So are you babysitting that tiger or does he live here?"

Cassidy sat down on a plain stone bench that stood near one of the trees. The trees had just started to leaf out, a brush of misty green contrasting their dark trunks. Torey took the opportunity to run in wider circles but never far enough for Cassidy to be out of sight.

"Babysitting," she said, watching Torey. "He has a foster mother, but sometimes she needs a break. She has four cubs of her own."

"I can see that. What happened to Torey's mother?"

Cassidy looked sad. "She died bringing Torey in. That was three years ago. Torey's dad kind of went to pieces after that. He and his mate had the mate bond, and some Shifters don't recover from that. Torey's dad . . . He killed himself."

"Damn," Diego said. "Poor kid." He watched Torey scampering in circles, chasing a butterfly. "I never heard about a Shifter committing suicide." Something like that would make the newspapers, or at least the files in Shifter Division.

"Eric kept it quiet, told the humans he died of natural causes," Cassidy said. "Our Guardian sent his body to dust right away, so there was no chance for human doctors to check."

"If it's a secret, why tell me?"

Cassidy looked up at him, her green eyes full of sorrow but also conviction. "Because you know how to keep things to yourself. Because you know when to bend rules. I've seen you do it for me. And you didn't do it for personal gain. None that I can tell anyway." She watched Torey again. "We don't need Torey getting taken away. This is the best place for him, where he knows everyone, not arbitrarily transported to another Shiftertown."

Diego nodded. "I get that." Their secret was safe with him.

"So, Torey's alone," Cassidy said. "His foster mother is unmated right now, so it was safest to put Torey with her." She smiled a little. "But he's a handful."

"Are you serious that Shifter males would try to kill him?"

Cassidy shook her head, her blond hair brushing her shoulders. Diego liked how close he had to sit to her on the bench, her warmth spilling onto him. "They won't. Not with Eric as Shiftertown leader—that means he has authority over all prides and clans here, regardless of species. Everyone obeys Eric, and besides, males only killed cubs like that long ago in the wild. But even though we're civilized now, the instinct is still there. If a male Shifter is drunk, or angry, or whatever, and loses control, he might hurt him, even without meaning to. So Torey needs to be in a safe household for a while, until he grows up enough to defend himself."

Diego watched the way her face creased in worry as she followed Torey's movements. He liked her concern. Hot, sexy, compassionate Cassidy.

"Why can't the little guy live with you?" Diego asked. "You don't have four other cubs to take care of. Do you?"

Cassidy laughed. "Listen to the worry in that question. No, we're cubless here, now that Jace has gone through the Transition. But even Eric has the instinct to kill another male's cubs, although I know he never would act on it. Besides, he's Shiftertown leader and our clan leader, and he has to be careful about who it looks like he's favoring. Torey's dad was pretty far down in the dominance chain, which means Torey will be too for a while, and if Eric privileged Torey by raising him in his house, alongside Jace—let's just say there would be issues rippling up and down Shiftertown."

"That's way too complicated for me," Diego said.

"From what Eric tells me, our jealousies and rivalries aren't too much different from humans'. We just acknowledge them with rules. We follow the rules; no one gets hurt."

"That explains why Shifters don't get arrested often. You're used to following rules. Even stupid ones."

"Easier than fighting every day of your life. Most of us live a long time, and we learned the hard way that keeping the peace is so much better than bloodshed." Cassidy looked down the strip of land to other cubs playing in the distance. "Humans shoving us into Shiftertowns sucks, but at the same time, it's helped us survive. Shifters were dying out. That's why most of us didn't fight coming out of the Shifter closet, or even taking the Collar."

Cassidy's Collar hugged her throat and looked damn good on her. Diego reminded himself that if it shocked her, it would hurt her badly. But still, the way the Celtic knot rested in the hollow of her throat, the way the silver links glistened under her hair, made Diego want to lean down and press his lips to it.

He closed his hands around the edge of the cool stone bench and changed the subject. "You said Jace went through *the Transition*. What's that?"

"It's like human puberty on steroids. I went through it, and I thought I'd die, but it's worse for males. It's your body deciding you're ready to fight, mate, and find your place in the hierarchy. Your metabolism goes insane, telling you to mate, mate, mate, fight, fight, fight. Right *now*."

Diego thought about his own rushed transition from boy to man and gave her a look of sympathy. "Looks like you made it. So did Jace."

"I made it because I had Eric. Our parents were dead by then, but Eric was good at knocking me down or even chaining me up when I needed to be. Trust me, it was self-defense on his part. I thought my body was going to spontaneously combust a couple of times. For Jace, both Eric and me were around to help him, but, Goddess." Cassidy took on a look of pure exasperation. "Jace's Collar went off ten times a day, and even that didn't calm him down. Poor guy. At least I got to Transition before the Collar."

Jace certainly looked amiable now. But all the Shifters did, even Shane, until they were pissed off.

"It was hell," Cassidy said. "But that's over." She blew out her breath. "Jace is ready to mate, but . . ." She opened her hands. "Not that many female Shifters to go around. It's a real blow when we lose one. Not as many females die bringing in cubs as they used to, but it still happens." She looked at Torey, her expression sad. "But you understand what Torey's going through, don't you? You lost your dad."

Diego remembered the utter shock of it, the jolt of the violence that had taken his father's life. Diego had been eight, Xavier six. They'd been stunned and grieving, but Diego hadn't understood until he was older what his mother must have gone through. Mamita was a strong woman—she didn't take shit from anyone—but she must have been devastated. How she'd held it together, held *them* together, Diego still didn't know.

"You lost your mate," he said to Cassidy. "Eric's died too, right?"

"Kirsten. Yes, bringing in Jace." She let out her breath. "That was tough."

"But Eric's still here. And you are. And so is my mom. You didn't take the way out that Torey's dad did."

"I had Eric," Cassidy said, as though it were that simple. "Eric had me, and he had to take care of Jace. And I bet your mom made it because she had you and your brother."

"That's true. I think I stayed alive when those meth-heads shot me and Jobe because I want to get them. And I will."

"Exactly." Cassidy drew another breath, as though she'd say something more along that line, then she let the breath out again. "I suppose we make choices for our own reasons. I feel bad about Torey's dad though. I should have been paying more attention."

"You can't see every sign," Diego said. Law enforcement had its share of suicides, and it wasn't always obvious until later that the person had been in that much despair.

"I'm Eric's second. It's my job to see them."

Diego's brows rose. "Your job?"

"It's what a second does. Noses into other people's lives to make sure everything's all right. So Eric doesn't have to take time away from liaising with humans and keeping three different species of Shifters from killing each other. I take care of the secondary problems. Like making sure Torey's new mom has time to cope."

Diego glanced at the house next to the Wardens'. "You seem to get along with your neighbors, the grizzlies."

"That's because Nell keeps Shane and Brody in line. All the bears, actually."

Diego remembered what Shane had said about Nell conceding leadership to Eric and Cassidy. "Why would she step out of the way for you and Eric? Bears are bigger than wildcats."

Cassidy shot him a sly look that seared his blood. "Because wildcats are fast. Nell won't try to take over. None of us would survive a fight like that, and we all know it. So we do what we do, and we don't worry about it."

They both watched Torey romp while Diego strove to calm down his body. "What else does a second do? You and Eric working together last night—that was amazing."

Cassidy shrugged. "Experience. I help Eric fight when necessary, but mostly I listen to people. I help the older ones, especially those who got stuck in this Shiftertown alone, apart from their clans. I take them shopping or do it for them, or just take them out to be a friend."

Diego felt a twinge of remorse. "And now that I've confined you to Shiftertown?"

"Don't worry, I'll work around it. Once I got over my hangover this morning, I realized that I need to cool it and not risk getting arrested again. It wouldn't just be me going to jail—the human police would come down on Eric, and there's too many Shifters dependent on us to risk us being thrown out of here."

"And the ritual you needed to do outside Shiftertown got done."

Cassidy smiled. "That too." She glanced past him. "Looks like your brother is ready to go."

Diego saw Xavier looking through the stand of mesquite

trees at them. Xavier waved when he saw Diego spot him, and Diego lifted his hand in answer. Xavier, his perceptive little brother, nodded once and went back into the house to wait for him.

Diego stood up, and Cassidy got up with him. Torey snarled and bounced as he attacked and shredded a weed.

Diego had promised himself that he'd hold himself back from Cassidy, but he'd forgotten how Shifters said good-bye.

Cassidy came against him, her arms going around his neck. Diego leaned down to her, unable to resist, as she held him tight and pressed her cheek against his. "Blessings of the Goddess go with you," she said in his ear. "Are you coming back to check on me tomorrow?"

Diego pulled away enough to look at her, but he kept his arms around her supple waist. His hands rested on her bare back, her skin oh, so soft.

"My captain made me promise I'd come and see you every day."

Cassidy's smile widened. "That's good. I'll make sure Jace has a fresh pot of coffee ready for whenever you arrive."

"Mighty hospitable of you, ma'am."

Cassidy pulled him close again, let her lips linger on his cheek. "See you, Diego."

It was all Diego could do to let her go, turn away, and walk across the yard. It was hard to walk with his pants having grown way too tight in the front.

He glanced behind him once and saw Cassidy lean down and Torey run and leap into her arms. She caught up the baby tiger, cuddling him and talking to him. Diego's heart squeezed, and he found it hard to breathe. He turned away again and pulled his coat closed over his pants so Xavier wouldn't make fun of him.

"You want to cut her probation short?" Captain Max asked Diego incredulously the next day. "Why?"

"She shops for shut-ins," Diego said.

Captain Max dropped into his chair, giving Diego his famous stop-the-bullshit look. "She can have a friend do that for her. It's only another week and a half."

"I didn't realize how many people Cassidy Warden actually took care of," Diego said. "I called her nephew this morning and asked him point-blank. She looks after all the elderly in Shiftertown. All the widows and orphans too."

"Widows and orphans. Dear God. Stop twanging the heart-strings, Escobar."

Diego grinned. "She really does. She's trying to get a kid settled with a foster mother, plus she helps three elderly Shifter females and one elderly Shifter male get groceries or fill out paperwork for the government or whatever else they need." Diego held up a folder. "It's in the file. Even Lieutenant Reid couldn't disagree."

"Yeah, I hear Reid can be a real asshole. He's pissed as hell at me for letting you have the Warden case at all."

"Well, then prepare to be surprised, sir. Reid agreed with me to ask that Cassidy's probation be shortened."

Captain Max stared. "He did?"

"Probably not out of compassion. I think he just wants his files back. Or me out of his sight. Both, probably."

"And you want me to sign off on this?"

"Cassidy Warden didn't intentionally break the law in the first place. She was scared and trying to hide."

Captain Max gave Diego a half-disgusted look. "You mean you like her, you think she's hot, and now you feel sorry for her."

"I can't lie, sir. She is hot. But Cassidy isn't dangerous. I don't think all the widows and orphans should suffer because humans decided that trespassing was a crime for Shifters."

Captain Max heaved an exasperated sigh. "Listen, Escobar. Personally, I agree with you. It's a dumb law, she didn't cause any damage, and no one cares about that rusty hunk of metal in the desert. But damn it, I hate Shifter Division down on my ass. They're the most anal, annoying shits on the planet. It's only probation, for God's sake."

"But Reid agrees with me," Diego said. "And his captain likes him."

Captain Max rubbed his hand over his balding head, climbed to his feet, and snatched the file out of Diego's hands. "All right. All right. We'll end your girlfriend's sentence early for good behavior. I'm sick of Shifter Division looking over my shoulder anyway. But she steps out of line even once—ever—it's on you."

"Yes, sir." Diego wanted to laugh in glee, but he confined himself to a quiet smile. He was looking forward to telling Cassidy that she was free to do as she liked.

Captain Max signed the forms, closed the file, and slid it back to Diego. "Diego," he said as Diego picked up the folder and started to leave. "Seriously, be careful. If you want to see this woman personally, it could backlash on you and your career. She's Shifter. Plus, you arrested her."

"I know that, sir. I'll be careful."

"See that you do. I almost lost you once. I don't want to lose you again."

"Yes, sir."

Too late for careful. Diego walked out of his captain's office with his file, reflecting that he'd just thrown away the excuse he had to visit Cassidy every day. He didn't like the thought that she might not want him to keep visiting now that she wasn't under restriction. Or Eric might not want Diego there. Eric had tolerated Diego because he didn't want to cause trouble for Cassidy. Diego was under no illusion that he and Eric were now friends.

He got a taste of dashed hopes when he called the Warden house to give Cassidy the good news. Cassidy wasn't there. Jace, who answered the phone, told Diego that Cassidy was over helping Torey and his new mom. But Jace would pass on the message. Jace also thanked Diego warmly for helping Cassidy out, then he hung up.

That was that. Diego stared at his cell phone a long moment in disappointment before he flipped it closed. Yep, he'd moved a long way past careful.

Diego's hopes rose again when his cell phone rang as he entered his apartment. He dropped the plastic bags of groceries on the counter and flipped open the phone. "Yeah?"

"Diego?"

Everything in the apartment seemed to brighten, but he kept his voice casual. "Hey, Cassidy, what's up?"

"Thank you."

Diego wanted to stand there and drink in her voice, the way she sounded truly grateful. He made himself start putting away the food, which mostly meant beer, along with some eggs and tortillas for breakfast.

"No problem. Just keep your nose clean, all right? The shitheads in Shifter Division are still jonesing to arrest you."

"I'll be careful." She kind of blew through the phrase, which wasn't reassuring, but for now he didn't care what Cassidy said. He only liked listening to her voice. "We're going to Coolers tonight to celebrate me getting sprung. Want to join us?"

Hell, yes.

Coolers was a Shifter club—that is, a human-owned club Shifters frequented. Thinking about Cassidy there, dancing in that tight blue dress, made his heart beat double-time. *This is why I'm glad I'm a man.*

"Diego?"

"What?" Diego shoved the fantasies aside. "Sure, I can meet you."

"Excellent. Ask Xavier to come too—Lindsay will be there." Cassidy laughed. "She only reminded me about ten times today to ask you that."

"Xavier. Right." Not as good as Cassidy begging him to meet her somewhere alone, somewhere dark, somewhere romantic, but he'd take what he could.

"I can't wait. We'll be there around ten. See you, Diego."

She hung up.

Diego stood staring at the phone, his heart beating off the scale, the plastic bottle of milk he held warming in his hand. When condensation rolled down his fingers, he jumped, shoved the milk into the fridge, closed the door, and hit his speed dial.

"Xav. We're going to Coolers tonight. Don't argue, just be there at ten." Diego clicked off in the middle of Xav's startled, "Sure thing."

CHAPTER NINE

By ten that night, Cassidy was so wound up she thought she'd have to shift and run around the parking lot to work it off. She settled for dancing, shimmying around the middle of the floor with Lindsay while male groupies drooled on themselves.

Coolers was one of the few clubs in town that let in Shifters. Most club owners didn't like the "element" Shifters drew, preferring to cater to rich tourists, but the Shifter-admitting clubs did a bang-up business.

Shifter groupies were humans who wore fake Collars, dressed in skimpy clothes or biker leather, painted on whiskers, and lived for contact with Shifters. Most groupies were happy to simply stand near a Shifter; others wanted full-on sex. Shifters, both male and female, were libidinous as a rule, so the sex seekers didn't always go home disappointed.

Cassidy did her best to ignore the groupies who wanted her in bed—or in a car or against a wall in the alley. She'd learned long ago that most of them didn't truly care about Shifters. They wanted the thrill of being with one, nothing more. A lot of the Shifters didn't mind—hey, if these humans wanted sex, fine—but Cassidy cared.

She understood the difference between sex for the thrill of

it and sex with love wrapped around it. The absolute joy of the second type made sex for the thrill of it empty and unfulfilling.

So, why was she was all charged up and excited about seeing Diego tonight? She was acting as giddy as a cub. Maybe because when Diego came tonight, he wouldn't be the cop checking up on her; he'd be a man coming to a club to unwind after work. A hot man who'd shared beer with her brother and with whom she'd talked about things close to her heart.

The air in the club changed. Cassidy knew, even before she turned in the dance, that Diego Escobar had just walked in the door.

He wore jeans and a leather jacket, definitely off duty, and he'd brought Xavier with him. Cassidy didn't miss how both of them slowed to check every part of the room before walking farther inside, at the same time taking care they weren't silhouetted against the open door.

"Oh, *yes*," Lindsay shouted to Cassidy. "Diego for you. Xavier for me. We compare notes in the morning, girl."

Cassidy wanted to yell back, *I didn't ask him here for sex!* But the thought of having Diego's tall body in her bed, if only for one night, sent the mating heat crawling up and down her body.

Diego and Xavier moved through the dark crowds on the dance floor to where Eric lounged against the bar. Diego walked with his usual ease, aware of every single thing around him while appearing to be relaxed. Xavier again was more restless but just as aware.

Lindsay grabbed Cassidy's hand. "Come on." She dragged Cassidy across the room at high speed, not that Cassidy wasn't willing to go.

Eric looked up at Diego, started to greet him, but just then Shane materialized out of nowhere to stand behind Diego, his growl rumbling even over the music. Shane's stance was predatory, angry.

Eric stepped to Diego's side, still acting casual, but Cassidy knew he could strike in an instant. Whether he'd strike down Shane or Diego remained to be seen.

When Cassidy reached them, she understood Shane's concern. She smelled it again, clinging to Diego like a mist, the sulfur and mint scent of Faerie.

* * *

Diego found himself reaching for the pistol in his hip holster as Eric, Shane, and Jace became a growling wall surrounding Diego and Xav. Stuart Reid's words flashed through his head.

You can't tame them, you can't trust them, and most of all, you can't be their friend.

Cassidy came up next to Eric, hot as hell in a white body-hugging dress that bared most of her long, curving legs. The woman was a walking wet dream.

Cassidy's eyes were changing from deep jade to a lighter green, her nostrils widening.

"Want to tell me what the hell is the matter?" Diego asked her. He felt his brother at his shoulder, saying nothing but ready if there was trouble.

Eric glanced at the humans around them, men and women with chokers around their necks, some of whom had painted whiskers on their faces or made up their eyes to look catlike.

"Let's talk about this somewhere private," Eric said.

"Sure," Diego said.

Eric gestured to a door at the back of the club, as nonchalant as ever. Shane, on the other hand, looked ready to kill. Diego hadn't seen Shane since they'd talked in the hall outside Cassidy's bedroom. He thought he'd gotten the bear-man to trust him a little, but there was no trust on Shane's face now.

Cassidy gave Diego a nod, as though trying to tell him everything would be all right, before she started toward the pitch-dark back of the club. Diego and Xavier made to follow her, but Shane stepped in front of Xavier.

"Not you," he said. "Just Diego."

Xavier faced Shane without flinching. "If my brother is going into a back room with a bunch of pissed-off Shifters, I go too."

Eric signaled to Lindsay. "Lindsay, keep Xavier company while we talk to Diego."

Lindsay slid to Xavier's side. "Sure thing."

"No offense, Lindsay, but no," Xavier began.

"Xav." Diego had the feeling that what he did and said here would be very, very important for a long time to come. "Give me five minutes."

"They can kill you in thirty seconds." Xavier's eyes were hard, the tough kid he'd been shining through.

"I give you my word that Diego won't be hurt," Eric said. "We just need to talk. Lindsay will be your hostage, our pledge of good faith."

"Hostage?" Xavier's voice went flat. "What the hell does that mean?"

Lindsay hooked a hand around Xav's arm. "It means that if they kill Diego, you have the right to kill me. Thanks a lot, Eric. I can think of way better things for me and Xav to do."

"Jace will stay with you too." Eric nodded at Jace, and Jace nodded back, unsurprised. "Also as my pledge."

"He means it, Xav," Diego said. He knew that Eric would never sacrifice his son. Eric had made that pretty clear the first night Diego had met him. Eric wasn't planning a kill.

Xavier exchanged a long glance with Diego and finally made a conceding gesture.

"Five minutes," Xav said. "Then I'm in there."

Diego squeezed his brother's shoulder and followed Eric to where Cassidy waited at a door beyond the bar. Shane stepped in behind Diego.

The door Cassidy opened led to a paneled, carpeted hallway. It was quiet back here when the main door closed, the hallway lined with rooms marked "Private." Why the Shifters had access back here, Diego didn't know.

Cassidy led the way. God, she was gorgeous. Her blond hair hung in a straight swath to the middle of her back, and her spike-heeled blue pumps made her legs look a mile long under that white dress.

Eric stepped around Cassidy to open one of the "Private" doors. Diego saw him jump in surprise, and he looked over Eric's shoulder into the room.

Two people were having sex on a sofa. Not Shifters. Though one wore a Collar, she was clearly a groupie, and the man wore no Collar at all. Or anything else for that matter.

Eric pushed his way in. "Get out," he rumbled.

The girl squealed and grabbed for her clothes, but the young man gave them a drunken smile. "Hey, join us. There's room."

Eric growled again, but the man paid no attention, sprawling on the couch in his naked glory.

Diego pulled out his badge and shoved it under the human man's nose. "Out."

The woman managed to hide herself as she fled through the open door. The young man eyed the badge, heaved a long sigh, picked up his pants, and shambled drunkenly after her.

Shane closed and locked the door behind him.

Diego tucked away his badge. "Five minutes," he said.

"You stink," Shane said. "Hell, I even started liking you."

"I took a shower," Diego said. "And my clothes are clean. Washed them last weekend at my mom's. She insisted."

Shane continued growling, claws showing. Diego knew he should be afraid—Shane could make short work of him, even with his Collar, and it remained to be seen whether Eric would stop Shane or not, pledge or no pledge.

But Diego felt no fear. Maybe because he'd gotten to know Eric and Cassidy a little, or maybe because he sensed that they, at least, were more worried and puzzled than angry.

Or maybe because they were on the ground floor. No heights, and Diego Escobar was one brave guy.

Cassidy stepped in front of Diego. "Leave him alone, Shane."

"Cass, he's been with Fae."

"Fae?" Diego asked. "What's Fae?"

"The Fair Folk," Eric said in his mild voice.

"You mean fairies?" Diego stared at Eric in amazement. "You believe that?"

"Of course we believe it," Shane said. "The bastards made us."

"They're real, Diego," Eric said. "I've fought the Fae. I almost died against them. They kill Shifters, and they laugh about it. They made sure we were put in these." He tapped his Collar. "They want us as we were—their slaves to hunt and kill for them. You've been in contact with one recently. I smell it on you now, and I smelled it when you came to the house yesterday."

Diego sniffed, but he couldn't smell anything but his own sweat and the sweet scent of Cassidy next to him. "I haven't met any fairies. I think I'd remember that."

Cassidy's jade eyes were full of worry. "They can look human, Diego. That hunter up in the mountains, he smelled like Fae."

"Cass," Eric rumbled.

"He needs to know this, Eric. If he's had contact with a Fae, he's in as much danger as we are." She turned back to Diego.

"Have you talked to anyone lately you didn't know? Or who looked suspicious?"

"How would I know? What do these fairies look like? Do they have wings?"

"No wings," Shane growled in disgust. "They have dark eyes. It's like looking into voids."

"They're blond or white haired," Cassidy said. "Very fair skinned. Plus, they can't touch iron. It makes them sick. They fashion their weapons from silver and bronze."

Diego considered. "I haven't talked to anyone off the force except during the drug bust I just finished, and all those guys carried plenty of iron. Or steel. Knives, pistols, machine guns, you name it. No one upchucking when steel handcuffs were slapped on them either. Could it be someone here in the club? Maybe someone I walked by when I came in. Or at the grocery store? I stopped for food on my way home."

"No." Eric shook his head. "It's faint, but I'm guessing you spent a little time with him or her, at least. Not here. I would have noticed a Fae in the club or in the parking lot."

Diego had gone to Captain Max's office before he'd left work tonight. But Captain Maxwell was about five feet six, with a fringe of brown hair, though he had very dark eyes. No blond hair or pointed ears—plus he always carried a Glock.

"It could have been a half Fae," Cassidy said. "They can look more human."

"This is too strong for a half Fae," Eric said. "The Fae scent wouldn't linger on Diego so much. I'd say full."

"Can't think of anyone," Diego said. His watch beeped. "Time's up."

Eric studied him thoughtfully, but Shane was still angry. "We can't trust humans, Eric. I always said so. Let me get the truth out of him."

"Leave it, Shane," Eric said.

"I think we're done here," Diego said. He turned around, only to find himself facing the wall of Shane. The man could move fast for someone so big.

Shane topped Diego by several inches. His face was changing into the bear-man's Diego had faced outside Cassidy's bedroom, his fingers again razor-sharp claws.

Diego looked straight into Shane's eyes. "Move."

Shane didn't move. Neither did Eric or Cassidy, though Diego sensed Cassidy ready to spring at Shane. Eric had laughed when Diego had refused to be intimidated by Shane, but he wasn't laughing now. The man was waiting to see who won the battle of wills, Diego realized. They were establishing dominance.

"Understand something," Diego said to Shane in a careful voice. "I know I can't fight you one-on-one. I don't have the strength. You could kill me right now, and I'm betting that your Collar wouldn't slow you down fast enough to save me. But I will promise that if anything happens to me back here, you'll be facing Xavier. Trust me, you don't want to. Xav might act like a guy who lives to party, but he's got a lot more anger in him than I do. If something happens to me, he'll go for you, and he won't stop for anything."

A spark jumped on Shane's Collar. Cassidy stood rigidly beside Diego, and Eric waited, quietly, for the outcome.

"Eric," Cassidy said softly. "Stop this."

Eric said nothing. Diego figured Eric would have a reason for not intervening, but he wasn't sure what it was. Was he testing Diego? And why?

"He's been with *Fae*, Cass," Shane said. "We can't trust him. *You* can't trust him."

Cassidy kept her gaze on her brother. "Eric, let me vouch for him."

Eric's quiet stance vanished. "No."

At the same time, Shane said, "Don't you dare let her."

"No, it makes sense," Cassidy said. "My fault for bringing him here tonight. My fault for bringing him to Shiftertown at all. There's a lot of Shifters out there, and if he's going to be safe from them, they need to know he's protected. You're leader, you're needed. You can't pay the price. But I can."

"Price?" Diego demanded. "What price?"

"Cass, no," Shane said, sounding anguished.

"Someone tell me what's going on," Diego said. "Now."

"Cassidy, don't do this." Now Eric was pleading.

"If he's going to be around Shifters, it's the best way. You know it."

Brother and sister exchanged a long look. For a moment, Eric's eyes held pain, raw and stark. Then they filled with understanding, even sympathy.

"This is what you want?" he asked quietly.

Cassidy stepped to Eric and put her hand on his chest. "This is what I want."

"It might not work out," Eric said in a warning voice.

"Then it doesn't."

The two exchanged another look, rife with emotion, then Eric nodded once.

"No," Shane growled. He brought up his claws.

Cassidy snarled. Her own fingers turned to claws, and she slashed quickly. Not at Shane—at her own hand.

Diego couldn't stop her. By the time he grabbed her, Cassidy had slashed three deep marks into her palm and turned her hand upside down over Eric's. Blood rained down to Eric's open hand.

"I swear by my blood," Cassidy said.

Shane's Collar sparked. "Damn it, Cass, no."

"It's done," Cassidy said calmly. "Let him go, Shane."

Shane looked devastated.

"Cassidy, what the hell did you just do?" Diego demanded.

Cassidy plucked a tissue from a box on a table and wiped her hand with it. "I vouched for you. Now, no Shifter in our Shiftertown will give you problems."

"What are you talking about?" Time was running out. Any second now, Xavier would try to burst in here, probably with LVPD's finest at his back.

Shane stepped solidly in front of Diego again. His claws had vanished, his face human again, and his Collar had stopped sparking. He looked angry but resigned. "Listen to me, human cop. If you make Cassidy pay for your mistakes, I'll kill you myself. I don't care about Collars or human law. I'll do it."

Diego could arrest Shane and confine him for the rest of his life for even saying that. But he was tired of the whole confrontation. "Just shut up, Shane," Diego said. "I'm not in the mood."

Shane remained fixed. Beside him, Eric took Cassidy's hands and kissed them. He gave her a worried and a loving look.

"I'd never let Cassidy pay for my mistakes," Diego said to all of them. "Understand that."

Shane's dark eyes were still filled with fury. "Understand *this*, Diego. Cass took a blood oath for you. That means that if you step out of line, if you betray any Shifter in any way to anyone, Eric will have to kill her."

CHAPTER TEN

Cassidy ran after Diego as he stormed down the back hall. As soon as they hit the club, he swung on her, his eyes glittering with rage.

"What crazy, fucked-up thing was that about?" he demanded.

"Diego." Cassidy reached for him.

Out of the corner of her eye, she saw Xavier start for them. Diego shook his head at him, warning him off. Xavier nodded once, took Lindsay's hand, and led her to the dance floor.

Diego took Cassidy's hand and turned it palm up. The slashes she'd made had already closed. Shifters healed quickly. "Trust me," she said. "It was necessary."

"Let me understand. If I do anything Eric considers a betrayal—to you or to him, or to any Shifter—he thinks he can kill you for it?"

"It won't come to that," Cassidy said. "The Shifters will know I wouldn't make a pledge lightly. But what you had with Shane was just a taste. If I don't protect you, you'll have dominance fight after dominance fight with every Shifter you meet. Some harmless, some violent."

"Damn it, Cassidy, Shifters can't touch me, no matter what

kind of dominance fights you think they'll start. They'll be arrested if they even try. I could haul off Shane for what he's done, and he'd be locked up forever, if they didn't terminate him."

"Instinct doesn't always listen to reason, Diego. If Eric lets me do this, then he's essentially saying he backs me up. Shifters will know to leave you alone."

"Eric's word is nothing. He can't kill you. He'd be executed—fast. He has to know that, and the Shifters do too."

Cassidy kept shaking her head, knowing Diego couldn't understand. "Eric is my pride leader and my clan leader. His word is law to me."

"No, it isn't. Even my word isn't law—I just enforce what's on the books. If Eric touches you, he'll be arrested and executed before he knows what hit him. They'd make a special example of him, since he's your Shiftertown leader."

"That doesn't matter. Eric will honor the pledge." Cassidy stepped closer to Diego and put her hand on his shoulder. She caressed, loving the hard muscle beneath his coat. "You were willing to vouch for me when your Shifter Division wanted to lock me up and not let me out. It's only fitting that I return the favor."

Diego lifted the hand she'd cut to his lips. "Not the same thing, Cass."

"Isn't it? What would have happened if I'd been arrested again? To you, I mean."

Diego shrugged. "Mark in my file. Disciplinary action, maybe. Suspension, depending on what it was you did. But Captain Max wouldn't shoot me for it."

"You did it because you decided to trust me."

Diego leaned to her, smelling good despite his brush with Fae—something she and Eric still needed to figure out. "And then you ran off again."

"I did what I needed to do, then I was finished. You'd never have known I'd gone if you hadn't popped up that evening. I wouldn't have betrayed you. And I believe you won't betray me."

"That's a lot of faith."

"I know." Cassidy put her other hand behind his neck. "Because of you, I can dance tonight in the club, celebrate with my family."

She wanted to touch him. The need to be near this man was driving her insane. Diego stirred every protective instinct she had and every mating instinct too. Maybe the crazy protective urge was because of Donovan. She hadn't been able to protect her mate, when she should have. She refused to let Diego die on her watch as well.

Cassidy also wanted the Fae scent off him. Other Shifters here would worry about it, even though Eric would warn them off confronting Diego. She believed Diego when he said he hadn't encountered any Fae, to his knowledge. His confusion had been genuine.

She lifted herself up on tiptoe and spoke into his ear. "Dance with me."

Diego's eyes went soft. He lifted her hand to his lips again and led her to the dance floor.

The music was wild and rocking. Groupies were dancing with Shifters, Lindsay twirling herself around Xav. Xavier was a good dancer, body relaxing as he let himself enjoy it.

Diego tugged Cassidy toward a more deserted corner of the floor. She turned to him, put one arm around his waist, and rested her unhurt hand on his shoulder.

There was a slow beat in the music underneath the fast one, and Cassidy started to sway to it. Diego caught on and stepped into the dance with her.

He knew how to dance, this man, knew how to move his body with controlled power. He guided Cassidy in slow circles around the rapidly gyrating couples in the darkness. Those around them danced to the rapid beat; Diego and Cassidy swayed together in their own rhythm.

Cassidy touched Diego's face, his jaw rough with dark whiskers. She came against him, resting her head against his cheek, letting her own scent mark him and erase the stink of Faerie from his skin.

Around and around they stepped, in slow, sensual rhythm. Diego's hands rested protectively on her hips. Cassidy lifted her head, and Diego looked down at her with sin-dark eyes. She kissed him.

Diego's hot, firm lips moved under hers, but he wouldn't open to her. He broke the kiss when she tried again.

"Not here," he said.

He stirred the challenge in her. Cassidy wrapped both arms around his neck. "Where then?"

"How about if I drive you home? You can explain more to me about these Fae on the way."

Cassidy smiled up into his face. "Let's finish the dance, first."

"Happy to, *mi ja*."

Cassidy put her arms all the way around him, feeling his body move in liquid grace. Across the dance floor, Lindsay grinned and gave Cassidy a thumbs-up behind Xav's back. Cassidy smiled at her and rested her head on Diego's shoulder.

E ric watched Cassidy and Diego for a time, happy that his sister had found someone to draw her out of her grief, and at the same time worried as hell. Diego was human, which brought with it a bucketful of issues. Shane trying to challenge him was the least of it.

Cassidy's pledge meant that the rest of the Shifters would leave Diego and Cassidy alone for now, which meant Eric could turn his attention to the other person in the club who was distracting him tonight.

A young woman sat by herself in the shadows at the back of the club. She'd come in with friends, but they'd soon deserted her to dance. She'd waved her friends off, telling them to enjoy themselves, while she remained alone at their table, sipping a drink.

She had dark hair and wore a slim blue dress, nothing too sexy—a woman determined not to draw attention to herself. Wasn't working. She had thick dark hair that a male would enjoy under his hands, a fine-boned face, strong limbs, and a sexy shape her dress couldn't hide. Her slender neck was bare of any Collar—real or Shifter-groupie fake.

She'd made sure not to get too near any Shifters; Eric had watched her making sure. Even now, she pretended not to see Eric leaving Shane to walk toward her, as though Eric would ignore her if she ignored him.

But *what* she was screamed itself at Eric. Eric needed to talk to her before any other Shifter noticed her.

She didn't look up at him, didn't react at all until Eric dropped into the chair next to her. "Who are you?" he asked.

She pretended to ignore him as she picked up her drink. Her eyes were deep blue, Scottish blue, like a loch in the summertime. She was sensual, beautiful, and very out of place. What this flower of the Highlands was doing in a seedy bar in the back streets of Las Vegas, Eric had no idea. But he would find out.

Eric leaned forward and rested his arms on the table, blocking the view of her from everyone else in the club. "What are you doing in here?" he asked.

The woman set down her drink and poked the slush of it with her straw. "It's a club. What do you think I'm doing here? I dance, I drink."

"You've been sitting here since you came in, trying not to be seen. Who talked you into coming? Or do you enjoy walking the edge?"

She flashed him a glance, then returned her gaze to her drink. "It's my friend's birthday."

"And she wanted to hang out with Shifters?"

"She's fascinated by them." Another glance, this one trying to be dismissive. "Can't think why."

"I take it your friend doesn't know that if she wants to see a Shifter, she doesn't have to look any further than you?"

The woman froze. Her blue eyes flickered the tiniest bit to Shifter before she caught herself and forced them back to human. "I don't know what you're talking about."

Eric reached to touch her throat. "How did you avoid it? The Collar, I mean."

She pulled back. "Get away from me, or I'll scream for the bouncer. I'm not kidding."

"The bouncer tonight is Brody," Eric said. "He's a Shifter— one of my trackers, in fact. He'll do what I tell him."

"Please, just go away."

Eric caught her chin between his thumb and forefinger. "This is my territory, sweetheart. Every Shifter in this city is under my jurisdiction. That makes you one of mine. Mine to decide what to do with."

The woman jerked away. "Arrogant bastard."

"That's what my sister calls me. And she's right. But I'm

still leader, and you're Feline." Eric drew in her scent. "A Feline female who's hit her mating years."

Her sudden, deep blush confirmed it.

Not that it wasn't obvious. Her mating need had smacked Eric's nose as soon as he'd clued in on her. His senses were a little more honed than those of other Shifters, but if any other Shifter male smelled her, she might not make it out the door. Females were too rare not to try for, and one alone, without pride, clan, or protection, would be fair game.

"I'm human," she said in a hard voice.

"You're Shifter, or at least half Shifter, passing for a human," Eric said. "Who sired you?"

Her flush deepened. "I don't know."

That could be true. Before the Collar, some Shifters hadn't been too choosy about where they dropped their seed. Probably more half breeds existed than humans knew about.

Eric leaned in. "My advice? Get the hell out of this club and don't come back. You're lucky I spotted you first. If any of the Shifters in here smell you—unclaimed, unmated, unprotected—I might not be able to stop them."

Her eyes sparkled with anger through her fear. Good. The humans hadn't cowed every bit of Shifter spirit out of her.

Eric touched the hollow of her throat, where the Celtic knot of her Collar would go. "You know what I could do, by rights? Claim you, take you home with me, snap a Collar on you, and confine you for endangering all Shifters. Make you mine in all ways."

The fear returned. Eric traced her throat, trying to soothe her, trying to make her understand her danger. And that he would protect her from all danger.

He liked that her throat was bare, though. Knowing she was free made his heart sing.

But how long could she last before the humans figured out what she was? She'd be exposed, arrested, maybe killed. Or, if another Shifter male found her, she could be taken and claimed by him. By not being raised Shifter, she wouldn't know how to resist, or even that, by Shifter law, she could.

She sat still, fury and fear mixed in her eyes. Her beautiful, beautiful blue eyes.

Eric leaned closer still. He inhaled her scent and exhaled

his own onto her. His mark. He nuzzled her cheek, breathing softly on her skin.

"What are you doing?" she demanded, but she didn't shrink away.

"Helping you."

"How is sniffing me helping me?"

Eric sat up. She smelled good, and now her scent was on him, and his on hers. "I scent-marked you. If other Shifter males try to go for you, they'll scent me and back off." In theory. It would be more difficult to protect her when she lived outside Shiftertown, but the scent mark would make whatever male tried to mate-claim her hesitate, giving her time to escape.

"Scent-marked? What the hell does that mean?"

Eric ignored the question. "When you decide you want to come in, you find me," he said. "I'll make it as painless for you as possible. Understand?"

"Understand me. I don't want to have anything to do with Shifters. Ever."

Eric put his hand on her arm. Her skin was soft, the bones fragile but still strong. Shifter strong. "You didn't choose this, I know. But you're Shifter, and you're stuck with it. You're going to need me."

"I don't even know who you are."

"Yes, you do," Eric said.

Her two friends came giggling back. They stared in delighted awe as Eric stood up, six feet six, tattoos, Collar, and all.

"*Iona*," one of her friends said. "You work fast. Aren't you going to introduce us?"

"No," Iona said.

Eric flashed a smile at the two women. "Eric Warden. Next round's on me. Except for Iona. She's leaving."

The friends looked excitedly curious, Iona angry.

Eric took Iona's hand and pulled her from her seat. Now the friends looked envious.

Iona glared at Eric, but she chose to be smart. She followed him without fighting him around the edge of the dance floor, Eric avoiding all Shifters.

Jace, at the bar, looked their way, but at Eric's slight shake of head, Jace went back to flirting with a Lupine who laughed at him from his other side. Jace would question, and Eric faced the possibility of having to lie to his own son. If even a breath of Iona's existence got out, she would be in grave danger.

Eric guided Iona out the back door to the cool of the parking lot. "Where's your car?" he asked.

Iona tried to pull away, but Eric's grip was unshakable. "My friends won't have a ride if I leave."

"I'll make sure they get home. Where?"

Iona heaved a sigh, which lifted her chest under the nondescript dress. Eric wanted to peel off that dress and find out what was underneath.

Iona led him to a small red pickup, an almost cute truck. She fumbled with the keys. Eric took them from her and unlocked the door. "How much have you had to drink?"

"Nothing. My margaritas were virgin. I'm designated driver."

"Good." Eric opened the door and put his hand under her elbow to lift her inside. The simple touch stirred fires in him, stoking embers he'd thought had long ago turned to ash. He gave her the keys and shut the door. "Go home. Stay away from Shifters and out of Shifter bars if you want to keep passing for human."

"You think?"

Without thanking him for not telling every Shifter in the bar that an unmated, unprotected female sat in their midst, Iona shot him an annoyed look, started the truck, and backed out of the parking space.

One final glare as she straightened the truck, then Iona gunned the engine. Red taillights flashed as she turned from the entrance, and then she was gone.

Eric was left alone in the dark parking lot, breathing in exhaust and dust.

"Iona," Eric whispered. The name tasted good in his mouth. *Iona.*

He'd see her again. He'd make sure of it.

Diego watched Eric leave the club with the woman in blue, Eric leaning in very protectively to her.

"Who was that?" Diego asked Cassidy.

Cassidy was looking too, curiosity on her face. "I have no idea."

The music segued into the next song, also fast-paced. Whatever happened to slow dancing? "Want to get out of here?" Diego asked her.

Cassidy smiled up at him and touched his lips. "I think so." She kept smiling as Diego put his arm around her, resting his hand on her curved hip. "You've seen where I live," Cassidy said. "Now that I'm off probation, how about showing me where *you* live?"

Diego's heart beat faster. He could take her home, slide her out of that clingy white dress, run his hand down those long legs . . .

He thought about Captain Max's warning, but at the moment, Diego didn't care. He just knew that Cassidy was tall and sexy and warm against his side. His own business who he saw off duty.

Xavier was still with Lindsay, still dancing, Xavier laughing and having a good time, as usual. Diego knew Xav would be all right, though. His brother knew how far to go and when to stop.

The parking lot was well lit, but there was no sign of Eric when they ducked outside. Brody, acting as bouncer, gave them a nod. He watched Diego sharply, likely having heard every word of what had gone on in the back room by now. But he said nothing and didn't try to stop them.

Diego's T-Bird waited in the middle of the parking lot. Shifters' cars, older but well kept, were parked in one defined area, while the human cars, mostly new, mostly expensive, sprawled everywhere else.

Diego unlocked the car. Cassidy got inside, slid off her shoes, and put her feet on the seat while Diego went around to get in on the driver's side. He put the keys into the ignition but didn't start the car, resting his hands on the steering wheel. It was quiet, almost peaceful out here after the noise of the club.

"So tell me more about these Fae," he said.

Cassidy wrapped her arms around her knees, her tight white skirt sliding up her thighs. "You're curious for someone who didn't believe in Fae half an hour ago."

"Things change. I read that Shifters claim Fae created them, wanting Shifters to be their hunters and fighters. Bred them how?"

Cassidy shrugged. "You don't want to know. *I* don't want to know. Fae have strong magic, and they're far more technologically advanced than humans—as long as the technology doesn't involve iron. Fae weakened with the rise of iron, and Shifters rebelled and got free of the Fae. You don't need me to tell you this. I'm sure it's all in the files at your police station."

"I thought the Fae connection was just a legend. The files were full of statements by biologists that Shifters are genetic aberrations."

Cassidy shot him a smile that made his uncooperative hard-on stiffen even more. "Thanks a lot, Lieutenant Escobar."

"I meant that in the best way."

Her smile deepened. Diego remembered the kiss they'd shared in the dark in her living room, the winding-up hot kiss he wanted again. He'd gotten another taste in the club, but he hadn't wanted half the Shifter population and his own brother watching him lick her mouth, tangle her tongue.

Cassidy slid across the seat to him. "I've been trying to cover the Fae scent on you," she said, touching his chest. "So the other Shifters will leave you alone. Want me to keep trying?"

The stiffness was definitely not going away. "Maybe you should," Diego said.

Cassidy rose to kneel on the seat, and warm, silken woman filled Diego's arms. He cupped Cassidy's hips and pulled her to straddle him as he opened her hot mouth.

He kissed her, each stroke going deeper, her tongue dancing across his in the best tango. Their mouths melded, lips moving, searing, seeking. She tasted like heat and honey. He ran his hand up her back, pressing her closer, still kissing.

Her lithe body rocked against his, breasts firm against his chest. Diego ran his hand down the leg that folded on the seat beside him, finding the sweet softness of her thighs.

"Cass," he whispered. "I can't get enough of you."

Cassidy made a little noise in her throat. Diego roved his hands over her back, found the catch of her dress, unhooked it. Bare back met his fingers.

A sound outside the window made Diego open his eyes. Eric?

Not Eric. Diego saw the barrel of a rifle, then heard a pop of the trigger and Cassidy's gasp as the tranq dart went into her side.

CHAPTER ELEVEN

Diego yanked the dart out of Cassidy the next instant, but too late. Cassidy wilted, unconscious, her weight pinning him to the seat.

Softly running feet sounded outside, getting away.

Diego lifted Cassidy gently onto the passenger seat, checking her pupils and pulse. She was all right, just deeply asleep.

Diego got out of the car, sliding out his pistol at the same time, took cover, and scanned the parking lot. There, a flash of movement between cars, someone sprinting with impossible speed to disappear behind the club.

Diego went after him, yanking out his cell phone as he went. "Xav, I have a situation."

"Where are you?"

Diego knew Xavier would be moving out of the club even as they spoke. "Parking lot. I'm in pursuit of a guy, tall, black hair. He popped Cass with a tranq rifle. She's in my car. Make sure she's all right."

"You got it."

Xav's voice vanished. Diego jammed the phone back into its holder and ran around the back of the club—to find noth-

ing. He heard a scrape and looked up to see a foot leaving the
ladder to the club's roof.

Hell, why can't anyone stay on the ground?

Diego stowed his gun and climbed the ladder. Halfway
up, his heart pounded so hard he thought he'd puke, and his
sweat-slick hands slipped on the rungs.

Don't look down. Don't look down.

Diego made himself keep climbing. One rung at a time.

I'm going back to the damn counselor. This has got to stop.

He was at the top. Diego had to consciously open his fingers to let go of the railing long enough to make the final step
off the ladder.

The man was all the way on the other side of the roof,
minus the rifle. Diego took cover behind the large cooling
units and drew his pistol. Just because the man had dropped
the rifle didn't mean he didn't have another weapon on him.

Diego worked his way rapidly across the roof, keeping
to cover. When he was five yards from the tall, slender man,
Cassidy's assailant suddenly spread his arms and leapt into
empty space.

"Ay!" Diego ran for the edge, stopping three feet from it, his
stomach roiling. He inched forward and peered over. Nothing.

"Damn it." Diego couldn't jump down to pursue without
risking breaking his legs—or neck. Back to the ladder.

He'd run a few feet when he nearly tripped over the tranquilizer gun. He touched it, his mouth going dry. The rifle had
come from LVPD. He'd checked out one of this exact make and
model two days ago, and besides, it had *LVPD* stamped on it.

Diego left it where it was, more interested in catching the
guy first. He'd send Xav up for the rifle.

Now to get down. As Diego approached the ladder, his
breathing came faster. And faster.

Idiota. It was just a ladder.

Diego stashed his Sig and gripped the bars, felt with his
foot for the first rung. It wasn't there. He panicked, his heart
hammering off the scale.

Cass. I have to help Cass.

First he had to find the effing step. His foot kept feeling for
it, missing. Had someone taken away the ladder?

It's bolted to the fucking building. Get a grip.

He was gripping—way too hard. Xavier would have to take up the chase. Diego couldn't even let go to call for help.

Somewhere in the dark parking lot, Cassidy screamed.

The sound spiked through Diego's dry-mouthed panic. He slammed his feet to either side of the ladder and slid downward, hands moving rapidly to keep up.

He had little memory of how he made it to the ground, but as soon as he touched it, he was off and running. His car door was open, Cassidy gone.

"Xav!"

Xavier ran up to him, breathing hard, looking grim. "Gone before I could get here. Scream came from that way." He pointed.

A wildcat—a big snow leopard—was already sprinting to the edge of the parking lot. Eric.

Diego grabbed a flashlight from his car and ran after him. Not far down the row of cars he found blood, black on the pavement. A few smears here and a few farther on. Diego's heartbeat thundered in his ears, and he ran faster. He would kill whoever had done this.

The parking lot ended at a chain-link fence, which had been kicked down in one place. Beyond was a huge vacant lot, where builders dumped whatever they'd dug up on other sites. Diego and Xavier climbed over the flattened fence, Diego's flashlight finding bloody spots on the ground.

Diego heard Cassidy cry out behind a mound of dirt mixed with stones, followed by Eric's wildcat snarl. Diego sprinted around the mound, Xavier right behind him.

Cassidy lay on her stomach, her white dress torn and streaked with dirt and blood. Sparks lit the darkness, an arc of blue white electricity crackling around her neck. Eric stood over her, but when he saw Diego and Xavier, he turned away and took off into the darkness.

Diego fell to his knees beside Cassidy and gently turned her over. Cassidy's eyes were open, the light green of her wildcat, and she breathed in shuddering gasps. As Diego cupped her cheek, the sparks on the Collar slowed and winked out.

Xavier moved past them, following Eric, his pistol out. Diego ran competent hands over Cassidy's limbs, something tight in him loosening when he found her whole and uncut. "Did he hurt you, *mi ja*? I can call the paramedics."

"No." Cassidy's hand closed on his, weaker than usual but still strong. "The blood's his, not mine. I tried to take down the son of a bitch."

Her eyes flashed to Shifter again, and her claws came out. Her Collar sparked, and she groaned.

"Easy." Diego stroked her hair. "What happened, sweetheart?"

"I woke up to find a Fae dragging me out of the parking lot. I clawed him, but the tranquilizer made me groggy. I'm only sorry my Collar went off before I could gut him." She sounded furious, not afraid.

"I'll find him, Cass, whoever and whatever he is. When I do, he'll be sorry he ever touched you."

Cassidy tried to sit up. "No, he'll kill you. Fae are dangerous."

"*I'm* dangerous, *amorcita*. And I told you, I don't believe in fairies."

"It doesn't matter. He obviously believes in you."

Diego helped her to stand. Cassidy swayed on her bare feet, and he put his arm around her waist. "How about if I drive you to a hospital?"

"No, don't. I don't want human doctors poking at me. I just need to rest."

Xavier materialized out of the darkness. "Saw no one," he said. "Footprints out the ass, but people use this field as a shortcut to everywhere."

Cassidy's laugh was weak. "You can't track a Fae. Not without being able to scent him. But that was him, Diego. The one that shot at us out where Donovan got killed. Damn."

She muttered the last word as her legs buckled. Diego swept her into his arms, having no intention of letting her walk across the glass- and rebar-strewn lot in her bare feet.

"Where's Eric?" Diego asked Xav as he strode back to the parking lot.

"Still searching."

Diego hoped Eric took care, but right now he was more worried about Cassidy.

He strode through the parking lot, Xavier right behind him. At the car, he settled Cassidy inside while Xavier stayed alert.

"Xav," Diego said. "He dropped his tranq rifle on the roof. Get it, will you? And then make sure all the Shifters in the club are all right and accounted for. This guy seems to be after Cassidy in particular, but he might go for any Shifter, who knows? I'll get Cassidy home."

"Sure thing," Xavier said. However much Diego and Xavier had fought as kids—especially when Xavier started messing around in gangs—they'd grown into a team, each instinctively knowing what the other needed. Xavier would save questions and explanations for later.

Xavier patted Cassidy on her shoulder, told her to take care of herself, and strode back to the club. Diego wasted no more time getting in and starting the car. He wanted Cassidy out of there.

Cassidy didn't speak much as they drove up Boulder Highway toward the freeway.

"You sure you're all right?" Diego asked her.

"I didn't give him the chance to hurt me." Cassidy moved over in the seat until her head rested on Diego's shoulder. "My Collar going off always makes me woozy."

She snaked her hand across his abdomen, sinking into him. Diego put his arm around her, cuddling her close as he drove.

Her snuggling against him made him more determined than ever to find the hunter trying to kill her. Fae or no, the guy would be damn sorry he ever messed with Cassidy Warden.

"You're sure it's him?" Cassidy sat in the front seat of Diego's car again the next day, looking fully recovered from her ordeal but still mad as hell. Diego had asked her to come with him tonight—she'd be able to recognize her attacker, if not by sight, then by scent.

"The tranq gun was checked out to one Lieutenant Reid," Diego said. "I didn't connect him with you saying I smelled like I'd been near a Fae, because I haven't talked to Reid in a couple of days. But I've been carrying his files around with me, and when I took them back down to Shifter Division yesterday, Reid was there. He doesn't look anything like how you describe the Fae, though. Not to mention the fact that he uses steel handcuffs and a Glock."

"If he isn't Fae himself, maybe he's working for one," Cassidy said. "Or he's half Fae, no matter what Eric says. They can use iron."

"Well, we'll ask him when he comes home," Diego said.

He looked across the busy street at an apartment complex that looked no different than the two- and three-story complexes that dotted Las Vegas. He'd driven here after he'd picked up Cassidy, wanting the confrontation with Reid to occur far from the LVPD building.

Cassidy waited beside him, restless. Her cropped white top showed off the stud in her navel, and her jeans rode low on her hips. She'd pulled her pale hair into a ponytail, which made the Collar around her neck more visible.

Diego had taken her home last night and left her in the capable hands of Nell, who'd come over in worry when she'd seen them arrive. Diego had wanted to stay, but Nell shooed him away, and Diego conceded that Cassidy needed to rest.

He'd gone back to the club to talk to Eric, who'd returned without finding anything. Diego fetched the tranq rifle Xavier had recovered, went home, and spent a restless night. This morning, Diego had investigated who'd checked out the tranq rifle and easily found the answer.

Stuart Reid, Lt., Shifter Division. He'd signed it out without hiding the fact.

Reid came to work as usual, but Diego deliberately hadn't confronted him, wanting to corner the man alone. What he wanted to do to Reid wasn't exactly regulation. Reid had neither sought Diego today nor avoided him—he'd simply gone about his business. Diego knew there was a chance he was wrong about Reid. If so, he'd apologize and leave the guy alone. If not . . .

Reid pulled up in an unassuming Chevy and got out, his hands full of grocery bags. It was dark now, and streetlights blared. Reid didn't close his blinds when he went inside, so Diego and Cassidy could watch him putting away his groceries like an ordinary man with nothing else to do on a Friday night.

Diego and Cassidy got out of the car and crossed the busy street. Diego led the way up to Reid's second-floor apartment. Second floors didn't bother Diego, as long as there were solid

stairs under him. Ladders, roofs, thirty-story balconies—
different story.

Cassidy came behind him, moving so silently Diego could
barely tell that she was there. But she was. He sensed her
anger but also her watchfulness. She had his back.

Reid answered Diego's knock without hesitation. "Escobar?" he asked, surprised. "What do you want?" He looked
past Diego at Cassidy standing behind him. "I see you've
brought your pet Shifter."

Diego pushed his way inside. Cassidy came in after him
and closed the door. Diego followed Reid into the kitchen,
walked up to the man, and smacked him lightly on the stomach. Reid flinched and grunted in unmistakable pain.

Diego had him pinned against the counter before he could
recover and yanked up the man's shirt. Four deep, red gashes
slashed across Reid's abdomen, the skin around them dark
with bruises.

"Thought so," Diego said. He pulled his gun from its holster and pressed it to Reid's chin.

CHAPTER TWELVE

Reid's hand flashed to Diego's unnaturally fast, and beyond-human strength crushed Diego's wrist.

Diego gritted his teeth but didn't move. "Let go or I'll pull this trigger, I swear to God."

Reid stopped the pressure but didn't release him. "Stay the hell out of my business, Escobar."

"Fuck that. You tell me why you shot at Cassidy and tried to drag her away last night. Tell me exactly who you are and why you want her."

"I need the blood of a Shifter."

Diego heard Cassidy's faint gasp behind him, and he ground the pistol barrel into Reid's jaw. "That was the wrong answer."

Reid's eyes flashed black with rage. "You can't understand, human. You stink like them, the bloody beasts of burden. You were all over her—it's like kissing a cow."

Diego's fury rose, the one that had had him tearing IV needles out of himself when he'd been in the hospital after being shot. "You tell me why you want Shifter blood, or maybe I'll just shoot you for the sick and twisted bastard you are."

"I need the blood for the ritual. So I can get back."

"Get back where?"

"To Faerie."

"What?" Cassidy was right next to him. "What are you talking about?"

Diego glared at Reid. "How the hell did the psych testers miss you?"

"You can't ever understand," Reid said. "I have to leave this place. I want to see my home again, no matter what it takes."

"You'll die if you touch Cassidy—or any of the Shifters. In fact, how about I arrest you for attempted murder right now?"

"I wasn't going to murder her, until she sliced me." Reid glared at Cassidy. "Now I want to bathe in her blood."

"Wait, Diego." Cassidy stepped up to Reid. "What do you mean? You need blood to get back to Faerie?"

"I'm locked out, aren't I? I searched for years for a spell, hunting down every true Wiccan coven I could, looking for the ones who'd saved the ancient Fae lore. After scouring Ireland and Scotland for decades, I found the spell here, in Las Vegas, of all places. An old woman of Irish descent had a grimoire that had been handed down through her family for centuries. That grimoire contained some rites of the ancient Fae, and had a lot to say about Shifters. They certainly hated you. The grimoire has a spell to get me back through the gates, but I need Shifter blood to work it. Lots of blood. I never got to use your mate's."

Diego felt Cassidy's rage at the same time her hands came up, fingers changing to claws. *"You killed Donovan?"*

"I never touched him," Reid said, but Cassidy was already shifting.

Her limbs became strong cat's limbs, her shirt tearing, her face contorting to the cross between Shifter and wildcat. Diego grabbed her and tried to hold her back, but she was too strong. Cassidy ripped herself out of Diego's grasp and lunged at Reid, claws and teeth poised for the kill. Sparks danced along her Collar, and she snarled in pain, but she didn't stop.

Sudden light flared, whiter and hotter than the Las Vegas sun. Cassidy fell back, and Diego shielded his eyes with his arm.

The light vanished. Diego lowered his arm to see Cassidy

standing there, still in her half-shifted form, Collar sparking, staring at the place Reid had been. The only thing missing was Reid.

The front door was still closed, but Reid wasn't in the apartment. Diego checked it, room by room, gun ready, but there was no sign of Reid. He'd simply vanished.

When he came back to the kitchen, he found Cassidy, human again, sitting in one of Reid's ordinary kitchen chairs, the man's groceries spilling over the table. Her Collar had stopped sparking, but her hands were over her face, and she was weeping.

Diego holstered his Sig and crouched next to her. To see this beautiful, brave, strong woman crying wrenched his heart. "Cass. Shh." He stroked her hair.

"He killed Donovan," she said brokenly.

Reid had claimed not to have touched him, but Diego knew what Cassidy meant. Whether Reid pulled the trigger himself or had someone else do it was irrelevant. Reid knew about the death, had been involved.

Diego kissed Cassidy's cheek. Her green eyes were wet with tears, and Diego nuzzled her. "I'll get him for that, Cass. I promise you."

She looked up, the anger in her like fire. "*I'll* get him. I'm going to find out exactly what he did and who helped him, and I'm going to gut them all."

Diego said nothing. He kept on stroking her hair, trying to soothe her, while she wept in rage and grief. He knew damn well that if Cassidy touched Reid, or anyone else, she'd be dead, possibly her whole family with her. He couldn't let her hunt him.

On the other hand, Diego could round up these people and show her Reid's body on a platter. He had the power to make that happen, and he would. He'd do anything, he thought, anything at all, to ease the hurt and grief he now saw in Cassidy Warden's beautiful eyes.

The Shifters were getting used to Diego's T-Bird moving through the streets of Shiftertown. Several waved as Diego drove by, and Diego knew enough by now to make sure he lifted a hand in greeting back.

Nell, on her front porch, watched Diego and Cassidy emerge from the car, Cassidy's shirt torn from her sudden shifting, and came alert. "Everything all right, Cass? You need me?"

Cassidy shook her head and went on into the house.

"She's all right," Diego said. Nell watched in suspicion, but she stayed on her porch.

The door to the Warden house stood open, the screen door letting in cool spring air. It was a beautiful evening, a reminder that they had only a month or two to enjoy the fine weather before triple-digit temperatures struck.

Cassidy walked right through the living room, heading for her bedroom, ignoring the tangle of two leopards that lay on the floor, dozing together like house cats.

The smaller of the wildcats—probably Jace—lifted his head and yawned, red mouth and long white teeth flashing in the dusk. He rose, still in cat form, and wandered down the back hall after Cassidy.

The larger cat rose, stretched, and became Eric. "Diego," he said. "Sit. I'll get you a beer."

Weird to watch a man saunter toward the kitchen, unworried about his naked ass.

Cassidy came out of the back again, but not as her human self. She was her wildcat, the beautiful snow leopard she'd been out in the mountains. Except that now she looked sad, so sad. When Diego sat on the sofa, she climbed up next to him, settled down, and draped her front paws over Diego's legs.

Diego thought about how she'd cried in Reid's apartment and how she'd been last night after she'd fought Reid and her Collar had gone off. She'd been tired, hurt, broken. Diego stroked her, trying to comfort her.

Her coat was soft, studded with little black dots, which were almost lost in creamy white fur. Cassidy sighed a little, her eyes drifting closed.

Eric plunked a beer on the table at Diego's elbow. A swift glance showed Diego that Eric had pulled on a pair of sweatpants, and Eric didn't hide his amusement that Diego had checked.

"She all right?" Eric said, looking at Cassidy. "Was he the guy?"

Diego rubbed Cassidy's throat. "We found him, yes. She

tried to attack him, her Collar went off, and he vanished. Into thin air."

Eric paused a second, then half fell into a chair and put his feet on the coffee table. Cassidy looked up at him, but she stayed cat.

"Tell me," Eric said.

"He's a cop in Shifter Division," Diego said. "Stuart Reid. He'd been assigned to watch you and your family. I had to talk to him sometimes about this case, which is why you smelled him on me."

"A cop?" Eric stared. "Can't be. We're after a Fae."

"We cornered him tonight in his apartment, and he had wounds that Cassidy gave him last night. He admitted he attacked her and said something about needing Shifter blood for a ritual. Claimed he was trying to return to fairyland."

"Faerie," Eric said softly. "Shit."

Jace came out of the back, dressed in jeans and a T-shirt. "If he's a cop at the police station, why didn't Cassidy smell him when she was there? Why didn't you, Dad? Or me?"

"I never took Cassidy anywhere near Shifter Division," Diego said. "We were in the interrogation rooms I always use, which are on a different floor. I hadn't talked to Reid at all before then. Most of us never have much to do with Shifter Division."

Jace put his feet on the table in a manner identical to his father's. "There's still no way a Fae could live here and be a police officer. Iron makes them sick, kills them with enough exposure. That's why they retreated to Faerie centuries ago and now avoid most interaction with the human world."

"Half Fae can, Jace." Eric's voice was quiet. "There's enough immunity in their non-Fae halves to allow them to tolerate iron. That's why they're so dangerous." He took a sip of beer. "I need to talk to this cop."

"He vanished." Diego said. "Disappeared with a burst of light. Is that a Fae thing?"

Eric shook his head. "I haven't heard of half Fae being able to appear and disappear at will, but who knows? I don't know a lot about Fae magic."

"I don't know anything about any magic," Diego said. "But I know about the shit people do to each other."

Eric regarded him a moment. "Something happened to you, Diego, something beyond your partner being killed, even your father being killed."

"A lot of things have happened to me." Diego's old anger stirred. Cassidy looked up at him, as though sensing his pain, and Diego went back to petting her. She needed the comfort as well. "But they're not what I'm talking about right now. I want to get Reid. I'm happy to arrest him and lock him up, but first I need to find him."

"I'll send some of my trackers to his apartment to have a sniff around," Eric said. "So we can start looking."

"I already sent Xav over there to keep an eye on the place. Reid might not go back there, though, now that we know where to find him." Xav, as angry as Diego about last night's attack on Cassidy, had been happy to help.

"Reid doesn't need to go back," Eric said. "My trackers can fix on his scent and use that to search him out."

Diego shook his head. "I can't let you start an all-out hunt. Reid's still a police officer, and if you hurt him or kill him I might not be able to help you. Cops hate cop killers, even if the cop is a criminal himself."

Eric gave him a hard green stare. "I can help you find him, Diego. I have resources you don't."

"I know that, and I appreciate it. I don't mind some assistance, Eric, but you have to let *me* take him down."

"Fair." Eric's voice was mild, but Diego knew better. He'd have to watch him.

Cassidy growled, a throaty rumble, gave Diego's hand a lick with a rough tongue, then languidly climbed off him.

Her cat was beautiful. Diego thought about the *cow* crack Reid had made and decided to break one of Reid's limbs for that.

Cassidy made her way down the hall to her bedroom. Eric suddenly slammed his bottle to the coffee table and climbed to his feet. "I'm grilling outside," he said. "Stay for supper."

S hifters couldn't do something as simple as cook out. The whole family got involved—Jace grilling buns and putting together the extras, neighbors drifting in to lend a hand or contribute food, and earning themselves an unspoken invitation.

Shane's mother, Nell, came over with a luscious-looking pie. "Blackberry," she said as she passed Diego. "Bears' favorite."

Diego planted himself at the cooker and watched Eric spreading steaks across the grill along with burger patties. Expensive steaks, if Diego were any judge.

Eric had sent his trackers to Reid's apartment as promised, but he'd instructed them, with Diego standing next to him, to let Xavier take point. Brody and company already liked Xavier—most people did—and agreed. Xav told Diego on the phone that he also didn't think Reid would show his face at the apartment again, but said he'd work with the trackers and keep them cool.

Diego picked up a spatula and flipped a burger Eric didn't reach in time. "Next time I'll bring you some of my mom's adobada. You'll sweat into next winter."

"Sure, human. We need that in this climate from hell."

"Spicy foods cool you down. Scientific fact."

"Right." Eric poked at the meat. "I bet you thought we ate everything raw."

Diego shrugged. "I figured you hunted it down and dragged it home."

"I've done it. Back in the wild, when there was nothing else." He gave Diego a serious look. "Then we discovered barbeque sauce."

Diego chuckled as he took a drink of beer. Then Cassidy walked out of the house, and all coherent thought left him.

She'd changed back to her human form and now wore a white sleeveless blouse, ass-hugging jeans, and sandals with a hint of heel. She'd brushed out her hair, and now it hung past her shoulders, parted simply in front.

Cassidy's tall body swayed as she walked. She didn't parade herself; she simply moved without hurry, as she walked to the cooler on the back patio, and all her curves moved in perfect harmony.

Diego wasn't the only one watching her. Every male within range stopped and stared as Cassidy extracted a beer from the cooler, opened it, lifted the bottle to her lips, and took a long, slow drink. It was like watching heaven. Diego followed the beer spilling down her lucky throat, imagined the sweat on the bottle's neck as her mouth slid around it.

"Mating need," Eric said without looking up from the grill.

Diego jumped. "What?"

Eric gestured with his fork at the males whose gazes riveted to Cassidy. "Cassidy is of cub-bearing age, and she's no longer mated. Males outnumber females around here five to one. Whenever Cassidy walks outside, every unmated male around zeros in on her."

Diego saw that. Blatantly or subtly, the men watched Cassidy. "And you let them?"

"They can look all they want, but it's Cassidy's choice. The males can claim her and fight each other to the death for her, but she can still turn down the mate-claim. The high ratio of males to females means that the females get to be choosy."

Diego frowned at the hungry stares trained on Cassidy. "What if they don't wait for her to be choosy?"

Eric flipped a steak. "Cassidy's my second, plenty dominant enough to make anyone she doesn't like back off. Plus, she's my sister. Anyone touches her against her will, they know they'll answer to me. And, trust me, they don't want to."

Diego didn't have to be Shifter to understand. Eric wouldn't need to threaten or even look belligerent. Just as in the neighborhood that had spawned Diego, the people here knew who ruled, who could do what, and what would happen if they disobeyed the unspoken rules.

The difference between Diego's world and Eric's was that Eric implied he'd respect his sister's choice. The man who had ruled Diego's neighborhood had pretty much kept his sister away from all comers, whether she liked it or not. She'd tried to kill her brother one day, just to get away from him.

Cassidy smiled over at Eric and Diego, oblivious that she was the topic of conversation. She came to them and clicked her beer bottle against Diego's. Diego had a hard time breathing.

Cassidy slipped her hand under Diego's arm. "Take a walk with me."

Eric turned back to his burgers and steaks, and Diego let Cassidy move with him to the edge of the party. A few more steps, and they were in darkness.

"I know you and Eric are talking about tracking down Reid," Cassidy said. "I also know that Eric will try to keep me out of it. But *I* want to find him."

Cassidy's voice held an edge. Diego recognized that edge, having heard it many times from himself.

"I'm going to kick his ass for touching you, Cass," he said. "I want to, and I can. And if he had anything to do with Donovan's death, I'll get him for that too. I promise you."

Her eyes glittered in the darkness. "Are you going to shut me out too?"

"No. But you were ready to kill Reid tonight. If he hadn't gotten away, you'd be in deep shit—so deep I wouldn't be able to get you out of it. You have to let me do this my way. I'll gather evidence against him to make the charges stick. If I'm careful, I can get Reid convicted for murder, not just assault and abduction. Trust me, I want him to go down."

"We have to find him first."

"I'll find him," Diego said with conviction. "Xavier and I are good at what we do, we have your brother's trackers, and Eric seems to be good at what he does too. Between all of us, Reid doesn't stand a chance."

Cassidy's face softened, but he saw the sadness in her eyes. "Diego . . ."

Diego put his hands on her shoulders. "Believe me, Cass, I'm going to get Reid for even trying to hurt you. And if he had anything to do with your mate's death, he'll pay for it. And if he didn't, I'll find out what really happened to Donovan, and make whoever killed him pay for it. I swear to you."

She looked perplexed. "Why would you do all this for me?"

Because he understood what she was going through. Someone had killed a person she loved and gotten away with it. Donovan's death must be an open and festering wound for her, and Diego wanted to heal her.

Diego knew damn well he might never run to ground the men who shot Jobe, might never have the satisfaction of taking his vengeance. But he could at least do this for Cassidy.

Diego squeezed her shoulders. "I'm doing it because you have a great ass."

Her answering smile flared. "Lots of women have great asses, Diego Escobar."

Diego slid his hands to the ass in question. "But I like yours best."

"Yeah?" Cassidy's touch flowed to his own buttocks. "Yours is pretty nice too."

Diego caressed her, finding her firm and sweet. "This is dangerous."

"I like dangerous."

He touched her Collar, which felt smooth and cool, like an innocent piece of jewelry. "You all right?"

"The Collar didn't have time to do much damage today. You petting me helped. A lot."

Her smile sent fires through him. Diego touched the Collar again. "I don't like to see this hurting you, *mi ja.*"

Cassidy looked up at him, her eyes full. "Thank you, Diego." She reached up to him, mouth hot, and Diego kissed her without hesitation.

CHAPTER THIRTEEN

Cassidy wrapped her arms around Diego's neck and melted to his heat. They swayed together, mouth to mouth, body to body. Cassidy's hurt, guilt, and anger receded as she sought him hungrily.

Diego's mouth was scorching. He opened to her, lips moving on hers, his tongue sweeping in. He pulled her against him, and she felt his obvious wanting, hard and without shame.

Cassidy cupped his buttocks, the fabric of the dark pants he wore for work catching on her fingers. She slid a hand up his chest, feeling his heart beating hard beneath her touch, and worked his tie loose. She liked the heat under his suit coat, felt the frustrating restraint of the leather holster tight against his side. She wanted to touch all of him.

She moved the loosened tie and popped open the first buttons of his shirt. She felt his damp throat, his smooth skin above his T-shirt, curls of hair touching her fingers. Cassidy broke the kiss to lick the hollow of his throat, his dark skin beckoning.

Diego ran his hands through her hair. She'd loved how he'd petted her when she'd been in cat form on his lap, in smooth, comforting strokes. He'd been a friend soothing her hurts, nothing sensual.

Now was *all* sensual. Diego ran his hand down to the small of her back, pulled her up to him, opened her mouth with his. He slid his fingers beneath her waistband, the low ride of the jeans letting him find the elastic of her panties and caress beneath it.

Out here, in the darkness, alone, Cassidy could drink him in. No shame, no worries. This man was awakening her mating frenzy—awakening *all* her emotions—for the first time in a long, lonely while.

Diego's teeth scraped her lips, and Cassidy scooped herself into him, loving it. She wrapped her arms around his neck and pulled him close while his fingers did their dance on the mound of her buttocks.

Something bounded out of the darkness, swerved past them, kept running. Wolf, by the scent. Diego broke the kiss as another wolf charged after the first. The two ran through the scrub, noisily disappearing into darkness again.

Diego looked around, breathless. "What the hell was that?"

Cassidy too tried to catch her breath. "Lupines. Those two just mated. They're in a mating frenzy."

"Mating frenzy?"

Cassidy kept her arms around Diego's neck, not wanting him to step away. "The need to mate—constantly. Mating until you fall dead asleep. Then waking up and doing it all over again."

Diego smiled his hot smile. "Must be something in the air."

"Must be."

Diego kissed her again, leisurely this time. He finished by brushing light kisses to her lower lip. "Cass . . ."

He was going to ask to sleep with her; she saw it in his eyes. He wanted her. Cassidy would say yes, and she'd love it. It would tear her up inside, because Donovan had been her mate, and she'd never forget that. She was confused, and scared, but still she knew she'd say yes.

A shrill peal cutting the air had Cassidy almost lifting off the ground. She gave a nervous laugh as Diego pulled his cell phone from his pocket. He studied the readout and gave it a regretful look.

"Sorry, Cass. I have to take this."

Cassidy nodded, folding her arms over her stomach as

Diego backed away. He touched the corner of her mouth, still looking regretful, then he turned and headed toward the house as he answered the phone.

Cassidy hung back to watch him walk away in measured strides, a man sure of himself. She liked that he never apologized for kissing her, nor tried to joke about it or express any shame about it. He kissed her because he wanted to. And he enjoyed it. If the phone hadn't rung . . . Would she have been sorry for going home with him? Or just loved it?

"Damn, girl." Lindsay materialized out of the darkness. "I saw that luscious kiss. On a scale of one to ten, I'd give you an eleven."

"That good, was it?" Cassidy asked distractedly.

"That *hot*. Lip-smacking, I'm-pea-green-with-envy hot." Lindsay bumped her hip against Cassidy's. "What are you going to do about it?"

Cassidy's throat felt tight. "I don't know yet."

"You don't know? I do. You're going to go for it. Diego has no human mate, he's gorgeous, and best of all, he has a brother. For me."

Any other time, Cassidy would laugh at her, but she was too wound up. "Part of me wants to." She let out her breath. "All right, most of me wants to, especially the relevant parts of me. But I'm not sure it's a good idea. It's still too soon."

"Cass, Cass, Cass." Lindsay shook her head. "You don't have to have the mating ceremony with him. You don't even have to see him again if you don't want to. But you're throwing off pheromones so hard, you're making me itch. I'm starting to have dreams about Shane and Brody. At the same time. Don't do that to me. I only want to think about pretty Xavier."

Cassidy unbent enough to grin. "You want me to jump Diego's bones so *you* will calm down?"

"Yes. You owe it to me as your best friend."

"What you're really saying is that I should get Diego out of my system."

"Amen, girlfriend."

Lindsay had a way of putting things in perspective. Cassidy watched Diego standing between her and the house, having stopped to talk hard into his phone.

Getting Diego out of her system was probably a good idea.

But remembering that searing, masterful kiss he'd just given her, Cassidy knew it would never be that simple.

Cassidy started back for the house, ignoring Lindsay's *Atta girl* behind her.

Diego finished his call, closed his phone, and waited for Cassidy to catch up to him.

"Cass, I'm sorry, I have to go. There's something I need to take care of."

Cassidy's heart beat faster. "Was that Xavier? Did they find Reid?"

"No." The warmth in Diego's eyes had gone, and he seemed distant now, closed off. "It's a different case. I need to go talk to somebody." He leaned down and brushed a kiss to her lips. "I don't know how long this will take."

Meaning he thought he wouldn't be coming back tonight. Cassidy folded her arms, trying to suppress her disappointment. "I understand."

Diego cupped her cheek. "See you tomorrow?"

"Sure."

Diego smiled again, but absently, as though his thoughts were far away. He kissed her lips again, then turned and left her.

She watched Diego walk to the house, pause and say good night to Eric then Nell, who sat on the Wardens' back porch in an Adirondack chair, and duck inside. As Cassidy reached the porch she heard Diego's Thunderbird roar to life then rumble away down the street.

Eric gave Cassidy a brief, one-armed hug as Cassidy passed him. She returned the hug then sank down into the chair next to Nell's. Cassidy's mouth was still hot from Diego's kisses, and her entire body throbbed.

"You look unhappy, Cass," Nell said. "What did the human do? Or, wait, maybe it's something he *didn't* do."

Cassidy shrugged. "Not his fault. He has a demanding job."

Nell crossed her strong legs and sipped from her beer bottle. "Don't hit me with your bullshit, sweetie. You're upset about it. But you need to remember, he's not Shifter. Most humans hold themselves back, no matter how much their needs scream at them. That's why they have so many psychologists."

"Some Shifters are holding back too," Cassidy said.

Nell patted her hand with her large one. "I know it's tough, Cass. I lost a mate myself. I know what you're going through."

"I know. Thanks, Nell."

So much loss. That was why Shifters had agreed to human strictures, so they could recuperate from all the loss of their past. To recover, lick their wounds, strengthen. The humans thought they'd confined Shifters and controlled them with the Collars, but Shifters had learned to find strength in communities. They were rebuilding themselves behind the fences humans had erected for them.

Nell lifted her beer bottle. "Doesn't stop me from wanting a good shag, though. Embarrasses Shane and Brody, but too bad for them."

Cassidy had to laugh. "They'll get over it."

"My boys try to intimidate the hell out of any male I show interest in. Not that males aren't intimidated by me already. Damn, I wish I were petite."

Cassidy squeezed Nell's hand. "Males don't like alpha females."

"I know that, the shits. Until there's a fight. Then they want us to save their asses."

Cassidy shook her head. "Males."

"That human of yours is no submissive himself, you know."

"I figured that out the day I met him," Cassidy said. "I saved his life, and it seriously pissed him off."

"Yeah, I heard the story. Alphas don't like to show weakness, especially to their females."

Cassidy thought about that for a while, and also about the phone call that had made Diego back away from her, away from Shiftertown. He'd said it had nothing to do with Reid, but Cassidy wanted to know what it was about. Whatever it was had upset him, though Diego had tried not to show it. She'd scented his distress.

"Is Brody busy, Nell?" she asked.

"Brody? Sure you don't want Shane?" Nell gave her a hopeful look, one she'd been giving Cassidy since they'd all moved to Shiftertown.

Cassidy sighed. "Nell, you know I like Shane, but . . ."

"But you aren't interested in him as a mate. I know. I

wouldn't mind having you for a daughter-in-law, Cass, that's a fact. But I understand. The mate bond can't be forced, and now this human has caught your eye."

"Diego was good to me when he didn't have to be."

Nell snorted with laughter. "Oh, please. You mean he's majorly hot. I have eyes, sweetie."

Cassidy couldn't help her grin. "Well, that too."

"Go. Get Brody. Do what you have to."

Cassidy leaned down, kissed Nell on her smooth cheek, and walked through the darkness to the house next door.

Diego drove around the last corner and felt like he'd traveled backward in time. The same houses were still there, the same liquor store with men and women standing idly in front of it, slot machines inside flashing white and red lights into the night. He could swear the same homeless guys hung around the Dumpster on the other side.

Diego had left this street fourteen years ago when he'd enlisted in the Marines, vowing he wouldn't be back. He had to come back, of course, from time to time. First to move his mother and brother out to the house his mom lived in now. Then, once he'd become a cop, his job had brought him back. Diego knew the streets and the people, which made him an asset to the LVPD.

One person Diego knew was Enrique Gonzales, a former gang leader who had made the young Diego's life an unmerciful terror. Diego now approached the one-story row apartments where Enrique lived with a feeling of pity.

Enrique was dying. He'd contracted HIV from a shared needle a while back, and pancreatic cancer was taking him. Not long now, probably. A month or so at most.

The man lived in the same apartment his parents had, they having succumbed to disease years ago, bodies worn down by drugs. Enrique's sister had fled the neighborhood the night she'd tried to kill him.

Enrique lived alone, getting money to pay for his needed medication by selling information to the police. Enrique knew everyone and had many connections, and he'd stopped worrying about people killing him for being a nark.

Diego took a step back when Enrique opened the door. Enrique had never been the cleanest of guys, and the house had always smelled. Now with Enrique alone and uncaring, the stink was bad.

A Shifter would run away howling. Maybe that was why Shiftertown was so damn clean—anything else offended their superior senses of smell.

"*Hola*, Diego." Enrique shuffled away from the door. Formerly a huge man, he'd lost so much weight that his flesh sagged on his bones. "I got beer somewhere," he said in Spanish.

Diego followed Enrique into the living room. "No, thanks."

Diego took out a roll of cash, five hundred dollars, all twenties, and handed it to Enrique. Enrique pocketed the money without counting it and motioned for Diego to sit on a threadbare armchair.

The state-of-the-art TV in front of the chair had its sound muted, but a movie rolled across the screen in vivid images. Enrique plucked up a remote, shut off the TV, and slumped into another chair.

"It's sometimes hard to find people in Mexico," Enrique said, sticking to Spanish. "But I did it. They're holed up in a little town called La Nébeda. They're gringos, so they stand out, and they're stupid, so they *really* stand out. Want me to have them taken down?"

Diego shook his head, though his heart beat faster in hope. "Stay out of it."

Enrique shrugged. "Don't matter to me. I won't go to prison, won't have time to make the trial even. Doesn't matter what I do now. But I get that you want to do it yourself. They got your friend."

Enrique did understand, in his own way. "Keep it cool," Diego said. "And go in peace."

Enrique laughed, a harsh sound. "I'd rather go out fighting. You know, in a good battle. Don't know why you're so concerned about me, Diego. I was one of the reasons you ran out of here like you were on fire."

"You were taking way too much money from my mom, who was working her ass off just to keep me and Xavier fed. She says hi, by the way."

The man's laughter rumbled again. "Juanita Escobar is one tough lady. She gave me the money but told me what she thought of me. *You* were a shit. A mouthy, too-tough-for-your-own-good kid, which is why I kept having you beat up. Heh." He shook his head. "Look at us now."

Yeah, right, those were good times.

Diego stood up and moved to leave. "I appreciate the info."

Enrique looked up at Diego with tired eyes. "Why don't you shoot me, Diego? Right now. I know you're carrying. You always hated me. You can tell everyone I offed myself. Wouldn't be far from the truth."

Diego hesitated. Enrique was suffering. The pain in his eyes was real. He'd been a strong man—an alpha, in Shifter terms—though Enrique always put his own interests first. Eric, on the other hand, ensured that his family and everyone in his jurisdiction was protected.

Enrique had never protected anyone. He'd collected money up and down the street, had Diego and Xavier beaten if they didn't obey him, and threatened to shoot both of them if Diego's mother didn't pay him. Enrique had demanded even more favors from Diego's mother, but she'd managed to put him in his place over that.

"Tell you what," Enrique said. He reached into the drawer of the table next to him and pulled out a black forty-four, a big weapon. "I've got my piece right here. You can say I lured you over here, then I shot at you when you came in the door. You shot me back in self-defense. *Comprende?*"

He screwed a silencer onto the end of the gun before taking the wad of money out of his pocket and plunking it on the coffee table. "Send that to my sister. I know you know where she is."

"I'm not shooting you, Enrique."

"No?" Enrique grinned, dark eyes sparkling. "Too bad, because I'm shooting you."

Diego barely dodged in time. Two bullets thunked into the solid front door, right where Diego's head had been. Enrique shot again, but this time, Diego's bullet went dead center into Enrique's chest.

Enrique gasped. His pistol fell from his slack hand but he

managed to smile. "*Muchas gracias,*" he whispered, and then he died.

Diego holstered his pistol, put the roll of cash back into his pocket, and called 911.

He left in exhaustion hours later. He'd told the uniforms who responded plus his own captain that Enrique had lured him over with the promise of information about a drug case then shot at Diego when Diego entered the house. Diego hated lying, especially to Captain Max, but he couldn't tell them the true reason he'd visited Enrique tonight.

Captain Max accepted the story then told Diego to take some leave, to get over the incident. Diego didn't fight him.

He started his car and drove home. Out of the old neighborhood, leaving the past to return to the present. *Cassidy.* The present was so damn much better.

Cassidy had been waiting a couple hours in the pitch darkness of Diego's bedroom when she finally heard him open the front door and come inside. Any minute, he'd walk in and turn on the light, and find her sitting there in the chair beside his bed. He'd be startled, but he'd smile and walk to her, and maybe take her in his arms. She'd explain that she'd come to comfort him as he'd comforted her earlier tonight, just as friends, if that's all he wanted.

Diego entered the bedroom, and her heart beat faster. He could also grow angry for her presumption and ask her to go. It was the chance she'd taken, but Nell, and even Lindsay, had convinced her. Time for Cassidy to act on her needs and worry about later . . . later.

Diego didn't turn on the light. He shed his jacket and gun and holster, then headed straight for the bathroom. He did turn on the bathroom light, throwing Cassidy into shadow, before he cranked on the water in the shower.

Through the open doorway, Cassidy watched him peel off the rest of his clothes. His strong, broad back came into view, and she saw a jagged black tattoo stretching across his shoulders. Next, he stripped off his pants, and now she saw his powerful thighs and legs, his firm backside.

His cock hung, thick and long, but nowhere near erect. Whatever Diego contemplated as he prepared for his shower, it wasn't sex.

Diego stepped into his square shower stall. The frame was rubbed brass, the walls transparent glass. Steam wafted from it, and the mirror began to mist.

Diego had his back to Cassidy as he let the water spray his face, wet his black hair, and run down his body. Water beaded on his biceps as he pushed his hands through his hair. His back tapered to a fine, tight ass, all wet. The black hair on his legs became plastered against his skin, and water ran over strong feet.

He lathered with soap from the soap dish and started rubbing his chest and arms. Suds dripped down his back, sliding between his buttocks.

Cassidy's blood was on fire.

She silently rose from her chair and entered the bathroom on bare feet. She could move like the cat she was, and Diego never heard her.

She could see his profile now. Diego slid soap down his torso, lifting his balls to gently wash under them.

She was about to call out to him when Diego let out a low sound of anguish. Cassidy knew that sound, animal pain so deep it cut.

Diego leaned his arm on the wall, cradling his head. His back shook, his body rocking. Diego Escobar was crying.

It broke her heart.

Without bothering to undress, Cassidy opened the shower door and stepped inside with him.

CHAPTER FOURTEEN

Diego jerked his head up and swung to her, his pain screaming itself at Cassidy in the breathless silence. Instead of
demanding to know how she got into his apartment, Diego
pressed her against the tile wall and kissed her.

They were hot, needy kisses that left her gasping. His
mouth was a point of fire as their lips parted then met again,
and again.

Her hands roved his back, found the wet skin of his buttocks. The very short cream-colored dress Cassidy had put on
to come over here was soaked, and Diego so easily found the
zipper in the back.

She hadn't bothered with a bra tonight. Diego's hands slid
down Cassidy's bare back, scooping her to him at the same
time. His kisses were frenzied, the need in him strong. His
cock was hard now, rigid against his abdomen.

Diego pressed her wet hair back from her face, cradled her
in his big hands. "How did you know, *mi ja*?" he asked. "How
did you know I needed you?"

Cassidy shook her head, beyond words. She'd needed *him*.
But something had happened tonight after he left Shiftertown,
something that had hurt him.

She ran her hands down his back, putting every ounce of calming into her touch. *It's all right. I'm here. You're safe now.*

Diego shuddered. It was working, his heartbeat slowing, or at least coming down from its frenzied pace. He tilted her face to his, the heartache in his eyes burning.

Cassidy found herself lifted up the wet wall, the water pounding around them. Diego yanked her panties down, and Cassidy kicked them off.

She and Diego were face-to-face now, water all over them. Diego kissed her face and her throat, open-mouth kisses that scorched. He kissed her lips, opening her, taking what he wanted. Cassidy wrapped her arms around him and gave back.

He lifted her right leg, fitting it around his hips. Cassidy clung to him, drawing a sharp breath as his tip pressed her opening. Diego's eyes opened all the way as he shoved up into her in one quick thrust.

Diego kept kissing her, their hot mouths bumping, seeking, needing. He was huge inside her, stretching, burning. He felt so, so good.

The part of Cassidy that had died when Donovan had been killed blossomed like a long-dormant flower. She groaned. "Diego, *yes.*"

Diego backed her against the slick tiles, his kisses everywhere. A string of Spanish poured from him, words she didn't understand. His mouth was hot, his cock, so thick inside her.

Cassidy said his name, the only word that flowed through her head. She whispered it; she shouted it. She touched him all over, his broad back, the sleek line of the tattoo, his hard buttocks as he loved her.

In this position, he couldn't thrust much, but he filled her, and pushed higher and higher. Cassidy held on with hands and her leg around his hips, her head back on the tiles while he kissed her.

Diego was tight inside her, where he belonged. He felt good, damn good. Cassidy had no thought but of Diego, his breath, voice, body, heat. She was shaking, trying to draw him up into her, wanting him to stay there forever.

"No," he said, voice grating. He shook his head against the tile next to her. "No, not yet."

Cassidy touched his face, his skin so hot. The heat snaked up her fingers, moved through her blood, twined around her heart.

Squeezed tightly there, wove fingers through her emotions and held on. Not releasing when Diego lifted his head and softly kissed her. A bond on her heart, a need to be with this man whatever happened to him or to her.

The mate bond.

Cassidy gasped in shock. Diego fisted her hair in his hand, kissed her lips. "*Mi ja*," he whispered. "*Amorcita*."

Cassidy couldn't speak. It couldn't be. Not with a human. Not so soon after Donovan . . .

The mate bond didn't care. It wound happily around her heart as Diego shut off the water, lifted her into his arms, and carried her, both of them dripping, into the bedroom.

C assidy's beautiful jade eyes were on him as Diego set her on the bed.

It was a mess in here. They should be doing this in some lush hotel room, maybe in a mountain cabin or by the beach, with a roaring fire or Mai Tais or something. Cassidy deserved a more romantic place than Diego's cluttered bedroom and unmade bed.

Next time. Next time would be perfect.

Cassidy was beautiful as she lay back and watched him through half-closed eyes. Her body was beyond gorgeous. Generous curves, long legs, breasts a man could die for. Her skin was pale, the ancient Scots in her, the dusky tips of her nipples awaiting his mouth.

She'd come to him. Diego's entire body hurt with what he'd done, and Cassidy had come. She'd known he needed her and exactly how to ease his pain.

Diego climbed over her on hands and knees. Any thought that she shouldn't be here, that he shouldn't do this, didn't matter anymore.

Their mouths met again in hungry frenzy. Diego broke off to lick the side of her neck, and Cassidy nibbled his shoulder, her soft breasts pressing him.

Diego lowered his head to take one of her nipples into his

mouth. He suckled the velvet tip, teeth scraping the hard little point. Cassidy moaned, driving him wild.

"Cass," Diego whispered, just to say her name.

"Please."

The little whimper got him. He should be sated after finishing in the shower, ready to sleep, curled against her.

Not yet. Not by a long way. Diego nudged her thighs apart and found her still as ready for him as he was for her.

Diego lowered himself to her and slid straight into her. Her eyes flicked to light green as he entered her, her cat's eyes.

"Cassidy." Diego slid all the way inside, resisting closing his eyes as she squeezed around him. He wanted to see her face. "Beautiful."

Her eyes flicked back to the deep jade green he was falling in love with. She was hot inside, so damn hot. He'd never met anyone like her.

When he thrust in again, Diego lost his tight control. He squeezed his eyes shut and just *felt* her, her body so soft under his, sweet hot sin on his bed.

Cassidy forgot how to breathe. Diego closed his eyes and turned his head, water from his hair dripping to her shoulder. He was heavy on her, his strong body enclosing and overwhelming hers.

She loved it. His mattress was firm on her back, his long, strong body hot on hers. Diego was inside her, and he fit just right, as though he belonged there and always had.

Cassidy wanted more of him, and more and more. She begged shamelessly with her body, arching into him, running her fingernails down his back. He smiled, opening his eyes to look down at her again. Cassidy loved his eyes, dark enough to drown in.

The heat she'd felt in the shower tightened even more on her heart and fanned out through her body. It was hottest where they joined.

This shouldn't happen. Can't happen.

But it was, and her heart and body sang with it.

Diego smiled at her, his eyes wicked and warm. He kissed her, swallowing her next gasp.

Slow thrusts grew faster. Then faster. Diego kissed her face, her lips, her neck. Cassidy's hips moved to meet his, sensations flooding her. All thought shut down. There was nothing in the world but her and him, their heat, this feeling.

Body on body, skin sliding on wet skin. Diego *inside* her, part of her, the craving to be joined with him—forever.

"*Mi ja,*" he whispered. "My beautiful, beautiful Cass."

His warm voice brushed liquid syllables over her. She'd loved his voice since the first time she'd heard it.

Diego couldn't get enough of her. That little smile, her green eyes, the scent of her body, the feel of her around him. This was *right*. This was home.

Thought dissolved into frenzy. Nothing existed but feeling. Cassidy's softness, her squeezing him so hard, her bare foot teasing on his leg. Breasts beneath him, hot mouth, scent of her desire, hips rising to meet his.

Never stop, always be here. With Cassidy. With the woman who should be his. Now and forever.

Words came out in Spanish, the language of his heart. "My love, my soul. Always mine. Always, Cassidy."

No more words. Their bodies met and melded, kisses turning to fire. His blood burned. He wanted all of her, more and more. Mindless. Feeling. *Mine!*

Diego's body shot the last of his frenzy into her. She moaned, moving with him, just as frenzied.

Diego wanted to stay inside her forever, but he settled for lying on top of her and gathering her against him. She breathed a sigh and smiled at him.

The smile was full of warmth, of caring, Cassidy who'd come to save him from himself. The darkness that had dogged him and eaten at his heart had eased somewhat. Because of her.

Diego knew, as he kissed her again, that he had to have this woman in his life. For always. No matter what he had to do to get her there.

They made love twice more, and at the end, Diego was as awake and alert as he had been when they'd started.

Cassidy drowsed though, and he let her, liking the way she looked curled under his sheets. Diego finally rose, quietly so he didn't disturb her.

He did a quick rinse off in the shower, tucked a towel around his waist, and went out to see what he had in his kitchen. He should offer her chilled champagne, but he'd be lucky if he had a couple of Coronas in the fridge.

The noise he heard was soft, impossibly soft, but it raised every trained sense he had. Someone was outside.

Diego quietly closed the bedroom door, cutting off the glare of the bathroom light he'd never turned off. In the living room's darkness, he crept to the window and looked out.

His front door led to a small outside balcony that served as a doorstep for his apartment and the one next door. Open stairs ran from it down to the parking lot. At the bottom of the staircase, a shadow flitted into view and then almost instantly vanished.

Diego moved noiselessly across the living room, set the two beer bottles down on the counter, went back into the bedroom, and picked up his gun from the dresser.

Cassidy propped herself on one elbow. "What is it?" she asked sleepily.

Diego's heart beat swiftly, both with adrenaline and at seeing the beautiful woman he'd just had sex with rising from his sheets.

"Someone outside."

"Oh." Cassidy lay back down. "It's just Kyle, one of Eric's trackers. He's here to protect me. He and Brody."

Of course. Eric, rightly so, wouldn't have let her leave Shiftertown without them, not with Reid running around loose.

Diego put the gun back into its holster on the dresser. "How did you get in here, anyway?"

He hadn't cared when she'd suddenly appeared in his bathroom—it was enough that she was there—but he was calm enough now to be curious. The front door had been firmly locked when he'd entered the apartment.

Cassidy smiled, a wicked, tempting smile that made him want to crawl right back into bed with her.

"Kyle, the Lupine, is very good at picking locks. But he won't be coming in. I took his lock picks away from him."

"Devil." Diego turned off the light in the bathroom, shut the bedroom door, and came to the bed. It was warm under the covers with her. "Tell me something. Why is Brody one of Eric's trackers but Shane isn't? Or is he?"

Cassidy pulled Diego into the comfortable nest with her. "Shane is Nell's second. There'd be a conflict of loyalty if Shane worked directly for Eric."

"But not if Brody does?"

"Brody's lower in the bear hierarchy. And Eric has one male from each Shifter family working for him in some way. It's another way he keeps the peace between species."

"Your brother is too damn clever for his own good."

Cassidy shrugged. "He's a good leader, and he makes use of all his resources."

Of which, Diego realized, he himself now was likely one. But he didn't want to talk about Eric and his trackers. "Come here," he said.

Cassidy put her arms around him, and Diego held her close. He drew a long breath and let it out. "I killed a man tonight," he said.

Cassidy started, then she stroked his back, soothing. "Oh, Diego. What happened?"

He told her. Diego hadn't told the dispatcher the truth, or the paramedics, or the uniforms, or his captain, not even Xav, who'd come to the scene when he'd heard. But the story poured out to Cassidy, from what Enrique had been like at fifteen to the thirty-five-year-old pathetic wreck Diego had shot tonight.

Diego found his eyes wet with tears. "Enrique didn't think I would do it. He was going to shoot me for real. He smiled at me as he died, as though I'd finally measured up in his eyes." He rubbed his forehead. "Like I ever wanted that son of a bitch to approve of me."

Cassidy touched Diego's cheek. "He was an alpha who'd lost his power. Sometimes dying pride leaders do that, when their power has passed on. They hole up somewhere and ask a young alpha to fight them, so they can go with dignity."

Diego shook his head. "Enrique deserved to die ten times over for what he did to my family and to so many others. He doesn't deserve dignity. But tonight, I felt sorry for him."

"Because you have compassion. The best leader does. Strength without compassion isn't true strength."

Diego managed a smile. "Listen to you. Like I haven't

dreamed about shooting him in the ass all these years. Like I don't want to find the men who killed Jobe and rip them apart with my bare hands."

"Of course you do. Just like I want to rip apart the men who killed Donovan."

Diego pressed a finger to her lips. "Which you are going to let me take care of," he said. "Humans won't tolerate Shifters killing humans."

"Shifters do a lot of things without bothering about humans," Cassidy said.

"Don't tell me things like that. I'm a human cop, and if I know things, I'm obligated to act on them."

Cassidy licked his finger. "All right. This is a no-telling zone."

His blood heated. "*Dios*, you're sexy, Cassidy. Especially when you smile at me like that."

Cassidy widened her smile. "You're sexy too."

"Stop looking at me like that," Diego growled.

"What are you going to do if I don't. Restrain me?"

Diego shivered. "And don't make my mind go there."

"Go where?" Cassidy gave him an innocent look.

He leaned into her. "Dirty, naughty places. Like it did in that skyscraper when I slapped cuffs on you. Sexiest ass I ever saw in my life."

"And yet, you still took me in."

"Just doing my job, ma'am."

"I wanted to jump your bones in the interrogation room," Cassidy said.

Diego's mind conjured up about five good scenarios, all of them highly satisfying. "I wanted to jump yours. Let's just say that if the video had been running, we could have made a fortune selling it on the Internet."

Cassidy grinned. "Really? It would have been that good?"

Thoughts of Cassidy, coveralls open, on the ugly metal table, lingered in his head. "It would have been *damn* good."

"It was pretty damn good right here." Cassidy rolled her lower lip with her teeth. "Maybe still is?"

Diego rested his fists on the bed. "Are you saying you want more?"

"I'm saying I want *you*."

It was a good thing Diego had decided to take a few weeks'

leave to get over shooting Enrique. He wouldn't be able to walk after tonight.

He pushed Cassidy down on the bed, letting his tongue do some exploring. Cassidy's skin was fiery and salty, her breasts smooth, filling his mouth with her taste. Diego suckled and licked, then drew his tongue to her navel and flicked it over the stud there.

Cassidy laughed. "That tickles."

"Too bad, *querida*. What happens to this when you shift?"

"It just goes away when I shift and is there when I change back."

"Oh, right. How does that work?"

She shrugged. "A Basque woman in northern Nevada made it for me. There's magic in it, she said."

"Magic." The Shifters liked to talk a lot about magic and seemed very comfortable with it. But then, these were people who could move back and forth from animal to human form. Scientists tried to claim that the shape-shifting ability was genetics gone wrong, but there had to be more to it. "Pretty magical, all right."

Diego played with the stud with the tip of his tongue, liking it. Cassidy's flat stomach rippled with her delight. "Lindsay and me both got one, daring each other. I was pretty crazy when I was younger."

"Yeah? What about now?"

"You're starting to make me crazy again."

Diego warmed. "Good." He left the stud and licked lower, then lower, to the warmth between her legs.

Cassidy stiffened. "What are you doing?"

Diego raised his head. "What does it feel like I'm doing? I'm feasting on you."

Her eyes were round, her breasts rising as she half sat up. "I've never . . ."

"Been feasted on?" Something in Diego went tight. "Do you like it so far?"

Silently, she nodded.

"Then I'll keep doing it."

Diego lowered his head. Dear God, she tasted good. He drank her in, the beautiful taste of Cassidy, his damn gorgeous, sexy woman.

He rose up over her, hard and wanting her. Cassidy's face was languid with sex, but there was a stunned look in her eyes. Diego grinned at her. "Did you like that?"

"Hell, yes."

"Good. How about some more?" He lowered his head again.

Cassidy loved it. His tongue drove her crazy. Hot, wet, wild, beautiful. *"Diego."* Cassidy raised her hips, wanting more. And more.

Diego slid his arms behind her legs, pulling her toward him. He knelt over her, positioning himself, then thrust straight into her.

He was big, opening her, satisfying her. Cassidy never wanted it to end.

Diego feathered her skin with hot, leisurely kisses. He made love to her just as leisurely, as though they had all the time in the world, slow heat in the cool night. *"Amada mia,"* he whispered. "You are so beautiful."

Cassidy didn't understand all his words, but the mate bond did. It rose up in her to bind her to him, and it wasn't going to give her a choice about it.

Hours later, Diego woke in the warm bed with Cassidy when someone thumped on the front door.

He didn't want to get up, not with Cassidy backed into him, her buttocks nestling sweetly into his groin. Sunshine poured through the window to touch her hair—when had it stopped being night?

The thumping didn't end. Cassidy looked at him sleepily. "That's not the trackers," she said. "They wouldn't knock. And if it was someone trying to hurt us, they wouldn't let them near the door."

Diego growled, but he got up, pulled on a T-shirt and sweatpants, and made for the living room. He relaxed when he recognized the silhouette outside his living room window, and unlocked and opened the door.

"Hey, Diego," Xavier said, walking in. "Ready to go?"

Diego rubbed his head. "Go? What time is it? What *day* is it?"

"Saturday." Xavier strode into the kitchen in his gray T-shirt and jeans and frowned at the two beer bottles still sitting on the breakfast bar. "We're supposed to go to Mamita's."

"Oh, yeah." Real life, which had seemed a million miles away, rushed at Diego with lightning speed. Last night, when Diego had talked to Xav, Xav had reminded him, but that seemed a lifetime ago. Xav had said he'd turn sitting on Reid's place over to Eric's trackers, because missing Mamita's Saturday breakfast wasn't an option. Mamita had made that clear a long time ago.

Xavier's gaze was on the half-open bedroom door. The bed was hidden but not Cassidy's shoes resting lazily on the floor.

"Aw, hell, Diego, you've got Cassidy in there. Why didn't you say anything?"

Diego stepped to the bedroom door and pulled it shut. "Keep it down."

"You should have used the signal. I'd have left you alone."

Diego and Xavier had worked out a signal when they'd moved into their own places years ago. If either had a woman spending the night, one front window blind was to be completely closed, the other to have the slats half open.

"There wasn't time," Diego said. "Give me a minute."

Xavier strode to the refrigerator, looked inside, and shook his head. "You'll starve Cassidy to death. Tell her to come with us and have one of Mamita's spectacular breakfasts."

Diego imagined Cassidy meeting his mother and how that would go, on both sides. But he *did* want Cassidy to meet his mother. Cassidy was special, and his mother would realize that.

Diego opened the bedroom door, ready to invite Cassidy and offer her first dibs on the shower.

He faced an empty bedroom. Cassidy's dress and panties still lay in a heap on the bathroom floor, but she was gone.

The window by the bed was wide open. Diego went to it and looked out. Two years ago, he'd have hung all the way out, but now he stayed a safe foot back on his solid floor and scanned the narrow alley below. He saw nothing but a few stray newspapers caught between the apartment building and the block wall that separated the property from an empty desert field. The apartment's back wall was sheer, but a large wildcat

could have easily leapt down, scaled the far wall, and faded
into the field on the other side.

Damn. The disappointment cut deeper than he'd have
imagined.

Diego showered and dressed while Xavier flipped chan-
nels on the television. Diego left the back window open when
he and Xavier headed out. It was unlikely a human being
could scale the sheer wall that led to his bedroom, and Cassidy might want her clothes back.

Cassidy waited, crouching in the scrub of the empty lot,
until she saw Diego's T-Bird drive off. She knew he was
unhappy with her running, but the mate bond sneaking up on
her had terrified her, and she needed to retreat and think about
it. Meeting his mother while the mate bond toyed with her
was not something Cassidy was ready for.

She'd seen Diego looking out the window for her, confused
and irritated, and she didn't like how that made her feel. But
she'd make it up to him. Cassidy would call him later, invite
him back to Shiftertown, explain.

*I'm trying to protect you, Diego. Just as I did when I took
that blood pledge to keep the other Shifters off your back.*

Eric hadn't been happy about that, but he'd understood.
Eric could be tough, but he had wells of compassion.

The back alley was quiet. Brody and Kyle were waiting
farther back in the desert lot, impatient and wanting to get out
of here. She sent them a low growl to cool it a minute while
she flowed quietly to the top of the wall.

From there, it was an easy leap through the back window
Diego had so thoughtfully left open for her. She'd need her
clothes if she wanted to drive home.

Cassidy landed on the bedroom floor with a light thump.
She started to shift into her human form when a sudden smell
assaulted her nose.

Fae.

She froze for a split second, then she sank back into her
wildcat. The Fae was moving around the living room. Cassidy slid noiselessly around the bedroom door, keeping to the
shadows.

It was him all right, tall and slim, dark-haired, and stinking of Faerie. Reid.

He didn't see Cassidy until she leapt.

Reid whirled, eyes full of fire. Cassidy's Collar went off, biting pain deep into her, but she opened her mouth and went for his face.

She felt something bite into her side, and found herself spinning, dizzy and sick, the world blurring before her eyes until it snapped and went dark.

CHAPTER FIFTEEN

"She climbed out the *window*?" Juanita Escobar said from the stove. "I've heard of men doing that when the husband comes home, but not a girl with nothing to hide."

Xavier had told their mother the whole story with a grin on his smart-ass face.

"Xavier probably scared her," Diego said. He sipped coffee, which was wonderful. The only coffee he'd found that came close to Mamita's was Jace's. The fried potatoes, beans, and eggs she was whipping up for breakfast chilaquiles would be even better. "Cassidy's shy," he said.

Xavier's eyes widened. "The woman who broke into your apartment and waited for you to come home to have sex with you is shy?"

"You should have brought her with you, Diego," Mamita said sternly. "You should have called for her to come back."

Xavier laughed. "Here, kitty, kitty."

The trouble with being head of the family meant having no privacy whatsoever. "Leave it alone. Cassidy obviously didn't want to make a big deal of it. Fine, we won't make it a big deal."

"How can you know what she does and doesn't want to do?" Mamita asked. "She's a Shifter, not a human. She probably reacted instinctively, like a cat who doesn't know who's approaching it. They hide first, and then they investigate."

"Call her, Diego," Xav said. "Tell her everything's all right."

"Or, I could give her some space," Diego said irritably. The problem was, he kept thinking about Cassidy's beautiful body, her kisses, and her throaty, sexy voice. He couldn't *stop* thinking about her.

His mother started layering the egg mixture with crisped tortilla pieces, then cheese. "Sounds like she doesn't want space; she wants reassurance. Call her, Diego, then go get her and bring her over here. I want to meet her."

Diego held on to his patience. "I can't guarantee she'll want to meet you."

Mamita gave him a pitying look. "Ask her. If a girl agrees to meet a man's mother, then she's serious. If she doesn't, then it was a one-night stand, and you're better off knowing right away so you won't break your heart."

"There's no question of me breaking my heart." The pang in it betrayed Diego's lie.

His mother's look turned sharp before she went back to the chilaquiles. "You let me be the judge of that. You're thirty-two, Diego. It's time you started seriously looking."

"Mamita wants grandchildren," Xavier said, his grin back.

"And don't you laugh at your brother, Xavier Escobar. It's time you started looking too. Enough with you two pretending to be bad boys. You don't play the parts very well, and you need someone to look after you."

"Oh, man," Xavier said, shaking his head. "Now my own mother's telling me I'm not macho."

"You're not," Mamita said. "Neither of you has ever had a serious relationship. You're both afraid to commit, and you're both lonely. I'm your mother. I know."

She had a point. But Diego refused today to be dragged into the perpetual why-don't-you-find-a-nice-girl-and-settle-down argument.

He hadn't found a nice girl and settled down because, first, there hadn't been time for it, and now, his job had him jaded. Women either wanted something from him—leniency, protection—or they shied away from marriage to a cop. Being a law enforcement officer was dangerous, the hours and pay were crappy, and the divorce rate was high. He'd gotten around the problem by simply not thinking about it. Xavier, the same.

Diego pulled out his cell phone. "I'll call Cassidy and make sure she's all right. Happy?"

He'd planned to do that anyway but not while his mother and brother watched him and listened to every word.

Diego turned away to seek some privacy, but before he could, his cell phone rang. He blinked in surprise at the read-out before he flipped it open.

"Hello?"

"Diego. It's Eric. We've lost Cassidy."

Diego went still while something cold and painful clenched inside him. "Lost her? What the hell do you mean, *lost her*?"

Eric's tone held rage, ferocity, and fear. "Brody told me she went back into *your* apartment, and then she vanished."

"What are you talking about? How could she have vanished?"

"I don't know, but it stinks of Fae all over your damn apartment. What the hell, Diego?"

"*Dios*, Eric, I don't know. Cass ran off before I could stop her. Weren't your trackers supposed to be protecting her?"

Eric growled—a wildcat growl, nothing human. "We can point fingers all day, but we have to find her."

"No kidding. I have an idea where to start looking."

"Yeah, so do I. Meet me out there, all right? Bring as much backup as you can."

Diego shut off the phone, his heart racing like crazy. He turned around to find his mother and Xavier staring at him, having heard every word.

"Go find her, Diego," Mamita said.

"I intend to. Xav, can you help?"

Xavier didn't even cast a longing glance at the chilaquiles. "Sure thing. Let me get my stuff."

Diego put his hand on his brother's shoulder, walked him out of the house, and spoke to him in a low voice. "Do you still know how to make pipe bombs, like you did when you were in that gang?"

Xavier looked offended. "I told you, I wasn't in the gang—" Xavier broke off as Diego shot him a don't-bullshit-me-now look. "Yeah. I remember."

"Good. Put something together."

"What do you have in mind?"

"Diversions and a damn good scare. And firepower if we need to take this guy down."

Xavier grinned. "You got it, Diego." And he went to get ready.

C assidy woke to find herself flat on her back on cold, hard stone. Her hands were bound and stretched above her head; her feet were likewise bound. She was naked and in her human form.

She had no idea where she was. She could tell only that it was a dark place, cold, smelling of stone and mud. And Fae.

There he was. Across the room, backlit by a few candles— why candles?—was Reid. Tall, thin, but with black hair and dark skin. Fae, definitely, but like no Fae she'd ever heard about.

Cassidy clenched her hands. The chains were solid but she was strong, and if she could shift to her wildcat . . .

She relaxed her body and summoned the shift.

And screamed as her Collar went off. But not just the Collar. Electric pain shot through her from wrists to ankles, wrapping her like white-hot bands of wire. They would slice her in half, and she would die in so much pain she'd welcome the darkness.

Dimly she saw Reid turn to her, eyes glittering black in the candlelight. Cassidy forced herself to calm.

Diego. Think about Diego. His warm smile, the way he spoke in liquid tones, the things he whispered to her as he lay with her, touching her, kissing her.

The strong warmth of the mate bond. The mate bond that shouldn't exist.

Cassidy took a deep breath. When she exhaled, the arcs of pain slowed, then stopped.

The mate bond warmed her, tried to soothe her hurts. It wouldn't be able to completely—nothing would. The only thing that would calm her thoroughly was the touch of Diego, her mate.

Reid came to her. He'd changed to more casual clothes than he'd been in when they'd confronted him in his apartment—

jeans, a gray hoodie jacket, and no shirt underneath. He looked like an ordinary human, except for that smell of Fae.

Cassidy's instinct to kill rose again. She suppressed her urge to shift, knowing that would only bring back the pain. But she had to break out of these chains.

Reid didn't speak to her. He leaned over and ran his gaze along her bare body, as though contemplating where to make the first cut.

Cassidy snarled and lunged. She felt the shackles give. And then her Collar went off, and again the escalating pain swept her body.

She slammed her eyes closed and fought off the pain one breath at a time. When she could speak, she said, "What did you do to me?"

"Wired your Collar to a Taser," Reid answered in calm voice. "When it goes off, it triggers the Taser and sends a shock along the chains."

Goddess, help her. "Do you get off torturing Shifters? Does it get you high?"

"No." Reid sounded, if anything, anguished. "I hate it."

"Oh, that's nice. Then why are you doing it?"

"I need you to bleed out without fighting me. It's nothing personal."

Cassidy jerked upward instinctively, then gritted her teeth and sank down before her Collar could go off again. "Well, it's personal to *me*."

"I know. I'm sorry. But you're Shifter."

"And to you Shifters are animals. Bred to do your fighting and hunting so you don't get your hands dirty."

Reid's eyes flashed in indignation. "*I* didn't breed you. *My* people didn't. That was the *hoch alfar*, the full-of-themselves bastards. Playing with nature to prove they could. I am glad the Shifters broke from them and made them pay the price." His anger and derision rang true.

Cassidy stared at him in confusion. "Your people? What do you mean, *your people*?"

"The *dokk alfar*."

"I have no idea what that means."

"You wouldn't."

"Enlighten me," she said.

"There isn't time. I have to kill you, Cassidy. I'm sorry, but it's the only way."

"Like you killed my mate?"

Cassidy drew another breath as her Collar started to tingle, tried to calm herself into the mode she assumed as second in command to Eric.

"Tell me," she said, in the most composed voice she could manage. "Tell me why you're doing this, if you hate it."

Reid sounded less derisive, more broken. "They threw me out of Faerie, the *hoch alfar*. Your blood, I told you, Shifter blood, will send me back there. Nothing else will. I'm sorry."

He lifted a long iron-bladed knife that glittered in the candlelight and touched it to Cassidy's stomach.

Eric, Jace, and Shane were already parked on the dirt road halfway up the mountain when Diego and Xav arrived in Xav's F-250. Diego knew without Eric mentioning it that all his trackers had already fanned out, covering the hills around the rock outcropping where the sharpshooter had pinned them down the other night.

"He's in there," Eric said without greeting them. "I smell him. How did you know Reid would bring her here?"

"Because he was so fucked-up eager to grab her here when she came the last time." Diego started taking weapons out of the truck. Besides his Sig, he holstered a Taser, and so did Xav. "Plus this was where Donovan was killed, and Reid was involved. There's something special about this place for him."

Eric nodded. "I thought that too."

While they spoke, Xavier hiked a little away from them and started unloading his backpack.

"What's he doing?" Shane asked.

"He's going to create a diversion," Diego said. "Reid won't abandon his fortress unless he has to. But we'll flush him out. When we do, you, Eric, and your guys grab him while I go in and get Cassidy. Even if we only scare him into vanishing, we still get Cassidy."

Rescuing Cassidy was the main objective, at least in Diego's mind. Finding Reid and stopping him, secondary.

"I'm going in there with you," Shane said. He stood in front of Diego, big arms folded. The guy was huge.

Shane also loved Cassidy. Diego saw that. But he loved her enough to take her rejection and still make sure she was safe and happy.

"Yeah, that would be good," Diego said. "We save Cassidy."

Shane nodded silently but didn't move.

Eric squeezed Diego's shoulder, his big hand strong. "I appreciate your help, Diego. I'll put my trackers in position. We'll be ready."

Diego still blamed Eric's stupid trackers for Cassidy getting nabbed in the first place, but they could battle that out later. Right now—Cass.

Find her, take her home, hold her, love her. Never let her go.

Diego touched his earpiece. "Xav. You ready?"

"Almost there."

Eric silently stripped down. Diego averted his eyes, but the sight of grown men suddenly removing their clothes no longer startled him. Shane stripped too, the guy so massive he'd make the most powerful wrestlers burn with envy.

Both men shifted at about the same time. Shane was close to Diego, and suddenly the space next to Diego was filled with grizzly.

Shane's bear lips rippled as he growled, and he fixed a black-eyed stare on Diego. *Dios*, the man was scary, even with the Collar gripping his big neck. Shifter bears were larger than their natural counterparts, which meant Shane was gigantic. Any hikers meeting *him* in the woods would run away, peeing themselves.

Eric, in his wildcat form, let Diego fix an earpiece to his tufted ear. Eric wouldn't be able to talk back, but at least Diego could keep him informed of what was going on. Eric didn't look happy about the procedure, but he put up with it and slipped into the woods.

Xav jogged back to them soon after Eric disappeared. "Small charges, but they'll make a lot of noise." He stopped and stared at Shane. "Holy shit."

Shane glowered right back at him. Xav drew a deep breath. "Remind me never to piss you off, Shane."

Shane gave a grunt that might or might not have been a laugh, and turned away. He padded toward the rocks, with Diego and Xavier following noiselessly. They stopped on Diego's command and crept toward the rock cave under the shadows of the closest trees.

"Eric," Diego whispered. "We're in place."

A faint growl sounded through Diego's earpiece, Eric's answer. Diego and Xav positioned themselves on either side of the rock entrance with Shane in the shadows. Diego prayed to any saint willing to listen that this was going to work, then he drew a deep breath.

"Now," he said to Xavier.

Xav pressed his detonator. Something flashed, then boomed in the middle of the clearing. The sound jolted Diego, and the wildlife took off. Wings fluttered and brush exploded as rabbits, birds, and deer fled the sound.

Nothing came out of the rock cave.

"We're going in," Diego said.

Xav nodded once, ready. Before they could move, Shane came charging out of the shadows—silent death—and ran straight between the rocks that marked the entrance. Xavier and Diego exchanged a swift glance and ran in after him, weapons ready.

Cassidy was there. She lay on her back on a flat stone, bound hand and foot. Red candles ringed her, all lit, throwing weird shadows onto the ceiling.

"Diego," she shouted. A warning, not a plea.

Reid dropped on them from above, the man in jeans only. He wasn't big, but he was wiry, his arms strong as they wrapped around Diego and pinned his firing hand.

Shane didn't care. He charged, knocking both Diego and Reid to the rocky ground. Several tons of bear landed on them, razor sharp claws coming down.

Reid screamed. Diego felt Reid growing hotter even as he brought his weapon around, saw light filling the cave. The man was about to vanish.

This is going to hurt, Diego thought, just as he stuck his Taser against Reid and pulled the trigger.

CHAPTER SIXTEEN

There was nothing like waking up with fifteen hundred pounds of bear on top of you. Diego shoved, but Shane was still out.

He heard another crackle of Taser, smelled more burning flesh, then heard Xav's voice. "No, you're staying down."

"Diego?" That was Cassidy.

Diego slithered and slid out from under the unconscious grizzly and climbed to his feet.

Xavier stood over Reid, Reid out on the floor, his bare torso covered with sweat, blood, and dirt. Cassidy lay naked on the stone, very still, as though afraid to move. Diego limped to her, holstering the Taser he still held and kicking candles out of his way.

Chains wrapped Cassidy's wrists and feet, and wires ran through those up and down her body to her Collar and then to a Taser. No wonder she didn't want to move. If she set off the Collar, she'd light up the chains as well.

"I'm sorry, Diego," she murmured.

"Why are *you* sorry? Reid did this, not you."

Diego felt along her Collar for the connections—simple

ones, he was happy to find, but Reid would pay for every one of them.

"I shouldn't have gone back into your apartment without checking it out, first. I knew Reid was still out there somewhere. I should have had Brody come with me."

Diego gently pulled wires from the Collar. "Don't beat yourself up, Cass. I'm kind of wondering why you went out the window in the first place. My mom's chilaquiles aren't that bad."

"I'm Shifter."

Diego finished with the wires and worked on the chains. They were locked in place with small padlocks. A quick search produced no keys, but small locks like these were nothing to a boy who'd been trained to break into cars by age ten.

Diego picked them carefully. "I'm not going to hide you," he said.

"No, but humans and Shifters don't mix well. It's hard on the human."

"You want to let me worry about that?"

"I've seen it happen, Diego. Humans lose their jobs, get shunned by their families. Don't risk that for me."

Cassidy was the one bound hand and foot, and she was worried about *him*.

"Mamita wants to meet you. She's not going to shun you. As for my career—an asshole from my office kidnapped you and wrapped you in chains. I'm not the one losing my job."

The last chain fell from her wrists. Cassidy rose with a groan, but her arms went right around Diego.

Diego gathered her to him as he helped her to stand, then they held each other. Cassidy buried her face in Diego's shoulder, her embrace strong and warm. Diego was happy to hold her and soothe her, which helped soothe him.

He leaned into her, rubbing her skin, absorbing her warmth. Animals tended to cuddle together for reassurance, and Diego thought they were pretty smart.

A rumble filled the little cave. Shane rolled up from the floor, waking up and fighting mad.

"Easy," Xavier said. He turned the Taser on him.

Shane opened his mouth and roared.

He's like a bear waking out of its hibernation sleep. He doesn't know who we are.

Diego brought out his own Taser again. "Xav, give him a chance but take him down if you have to."

Cassidy stepped away from Diego. Though her body was covered with dirt, her hair a tangled mess, she stood straight and strong.

Shane swung around to Diego and Cassidy with a long, low snarl. He charged.

Cassidy pushed Diego behind her. "Shane!" she said. "Stop."

Diego grabbed Cassidy and tried to move her, because Shane wasn't stopping. The bear's Collar was going off, sizzling all over the place, but he kept coming.

Cassidy held up her hand. "Shane. Stop, *now.*"

Shane's gaze snapped to Cassidy's. Awareness slammed through his eyes, followed by an oh-shit look. Shane stopped so fast he skidded on the mud, paws shoving over the last of the candles before he crashed into the stone slab and went still.

Cassidy went to him. "Shane? You all right?"

Shane sat back on his bear haunches, shaking his head. Cassidy leaned down and stroked his fur.

Now there's something you don't see every day. A gigantic grizzly sitting on the stone floor, splashed with wax and dirt, growling as a beautiful woman petted him on the head.

Shane shifted back to his human form, growling and groaning all the way. "Ow." Now he was a very large naked man smeared with wax and dirt, with a beautiful woman petting his head.

"You OK, Shane?" Diego asked.

"Yeah." Shane rubbed his face, gently pushing Cassidy away. "Good shot, Diego. Did you get the shit?"

"He's still out," Diego said.

Reid lay motionless, Xavier returning his Taser to him.

"I'll kill him," Shane said.

Diego shook his head. "Get in line."

Cassidy returned to Diego, arms stealing around his waist as though she couldn't not touch him. "I want to talk to him. How can we keep him from vanishing?"

Eric came through the entrance, shifting as he rose to his

full height. He took in the scene and went at once to Cassidy. Cassidy turned her embrace to her brother, the two holding each other tightly for a moment. There was nothing sexual in the contact—just two people who loved each other, happy to see each other whole.

Eric broke the embrace, rubbing Cassidy's shoulders. "Have Diego and Shane take you home. The Fae is mine."

Diego had heard that phrase often enough to know what it meant. Eric wanted them all to leave so he could kill Reid in private. Whether Reid died swiftly or lingered, Eric would finish him, Collar or no.

"No," Cassidy said. "I want to face him."

"Too dangerous," her brother answered. "He's obviously after you, Cass, and needs to be dealt with."

"He killed Donovan." Her voice filled with emotion. "He killed my *mate*, Eric. It's my right."

Shane broke in. "He's a fucking Fae and a Shifter hunter. I say let Eric . . . um . . . talk to him."

"No." At Diego's sharp word, everyone turned to look at him—all but Xavier, who kept his gaze on the captive.

"This isn't the wilds of Scotland in the Middle Ages," Diego said. "Reid is a cop—a human cop as far as other humans are concerned. If it's even rumored that a Shifter gutted him, all Shifters will pay."

Eric growled. "So what do you propose, human? He's *Fae*. Our enemy. You want us to let him get away with what he's done?"

"No, I want you to let me deal with it."

"You can't," Eric said.

"You'd be surprised what I can do."

They faced each other, Shifter to human. Eric was going to make this a dominance thing, but Diego didn't give a rat's ass about dominance. Reid would pay for touching Cassidy—but if Eric ripped into him, all the Shifters, including Cassidy, would be punished for it.

"Eric," Cassidy said softly. "Diego's right."

Eric dragged his gaze from Diego and pinned it on Cassidy. "I don't want you facing this guy either, Cass. Don't even think about it."

From the look on her face, Cassidy was definitely thinking

about it. "At least let me talk to him," she said. "I need to talk to him."

"She needs closure," Diego said. "Trust me, I know this."

Eric's gaze was right back on Diego. "You think I don't understand? I've been alive for three times as long as you have. I lost my mate and was left with a cub to raise on my own. I've been hunted and rounded up, chained down so humans could perform experiments on me. Don't tell me I don't understand about revenge."

"Um, ladies and gentleman," Xavier said in the corner. "Reid's waking up, and this man can vanish himself. Our question is—how do we keep him contained while you argue about who gets to do the honors?"

"You said iron hurt Fae," Diego said, "but Reid obviously works just fine around iron. What about silver?"

"Fae love silver," Cassidy said. "The purer the better."

"That's good," Xavier said. "Because I don't have any pure silver sitting around waiting to be used on a Fae."

"Tranq him," Diego said. "And we'll take him to my place. We keep him drugged until we decide what to do with him."

"Fine," Eric said. "But we take him to Shiftertown. No, don't argue with me. We have a better chance of hiding him there. No human neighbors to wonder why there's Shifters all over your place. And if he tries to escape, there will be nowhere for him to run."

Diego conceded the argument. He went back to Xav's truck for the same tranq rifle Reid had checked out of Shifter Division days ago, brought it back inside, and took a lot of satisfaction from shooting the dart into the side of Reid's ass.

Cassidy found herself once more watching Diego drive, this time in Xavier's truck. Eric was in his own car with Xavier, and in their trunk was Reid, bound and tranquilized.

Cassidy wore sweats that Eric had thoughtfully brought for her. Her dress must still be at Diego's. The mate bond kept squeezing her and humming happily. Diego had come for her. He'd known where to find her, and he'd come.

She reached over and rested her hand on Diego's arm. Just

touching him made her feel better. Diego glanced at her, his eyes full of warmth.

Cassidy wrapped her hand more firmly around his arm and sank her head into his shoulder. The hunt, the fight, had only stirred his warmth, she felt. Diego wanted sex; she could sense it and scent it. He'd wait until they were finished with this business, until he was certain Cassidy was safe. And then . . .

The mate bond was helping to keep down other things inside her. Rage, grief, the need for vengeance. They swooped at her, one after the other, but the mate bond kept them from driving her into a killing frenzy. She closed her eyes and breathed Diego's scent. Comforting. Warm.

At the Warden house, they unloaded the unconscious Reid, not without drawing attention. Shifters had no concept of minding their own business. They came out of houses and stood watching curiously as Diego and Xav carried Reid into the house.

Nell came over from the porch next door. "That him?" she asked Cassidy.

Eric had gone inside closely after Diego and Xav. The trackers on their bikes and Shane in his truck were just pulling in.

Cassidy couldn't speak, emotions now overwhelming her. Nell, understanding, pulled her into a hug, her arms strong. "I know, honey. I know. Want me in there with you?"

Cassidy wiped tears from her eyes. "No. Thanks. I have to do this."

Nell gave her a quick squeeze. "All right, but if you want me, you just yell. I'm good at getting men to confess their sins. I've had all that practice with Shane and Brody."

Cassidy smiled but at the same time blinked back more tears. "I'll be fine."

But would she?

Cassidy went inside to find that they'd tied up Reid on the floor, in a space cleared in the living room. Xavier sat backward on a wooden chair to watch him, both a Taser and a regular pistol in his hands. Eric waited on the other side of the room, Jace beside him. Diego stood above Reid, the tranquilizer rifle resting easily in his arms.

Cassidy halted at Reid's feet, her emotions churning. She

wanted to kill him, at the same time she wanted to pound on him until he begged her to stop.

Diego reached over to the dining room table, grabbed a glass of water that had been resting there, and poured the water over Reid's face.

Reid coughed, and his eyes fluttered open.

Diego cocked the tranquilizer rifle and pressed it into Reid's stomach. "First question. Who are you, really?"

Reid's eyes were glassy as he stared up at Diego. He blinked, trying to focus. "You know me. Stuart Reid. I'm *dokk alfar*."

"What the hell does that mean?"

"That's what he said to me," Cassidy said. "In the cave. He said his people were the *dokk alfar*. He called the Fae the . . . something that sounded German."

"*Hoch alfar,*" Jace said, breaking in. "It's of Scandinavian derivation. It means, literally, *high elf. Dokk alfar* can be translated as *dark elf.*"

"There's elves now?" Xavier asked. "What is this—*Lord of the Rings*? Pointy ears, long hair, bows and arrows?"

"Goddess, you're ignorant," Reid sneered.

Cassidy scented it, Reid's body heating into the flare that built right before he vanished. "Diego."

Diego dug the rifle into Reid's stomach. "I can tranq you before you can fire up. Just stay here and answer, or you're going to have one hell of a hangover."

Jace came to them, still interested in Reid's revelation. "Where do you think Tolkien got his ideas for his elves? From the legends of the Fae—from Celtic, Norse, and Anglo-Saxon stories. I've never seen a dark Fae, never knew they existed."

"They exist," Reid said. "*I* exist."

"So, you're not half Fae," Eric said.

"No." He shot Cassidy a derisive look. "I am pure."

Cassidy had had enough. She advanced on him, ready to shift, ready to gut him.

"Why Donovan? Why *him*?" The last word robbed her of breath. Grief, rage, sorrow, confusion took hold of her. "And don't you *dare* say he was only Shifter."

To her amazement, Reid looked ashamed. "He wasn't supposed to die," he said. "I'm sorry. Those hunters killed him before I could stop them."

CHAPTER SEVENTEEN

Cassidy advanced again, unable to stop herself, the bare floor cool on her feet. "What are you talking about? You told me you needed his blood. And my blood. Nothing *personal*, you said."

"Shifter blood, yes." Reid's face was pasty, his breathing shallow. "I was going to take an un-Collared Shifter. These hunters had bagged un-Collareds before, and I paid them to do so again. I told them to keep the Shifter alive. But when I got there . . . when I got there . . ." A shudder went through him. "They'd shot him and pulled off his Collar. Stupid. Stupid. And then, when I knew that I'd have used his blood anyway, if the police hadn't come too soon . . . I knew then . . . what I'd become. What they'd made me become . . ."

Anguish flooded his voice as much as it flooded Cassidy's. The man moaned, his head dropping back to the floor.

Cassidy could scent his fear, his despair, and over that, his vast shame. It wrenched at her heart; at the same time, she could find no forgiveness. Donovan was dead. That was all.

Eric and Jace twitched with the heightened emotion in the room, but Diego was coolness itself. He stuck to essentials.

"What who had made you become?" Diego asked.

"The *hoch alfar*," Reid said. "The fucking *hoch alfar*, who do you think? They took me because I was a danger to them. They killed my family and put me in this place. This *human* place."

Diego prodded Reid with the rifle. "A little bit more. If you're one of these dark elves, how did you join the police force? How do you have a name, a home, a social security number?"

"I've been here a long time. So long. Fifty human years. They exiled me. And for what? So that my *dokk alfar*, who lived in the land the *hoch alfar* warrior wanted, wouldn't get in his way. I fought him. I'm very strong, a damn better warrior than any of *them*. I led my people against them. But in the end, there were too many. They killed my family and friends most loyal to me. They took me—the one who dared rise against them—and they shoved me here. To die, they thought. Stupid *hoch alfar*, think *dokk alfar* can't take iron. Hell, we *invented* iron."

"So you found yourself here," Diego said, still calm. "What did you do then?"

Reid shrugged, as much as he could while bound hand and foot. "The humans didn't notice any difference in me from themselves. They don't believe anything until it's shoved under their noses. I blended in. I became Stuart Reid. Paperwork was easier to fake fifty years ago. I've been Stuart Reid for a long time, moving before people caught on that I age more slowly than humans do."

"And you tried to go back?" Diego asked.

"I tried, I tried, and I couldn't. It doesn't work for me to go to the weak places on the ley lines—the stone circles and whatever—which is how the *hoch alfar* cross. It doesn't always work for the *dokk alfar*. The magic is different. So I searched for humans who knew Fae lore, as I told you. The ritual I found in that grimoire used the blood of a Shifter, in a spell performed at the spring equinox. It's supposed to open the gate."

"Great," Jace said softly.

"I'd already been a police officer for a while," Reid said. "I was good at it. In my world, I was a warrior and an enforcer. I easily passed the tests to get into the police. Once I found the spell that used Shifters, I got myself transferred into Shifter Division. I figured it was just a matter of time before I found an un-Collared Shifter that I could use. When the hunting law changed, I saw a way to speed up the process. I found some hunters experienced in tracking down un-Collared Shifters and paid them to help me. Except, they were hot to kill any Shifter, Collared or otherwise. They shot Donovan Grady before I could stop them, then pulled off his Collar to try to fool the cops . . ."

The speech, delivered rapid-fire, faded.

In the silence that followed, Cassidy could hear Nell talking to Shane and Brody outside. Warm, family conversation, so different from the anger and fear in this room.

"Are you telling me you would have let Donovan live once they'd captured him?" Cassidy asked. "As desperate as you were?"

"I don't know."

"Why did you try to kill *me*? Not just any Shifter, but me in particular?"

Reid met her gaze with eyes like the black of space. "I knew you were his mate. I learned all about you and your family. I became an expert on you. I know that Shifters perform a ritual on the one-year anniversary of a death, and I knew you'd come out there again, right at the equinox. I told myself that you were so unhappy that it wouldn't matter if the spell killed you. I justified it like that. But when I shot at you, I missed, and you ran. I chased you, so obsessed about doing the damn spell that I didn't care about anything else. I realized, right then, that the *hoch alfar* had broken me. They'd made me become a *dakhlar* who'd sacrifice an innocent being for my own benefit. I'd grab you, use the spell, and deal with my guilt later."

Cassidy put her bare foot on his thigh. "Why did you keep hunting me after I eluded you the first time? I went back to finish my ritual, but I brought plenty of guards, and we were alert for you. We almost got you that night. There must have been easier targets."

Reid shook his head. "I told myself it had to be you, and you alone. To put you out of your misery, I reasoned. I thought you'd be happy to die."

Cassidy rolled her foot on his thigh, increasing the pressure a little. He looked so pathetic, wrists and ankles bound with plastic ties, Diego with the barrel of the rifle in his stomach, Xavier watching with double weapons. Here was the man responsible for her mate's death, at her feet, and now her victory tasted hollow.

Jace spoke behind her. "You're talking as though the Fae have qualms about killing Shifters."

Reid lifted himself halfway up. "No, no, the *hoch alfar* don't care about killing Shifters. They'll kill anything that gets in their way—they'll do it for amusement. I know that, because I watched them do it to my mate and my children."

Cassidy took her foot from him. "Diego, let him go."

Diego shot her a surprised look. "He'll vanish. We might never find him again."

"Let him. I want him gone. I don't want to look at him anymore."

Eric's voice rumbled. "He caused Donovan's death, Cass. No matter how he tries to spin it, he's guilty of that. It's your right to do what you will with him."

"I know." Cassidy looked back at Eric, her heart bleak. "And I'm exercising my right."

She'd wanted Reid to be gloating, rubbing his hands like a villain, so she'd feel triumph when she ripped out his throat. Instead she found a creature of shame, anger, and emptiness.

Diego held her gaze. "There's nothing to say he won't try to kill another Shifter if we let him go."

"He won't," Cassidy said. "We'll make sure of that."

Diego's eyes held compassion. Only last night, he'd dispatched one of his old enemies, one he'd grown to pity. Diego understood.

Cassidy and Diego looked at each other a moment longer, then Cassidy turned and walked out of the house. She didn't bother with shoes; she walked barefoot outside to the swath of grass and brush down the common. She walked past houses of her friends and extended family, and Donovan's friends and family. She walked all the way to the eight-foot-high cinderblock wall that marked the end of Shiftertown. Why humans had built the wall, she never understood—nothing but scorching desert lay beyond it.

Cassidy leaned on this wall, soaking the cool of it into her bones.

Donovan's killer. Hers to kill, quickly or slowly. Her right as the mate whose mate bond had been broken by murder. Even Donovan's mother didn't have the bond that Cassidy had shared with Donovan. The vengeance kill belonged to the mate.

Cassidy knew that more lay behind her sudden despair besides Reid not being the evil killer she'd wanted him to be. Reid was responsible, but his finger hadn't pulled the trigger. Those human hunters were still at large, still fair game, still hers.

She knew damn well that part of her grief was for the severing of one mate bond and the beginning of another.

How could this happen so quickly? Eric had lost his mate, Kirsten, when Jace had been born, and Eric had never shown any inclination to mate again. Having offspring lessened the mating instinct, that was true, but though Eric occasionally had casual relationships with females, he hadn't made another mate-claim, hadn't even voiced the inclination to.

Cassidy had thought she'd be like him, letting forty years go by before she even declared herself interested again.

Then she'd met Diego, a human who'd bound her and arrested her for little more than being Shifter. But he'd made Cassidy start erasing Donovan from her heart.

She couldn't. She wouldn't.

And yet, the mate bond sang.

Cassidy screamed to drown it out. She beat her fists on the wall, the cement grating her skin. She slapped her palms to the stone, over and over, her frustration, fear, and anguish boiling out of her.

"Stop." Diego's warm voice was in her ear, his strong hands closing over hers. He pulled her from the wall and gathered her into his arms. "Don't, *amada mia*."

Cassidy turned to the strength of his embrace. "I loved him. I *loved* him."

"I know."

"I don't want that to go away."

"Is that what you're afraid of?" Diego asked.

She nodded, tears flooding her eyes. "Donovan deserves to be avenged. And I couldn't do it."

Diego pulled her close. "Don't, *mi ja*. We think that if we keep hunting, keep trying to fix what hurt them, they'll stay alive somehow. But that's not what keeps them alive. It's us, remembering the good of them."

"Oh, Goddess, Diego, I don't want to forget him."

"You never have to."

She looked up at him again. "I'm feeling the mate bond for you. It's erasing the one I had for him. I don't want that!"

"Mate bond?"

"It's what Shifters feel for each other when the mating is right. It's a magical thing—a Goddess thing."

Diego's black brown eyes were as dark as night. "And that's what you feel for me?"

"Yes."

Diego gazed down at her, his lips parted. Cassidy cursed herself for babbling it all out to him. He was human—how could he understand? Maybe the last thing he wanted was a Shifter woman confessing she considered herself emotionally bound to him.

The next thing she knew, Diego was crushing her into the wall, his body heat and scent all over her.

"Damn it, Cassidy," he whispered.

She opened her mouth to explain and found Diego's mouth silencing her with a strong, hot kiss. The cement wall scraped her back, but Diego was hard against her front, hemming her in, his body so damn hot.

Cassidy wanted him, and she didn't care who knew it. Her hands went to his buttocks, and she pulled him against her.

Diego's mouth was hot and hard, taking. Gentle fingers wiped away her tears while he kissed her like he couldn't get enough of her.

He tugged the laces that held up her sweatpants. She wore nothing under them, so when he yanked them down, his fingers could sink right into her heat.

So erotic, to be against the wall while the hottest man she'd ever met started her toward ecstasy.

Cassidy tugged at his belt, then his zipper. Diego almost ripped his pants open, and then she was rising against the wall, Diego holding her firmly. Hard and blunt, he slid into her, high up inside.

As in the shower, he couldn't move as much in this position, but he was inside her, holding her so tightly against him. The mate bond surged, its warmth starting in the place they joined and entwining her heart.

"Diego."

He opened his eyes. They were dark, like starless night, and yet warmer than anything she'd ever seen in her life. Cassidy could see all the way inside him, she thought, and he was letting her.

Diego, I'm falling in love with you.

Diego's head went back as he felt his pleasure, and his eyes closed, but that didn't shut him off from her. He was giving her everything, all of him. She barely noticed the harsh wall at her back with Diego's arms around her and his wild heat inside her.

His seed scalded her even as she hit her own climax. Diego opened his eyes again, cupping her face, the liquid sound of his voice pouring over her. He stared right into her heart, and Cassidy, much to her anguish, let him.

D amn, she was so beautiful. Diego eased off his climax by kissing Cassidy's face, every inch of it. He could have lost her today.

He kissed her again, her lips and chin, while he slowly and reluctantly withdrew. "If this is the mate bond, I like it."

"It's more than that." Cassidy sounded worried about it.

Diego stayed pressed against her, loving the heat of her against his groin. "No problem. We can go out to dinner sometimes too."

"Diego." The word ended on a sob.

Diego smoothed her hair, kissed it. He thought he understood what was up with her. Cassidy had lost her mate—her true love. She feared that falling in love again meant she'd not really loved Donovan.

Not true. The heart, the human one at least, could form strong bonds with many people. Diego loved his mother and his brother, and what he'd had with Jobe could be called love—not in a gay way, the macho side of his brain quickly added, but in a best-friend-a-guy-could-ever-have kind of way.

Affection and love. Diego would die for these people. He'd have preferred to die for Jobe instead of the other way around.

"Cass," he said. "I've fixed on you. I don't know if that's the same as your mate bond, but I'm willing to believe it is."

"I don't know what it is."

Cassidy had stopped crying, but she sounded confused.

"I'm willing to wait until you figure it out," Diego said. "Hell, I'll try to help you figure it out. And if we have to enjoy screwing each other every day until then, fine with me. I've got the strength."

There it was, Cassidy's smile, the spirit returning to her eyes. "You're full of yourself, human."

"You think I don't have the stamina for a Shifter?"

She pretended to consider. "You're not bad so far."

"*Not bad so far*. Evil woman." Diego moved his hips, enjoying the hot feel of her. "My life has been crazy since I met you, *chiquita*. I think I needed waking up."

"You know your pants are down around your ankles, right?"

Diego grinned. "Yours flew off in the bushes somewhere."

"Pants around your ankles looks funnier. Especially since you're wearing socks."

Diego let his gaze rove Cassidy in only a sweat jacket, her strong, slim legs bare. "You look better." He let go of her long enough to pull up his jeans and fasten them. "Want to come home with me?"

She smiled, making his heart warm, then her smile faded. "Only if Reid is contained."

Real-life problems came rushing back. "There's still a lot of things I don't get about him. Like what is so special about that rock cave? It's not very big, it's in the middle of nowhere, but he keeps going back to it."

Cassidy broke from him to fetch her pants. Diego's thoughts stumbled to a halt. Her hips moved in the most delectable way as she bent to slide the sweatpants over the sweetest ass he'd ever seen in his life.

"I can tell you're a good detective," Cassidy said, tugging the ties together. "You don't close the case once you've beaten the suspect into submission."

He forced his brain to start working again. "We shouldn't let him go, Cass. Like I said, what's to say he won't get over his remorse and try to kill another Shifter?"

"I know, but . . ." Cassidy stopped, still holding on to the ties of her sweatpants. "I've wanted to kill him for a long time. But all of a sudden, it seems like the wrong solution."

Diego's thoughts switched to the dingy living room with Enrique, his state-of-the-art electronics surrounding a sofa that held thirty years of soil. Diego had wanted to kill Enrique so many times when Enrique had been a dangerous and deadly gang leader. Last night, Diego had held the power and strength, and Enrique had seemed pathetic, a waste of time.

Maybe Cassidy felt the same way about Reid. However, Diego still didn't trust him. All this talk about *hoch alfar* and *dokk alfar* and gates to Faerie seemed like so much fanciful bullshit. Diego liked to deal in the concrete.

And he would, he thought as he slid his arms around Cassidy's waist. Just as soon as he got done kissing Cassidy.

Reid was still in the living room when they got back. The man sat on the floor with his back to the wall, his runner's legs drawn up under him. He looked at the carpet, as though not very interested in anything around him.

"He asked for my protection," Eric said.

Cassidy looked amazed. "Did you grant it?"

"Haven't decided yet."

"What does that mean?" Diego asked.

Ever since Cassidy had sliced open her hand to pledge that she believed in Diego—and if she was wrong, Eric could kill her—Diego realized that Shifters took their oaths and promises seriously. Just saying, *Sure, I'll return your library book for you*, might have dire consequences.

Eric lounged back on the couch, his feet up, as though the morning hadn't been all that interesting. "If he were Shifter, and I granted my protection, that would mean I gave him the same status as someone in my pride. Meaning I protect him with all my strength. Meaning I expect him to show me the same loyalty I expect from those in my pride."

"But because he's not Shifter . . ."

"I haven't decided. Plus there's the whole fact that I still want to kill him."

"If anyone kills him, it will be me," Diego said. "Where's Xav?"

"Next door. He's talking to Shane."

Reid lifted his head. "Escobar, I've never liked you, but you're a good cop, and you're trustworthy. I'm not asking for forgiveness. I'm asking a Shifter for protection. That's my way of pledging I won't try to hurt them anymore."

Cassidy folded her arms. She'd shown compassion, but her compassion didn't make her weak. "You told us you needed Shifter blood for a spell."

"I'm willing to try to find another way, look for another grimoire and more spells. There has to be some way I can trick the *hoch alfar* and cross back into my world, without me having to be a monster to do it."

Diego sank down on his heels to look Reid in the face. "You can vanish whenever you want. Why can't you vanish back to your world?"

"Do you think I haven't tried that? I can teleport, but only in this world. The funny thing is, when I was home, I couldn't do it. Many *dokk alfar* can, but I never manifested the talent."

Eric gazed down at them from the couch. "Interesting. Maybe that has something to do with why you can't get back."

"You know about these things?"

"Not really." Eric yawned and stretched, like a lion preparing for his post-hunt nap. "But I know someone who knows someone who might know something. I'll talk to them this afternoon."

"You'll give me your protection?" Reid's voice was full of hope.

"For now."

Cassidy relaxed. "Thank you, Eric."

Eric lifted his head, still the lion who could come alert at any second. "It also means that if he breaks any part of his word, I get to rip his head off. Don't worry, Diego, I'll do it discreetly."

Eric sank back down and put his arm over his eyes, finished with the business at hand.

"You see?" Reid said to Diego. "The Collars are useless when they really want to do something."

"If you despise Shifters, why are you asking for Eric's protection?" Diego asked.

"Because I'm not a fool. The Shifters here would kill me without it, and my greatest wish is to return home. I'm willing to do what it takes. I'm not a killer. I only want to go home."

Whatever truth was in Reid, he at least believed what he said. Diego himself was not sure what to feel.

He rose to his feet. "If Reid is staying here, I want Cassidy with me."

Eric moved his arm enough to peer at Diego around it. "You don't have to ask my permission."

"I just don't want you talking about ripping *my* head off."

"Cassidy's a grown female. She can do as she pleases."

"Cassidy's standing right here," Cassidy said, hands on hips. *Dios mio*, she was sexy when she did that.

Diego shot her a grin. "I asked you before, want to come home with me? Or better still, to my mom's house? There's some things I still need to take care of."

CHAPTER EIGHTEEN

His mother's house. Cassidy wasn't sure how she felt about that as she slung an overnight bag into Xavier's truck.

Diego was talking in a low voice with Xav a little way away from the truck. Cassidy worried a bit about leaving Eric and Jace here alone with Reid, but, interestingly, Nell had volunteered to stay over and watch him. She looked delighted, Reid apprehensive. Nell wouldn't rough him up *too* much. Maybe.

Cassidy got into the front seat, leaving the door open, and waited. She pretended to study her hair in the visor's mirror, but she strained her Shifter hearing to listen.

"You sure, *hermano*?" Xav was saying. "Enrique's word isn't necessarily reliable. He could be luring you down there for a reason. A dying man's last nasty trick."

"I can't not check it out. First lead I've had in a long time."

"If the captain finds out, you are dead meat. I like you, Diego. You're not bad, for a pain-in-the-ass older brother."

Diego shrugged. "Captain Max told me to take some leave. Nothing says I can't go to Mexico for a vacation."

"Yeah, but most people vacation in Mazatlan or Cabo. Not some bandit town in the middle of nowhere. Besides, what about Cassidy?"

Out of the corner of her eye, Cassidy saw Diego look her way. She busied herself rubbing at an imaginary dirt mark on the corner of her mouth.

"With Reid here, Cass will be good at Mamita's," Diego said. "Especially with you to look after her."

"No way, Diego. If you're going down there, I am too. You'll do something stupid and end up in some Mexican jail, and we'll never see you again."

"It's true that I could use your help. After I make sure Cassidy is safe."

"Good. I'm with you."

"Just don't tell Mamita."

Xav laughed. "You got that right."

Cassidy put up the visor as they approached and pretended she hadn't heard a word.

She wasn't sure why Diego wanted to go to Mexico on the word of this Enrique, the one he'd been forced to shoot, but she sure as hell wasn't letting him go alone.

C assidy did want to see the house that Diego called home. She knew from what he'd told her that he hadn't grown up in the modest house in Boulder City he took her to, but even so, Cassidy knew it was a home the minute she walked in the front door. Just as the house she lived in with Eric and Jace in Shiftertown was now home, so was this one. Loved ones were there, the people with whom you shared sleepy mornings around the breakfast table, who didn't mind that your hair was a mess or your clothes unkempt.

Comfort and love. This house rang with it.

Diego hugged his mother, a woman half his height, with a firm embrace. "Mamita, this is Cassidy."

Cassidy found herself under the scrutiny of a sharp-eyed, dark stare. The stare wasn't unfriendly, just interested and assessing. *So, this is the woman sleeping with my son.*

"I heard you jumped out the window when you heard Xavier coming," Juanita Escobar said.

Cassidy's face heated to roasting. "I wasn't sure who it was, and I didn't want to cause trouble for Diego."

"Because you're Shifter." The small woman nodded. "I

understand that. Gang warfare is the same all over, even though humans and Shifters might not admit that's what it is. Don't be found with the wrong people."

"Something like that," Cassidy said.

"Diego won't let anything happen to him because of you. Or to you because of him." Juanita held out plump arms. "Diego tells me that Shifters don't worry about showing affection. Very sensible. Come here, *mi ja*."

Cassidy surrendered to her hug. The small woman held her tightly, and Cassidy returned the embrace.

"Now," Juanita said when they parted. "That's done with. I made another batch of chilaquiles, since these two boys ran off without eating any. We'll have them now."

Cassidy admired herself for her patience all the way through the flavorful dinner. She listened to Diego and Xav banter, answered their mother's questions about Shifters, and praised Juanita's food. Not until after she'd helped Juanita do the dishes, while the brothers went outside for an impromptu game of basketball, did Cassidy have the chance to confront Diego.

She walked out to the front driveway where they played in the growing twilight. Diego had his shirt off, Xav keeping his on—so they could tell which team they were on, she supposed. Not that she minded watching Diego's well-honed muscles play under his dark skin.

Diego dribbled the ball, keeping his back to Xav, while Xavier tried to get around him. Diego shot, but the ball hit the rim of the hoop and bounced off. Cassidy dashed in, jumped, and tipped the ball into the ring.

Diego whooped, laughing, lifted Cassidy off her feet, and whirled her around.

"Hey, no fair getting help from your girlfriend," Xav said, catching the ball. "Your *tall* girlfriend."

"We make a good team," Diego said. He set Cassidy on her feet and kissed her lips, turning the swift kiss into a lingering one.

Cassidy liked him like this, smiling, relaxed with his family. Happy.

"Diego, we need to talk," she said.

"Uh-oh," Xav said. "Never a good way to start a conversation."

"You're in on this too," Cassidy said.

Xavier raised his hands, the basketball still under one arm. "What did I do? Whatever Lindsay told you, I only danced with her, I swear. That's all. So far."

"Nothing to do with Lindsay." Cassidy took the ball from him, set up a shot, put it through the hoop, and caught the ball on its first bounce. "It's about Mexico."

Diego shot Xav a look, and Xav shook his head. "I didn't say a word. When would I have had time?"

"Shifters have good hearing," Cassidy said. "You're going to Mexico to find the guys who killed your partner, aren't you, Diego? That Enrique guy told you something about them, and you're leaving to check it out."

"Not so loud," Diego said. He retrieved his T-shirt and pulled it on. "I don't need Mamita worrying."

"Or chewing out your ass," Xav said.

"I understand why you want to go," Cassidy said. "For the same reason I went after Reid; for the same reason I still want to find the human hunters. But I'm not letting you go without me."

Any humor in Diego's eyes vanished. "Like hell I'm taking you to Mexico. It can be fucking dangerous down there, and you're a Shifter. You can't exactly go back and forth across the border. Hell, getting permission to go from state to state is tough for a Shifter. You want to end up in some Shifter Division cell, in *Mexico*?"

Cassidy waited for him to finish. "How were you planning to get there?"

"Xav's truck. We'll probably need four-wheel drive for where we need to go."

"Conspicuous. Why not fly in as close as you can and find transportation from there?"

Diego shook his head. "Because I'm not a rich boy with a private plane."

"If you let me come with you, I can provide the plane," Cassidy said. "And the pilot."

Diego blinked. "How?"

"First, promise you'll take me with you."

"Cass . . ."

Cassidy folded her arms and waited. At the beginning of the week, she'd have never admitted to Diego, a human, that Eric knew people who could help with clandestine trips, but things had changed. Diego had saved her life—more than once—and he hadn't had to. He'd kept her from being locked up by Shifter Division, helped her with Reid, and understood what she was going through.

Diego watched her a moment, then he let out an exasperated sigh. "All right, but only because I'm desperate. And you'll stay far out of the way if we find these guys."

Cassidy smiled and gave him a nod. Not that she'd agree to that restriction. But she'd argue that point once they found them.

Cassidy's pilot awoke every one of Diego's cop suspicions. Diego had assumed that the contact to secretly fly Shifters where they wanted to go would come through Eric, but Cassidy blithely made a phone call, then directed Diego to drive them out east of town.

Once the city dropped behind them, Cassidy directed Diego to a little-used highway, which sped them out to the middle of nowhere. Dramatic scenery surrounded them, stark, knifelike hills, wide sky, white desert.

They made another turnoff to a dirt road, which was wide and well graded. Beyond a few deep washes, the road ended in a flat stretch between hills. A trailer house stood incongruously in the middle of this dusty field, with two small planes parked behind it.

The slim man who walked out to meet them—armed with a handgun on a belt holster—broke into a smile of delight when Cassidy got out of Diego's car.

"Cassidy," he bellowed in a voice too large for his wiry build. "How are you, girl?"

"Just fine, Marlo."

Cassidy walked right up to him and embraced him, which Diego didn't like. He knew by now that this was the normal Shifter way of greeting, but Marlo seemed to enjoy it a little too much.

"This is Diego," Cassidy said. "He's the friend I mentioned who needs the ride."

Marlo looked Diego up and down. "He looks like a cop."

"He is a cop. How can you tell?"

"Experience. He's not a drug runner."

"You'd better not be either," Diego said.

Marlo's eyes narrowed. "You want my help or not?"

"Not if you're a drug runner, no." Drug runners might think about only the money they were making, but their product ended up in kids who died. Diego would never look the other way for that.

"I gave up that shit a long time ago. Too dangerous, too stupid. Now I'm just a pilot for hire, for people who need to get places in a hurry."

"Like Shifters?" Diego asked.

Marlo spread his hands. "I believe in freedom and equality for all. Why should Shifters not be allowed to travel like anyone else? So, if they need a ride, they call Marlo. Cassidy vouched for you, so I know you won't be reporting this to your cop friends."

Cassidy had been vouching for him a lot, lately. "I need to go down to a place in Mexico, in Durango," Diego said. "Can you get me there?"

"Sure. How many passengers?"

"Three—me, my brother, Cassidy."

"And Shane," Cassidy said.

Diego shot her a look. "What?"

"Eric would kill me if I left without Shifter protection." Cassidy's answer was serene. "Besides, we might need him."

Shane could turn into a fifteen-hundred-pound grizzly bear, true, but if Diego's prey was armed to the teeth, which they would be, being a grizzly might not help him.

"It might be too dangerous even for Shane," he said.

Cassidy cocked her head. "Then it's too dangerous for you."

They shared a look, Cassidy's determined. "If we get Shane killed," Diego said, "his mom will never forgive us."

"Nell understands danger like this. Besides, if you or Xav get killed, I can imagine what *your* mom would say."

"She'd go on a rampage. I know. Fine. Four passengers."

"Four thousand dollars," Marlo said.

Diego swung around. "What?"

"Hey, I said I was for hire, not a charity. I have to buy fuel, maintain my plane, take you down to the middle of nowhere in dangerous country. A grand a piece, that's my price."

Diego started to argue, but Cassidy broke in. "Call Eric. He'll get it to you."

"Don't," Diego said. "I'll spring for it, but, Cass, I really want you and Shane to stay the hell home."

"No." Cassidy came close to Diego again. She touched his face, firing his blood. "Take this as my gift to you, Diego. I understand why you need to go. Let me do this for you."

"Where is Eric going to get four grand?"

Cassidy's eyes flickered, but she didn't look away. "Let Eric worry about that."

She cradled his face between her hands, her eyes darkening, then she gave Diego a long kiss.

The fire leapt. This woman was fine, like a diamond he'd stumbled upon in a sea of sand. He opened her mouth with lips and tongue. Cassidy kissed him back, the taste of her wild.

Marlo chuckled beside them. "Looks like you mean business, Cass."

Cassidy broke the kiss and grinned at him, but she didn't look all that embarrassed. "Take it, Diego," she whispered.

It was important to her. Diego saw that in her eyes. He'd discuss it with Eric later—such as how Shifters who weren't allowed to have decent jobs would be able to cough up four grand—but Diego nodded. Cassidy kissed him one more time.

When she did that, Diego stopped worrying about petty details like money, getting to Mexico on an ex-drug-runner plane, and what he'd do when he got there. *Dangerous*, he thought. *I'm liking forgetting way too much.*

At Diego's house that night, they slept in separate bedrooms. Diego bunked with Xavier in the room that had been Xav's, and Cassidy stayed in Diego's old room.

Diego's mother had placed on the dresser a photo of a very young Diego in his Marines uniform and one of him when he'd graduated from the police academy. Juanita had also framed his military service medals and his commendations both from the Marines and the police. A proud mother honoring her son.

Cassidy touched each medal, reading the certificate that went with it, trying not to think of Diego lying warm and solid in a bed in the next room. Cassidy tried to shut out the mating frenzy that was winding her up, but when she at last climbed into bed and slept, she dreamed of only Diego.

"Sure this thing's safe?"

Shane looked nervously out the window as they glided south, following the Colorado River as it snaked between California and Arizona. The view was beautiful, the plane far smoother than Diego had feared it would be.

"Yep," Marlo called back from the pilot's seat. "Just tuned it up."

"I don't like to fly," Shane said. "If Shifters were meant to fly, they'd be able to turn into birds."

"So, why can't they?" Xav said, looking up from his magazine.

"Huh?"

"You have big cat Shifters, wolf Shifters, and bear Shifters. Why not raptors, like eagles or hawks?"

Shane stared at him. "Hell if I know."

"The Fae created us," Cassidy said. "They chose the animals. Who knows why? Or why not?"

"I guess an elephant would be tough," Xav said. "You'd need a lot of space. Or whales. What if you shifted in the middle of the ocean? You'd need to stash scuba gear somewhere."

"Very funny," Shane said.

Xav chuckled and returned to his magazine.

Diego found Cassidy's gaze on him from where she sat beside him. He didn't mind looking down into her gorgeous eyes, but he wondered why she kept looking at him. Different looks every time. Coy, frank, thoughtful.

The trip was long enough for napping. Diego rested his head against the window, not minding the miles down to the ground. Airplanes didn't bother him either, he'd discovered. But then, they didn't have balconies.

Cassidy curled up nicely into his side. He draped his arm around her and dozed off, happy with her against him.

They landed after dark, on an airstrip Diego couldn't believe Marlo could see. But the man brought the plane down with only a few bumps, and then they stopped.

Hot, dry air wafted over them as they climbed from the plane. "Where are we?" Diego said as he stretched.

"About forty miles from your little town of La Nébeda."

"*Forty* miles?"

"Yep," Marlo said. "I figured you didn't want to get too close to whoever it is you don't want to see you coming. Planes landing near a town that small are going to be noticed. My friend here has a jeep that can take you in."

Marlo wouldn't leave his plane, so Marlo's friend at the airstrip gave Xavier keys to a rusty but sturdy jeep, and Xavier drove the four of them to the town. Shane sat in front with Xav, and Diego and Cassidy rode together in the back.

This part of Mexico was definitely off the tourist path. It was the territory of drug runners, human traffickers, and people looking for a place to hide. There were no resort hotels for rich Americans here, just long stretches of empty roads and bad men with guns.

"I want the two of you to keep out of sight the best you can," Diego said to Shane and Cassidy over the whine of the engine. "Who knows how people here will react to Shifters?"

"I'm here to back up Cassidy," Shane said. "So where she goes, I go."

"Then you'll both stay out of it," Diego said.

Cassidy didn't answer, but the stubborn way she wouldn't look at him told him much.

The town, when they reached it, was nothing but old buildings, open bars, dogs, and insects. This was siesta country, where everyone slept during the heat of the day. The sun had gone down an hour ago, and people were emerging now into cool darkness, the town coming to life.

Lights were brightest in the cantinas, three of them in this tiny town. Xavier parked the jeep in the dark at the end of one street, beyond one of the cantinas. Diego climbed down and checked the stash of guns in the back. Shotguns, three of them, in addition to Xav and Diego's handguns.

"Shane, can you shoot a gun?"

"I've done it," Shane said. "I don't like to. Claws are better." He scratched the air, his dark eyes gleaming, sending Diego a sly grin.

"You might have to use a gun if things go bad," Diego said. He handed Shane one of the shotguns. "Shoot to defend Cassidy, and then get her the hell out of here."

Cassidy hopped out of the jeep and finally spoke up. "Screw that. I'd not leave you to die. That's not why I helped you come here."

Diego checked his gun's magazine and stashed spare ones in his pockets. "I want to bring these guys in, Cass," he said, "but to be honest, I don't know if I'll be able to."

Cassidy put her hands on her hips. "*We'll* be able to. The four of us together. These men killed your partner, and they deserve to be brought to justice. Shane and I are fighters. Use us to fight."

"Hate to say this, Diego," Xavier broke in, "but she might be right."

Diego worked with women all the time. One of the toughest detectives he knew was a female lieutenant in homicide. No one questioned her competency or made jokes at her expense—not twice, anyway. Cassidy was just as competent as that lieutenant, probably more so. But the difference was, Diego wasn't falling in love with the homicide detective, didn't feel as though he'd protect her with everything he had in him and then some. If something happened to Cassidy, Diego knew it would kick him like nothing else ever had. Not even losing Jobe would compare.

"She'd make good bait to draw them out," Xavier said.

Both Shane and Diego stared at him. "You mean a honey trap," Diego said.

"It's a good idea," Cassidy said, moving to stand next to Xavier. "If *you* go muscling into the cantina or wherever, Diego, they'll know what's up right away. They'll run or fight. If *I* go in . . ." She opened her hands. "I can draw them out, right into your waiting arms. You tie them up and take them to jail."

"No," Shane said, at the same time Diego said, "It's too risky."

"It will work," Xavier said. "Think about how we wrapped up this last case, Diego. Jemez went into the dealer's house with her big brown eyes and her short skirt, and those guys fell all over themselves trying to impress her. She got more evidence in one afternoon than the rest of us did in months."

"I know, and I didn't like sending her in there either," Diego said. "Honey traps can be dangerous."

Cassidy slanted a smile at him. "I'll be sure to be sweet."

Damn it. Diego shook his head. "We can't trust them to react the way you expect them to."

Cassidy's good-humored look vanished. "I haven't always lived in Shiftertown, Diego. In the wild, Eric and I fought other Shifters to protect our family. Sixty years ago, a world war came close to our shores, and we fought then too. We might not have worn uniforms or used guns, but we crossed the North Sea, joined the underground movements, and sure caused a lot of trouble." She grinned. "They never had any idea how Eric and I did what we did, but we did a lot of damage. Those were fun times."

CHAPTER NINETEEN

Cassidy saw the anger in Diego's eyes and knew she wasn't convincing him. Diego had the instinct to protect, and right now he wanted to protect Cassidy.

"At least let me scout," she said. "I can entice them out without even going near them."

Diego's brows drew even closer together, and Shane didn't look much happier. *Males.*

Cassidy hooked an earpiece over her ear, brushed her hair around it to hide it, and tied a silk scarf she'd brought with her over her Collar. "If I even think something is going wrong, I'll yell, and you come running. With your big guns." She winked at Diego.

Xavier chuckled. "I like her."

Shane wasn't laughing. "I'll come running too. And I don't need a gun."

Diego at last conceded—on condition that he kept an eye on her and she kept the damn earpiece on all the time.

He'd told her about the guys he was looking for, and on the plane, Diego had pored over the photos he kept in a file he hadn't told his captain about. He'd carefully hoarded information, showing the same obsession with which Cassidy had tracked data about the hunters who'd killed Donovan. Only, Diego, with his resources, had been able to find out much more about Jobe's killers than Cassidy had about Donovan's.

Cassidy was determined to help Diego take his vengeance now, to ease his pain and his guilt. That hurt in his eyes hurt her too.

She approached the first cantina, cautious but not worried. This was a much easier mission than sneaking into Nazi supply tents to sabotage them. Back then, she'd slunk through the night with explosives strapped to her wildcat body. Tonight she simply walked into the cantina.

The cantinas in this town were open-air, the weather so mild that people preferred to sit outside or in the bar where one stone wall and a roof divided the place from shops beyond. Not many people were there tonight, which was odd. The town was small, but the cantina was nice enough, brightly painted and fairly clean. Besides, other than the cantinas, there was nowhere else to go.

Cassidy didn't note what was missing until it struck her that there were only men in this bar, no women in sight. The drug runners all were white Americans, and Cassidy saw no white Americans here. Everyone was native, and no one looked up when she swept her gaze around the cantina.

Very odd. Cassidy should stand out like a sudden wash of water in a desert.

She left the first cantina without pausing and walked on down the street toward the second, and larger, one. Her Shifter senses were very aware of Diego, Xav, and Shane in the shadows, watching. The three men were too wound up for this. Eric would have been a ghost.

Cassidy's personal plan was a bit different from the one the males had discussed. She'd find the dealers all right, but she'd make them pay for what they'd done to Diego in a more basic way. This town was far from human law courts and rule books, which was why criminals tried to hide out here, and so, Cassidy would apply Shifter law.

The men they stalked had killed Diego's best friend plus shot Diego and left him for dead. Cassidy's mate bond was building for Diego, and these men would learn what happened to people who hurt a female Shifter's mate.

She walked casually into the next cantina. Men in this one lifted their heads and watched her, but they looked more worried than curious.

Strange. Cassidy was a young woman alone, obviously way out of her territory, and *they* looked worried.

One of the drug runners Diego sought was sitting at the bar. His skin was sunburned, and he'd grown a scratchy beard, but she recognized him from his photo. He was a big man, almost as big as Shane, and much of the skin his biker vest showed was inked.

The man saw Cassidy and gave her a hard stare as she approached the bar.

"You shouldn't be in here," he said to her in English.

Cassidy ignored him, rested her arms on the bar, and spoke to the bartender behind it. "Do you understand English, *señor*? Do you have a phone I can use?"

She smiled at him, trying to look like a clueless tourist who'd taken a very wrong turn while heading for her beach resort. The bartender looked blank. The man in the biker vest spoke to him in rapid Spanish.

The bartender shook his head. "*No, señorita. No teléfono.*"

Cassidy turned her smile on the biker. "Do you have a cell phone? Can I borrow it?"

He was supposed to smile back at her. Leer, actually. Suggest he let her use the phone outside or somewhere more private. Instead, the man clutched his bottle of beer.

"You should get out. Out of here, out of town. Fast."

"Why?" Cassidy asked, sitting down. "I like this place. So festive."

"*Cassidy . . .*" came Diego's whisper in her earpiece.

"Maybe you could take a look at my car," she said to the biker. "See what's wrong with it?"

The man perked up. "You have a car?"

"Yes. It broke down. I'm so happy I was close to this town. The map I had made no sense at all . . ."

The biker abandoned his seat with amazing speed and closed beefy fingers around Cassidy's arm. His grip was hard, but the look in his eyes was the wild one of a man who'd abandoned hope and then suddenly found it dangling in front him.

"Take me to your car. Hurry. I'll fix it, and then you'll need to get the hell out of here. But only if you promise to take me with you."

Cassidy looked him up and down, pretending to be a silly rich woman contemplating giving a ride to her auto mechanic. "I don't know. I had it detailed before I drove down here."

"Please."

The man was big, taller than Cassidy, but she smelled the fear on him. Waves and waves of fear.

She likewise scented fear on the second biker who came into the cantina, another of the gang Diego hunted. The second man frowned at his friend, then at Cassidy. "What are you doing?"

"She has a car," the first man said to him.

"Yes, and I need help fixing it," Cassidy said. "Does this road go back to Mazatlan?"

The second man gave the first a warning look. "You sure *he* didn't send her?"

Cassidy blinked. "Sure who didn't send me?"

"I don't think so, man," the first biker said. "Look, she needs to get out of here, and so do we."

The first man started steering Cassidy out of the cantina. Cassidy nearly gagged on the smell of his fear, but she guided him down the street, toward the jeep waiting with Diego in the darkness.

Both men walked fast, propelling her along. She noticed they also made sure to stick to deep shadow, letting no stray light from any of the crumbling buildings touch them.

"Maybe I should stay here for the night," Cassidy said. "Is there a resort anywhere nearby?"

"No, sweetie," man number two said. "I'll drive you to a resort. Any resort you want. Promise. Now, where's your car?"

"There." Cassidy pointed to the jeep, waiting alone.

Both men rushed for it, and Cassidy had to run to reach it with them. The first man jumped into the driver's seat. "Keys?"

"Here somewhere." Cassidy pretended to fumble in her pockets.

"Never mind." The man reached under the steering wheel, ready to break his way in.

And found Diego's shotgun in his face.

"I knew it," the second man said, his voice a terrified whisper. Shane and Xavier closed behind him. "It was *him*."

The first man was just as terrified, but not because of Diego's gun. Both men were looking straight at Shane, and the fear in their eyes was boundless.

Diego cocked his weapon. "Do you remember me?" His voice was quiet.

The first man stared back at him, first in mindless panic, then in recognition. "Shit!"

His friend swung around, saw Diego, swallowed. "Aw, man. Just when I thought things couldn't get any worse."

The first man put his hands on top of his head, in perfect position for someone being arrested. "No, man, it's OK. He's a cop. He'll arrest us and get us out of here. We surrender, all right?"

Diego exchanged a glance with Cassidy. Cassidy shrugged. "Something's scared them bad," she said, "and it's not you."

"I'm hoping it's me," Shane said.

"Come on, let's go," the first man said. "Before *he* finds out."

He, again.

"Where are your friends?" Diego asked, not moving the gun. "My intel said there were four of you down here. I want you all."

"Gone," the first man said. "They're gone."

"Gone where?"

Their fear escalated, the men stinking with it. They hadn't bathed in a while either, so the smell was overwhelming.

"They're dead, all right?" the second man nearly shouted. "Dead. He had them killed."

Diego still didn't move. "I want them."

"Come on, man," the first man said. "I'll show you where we buried them. What was left of them. But we gotta go. *Now*."

"Diego," Xavier said.

Diego's face was like stone. Cassidy took the shotgun Shane was holding unsteadily and touched it to the second man's cheek. She leaned to him, letting her eyes go Shifter. "Who is it that you're afraid of?" she asked.

The man gasped. "You're one of them."

Cassidy moved her scarf so he could see her Collar. "If you

tell us the truth, you'll be fine. Lie to me, and I'll put up with the pain. I've done it before."

The man eyed her Collar. "No, wait, you're different." His gaze flicked to Shane and his Collar. "You're not with them."

Cassidy wanted to scream, *Them who?* when Shane sniffed the wind.

"Aw, hell, Cass, you smell that?"

Cassidy did, and every hair on her body stood up.

"Can't smell anything over the current BO," Xavier said.

"Diego, get into the jeep and drive." Cassidy pushed Xavier and his captive toward the backseat. "Just go."

Diego gave her a hard look but, Goddess bless him, he didn't argue. Diego shoved the first captive over and started up the jeep while Xavier pushed the second man into the backseat. Shane boosted Cassidy over the tailgate to the small space behind the seats.

Before Shane could climb in, they came. Out of the darkness, eyes shining in the jeep's headlights, they came, bodies low to the ground, the smell overwhelming.

"Shifters," Shane said as he dove over the tailgate. "Diego, gun it."

"Shifters?" Xavier asked as the jeep leapt forward. "What the fuck?"

"Ferals," Cassidy shouted. She hung on as Diego U-turned the jeep in a scattering of dirt. Every single one of the Shifters in the darkness had gone feral.

And every single one of them charged.

Eric had put Reid under his protection to reassure Cassidy, but he did not trust that Reid, once he felt better about himself, wouldn't try to find another Shifter to bleed out for his spell. Reid might think twice about going after Collared Shifters, especially those protected by Eric, but there was an un-Collared Shifter running around Las Vegas, just waiting to be caught . . .

Iona Duncan.

Eric had put together the information on her himself the last couple of days, not wanting even his trackers to know that she was Shifter.

Iona owned, with her mother and sister, Duncan Construction, a company that built both residential and commercial buildings, nothing flashy, just serviceable. They'd been one of the few companies that kept going after the real estate crash, though they had to be hurting like everyone else. Humans put too much faith in building booms.

Iona's mother was human, her father, an unknown Feline Shifter. Eric kept pretty close tabs on the Felines in his Shiftertown, and he knew that Iona's father didn't live there. Iona was just beyond thirty, which meant a few years past her Transition. She'd been born before the Collars, before Shiftertowns—her mother might not even have known until after Iona's birth that the man who'd given her a daughter had been Shifter.

Iona stayed pretty low-key. She worked in the company's office and didn't often go to the building sites. She had a few select friends and confined her entertainments to simple outings with them or with her mother and sister.

And she was feeling the mating heat.

Eric had scented it on her at the club and knew it was only a matter of time before it started to drive her insane. She wouldn't understand, and Eric needed to get to her before her instincts did her too much damage.

All Shifters learned careful control of their animal instincts from the time they were cubs, but Iona, who hadn't been raised Shifter, wouldn't have had that training. There was a good chance that her mating heat would drive her into becoming feral—Shifters who'd given in to their animal side, who'd become more animal than human, who could control no instincts at all. They mated, and killed, without restraint.

Tonight Iona had gone to the Forum Shops at Caesars Palace with her friends. Shifters weren't allowed in the gigantic mall, but Eric was perfectly welcome to linger outside on the Strip in front of Caesars. He knew that Iona and her friends would come out that way, because his research told him they liked to walk down the street afterward and watch the dancing waters at the Bellagio.

Eric lingered, leaning on the railing, his leather jacket hiding his Collar. Next to him, men called out to passersby, thrusting leaflets for exotic dance clubs at anyone who looked interested.

One of the flyers lay at Eric's booted feet, showing a photo of a Shifter woman, bare, her hands hiding her breasts.

Shifter women did dance in clubs, seeing nothing shaming about nudity and liking the tips. Some of the male Shifters didn't like it, though, and Eric had to intervene with brothers angry that sisters were dancing for money. Granted, some males still thought Shifter females should be sequestered and used as cub-making machines, as they had hundreds of years ago.

Times change. We need to change with them, or we die.

Iona's friends came out of the shops and strolled up the long walkway to the street. Iona wasn't with them.

Damn it.

Eric strode down the length of the walk, passing Iona's friends without looking at them. In the pressing crowd this fine night, no one noticed him.

He could tell that Iona hadn't come out this door at all, because her scent was nowhere near it. Keeping his head down, Eric ducked inside with the rest of the tourists, hunkering a little so his height wouldn't give him away.

He took an escalator down, patiently waiting on the moving stairs instead of shoving his way through the crowd. At the bottom, he searched the crowd, letting his nose lead him in the right direction once he'd picked up her scent.

He found Iona outside a chocolate shop, staring at the exotic confections within.

Eric stopped to watch her. Iona's black hair was caught in a simple tail, her lean body fine-looking in jeans and blouse, her high-heeled boots making her legs long and sexy.

Beauty. Un-Collared. Free.

Her scent screamed at him. Unmated female, rushing headlong into mating need with no idea how to contain it.

Eric knew from living with Cassidy that females tried to damp down mating need with food—chocolate, ice cream, cake. Shifter women worked off the calories fast, their metabolisms quickly burning the sugar. Probably why Iona was drawn to the chocolate shop.

Iona was so fixed on the chocolates that she never heard Eric, never smelled him. He was simply there between one moment and the next, filling her vision and her space.

She saw him, and her mouth went dry. Not again. She hadn't been able to concentrate on anything since meeting him at the club, as though he'd invaded and taken over every thought. Stalking her in her head. She didn't want to see him again.

And yet, every one of Iona's female instincts came alert at Eric's tall body, hard face, dark hair, and most of all, his eyes. They were jade green and held fathoms of thought. Those eyes could see all the way down inside her, uncovering things Iona hadn't been aware of herself.

Not that she was going to let Eric and the confusion he stirred cow her. Iona turned to face him, no avoidance.

"Shifters aren't allowed in here," she said. "Tell me what you want, before I call security."

His smile licked wicked delight up and down her body. "Go ahead and call. You know I can out you a hell of a lot worse than you can out me."

"Why shouldn't I call them?" Iona said, her lips stiff. "You're obviously following me around."

"Why didn't you stay with your friends?"

"None of your business."

Eric nodded at the tiers of confections. "They look good, don't they?"

Iona glanced at the enticing chocolates, and her mouth started to water. She'd been walking by, and then she hadn't been able to keep walking by. She'd told her friends she'd catch up to them, saying she needed to buy a gift for her sister or mother—some excuse.

"The scent," Iona said. "I don't know why it fascinates me. I like looking at the shape of the chocolates, imagining how they'll taste in my mouth." Smooth, dark, delicate, music on the tongue.

Eric gestured to the shop door. "Come on. I'll buy you some."

No. Iona couldn't let him do anything for her; she couldn't even stand next to him.

Eric shrugged and walked straight into the shop, not bothering to see if Iona would follow him. Iona didn't want to. She resisted with all her might, but she sighed as her feet took her inside after him.

Eric did a good job, she saw, of hiding his Shifter-ness. The fact that he was Shifter screamed itself at Iona, but Eric rounded his shoulders so he didn't look so tall, hid his Collar behind his high-necked shirt and jacket, and didn't even look up at the perky young clerk.

He let Iona pick out what she wanted, playing the part of the patient boyfriend waiting for his girlfriend to make up her mind. Iona chose chocolate after chocolate, indulging in exotic flavors and fillings, all of which the clerk put into a pretty box, then a pretty bag. Eric handed over some cash, took the bag, and steered Iona out of the shop.

His hand on her arm sent electric heat through her body. Iona tried to jerk away once they were back inside the mall. "Don't touch me," she said.

Eric let go, but not because Iona commanded it. He did only what he wanted to.

"Come on," he said. He started off in the direction opposite the one her friends had taken.

Iona followed him. He had the chocolate. She *needed* that chocolate.

How a Shifter knew the back doors out of the Forum Shops, Iona didn't know, but Eric led her through an obscure hall and outside into a shipping bay. It was dark here, the only light coming from the stars overhead and the distant glow of the parking lot.

Eric held up the bag. "Want one?"

Iona could barely breathe. "Yes."

Eric made short work of the clerk's lovely bow and opened the box. Two trays of eight beautiful chocolates nestled inside.

Eric lifted out the first one. Iona smelled it, liquid chocolate with candied violet inside.

She started to reach for it, but somehow she found her back against the wall, Eric in front of her. He touched the chocolate to her lips.

Iona closed her eyes, trying to resist, but her lips parted, and Eric slid the piece into her mouth.

CHAPTER TWENTY

Darkness, chocolate, smoothly bitter like coffee slid over Iona's tongue, followed by the bright sweetness of the violet. Iona hummed softly as she chewed.

"Another?" Eric asked.

"Yes," she whispered.

What was the matter with her? She should stop this, smother him with invective, then hurry away. Instead, she let Eric trace her lips with a second piece of chocolate before he popped it inside her mouth. This one was laced with chai—smoky, sweet, sharp.

Eric touched the corner of her mouth. "Good?"

"Yes. Give me more."

"I will." He leaned so close, his breath touching her lips. "You're feeling the edges of the mating need. The chocolate will ease it, but only for a little while."

What the hell was he talking about? Iona wanted the chocolate because it was chocolate.

She opened her eyes. Eric stood against her, body heat all over her, his scent . . .

Iona inhaled. She smelled the night, wildness, musk, and

chocolate. Her body went tight, the craving for the sweet
darkness transforming into a craving for Eric.

No. Eric was the enemy, a Shifter who wanted to capture
her and take her into his fold. He'd expose Iona, put a Collar
on her, ruin her life.

And yet, the craving didn't leave her.

"Another," she said.

Eric lifted the next chocolate, this one laced with chiles,
and tucked it inside her mouth. Warm spice laced with sweetness danced over her tongue. At the same time, Eric touched
his lips to the corner of her mouth.

Iona turned her head and took the kiss full on.

Her world melted. She found herself against the wall,
Eric's warmth covering her body. Eric's taste fused with the
chocolate, his tongue strong inside her mouth.

She lifted her hands to his neck, meeting the leather of his
coat. Upward to his hair, short and silken under her hands.

Eric's body was large, solid, warm in the cool air. His mouth
brushed hers once, twice, opening each time. Iona stroked his
hair, but Eric didn't touch her. He kept one hand on the wall,
the other still holding the precious chocolate.

Iona wanted him. In her apartment, alone. Tonight. Wanted
him touching and stroking her, letting her touch and stroke his
bare body in return.

She wanted to feel her mattress at her back, his weight on
her, while his hands lifted her breasts, brushed between her
legs, made her on fire for him.

Iona turned her head, breaking the kisses. "What are you
doing to me?"

Eric remained close, his body heat like a blanket. "Nothing." The word touched her lips. "Mating need. All Shifters
go through it."

"I'm only half Shifter."

"Doesn't matter. The Shifter side breeds strong." He
leaned closer still, the length of his body against hers. "Come
home with me, Iona. I'll help you through it."

Seduction with chocolate. And Eric.

Iona sucked in a painful breath. "Forget it, furball," she
made herself say.

To her surprise, he chuckled, a warm sound, and kissed

her again. Their mouths sought each other's, heat, spice, and chocolate melding.

Iona wasn't afraid. She should be, of this man who followed and watched her, who'd brought her out here in the dark, alone, and fed her chocolate. He made her body hum.

Eric eased out of the kiss, and Iona couldn't suppress a faint moan of disappointment as he lifted himself away from her.

He touched her lips. "I'll bring you in sometime, my Iona," he said. "It would be easier if you didn't fight me."

Iona drew a shaking breath. "I've lived as human all my life. I can keep doing it. If I feel the need to go Shifter, I'll call you."

Her bravado didn't impress him. "How often do you shift?"

"What?" It had been a while, and didn't that make her feel itchy? "When I can. I don't always have the opportunity."

"Do it at least twice a week. Run it off." Eric brushed a stray bit of chocolate from her lower lip. "But when you do go out running, you call me. It's dangerous out there without a Collar, and you need protection."

"Sure, Eric. But who protects me from you?"

Again the laugh, dark and warm. "I'm your alpha, love. You have no clan or pride, so I'm it by default, as ranking Feline in the area. I protect you—from everyone. Including myself."

"Now, why doesn't that make me feel better?"

"You call me." Eric handed her the bag of chocolate, and she felt another twinge of disappointment. Him feeding her had been . . . delectable. "Now, I'm taking you home."

"I'm meeting my friends."

"Call them and tell them you're going home." Eric leaned in again. "There's bad stuff out there, Iona, and bad people. You have no natural defenses against them." The look in his eyes was one of true worry, not just the you-obey-me-because-I'm-dominant crap. "I don't want you dying on my watch."

"Dying?"

"Yes, sweetheart. The Collars don't mean we've given in to the humans. We chose captivity to save ourselves, and some of those without the Collar are getting wilder and wilder. If they let the animal take over, they go feral. Not a good thing. You feel the wildness though, don't you?"

Of course Iona didn't. She'd grown up like a normal girl—playing with toys, skateboarding, jumping rope, riding horses. Although the horses had always been a little nervous with her. Then she'd become a teenager and discovered that she liked clothes, makeup, shoes, and boys.

Normal. Sure.

Iona smelled the chocolate, winding around the hard craving inside her, and she shivered.

"You feel it," Eric said.

Damn him. "How do I make it stop?"

"It will stop when you mate. When you and your chosen spend days together. When your body is convinced it's doing the job it was made to do, which is to produce cubs."

She stared at him. "How nineteen fifties of you. I have a life, a career."

"You can still have a life. Just one with lots of sex. And cubs."

"Oh, sure. While the men do whatever they want. I've heard *that* before."

Eric leaned to her again, and her mouth watered. *Need chocolate!*

"Males have the same frenzy, sweetheart," he said. "*I* have the frenzy." He traced her cheek. "So whenever you feel the need to dampen it a little, you come and find me. We can help each other."

He was offering to help her ease the pain with lots and lots of sex. Iona should be insulted, not tempted.

She was tempted.

"Give me another piece of chocolate," she said.

Eric plucked her cell phone from her purse and started punching buttons, one-handed. "I'm putting in my number. When the need gets bad, you call me. If you want to go running around as a wildcat, you call me. You want anything at all, you call me."

"I want the chocolate."

Eric laughed. He slid the phone into to her purse and took back the bag of chocolates. He found one laced with citrus and held it up to her. Iona put out her tongue and drew the chocolate into her mouth.

Eric's eyes went dark as he watched her, but he didn't try

to kiss her again. She craved the kiss, but she didn't let herself reach for him.

"Come on," Eric said once she'd finished. He took her arm and kept hold of the bag of chocolates. "You're going home."

D iego gunned the jeep straight through the Shifters. Wildcats, wolves, bears—there were so many of them.

The Shifters leapt out of his way. Diego fishtailed as a wildcat tried to jump on the back of the jeep. The wildcat became dislodged, but not the bear that reached for Cassidy.

Shane roared, half changing, clothes ripping, and went for the bear. Diego saw Cassidy stripping off, heard her growls.

If Diego could get the jeep up to speed, they could beat the Shifters back to the plane. Even Shifters could run only so fast. But the jeep, ancient and worn out, gasped and chugged along. Diego drew his pistol.

A bear charged out of the darkness straight for the side of the jeep. Xavier brought up his shotgun and fired.

At nothing. The Ursine hit the dirt, the shot missing. The bear, a giant of a thing, regained his feet and swiped the shotgun out of Xavier's hands.

In the next second, the bear had swept Xavier out of the jeep. Xavier fell and hit the ground, rolling, rolling. He'd try to get to his feet, snatch out his pistol, fire.

Diego hit the brakes, and the jeep swung around. The biker in the passenger seat held on, swearing and praying, his eyes closed.

Cassidy was out, her wildcat racing back to help Xavier. Shane rose on his hind legs, scraps of clothes clinging to him, the grizzly roaring his rage.

Diego grabbed his shotgun and jumped out, weapon ready, as he ran back to Xavier. Xavier made it to his feet, but the bear and now several wolves surrounded him.

Xavier didn't want to shoot. Diego saw that in his stance. He liked Shifters, now that he'd gotten to know some, and he didn't view them as dangerous animals that needed to be contained. He wanted there to be a way out that didn't involve death.

Cassidy and Shane simply attacked them.

Shane hit the bear that held Xavier, and Cassidy went for one of the wolves. Diego ran on toward them, his heart in his throat.

Cassidy's Collar went off as soon as she landed on the back of a wolf, her claws extended, but she kept on fighting. Shane, same thing.

But they'd tire, and the pain of the Collars would break them soon. The other Shifters were many, strong, and not restricted by Collars. Shane and Cassidy were like declawed tabbies trying to fight a horde of angry alley cats.

Diego heard the jeep behind him roar to life. The drug runners. Of course they'd steal the jeep and run out of there to save their own asses.

But they weren't fast enough. A few bears broke off and rushed the jeep. They didn't try to stop it or grab the men inside, they just tipped the damn thing over.

The engine whined, gurgled, and died. The bikers tried to run, but the bears and wolves were on them.

Diego took aim at the Shifters surrounding Xavier and fired. One bear fell, moaning. Diego cocked the gun one more time before it was knocked out of his hands. He found himself facing a wild wolf, with crazed eyes, brown teeth bared, its breath horrific.

Diego fought. His body took over, the lessons and experience of hand-to-hand combat closing down his brain. To think meant to die.

He'd never in his life gone hand-to-hand with a gigantic wolf, but the same principles applied. Go for the vulnerable spots, take down the assailant as fast as you can.

The wolf's muzzle was vulnerable—if Diego could get past the teeth. Likewise the throat, the legs.

The wolf's front claws tore open Diego's skin, raising welts of pain. Diego ducked and came up under the wolf, jabbing a hand into the wolf's throat. It fell back, choking.

Cassidy's Collar shocked and arced in the darkness. She howled as another wildcat and bear joined her fight to keep Xavier safe. Xavier was firing now, Shifters screaming as he hit them.

Diego dove for his shotgun. It was snatched out of his reach by a bear, who half shifted and rose to his full height. The thing smelled like urine.

Diego rolled into the darkness. Like hell he was getting shot in the stomach twice in his lifetime by the same kind of gun.

The Shifter brought the gun around like a club and caught Diego on the temple. Diego ducked in time to keep the blow from doing full damage, but the world spun around him.

Shane knocked the half-shifted bear away from Diego, but Diego felt himself losing consciousness. The last things he saw before he passed out were at least a dozen Shifters dragging his brother away, followed by Cassidy's wildcat sprinting after them into the darkness.

"Shifter woman, I claim you."

The speaker was a bear Shifter, in human form now. The gigantic man's skin was covered with tattoos, his shaggy hair and beard touched with gray. At least he'd put on a pair of pants, tattered BDUs.

All the Shifters in the abandoned building wore clothes of some form or other, but none had offered clothing to Cassidy. She'd chased them and tried to get Xavier away from them, but she'd been beaten down by five Lupines and a Feline, plus the shocks from her damned Collar.

The Collar was silent now, and Cassidy sat cross-legged on the dirt floor, holding in the Collar's aftermath pain. Xavier lay on a blanket next to her, unconscious, his head caked with blood.

Cassidy looked up at the bear Shifter, meeting his eyes. It was difficult to lock gazes with him, because he was definitely the leader here, and he had dominance. Plus he was just so tall, and her neck hurt. But Cassidy knew that if she looked away, if she betrayed any submissiveness to him, she was done for.

A male might hesitate to force an alpha female who was not afraid to fight him, because she could do him a lot of damage. But he'd not hesitate to force a submissive. A feral wouldn't anyway.

"When my alpha comes for me, you're not going to be happy," Cassidy said. "Trust me."

"Your alpha has to be a thousand miles away," the bear

said. She'd heard one of his trackers call him Miguel. Whether that was his true name or one he'd taken when he'd come to Mexico, she didn't know. "You have a Collar," Miguel said. "That means you don't live nearby. No one around here is Collared. They wouldn't dare take a Collar."

Cassidy clasped her knees to her chest, but she kept her voice nonchalant. "Felines, Lupines, Ursines, living together in the wild. Unheard of."

"We're just doing what you did," Miguel said. "Coming together, putting aside differences, only we didn't bow to humans to do it. The humans bow to us. No Collars. Just Shifters."

Living in a half-ruined building in the middle of nowhere in Mexico, terrorizing the locals and hiding like fugitives. No access to any stashes of wealth, it looked like. They either killed their food or had the local eateries give it to them free.

"Looks . . . cozy," Cassidy said.

"You're pretty strong. When you're my mate, we'll get that Collar off you, and you can be my second. Or third. Depending on how well you fight my alpha mate."

Cassidy rolled her eyes. "I reject your mate-claim. That's a no-brainer."

Miguel laughed. The two Feline trackers who were sitting as his bodyguards did too. The only other Shifters with them at present were another bear and a wolf guarding Xavier and Cassidy.

"Females around here don't reject mate-claims," Miguel said. "There are only so many females to go around, and you'll be mate-claimed by more than one male. But the first cubs are mine. After that, you can fuck whoever you want."

Cassidy wrinkled her nose. "Way to romance a girl."

"Romance is for humans."

Cassidy thought about how Diego whispered beautiful words as he made love to her. She'd take human romance with Diego over Miguel's disgusting statements any day of the week.

"I'm not standing up with you under sun and moon," Cassidy said. "Forget it."

Miguel laughed again. "None of those rituals exist here. We just mate."

"Taking off my Collar might kill me," Cassidy said. "Then I wouldn't be much good for producing cubs, would I?"

"I'll let you push out a few first, just in case."

Cassidy pretended to ignore that. Her heart was pounding, but she tried to suppress all emotion. No rage or fear. Miguel would be able to scent her fear and use it to break her.

Cassidy glanced around the barren room again. Wind blew through chinks in the ceiling high above. "This works for you, does it? Coming together, living in harmony, all Shifter races as one. Are you having more cubs, then, a better rate of survival? If so, where are they all?"

The slightest flicker of Miguel's eyes told her much. They weren't having the number of cubs they thought they would.

Because they'd gone feral. *Feral* didn't mean the same thing as *wild*. It meant the animal instincts taking over, the human side being suppressed until the animal ruled, no matter what form the Shifter was in. Shifters were half beings, at their very best when each aspect of them worked in balance. Going too far in either direction wasn't good at all.

These Shifters had probably found each other after humans started forcing Shifters to take Collars. They'd have escaped before Shifters were put into Shiftertowns, choosing to stay wild, thinking they could beat the humans at their own game.

Nice idea to try to make it together. Shifters taking the Collars had found, to their surprise, that living in communities, even restricted ones like Shiftertowns, let them stop fighting for survival and learn to *live*. Shifters together had gotten stronger, their fertility rates higher, the incidence of losing females in childbirth much lower. Cubs had safe places to grow up now.

These Shifters had tried the same idea, but without Collars to keep the fighting down. Different species instinctively fought each other, but Collars, Shifters had found, let them live side by side in some kind of peace. That way Shane and Brody and their mother could be friends next door instead of Eric and Cassidy having to fight them every time they walked out the door.

The dominance fights in this Shifter enclave must be horrific. And ferals were even worse at reproducing than Shifters who'd lived alone in the wild. Life was hard on a female Shifter, as was childbirth.

"This is how you introduce fresh blood, is it?" Cassidy asked, as though simply curious. "Kidnapping females and mate-claiming them?"

"We went out to defend our town against incomers," the bear said. "You were an opportunity."

Cassidy had been trying to save Xavier's life. The last thing she'd wanted was for Diego to watch his brother die.

She glanced around surreptitiously, taking in the floor space, the exits. Windowless walls rose around them, with only one main doorway leading out into the night. The ceiling soared above her, pieces of it missing. It had to be a sixty-foot climb to the top. The light came from battery-operated lanterns, and the cooking fire was a gas camping grill. All stolen, she surmised.

A dark doorway stood beyond Miguel and his guards, the farthest point from Cassidy. The smell behind it was stuffy, enclosed, and it was also filled with pungent fear. Cassidy's hackles rose, instincts telling her she did *not* want to go in there.

Miguel nudged Xavier with his foot. "Who's the human?"

"My pet," Cassidy said. Shifter females in the wild had sometimes taken human male lovers, referring to them as *pets*. She figured Xavier wouldn't mind the lie if it kept him alive, if he were even awake to hear it. "You don't get to have him."

"Maybe I'll just kill him," Miguel said.

Cassidy coolly met his gaze. "If you let me keep him, I'll consider the mate-claim."

"You don't consider anything, Feline. I mate-claim you, and that's that."

"But if I get to keep my human male, I might be nicer to you and not hurt you as much."

Miguel chuckled. "I like you, Feline. We'll see. You be good, and you can keep your pet."

"How about some clothes?" Cassidy asked. "It's getting cold."

"I don't have any to spare. I'll have one of my females get you some tomorrow. If you're cold, you'll have to stay shifted."

Cassidy didn't want to shift. She could think more clearly as a human, and she knew that the way to win with Miguel would be to outthink him. The feral bear had the edge on her in terms of animal strength, plus Miguel was smart. How else would he have maintained dominance here, keeping three species of Shifters from killing each other? He'd have to be cunning and a quick thinker, even if things hadn't turned out the way he'd hoped.

Cassidy sighed. She stretched, letting her cat take over, and ended up sitting on her furry haunches.

She tamped down her fighting instincts with great effort. Her wildcat wanted to attack, but the minute she did that, Miguel and his boys would be on her, and five against one wasn't good odds. As much as these Shifters needed females, she sensed that they would kill her to stop her escaping. Even if they wouldn't mean to kill her, she'd be just as dead.

Cassidy closed her throat to keep herself from growling, and she lay down next to Xavier. He was still out, his face pale, and she wanted to growl again in worry. She curled around Xavier to give him as much of her body heat as possible, but she remained awake, and watchful.

CHAPTER TWENTY-ONE

"Come on, Diego. Wake up."

A huge hand batted Diego's face, and Diego cracked open his eyes.

He found himself on a dark dirt road, a jeep on its side not far away, with two men in biker vests lying limply next to it. A naked and mud-streaked Shane stood above Diego, about to hit him again.

"Stop," Diego said, voice hoarse. "I'm awake."

"Those ferals took Cassidy." Shane sounded like he wanted to cry. "And your brother. Cass could have gotten away, but she stayed with Xavier."

Son of a bitch.

Diego got himself to his feet. His head hurt, badly, but he wasn't dizzy. Yet. The shotgun lay not far from where he'd fallen, and Diego scooped it up as he walked toward the jeep.

He looked down at the drug runners he'd come to arrest. "Are they still alive?"

"Yeah. Bastards tried to leave us here."

"They know all about running away," Diego said. Adrenaline was flowing through him, dulling pain, honing Diego's thoughts to focus on one goal.

Get Cassidy and Xavier back.

Diego checked the ammo in his pistol, then started pulling the ammo boxes from the back of the fallen jeep. The jeep was dead, no fear of fire, but still he wanted all that explosive potential away from the gas tank.

Shane started to help. The man was stark naked, but Diego scarcely noticed as they lugged out their gear and assessed what they had. Interestingly, Shane didn't try to take over or demand that Diego obey him. Shane was waiting for Diego to tell him what to do.

"Call Marlo, tell him what happened," Diego commanded as they unloaded the last of the ammo. "We're going to need the plane ready to go."

"What are you going to do?" Shane asked him.

"Tie up these guys, then find my brother and Cass."

Shane stepped in front of him. "You can't go up against Shifters alone, Diego. The alpha will have trackers, they'll smell you coming, and they'll be ready."

Diego dragged his satellite phone out of the wreckage, relieved when he found the thing undamaged. He also found Cassidy's earpiece on the ground where it had fallen when she'd shifted. He handed the earpiece to Shane.

"Good to know. Help me with these guys and then call Marlo."

Together they pulled the drug runners away from the wreckage, and Diego handcuffed them. Shane walked away to get Marlo on the sat phone.

One biker swam to consciousness. "Are the Shifters dead?" he asked. "Are they gone?"

"Not yet," Diego said. "But they have my girlfriend and my brother, thanks to you trying to leave us behind."

The man lowered his head, pretending incomprehension. Asshole.

After Shane hung up, Diego and Shane marched the dealers back to the cantina where Cassidy had found them. Whatever patrons had been in there had vacated.

The bartender, who owned the place, protested. Diego answered him in Spanish. "If you want an end to your Shifter troubles, you'll help me," he said. "I'm going to get rid of them *and* your drug dealer problem."

He and Shane set the two bikers on chairs and shackled them together.

"The Shifters came two years ago," the bartender said as they worked. "Our own fault. The drug runners had taken over, fighting each other in our streets, ruining our lives. We put out the word that we needed help. The Shifters came down out of the hills, holed up in the factory that had never been finished, and took over. They got rid of the drug runners, all right."

"Then you had a Shifter problem instead." Diego checked both men's bonds and approached the bar. "What did the Shifters do?"

The bartender looked sad. "We have to give them anything they want. Food, clothing—our daughters. Some of them wanted to kill our sons, but the alpha, he said no. Said it would attract too much attention."

This was exactly what Reid had meant, Diego realized. *They can look human, and they try to act human, but if you don't treat them like the dangerous animals they are, you'll pay for it.* Humans had rounded up Shifters and slapped Collars on them, because they'd feared that something exactly like this might happen.

But these Shifters were different. *Ferals*, Cassidy and Shane had called them. Diego wasn't sure what that meant, but he couldn't imagine Eric or Nell or Lindsay doing things like this.

"What's this alpha's name?" Diego asked. "And what kind of Shifter is he?"

"He's a bear. Calls himself Miguel. He said he chose the name of one of the humans' archangels. Thought it was funny."

"Sounds like a smart-ass. Where is this factory?"

"Five miles west of here. There's only one road that goes there. Hard to miss."

"You're being very open about it."

The bartender shrugged. "What have I got to lose? The dealers used my place as a base, and then the Shifters laid siege to them here. They killed my brother and took my daughter."

"Did you all try to fight back?"

"Sure. The dealers left a pile of weapons. But the Shifters were too fast, too strong. We held out for a while, then . . ."

He shrugged, a man defeated. "If you're thinking of fighting them, you won't last long. Get out while you can—just some friendly advice. Go back to America where you can be rich and safe."

Diego had never considered himself rich, and he knew just how "safe" the streets of his city were. Everything was relative, he supposed.

Diego walked outside in the night to make another phone call, but he couldn't get through to Eric. Shifters were allowed to have cell phones, but they had old models without much power. Or maybe Diego's sat phone wouldn't connect with them for some reason.

Shane came out after him. He wore a pair of jeans that looked too small—a gift from the bartender. "You should get out of here, Diego, and let me take care of this. Have Marlo fly you back home."

"And leave Cassidy and my brother? No way in hell."

"I understand how you feel, Diego, but these are ferals. You have no idea what you're fucking with. One, you might be able to handle. A group of them, you can't."

"What does *feral* mean exactly—they didn't take Collars?"

"More than that. Even a Collared Shifter can go feral, but it's rare. The Collar usually stops the violence. Feral means a Shifter living by his animal instincts, suppressing the human ones. It usually starts with giving up bathing."

"Yeah, I smelled them."

Shane rubbed his lip. "But these are different from other ferals I've seen. Most of them run off on their own and eventually die. This is a *group* of ferals, different species living together. That's weird. We hated each other in the wild, couldn't get along. We barely get along now."

"Whatever they are, I'm not leaving. Cassidy went with them to protect Xavier. I'm not abandoning either of them."

Shane regarded Diego quietly for a moment, then nodded. "I see that. I'm glad."

Diego assessed the dark street. Aside from the few lights in the cantina behind him, the town was unnaturally silent and dark. He imagined it had been lively at one time, with the townspeople emerging from their houses at night, enjoying the cool evenings before having to face the heat of the day once more.

He slung the shotgun on its strap over his shoulder and loaded his pistol with a fresh magazine. The Shifters would know he was coming—Shane was right about that.

But like hell he'd let these Shifters do to Xavier and Cassidy what the drug runners had done to Jobe. Same situation, different place.

"What now?" Shane asked.

"We go find them."

Shane looked surprised. "You're not going to wait for Eric?"

"I can't reach Eric. I'll have Marlo start trying to get him, but we need to scout, find Cassidy and Xavier's exact positions, and figure out a way to extract them."

"I get that. But, like I said, we can't sneak up on them. This Miguel will have trackers everywhere, and these Shifters are going to be more animal than human."

"If they'll see us coming, we can use that. Do you want to shoot or shift? I need you in the best shape, so which one will least likely set off your Collar?"

Shane shrugged. "I've never shot anyone, so I don't know. I can only fight a few minutes with the Collar, and the hangover is a bitch." Shane already looked pretty green now.

Diego handed him the extra shotgun. "Then you shoot. Aim for the chest—think of it as a triangle from shoulders to groin, and aim for the middle. Doesn't really matter if you're a dead shot. We just need to take them down long enough to get Cassidy and Xav out of there."

Shane took the shotgun, holding it gingerly. "I'll try."

"If you think it's better you ditch it and shift, you do it."

Shane eyed the weapon. "Got it." Diego suspected he'd be ditching and shifting.

"We're getting her free, Shane," he said.

Shane nodded, giving Diego a look of new respect. "Damn right we are."

Cassidy didn't sleep. Xavier woke up, saw Cassidy next to him in leopard form, raised his head, and opened his mouth to speak.

Cassidy put a heavy paw on his chest and fixed him with a stern look. Whether Xavier understood her signals or simply was smart enough to realize that keeping quiet was best, he lay back down and said nothing.

The night dragged on. The Shifters were restless, going in and out of the building, fading in and out of the darkness. A female bear came in to see Miguel. She glanced over at Cassidy lying quietly with Xavier, and quickly looked away, but Cassidy smelled her fear. The female was worried that Cassidy would displace her.

Don't worry, honey. I am so out of here.

Diego would have contacted Eric by now. Help would be on the way.

Cassidy held on to that hope as night slid into day. The sun came up and things began to warm.

Miguel came to her as a sunbeam sliced down on her from a crack in the ceiling. "About time I made good on the mate-claim," he said.

Cassidy didn't bother shifting back to human. She gave Miguel a disdainful look from her cat's eyes and lowered her head to lick one paw.

Miguel laughed. "I like them with sass. Tastier when they go down."

Dangerous games. Forcing the mate-claim was against Shifter rules, but rules didn't always stop a Shifter in a mating frenzy, and Cassidy knew that in this place, Miguel made his own rules. However, making Miguel focus on the mate-claim would distract him from Xavier. If Miguel fixed on his frustration with Cassidy, Xavier might have a chance to run. Tricky, but it might work.

Cassidy yawned, putting every bit of nonchalance into it she possibly could. A female not very impressed with a male. She started grooming her paw again, and Miguel chuckled.

"Oh, it's going to be so good with you, sweetheart. So damn good." Still chuckling, Miguel walked away. Only when he was all the way across the room again did Cassidy let herself shudder.

Never with you, asshole. Not only are you an idiot, but, Goddess, you stink.

* * *

Diego managed to get the jeep running by dawn. He gave the drug runners their greatest wish when he and Shane loaded them into the jeep, and Diego drove back to the airstrip.

He shackled the bikers under a wooden awning just off the dirt runway and left them to be looked after by Marlo's friend. Marlo cheerfully got the plane running and he, Shane, and Diego took off, heading north and west.

They located the half-finished factory west of the village, right where the bartender had said it would be. A couple of walls had been built and part of a roof, but the rest of the building looked skeletal or had started to fall apart. No Shifters were in sight, but Diego knew they'd hear the plane.

After a few passes, Diego directed Marlo to take them back to the airstrip.

Shane was gloomy as they disembarked. "There's no cover at all," he said. "We can't sneak up on them, and even if we wait for dark, they'll smell us and hear us. Plus Shifters can see in the dark way better than you can."

"We're not waiting," Diego said. "The hottest part of the day will be what—at three or four this afternoon?"

"About that," Marlo said.

"We go in then. During siesta time, when the Shifters are napping."

"They'll still have the trackers guarding," Shane said. "And there's only two of us against who knows how many?"

"As you said, darkness won't give us any advantage," Diego said. "Daylight puts us on even sight footing, and as for the Shifters' superior sense of smell . . ." He grinned. "I bet the local market has a great selection of chiles."

Shane laughed and slapped Diego on the shoulder so hard that Diego nearly went to his knees. "I like the way you think, human."

"No stealth, just chaos and confusion," Diego said. "We don't have an army, but we can make as much trouble as we can without one."

Shane laughed again, but this time Diego ducked before the hearty swat could land.

Diego left Marlo with instructions of what he wanted the

man to do and when, and also to keep trying to get hold of Eric. Diego could do this without an army, but having one would be even better.

Cassidy watched the Shifters quiet as the temperature rose. The guards changed, the ones watching Cassidy and protecting Miguel yawning as they left.

That's the problem with letting yourself go feral, Cassidy thought. These Shifters had become nocturnal, snoozing in the light of day, prowling at night. Even Miguel was groggy.

If Cassidy were to make her move, it should be soon. Xavier was alert, but his wounds weren't good—the cuts looked deep, and his left arm was broken. Cassidy would be carrying him out.

From what she'd been able to ascertain, they were being kept in the heart of the structure, behind the stoutest walls. Daylight showed through the doorways and the high windows, revealing half walls and completely missing walls beyond.

This room was the most heavily guarded, of course. Miguel had shifted and dozed off, a huge brown bear snoring on the floor. Two trackers sat on either side of him—Lupines—eyes open, fully alert. Two Felines guarded the door leading to daylight, two more standing guard at the door leading to the darkness that Cassidy didn't like.

The smell from that opening bothered her. Too much fear. She had the feeling that the dark room beyond was where Miguel would stash her next.

Marlo's airplane had flown over earlier, not too low. The Shifters had watched the plane, but because it hadn't circled or returned, let it go. Cassidy had made herself not look up, remaining inert, uncaring.

She couldn't help her slight jolt when she heard it again.

Cassidy masked her interest with a yawn, but the guards came alert. One leaned down and spoke into Miguel's ear.

To Miguel's credit, he didn't wake up trying to tear his guard's head off. He opened his eyes, listened, and shifted back to human, fully awake.

"Your friends?" he asked Cassidy. "You think that the human and the Collared bear are coming to rescue you?"

Cassidy stayed wildcat and didn't answer.

Miguel got up and started for her. "I think it's time to make the mate-claim stick."

Damn. If he started on her, Cassidy would have to fight him. Fighting him would tax her strength and energy, which meant she might not have enough left for the dash out with Xavier. Plus her Collar would go off.

She drew a breath, trying to stay calm, and tried to draw on the techniques Jace had been teaching her to override her Collar. Cassidy knew she wasn't anywhere close to mastering it yet—the Morrisseys in Austin had been working on this for years, Cassidy only a few weeks.

Still, she closed her eyes, breathed deeply, and tried to clear her mind.

"Bring her," Miguel's voice grated through her thoughts. "And kill the human."

CHAPTER TWENTY-TWO

Cassidy opened her eyes and snarled. No time for medita-tion. She'd just have to fight through the pain.

She struck at the bear and the wolf that closed in on her. Her paw ripped across the bear's face before she felt the tingle of her Collar. But she couldn't stop for that. She had to protect Xavier.

The wolf went for her throat. Cassidy gave up and let her-self go. She became a ball of snarling teeth and claws. She struck and bit, swiped and ducked, using her Feline reflexes to out-jump, out-smack, out-leap her opponents.

Idiots. Miguel should have sent a Feline to take down a Feline. Bears and wolves outweighed her and had more brute strength, but Cassidy's agility kept them from pinning her.

She fought hard until Miguel's paw caught her on the side of her head. His bear was huge, almost as big as Shane. Cas-sidy stumbled, stunned, and her Collar bit pain deep into her.

Still she fought him. She couldn't let Miguel kill Xavier.

Miguel roared. He was finished playing. Cassidy struggled on against him and the wolf, her claws leaving deep gouges. The second bear had retreated, his face a bloody mess.

Miguel clamped his giant maw on the back of Cassidy's neck, huge teeth breaking through her fur. He started dragging Cassidy toward the dark doorway, from which issued a stench of fear and sweat.

The wolf was joined by a second, both of them circling on huge paws around Xavier. They were going to kill him.

Cassidy struggled, snarled, lashed, bit. Miguel held her fast. Damn him.

She did not want to go through that doorway. Despair and fear reigned there. *Not that door, not that door . . .*

Bright, blinding light. The *whump* of an explosion. More light. Cassidy's eyes screwed shut, and Miguel grunted and dropped her. Cassidy tried to scramble away, only to be stopped by a paw whacking her down to her side.

More light. A flash of brightness so intense it blinded her even though Cassidy had instinctively shut her eyes.

And then the stench. Not Shifters. Sharp raw smells— ammonia, gasoline, and pepper. So much pepper. Not pepper spray, but an explosion of nose-assaulting chiles, the kind that could burn your skin and make your eyes and nose run for hours.

To throw that over a Shifter . . .

She heard yowls and snarls, howls. Confusion.

Over it came another explosion of light, and in the middle of the light—as well as her streaming eyes could see—a man.

Not a Shifter. He was an upright man with black hair and eyes like midnight. He held a shotgun in competent hands, and he blasted Shifters left and right. Behind him came a very, very angry grizzly.

The Shifters weren't dying. They were falling, groaning, weeping, howling. Whatever Diego was hitting them with was making them insane with pain.

Two large paws locked over Cassidy. Miguel. Still up, still fighting.

He dragged Cassidy to the darkened doorway, caught her by the scruff of her neck, and tossed her inside. Cassidy shifted at the last second, the change painful this time, and caught the doorframe with both hands. Miguel shifted at the same time, rising tall to face Diego.

Diego just looked at him, no emotion, no fear, nothing in his face. He'd come to do a job, and he'd finish it. No questions.

"The woman is *mine*," Miguel shouted at him. "No matter what you do to my Shifters, she's my *mate*. I claim her."

"*I reject the claim!*" Cassidy yelled.

Her shout would have been good enough for civilized Shifters, but Miguel only smiled. "The claim is mine unless this puny human here wants to Challenge."

Diego would have no idea what that meant, but apparently he didn't care. Diego brought up his shotgun and aimed it at Miguel.

"Consider this a challenge," he said.

He fired. What hit Miguel was not a bullet, but scattered shot that smelled and burned. Miguel got it full in the face.

While Miguel was howling, Diego charged forward and grabbed Cassidy.

At the same time, the room filled with still more light, blinding and hot. A tall, lean man appeared in the middle of it—Stuart Reid.

Before Cassidy could register shock, Reid bent over Xavier and came up with the man across his shoulders. Another white-hot flash, and both were gone.

"Run," Diego said into Cassidy's ear, but his voice was still very calm. "Marlo set explosives. This wreck is coming down."

"No, wait."

Cassidy had glimpsed something important on the other side of the darkened doorway when Miguel had tried to throw her through it. She shook off Diego and charged through to stairs that led down into cool earth. The stench came from below.

What she'd seen on the stairs in the one moment she'd had to glance at them had been a child.

The cub had been about five years old, just old enough to shift, and he'd been naked and filthy. As she neared the bottom of the stairs, the smell got worse, and Cassidy found what she'd feared she'd find.

A big room—large enough, thank the Goddess, or Cassidy would have found worse than she did—spread out before her. Frightened eyes turned her way as she charged in.

The females. They were sequestered and naked, surrounded

by the children too small to be around the full-grown males. Shifter males would have the instinct to kill the offspring of rival males—as with the problem of Torey in Cassidy's Shiftertown—but the ferals wouldn't even try to suppress the instinct. Miguel had obviously gotten around that problem by sequestering all cubs until they were big enough to fight for themselves. Even worse, some of the women down here were human.

Only one person rose to meet Cassidy—the alpha female, Miguel's mate, who'd looked at Cassidy in such worry.

"Get them out," Cassidy shouted at her. "Now."

No one moved.

Damn it, there was no time. Diego's attack depended on surprise, chaos, swiftness. Miguel would figure out how to regroup, and then they'd lose the advantage.

"This building is going to blow," Cassidy said. "You have to leave."

The females still stared at her, every confidence they'd ever possessed having been beaten from them long ago.

"Miguel's down," Cassidy said. "He's finished. You're free."

"No!" The alpha's cry was anguished. "You bitch, what did you do to my *mate*?"

She launched herself at Cassidy, shifting along the way.

Cassidy shifted again, her bones aching, her Collar already slowing her down. But she knew how this had to end. She had to defeat the alpha, become alpha herself, before the rest of the women would follow her.

The female, an Ursine, was unhampered by a Collar, but she'd been weakened by living down here in the darkness. In the real world, she wouldn't have had the dominance Miguel had given her here.

The fight was swift. Cassidy's Collar snapped and sparked, pain biting deep. Cassidy tried to close her mind to it and pinned the female with her paw. She fought the instinct that made her want to snap the woman's neck, telling herself that whatever this woman had become, it wasn't her fault.

Cassidy knocked the female's head on the stone floor, and the woman groaned, the fight going out of her. Cassidy rose to her full height and shifted, pretending that the change wasn't agony.

"Miguel mate-claimed me," she said. "I just defeated your alpha, and unless someone else wants to challenge me, *I'm* alpha. And we're going. *Now.*"

Animal instinct was amazing. The females sat for a stunned moment, then the idea made it through their brains that Cassidy had strength and power and, most of all, could protect them. Even the human females figured that out.

They got up, gathered their cubs, and started for the stairs.

"Diego," Cassidy shouted upward. "We're coming!"

"Hurry it up, *mi ja*," Diego said, still sounding amazingly calm. "Marlo's a pyromaniac."

Cassidy herded the seven females and dozen cubs up the stairs. She'd have to come last, she knew, letting them know no one was getting left behind.

Cassidy caught the last, slow, crying little boy and sent him up the stairs after his mother. She grabbed the fallen alpha, who'd shifted back to human, slung her over her shoulder, and started up the stairs.

The Shifters were regrouping, looking for Miguel. Diego was propelling the women out of the gloom, Shane returning to help.

"Cass!" Diego shouted at her. "Hurry!"

Miguel was coming around. He saw Cassidy dash by with his mate over her shoulder, and came up with a roar.

Cassidy ran past Diego, who was walking through the big room as though he had all the time in the world. She emerged from the factory into sunlight and heat. Shane charged by her, crying cubs clinging to his back. Xavier was already out by the jeep, leaning heavily against it, Reid next to him. Some men from the village were there as well.

The bartender from the cantina saw the females coming toward them, gave a cry of joy, and launched himself at a dark-haired young human woman carrying a small boy. Father and daughter. Arms went around each other, the two crying and hugging.

Cassidy laid the alpha female on the ground next to the jeep then started back to the building. Diego hadn't come out yet. She hurt too much to shift, but fear kept her running on her cut and bleeding human feet.

Before she made it halfway back, Diego emerged. He was

dirty and bloody, his clothes ripped by claws, but he walked steadily toward her.

Behind him, the factory blew. Marlo's charges, one after the other, sent the remaining walls of the factory heaving outward, and an orange ball of flame rose high into the hot sky.

Diego shouldered his shotgun as he reached Cassidy, then he put one arm around her shoulders and gave her a swift kiss on her lips.

"Hey, *mi ja*," he said, his smile warm. "Need a ride?"

D iego didn't get a chance to speak to Reid until they reached the airstrip.

"How did you do that?" Diego asked Reid. Reid stood with him and Xavier under a corrugated tin shelter as Diego checked Xavier over. "How did you know exactly where we were and how to get in?"

"GPS," Reid answered. The man looked none the worse for wear, not even scratched or dirty. "Your pilot gave Eric the coordinates of the factory. I landed myself on the roof, looked things over, and figured out the fighting was worst in the main room. Got in there, saw your brother wounded, and pulled him out."

"Thanks, Reid," Xavier croaked. "I owe you."

"You owe me nothing," Reid said, and walked away.

Xavier groaned a little as he propped himself against the big water cooler Marlo had provided. "Reid is weird, but I'm grateful to him. Stop worrying about me, *hermano*, and go find out who those other guys Eric brought are."

A second, smaller plane sat on the end of the dirt runway. This one had contained Reid, Eric, a couple of Eric's trackers, and some Shifters Diego hadn't met.

The Shifter that seemed to be the leader had dark hair going gray at the temples, blue eyes, and the hardest stare Diego had ever seen.

"This is Dylan Morrissey," Eric said when Diego reached them. "From Austin. His son's the Shiftertown leader there. I asked him here to check out this feral problem."

Dylan looked Diego up and down, nostrils widening as he inhaled Diego's scent. He obviously tried to make Diego look away, but Diego was getting a little tired of this game. He met Dylan's gaze squarely and stayed put.

Dylan held out his hand, conceding. "Well met."

Diego took his hand. Dylan pulled him forward and slid one strong arm around Diego's back. A hug, but not quite. More an I'll-trust-you-for-now-but-don't-fuck-with-me kind of greeting.

"Diego blew up the ferals," Shane said. The bear had put a T-shirt on over jeans of the right size, and he grinned, showing all his teeth. "It was awesome."

"He blew up their base," Dylan said, sounding less impressed. "Whichever ones survived will try to regroup and start again, especially if the leader survived. I've come to prevent that."

"You by yourself?" Diego asked.

Dylan nodded, the man radiating self-assurance. "With a few of my trackers. I'll have my mate join me if I have to come down on the Lupines. They won't want to deal with her."

"I believe you," Eric said. "I've met Glory."

"Plus I brought Collars," Dylan said. "They'll take them."

"What about the females?" Cassidy moved to stand beside Diego. Someone had given her a dress decorated with bright red flowers, and her tall, sexy curves made the shapeless garment look good.

"They'll go back with us," Eric said. "I claimed them."

Diego gave him a sharp look. "Wait, what? What does that mean?"

"Their males are defeated, and I'm a clan leader," Eric said. "As leader and alpha, I can claim as many mates as I want. Don't worry—it's just a technicality to take them back safely to our Shiftertown. They're now off-limits to other males, and once I get them back home and put Collars on them, I'll release my claim. I promised them I wouldn't kill their cubs, so they're fine with me so far."

He'd promised not to kill their cubs. *Dios mio.*

"How do you plan to explain to the humans in Las Vegas that five new women and all those kids are suddenly living in your Shiftertown?" Diego asked.

Eric smiled, but there was no humor in it. "You let me worry about that."

"That lead feral, Miguel," Diego said. "He said he mate-claimed Cassidy."

Both Eric and Dylan turned intense gazes to Diego. "Did he?" Eric switched his stare to Cassidy. "Did Miguel survive? We haven't looked at the casualties yet."

"Diego Challenged him," Cassidy said.

Again, both Eric and Dylan looked at Diego.

Cassidy laid her hand on Diego's shoulder. "In front of witnesses, including Xavier. And I'd say he defeated Miguel, whether Miguel survived or not."

Eric wasn't smiling anymore. Dylan watched with keen interest.

"Anyone want to tell me exactly what you're talking about?" Diego asked.

Eric shrugged. "It's a little unorthodox. But Shifter law is Shifter law. Miguel made the mate-claim. You Challenged, you won. That means the mate-claim for Cassidy transfers from Miguel to you. Cassidy is yours to take as mate, if you still want her."

CHAPTER TWENTY-THREE

Diego didn't understand, Cassidy saw as they flew back north. She was exhausted, sick from the pain of her Collar, and worried about the females and cubs.

Five of the seven females had been Shifter, the other two, human women from the village. The cantina owner's daughter she'd seen welcomed with open arms back to her father, but the other woman had been shunned by her family. They claimed she'd been defiled by Miguel, and they didn't want her back. Cassidy saw the heartbreak in the poor woman's eyes, and she burned with anger for her.

Dylan, however, said the woman could go back to his Shiftertown—his son's mate was human, and that son was Shiftertown leader. The woman would be protected. Cassidy saw that the young woman was miserable, but she accepted the offer. She didn't have much choice. Diego asked the question about papers for her, and Dylan quietly said he'd take care of it. Cassidy believed him. Dylan was a take-care-of-it kind of male.

Eric would help the Shifter females, but Cassidy felt responsibility for them too. Her fighting and defeating their alpha meant something, even though Cassidy had done it to expedite the situation. She'd have to help Eric find them places to live and make sure they didn't have too much trouble adapting to Collars and to Shiftertown—and Shiftertown adapting to them.

For now, Cassidy let out her breath and snuggled a little closer to Diego. She so needed a nap . . .

Diego closed his arms around her. She turned sleepily to him, rewarded with his warm mouth on hers.

He stroked her hair—which had to be filthy—and kissed her lips again. "I almost lost you," he whispered. "I almost lost you, Cass. And Xavier, and it would have been my fault."

Cassidy sat up, his hurt winding around her. "It's not your fault the feral asshole Miguel decided to take over a human town. You didn't know he was down here."

"Enrique must have set me up—I'm betting he knew those Shifters were there."

"Possibly. But look at it this way. You saved the town." Cassidy batted her eyelashes at him and put on a sugary voice. "My hero."

Diego didn't smile. "You let your vengeance go when you had the chance to kill Reid. I hung on to mine, and you nearly died for it."

Cassidy snuggled into his shoulder again. "I let it go because Reid was so pitiable. In your case, the guys who shot your partner terrorized a town, and then were terrorized by the Shifters, who were even worse. You solved both problems, and it's finished."

"I know."

Diego didn't sound elated, but Cassidy understood. He'd held on to wanting to bring Jobe's killers to justice for a long time; he'd let it drive his life. The obsession of it kept him from seeing anything else. Now Diego's tunnel vision was gone, and he didn't know where to look.

Cassidy knew how he felt. The hunters who'd actually shot Donovan were still out there, but they were pathetic excuses who had been coerced by Reid, who himself had been driven by desperation. Life was more complicated than simply a kill for a kill.

Diego didn't speak much the rest of the trip, and he and Cassidy were both too busy to talk during the unloading. Cassidy had to help look after the females and their cubs—the cubs were both excited and terrified.

Diego left them at the airstrip to take Xavier to the hospital and the drug runners he'd arrested to jail, while Cassidy and Eric faced the task of getting the women and cubs back to Shiftertown undetected. Marlo helped with that too. The man had amazing resources.

Nell came out to meet them when they reached Shiftertown. She didn't even wait for Eric's explanation but waded in to the women and cubs with her no-nonsense attitude. The women had been so beaten down by Miguel that they were pitifully grateful for someone to tell them what to do.

It was late—actually early in the morning—by the time Diego arrived in Shiftertown. Cassidy had been able to grab a shower, but she ached all over, the aftereffects of her Collar making themselves felt.

"You should sleep," Diego said, after kissing her.

"There's still a lot to do."

Diego caught Cassidy as she sagged. "Cass. Bed. Now."

She stopped protesting when he lifted her and carried her into the bedroom. Relaxing in Diego's arms wasn't a bad thing.

Diego set her on her feet in her bedroom and started stripping her clothes from her. She'd already given the flowered dress to Nell, who'd admired it, and now Cassidy wriggled out of jeans and a sleeveless shirt.

Diego caught her in a long kiss. He'd showered too, sometime in the chaos, and smelled like soap and aftershave.

Why did remembering Diego walking away from that factory while it blew behind him, his face streaked with sweat and soot, excite her even more? The Shifter in her liked it. Battle was an aphrodisiac, Diego a warrior.

Cassidy tugged at his T-shirt until it came off, then she skimmed fingers over his hot skin. She was still sick and dizzy from her Collar, but touching Diego made her feel better. Cassidy leaned into him and rubbed her cheek on his chest. She heard his heartbeat beneath her ear, the even thrum that meant he was alive and hers.

She liked the wiry, dark hair on his chest. She rubbed her fingers through it, watching the curls wind around her fingertips. Her questing fingers found his flat, male nipple; she smiled to see it draw to a tight point under her touch.

Cassidy licked the hollow of his throat. Diego gripped her elbows with his warm hands, and his openmouthed kisses landed on her cheek, her neck, her breasts.

Outside her window, Cassidy could hear Nell explaining to some of the cubs that, yes, they were allowed to play outside now.

"That's why you went down to Mexico," Cassidy whispered to Diego. "So these cubs can now be kids without fear."

"They're out playing at four in the morning?" Diego asked. "Mamita would have my guts on a plate if she caught me out at four in the morning."

Cassidy chuckled. "They'll adjust." Her Collar hangover was starting to fade. She tugged the waistband of Diego's jeans. "Take these off."

Diego unbuttoned, unzipped, and let his pants drop. Cassidy slid her hands to firm buttocks under silk boxers.

"I love you with your pants around your ankles," she said.

Diego kicked out of them plus his boxers, and at the same time tugged down Cassidy's bikinis. As he came up, he skimmed her camisole up and off her.

There he was, naked, facing her. Soft lamplight kissed Diego's skin, muscles moving as he brought up his hands to cup her face. "I almost lost you," he said, eyes darkening.

"You keep rescuing me. It's embarrassing. Next time, I rescue you."

Diego kissed her again. Body to body, his hardness came tight against her abdomen, and his kisses opened her mouth. He cupped her breasts, and his kisses turned rough, teeth scraping her lips, hands so warm.

Diego lifted her and laid her on the bed, then came down to her. No seduction, no whispered endearments. Just a man who needed a woman. Cassidy welcomed him.

Diego's eyes widened as he moved inside her, *all* the way in. "*Amada mia*, you are so tight."

Cassidy smiled back. "You take up much space." He was stretching her, easing the Collar's pain, and making her ache a different way. "Don't stop doing that."

"I'm not going to stop. Never, ever, *mi ja*."

"Good. *Good*."

Diego thrust, his body warm and heavy on hers. Cassidy lifted her hips to meet his. Loving him felt so good, so *damn* good, an explosion of pleasure as he pushed inside again and again.

Cassidy moved under him, loving the hardness of him. His body was as hard as his cock, tight and fine, his kisses rough. Diego braced himself on the bed, the mattress dipping as he loved her. His breath came fast, and sweat dripped from his face.

Cassidy's head rocked back as the pleasure went mindless. She felt the fiery point where they joined, which spread waves of erotic joy. No smooth and sweet loving—Diego was making it wild and fierce.

Fierce. Cassidy liked that. She wanted more. His hard loving seared her, awakening secret needs she hadn't known she had. She wanted Diego in all ways, wanted to touch him, taste him, feel him becoming part of her.

Need. Mate. Love. Joy. Simple words for the feelings that lifted her and dropped her into an abyss of wildness.

She heard her voice ring out, crying his name, and his answer.

"Cass. *Amorcita*, you make me come so hard." His words turned to groans, and his eyes darkened as he went over the top. Cassidy wasn't quite there yet.

"Diego," she begged. "Please."

He reached between them, fingers finding and stroking her. *That* did it.

Cassidy heard nothing, saw nothing but his beautiful eyes, felt nothing but the glory of him inside her. She'd found a place where she would never hurt, never fear, never worry—a place she never wanted to leave.

Cassidy felt tears trickle from her eyes as they collapsed together, both of them breathing hard, both sweating, neither wanting to stop.

"Diego," she said. "My Diego."

He just looked at her, his eyes so dark and warm, before he stopped her words with his kiss.

*H*oly mother of God. Diego fell next to Cassidy on her bed, breathless, staring at the sunlight slicing across the ceiling.

That was . . .

Shit.

Cassidy rolled to him, curling around him, resting her head on his shoulder. The fall of her hair was like silk on his skin. Cassidy smiled once at him then closed her eyes and dropped into an instant and untroubled sleep.

Diego kissed the top of her head and rested his gaze on her now-serene face.

What a woman. She'd back-talked to that very scary feral bear, and instead of running away the instant the path was clear, she'd run back to rescue the cubs. And then she'd smiled at Diego like it was no big deal.

She'd stayed up the rest of the day and all night to settle the kids and their mothers in, and then she made love to Diego like a wild thing.

Damn, I love her.

"What am I going to do with you, *mi ja*?" he whispered, touching her face.

Diego could lose his job if he had a long-term relationship with Cassidy, lose everything he'd fought to gain since he signed on the dotted line that took him and his family out of their crap neighborhood. If he threw in his lot with the Shifters, Diego might end up as shunned as they were.

At the moment, he couldn't decide whether he cared.

Diego felt Cassidy's eyes on him. Deep green eyes, beautiful like a sunlit pond. "Sorry," she said. "I didn't mean to fall asleep. I guess I'm more tired than I thought."

"You battled Shifters, flew a thousand miles, and then helped calm down five terrified women and a bunch of kids. You're supposed to sleep."

"Not when I'm making love to you." Cassidy slid her hot, beautiful body on top of his, closing her hand around his already rising cock.

"Are you making love to me?" Diego asked.

"I am now."

She moved onto him, her body easily connecting with his. Diego cupped her breasts as he slid into her, loving the disparate feel of firm flesh and soft skin.

She rocked her hips, driving Diego deep inside her. *Where I belong.*

He loved looking at her—at her lush breasts, the dark tightness of her nipples, the curve of her hips, and the brush of gold between her legs. She was beautiful, sexy, full of fire.

And sexy. Wait, had he thought that already? Didn't matter. It bore repeating.

"Damn, *querida*. What you do to me."

Cassidy was beyond speech. She made sounds of passion as she rode him, and the hands that braced on his chest sprouted the tiniest bit of claw.

The small bite as she scratched him excited him. She was trying for control and losing the battle.

Now she was coming. Crying his name. The claws extended, Cassidy's wildcat wanting to join the fun. Diego drove up into her as he kept coming, and coming . . . never wanting to stop.

Cassidy collapsed on top of him, claws vanishing. Diego gathered her tightly against him as everything went still once more.

There were too many people in the house, Cassidy thought as she came out later that afternoon, yawning.

Eric, Jace, Shane. Marlo, for some reason. Xavier.

What was Xav doing here? He'd gone to the hospital, hadn't he?

The five men seemed to be deep in conversation in the kitchen. Jace looked up and saw Cassidy, went to her, and drew her into a hug. Cassidy held him tightly. Jace was so tall now, as tall as Eric. It was criminal that Kirsten hadn't lived to see Jace become such a fine man.

Jace let Cassidy go and gave her shoulder a loving squeeze. "Do me a favor, Cass," he said as he moved back to the kitchen counter to pour her some coffee. "Either buy me some earplugs or soundproof your room."

Xavier burst out laughing. His left arm was in a splint, and bandages decorated his right arm, neck, and the back of his scalp. "My brother, the yeller."

Cassidy felt herself blushing. "You all could have left the house."

"It was four in the morning," Jace said, handing her the cup. "And five. And six. Let a guy sleep sometime."

"I take it Diego's OK, then," Xavier said, still grinning.

"He's sleeping." Deeply, on his stomach, hugging a pillow, sunshine highlighting the jagged tattoo across his back.

"He deserves it," Shane said from the table. "That was a hell of a fight."

"Fun stuff," Marlo added, hands around a beer instead of coffee.

"Trust Diego to make a dramatic entrance to save his girl," Xavier said. "The big show-off."

Cassidy sipped coffee—rich, good, and hot, as only Jace could make it—as she sat down at the table. "Diego came for *you*, Xav. He knew I was protecting you."

Xavier laughed. "No, he came for you, *chiquita*. He only got *me* out because he knew Mamita would kill him if he didn't."

Shane nodded. "I have a mother like that."

"Tell Nell I appreciate her help," Cassidy said. "How do you feel about all those women in your house, Shane?"

Shane actually blushed. "I don't mind. One or two honeys I'd like to get to know better. Of course, Eric's claimed them all, and I'm sure not Challenging *him*."

They all looked at Eric, who lounged back against the kitchen counter, sipping coffee. He'd kept quiet until now.

"I'll release them soon," Eric said. "They need someone they can lean on while they take the Collar, but once they're stronger and more confident, they can choose who they want to be with."

"You're really going to make them wear Collars?" Marlo asked. "It will hurt them bad when they put them on, won't it?"

Eric stared into his coffee. "I have no choice."

Cassidy came alert while pretending not to. Eric usually announced his decisions with his head up, daring anyone to question him. Not bowed, without looking at anyone. Something was up.

Her attention moved instantly from Eric to Diego walking out of the back, fully dressed. Diego went for the coffee while Marlo lifted his beer in salute.

Xavier laughed. "Hey, *hermano*, I'm surprised you can still walk."

"Funny." Diego got coffee, put his arm lightly around Cassidy's shoulders, and gave her a kiss. No embarrassment, no regrets. Diego did things and wasn't ashamed of them.

"Where's Reid?" he asked.

"At my house." Shane wrinkled his nose. "I think my mom wants to keep him."

"Good. I need to talk to him. And then take care of some things." He kissed the top of Cassidy's head. "Job things."

Xavier lost his smile. "Want me to come with you?"

"No, I want you to heal. And I want Cass to rest." He squeezed her shoulder.

"Then you'd better leave," Xavier said. "She doesn't stand a chance of resting with you here."

Marlo laughed, and even Shane grinned. Cassidy found herself blushing, and Cassidy never blushed. Diego kissed her lips again and whispered, "See you later?"

Cassidy nodded. Diego, ignoring Xav's and Marlo's teasing whoops and laughter, left the house.

Cassidy missed him already, but she too had things to take care of. She touched Eric's shoulder as she went. Her brother, his expression still troubled, nodded, and Cassidy left the house.

CHAPTER TWENTY-FOUR

"I remember me telling you *not* to go after those drug run-ners." Captain Max was on his feet in his office, his face dark with rage. "Do you remember, Escobar? Do you know *why* I told you that?"

Diego had all kinds of answers, but he decided to keep quiet.

"Because the courts will have a field day, that's why!" Captain Max finished for him. "Everyone knows you have a vendetta against this gang, that they killed your partner. And then I hear stories that you turned vigilante in Mexico, shot up a factory or something going after those guys. How is that going to look when you take the stand?"

"I won't be taking the stand, sir," Diego said, fixing his captain with an unblinking gaze. "I never made the bust."

Captain Max stopped in mid-breath. "What the hell are you talking about? I have two men in my lockup looking scared to death, and their public defender's not looking much better. Don't bullshit me, Escobar."

"No bullshit, sir. I didn't arrest them. Lieutenant Reid did. He saw the two remaining gang members in a cantina while he was vacationing in Mexico, and he arrested them. I had nothing to do with it. It's all in Reid's report."

The report lay on Captain Max's desk, the file unopened. "I don't know what the hell game you're playing, Diego. I'll bust you back down to uniform, I swear to God."

"Reid made the arrest, sir. I promise you."

Reid had arrested the men at the airfield while Diego and Xavier kept out of the way. They'd all agreed not to alert the Mexican police and to quietly fly the guys back to the States. Less paperwork, fewer questions, and they would have had to search awhile to find police out there anyway. The drug runners had capitulated easily enough, wanting to get out of there as fast as they could.

Once they'd landed back in Nevada, Reid had gotten stuck with the paperwork, and Diego had taken his brother to the hospital then gone to Shiftertown, found Cassidy, and . . . had a night he'd never forget.

"You know I'll be questioning Reid pretty closely," Captain Max said. "Your brother too."

Diego nodded. "Reid is willing. Xavier wants to come back to work tomorrow, by the way. He's feeling better and has energy to spare."

"I'll see." Captain Max gave Diego a stern look. "If we get away with this, I *might* not kick your ass. But then again, I might. Remember that."

"Thank you, sir."

"Don't fuck with me, Diego."

"No, sir."

The captain scowled over the desk. "Aren't you still on leave?"

"Yes, sir. I wanted to come in and write up the last of my notes on Jobe's case. Finish it."

Captain Max sighed, becoming human for a moment. "It's been a long time coming, hasn't it?"

"Yes, it has."

"You talk to Jobe's family yet?"

"Plan to do that tonight." Diego would take Cassidy with him. That seemed right.

"All right," Captain Max said. "Get out of here, Escobar."

"Yes, sir." Diego grinned at his captain and left him.

* * *

Stuart Reid hated Shifters, and now he was surrounded by them.

Hate was the wrong word, maybe. Uncomfortable, definitely. He'd grown up trained to believe certain things, most notably that *dokk alfar* were superior creatures, and that he was damn lucky to have been born one. *Hoch alfar* were evil and should be slain on sight.

The *hoch alfar* had hated Reid, not only because they'd wanted his lands deep in the mountains, but because Reid could manipulate iron. He could make iron behave how he wanted it to, and weren't the *hoch alfar* afraid of that? That was another reason the *hoch alfar* had exiled Stuart to this overbright and overheated place, full of humans who constantly fought among themselves. The *hoch alfar* had fully believed they'd handed Reid a fate worse than death. And they weren't far from wrong.

Another of Reid's deep-seated beliefs was that Shifters, the fighting slaves of the *hoch alfar*, were not to be trusted. They were Fae bred, and though they'd had the cunning to break free of the Fae, Shifters had shunned Faerie and chosen to live solely in the human world. Anyone not wanting to live in Faerie had to be insane. The Shifters' own fault they'd been dying out and had to accept human restrictions.

In his years in Shifter Division, Reid had learned much about Shifters—how they pretended to be pathetic captives but seemed to survive just fine on subsistence-level jobs. They had resources somewhere, he was certain of it, and they were gathering strength. Reid didn't miss how Eric Warden manipulated the humans to remain top cat while seeming to give in to human demands.

The humans were fools if they thought they had Shifters under control. The only thing that stopped Shifters now were their Collars, and one day, Stuart was sure, they'd figure out a way to break that power.

Because of his ingrained mistrust of Shifters, Stuart had convinced himself that killing one un-Collared Shifter and taking its blood to get him back home would be justifiable. But when he'd seen Cassidy grieve, he'd realized what he'd done. *I, who thought myself so superior to the* hoch alfar, *have become just like them. I thought nothing of taking Donovan Grady's life—husband, brother, son, potential father. I did that. And I can never pay enough.*

So, when Eric had gotten the call from Marlo that Cassidy was in trouble, Stuart had been the first one out the door. With his talent for teleporting—something he hadn't been able to do in Faerie—he could get in and save her. He'd been happy to save Xavier too, while he was at it.

Helping Shifters and their friends maybe could atone for what Reid had done. His guilt had made him come over to Nell's this morning to see if he could do anything further for the women and cubs they'd rescued.

Nell put him outside on the patio to watch the kids play and make sure they didn't hurt themselves. The cubs, tiny things, not sure about their change in scene but more willing to accept it than the adults, ran about in wonder.

Nell, on the other hand, scared the hell out of Reid. She was crazy, that one, violence with a smile.

The younger woman who now wandered out the back door worried Stuart far less. She was the mate of the dead Miguel, and the look in her eyes was dead too.

Not dead, Reid thought as she sat down on the patio chair next to his. Empty. She was free and safe but had no idea what to do.

The Shifter looked over at Reid with dark blue eyes and sniffed. Her hands curled on her lap. "I thought I smelled Fae."

"I'm *dokk alfar*," Reid said. "Not the same as the bastards who made Shifters."

A spark of curiosity touched her eyes. "*Dokk alfar?* What's that?"

"*Dokk alfar* are the true, and first, Fae. We dwell in the deepest woods, in the earth itself. Our magic is the magic of nature. We don't have to build glittery castles and hunt unicorns and all that shit."

More curiosity. "So why are you here and not in the woods in Faerie?"

Bitterness lodged in his throat. "Because the *hoch alfar* decided to kill family and throw me out here. For fun. They thought I'd die in the human world, slowly and painfully. They're idiots. But they made it so I couldn't get back."

"Oh." The woman reached across the small space between their chairs with the Shifter instinct to touch. Her hand rested on Reid's, her fingers warm. "I'm sorry. I didn't know. No one's even told me your name."

"Stuart. Stuart Reid. That's as close to my real name as I can manage here. Humans can't pronounce anything."

The corners of her mouth lifted the slightest bit. "Tell me about it."

"Do you have name?"

"I used to. I haven't heard it in a while." She hesitated as though having to think hard to remember it. "Peigi. It's Scottish."

It was pretty. "How did you end up in Mexico with a bunch of un-Collared Shifters?" Reid asked her.

Peigi shrugged and withdrew her hand. "I believed in Miguel. I thought he was right when he refused the Collar and formed his own community of Collarless Shifters. I'd lost my family and no longer had a clan, so I decided to accept his mate-claim. I didn't want the Collar either." She touched her bare throat. "I guess I don't have a choice now."

The sad gesture stirred his sympathy. "So what happened? When did Miguel decide he'd take over the Mexican town and become an evil villain?"

"He went feral. I realize now that Miguel wasn't the most stable of males to begin with, and then his beast took over. His idea of having his own Shiftertown, where Shifters ruled, made sense to me when we started. We'd be free of human restrictions but have the advantages that Shiftertowns are giving the Collared Shifters—peace, stability, a better chance of having cubs that survive. It worked at first, but then . . ." Peigi shrugged, looking tired. "It all fell apart. Lots of fighting between species, even within species, and Miguel decided that females should be sequestered. For their own safety." Peigi's smile was wry. "Really, so he could have first pick, and we couldn't run away."

Now Stuart felt disgust. He hoped Dylan Morrissey hunted down Miguel, if Miguel proved to be still alive, and ripped his head off. "Now you're free of him. Are you all right?"

She shrugged. "I never formed the mate bond with Miguel. When I was young and silly, I believed it would form, but after I didn't conceive any cubs, Miguel started taking additional mates, who did have cubs. I had to battle to keep my place in the hierarchy, or he would have thrown me to his men to see what they could get on me, or he'd have had me killed. It became a struggle to live, every day. The day I let my place slip as top mate was the day I died." Peigi let out her breath. "Now it's over."

Stuart let her sit quietly for a moment. In his career as a cop, he'd seen the look Peigi now wore on the faces of women from abusive marriages, after their husbands had been killed or imprisoned with no hope of parole. The women didn't dance around in elation; they sat quietly, stunned, confused, unsure of what to do or where to go. Realization that they were free would hit them later. Many of them had grown so used to being told what to do every second of their lives that they were terrified of going it alone.

"Eric said he'd release all of you once you were settled in," Stuart said. "That he wouldn't make you his mates."

Peigi nodded. "That's what Nell told me."

"Would you want to stay with Eric?" Stuart asked.

Peigi's eyes flashed, the first fire he'd seen in her. "I'm thinking I don't want to be with anyone. At all. Ever again."

She leapt from her chair so fiercely that the heavy thing fell back, then she stepped from the porch and moved across the yard in long-legged strides, not looking at the playing cubs. She wore borrowed jeans that hugged her legs, and her now-clean tail of black hair bounced against a white blouse.

Stuart watched her for a time, as her swift walk turned to a restless jog. She was a fine-looking woman—for someone who could turn into a bear. Stuart quietly rose, left the porch, and followed her.

Iona Duncan pulled into her driveway after work, looking forward to unkinking her body and unwinding with mindless TV, or maybe digging into a good novel.

What she really wanted to do wound its way through her mind. Her wildcat wanted to come out and play, to feel the forest floor underneath her paws, to taste the wind.

Iona suppressed the wildcat with effort. She couldn't keep

driving up into the mountains without people getting suspicious, wondering what the hell she did up there. Even her mother was getting worried, and her mother and sister were the only ones in the world who knew what Iona truly was.

The wildcat wanted to come out, though. As Iona tried to unlock her front door, her fingers turned to claws, and she dropped the keys.

"Damn it."

She bent to pick them up and yelped when a strong hand scooped them up for her.

"*Shit*, Eric."

He was standing way too close, his scent and body heat making her wildcat shiver. His Collar glinted in the evening light. Eric shoved the key into the lock and opened the door. He kept unlocking doors for her, damn him.

Without invitation, Eric walked into Iona's house and looked around, Shifter-style, to make sure nothing waited for them inside. He looked back and gave her a nod that it was all right to enter.

Iona strode to him. "Eric, you cannot come into my *house*."

"I'm already in. Shut the door before your neighbors see you with a Shifter."

Iona slammed the door and dumped her purse on the table in the foyer. The mirror above the table showed her black hair mussed, her blue eyes wide.

Eric had already moved to the back, into the kitchen, to pull down the blinds in there. "Nice place," he said. "You own this?"

"Of course I do," Iona said, following him. "I bought it myself."

His jade green eyes almost shone in the dim light. "Shifters aren't allowed to own houses."

"I know that. Why do you think I don't want you going around telling people I'm half Shifter?"

Iona couldn't have him here. Eric took up too much space, the tall, hard-bodied Shifter pushing her cozy kitchen into the background.

"What do you turn into?" he asked.

"What?"

"Your wildcat. What does it look like?"

The wildcat in question started to push its way out again. Iona fought it back. "Panther. Mostly."

Now Eric was in front of her, hand scooping back her hair. "Black haired. With blue eyes?"

"Yes."

"I'd like to see it." Eric leaned closer and inhaled her scent. "I'd like to see you."

"Why?"

A smile tugged the corners of his mouth. "I'd like to let my wildcat out to chase you, to tussle with you." He nuzzled her. "Maybe more things, Iona."

Heat swirled along every limb and settled low in her belly. "I don't go wildcat in the house," she said with difficulty. "I don't want to break anything."

"Where do you go, then?"

"Out in the mountains. I have a place."

Eric's nose touched her temple, followed by a brush of lips. "Next time, I'll go with you."

"No."

"It's too dangerous for you to go out alone. There are hunters looking for any excuse to shoot a Shifter. You need to stay safe."

"I'd be safer if certain Felines didn't come sniffing around my door."

Another smile. Iona wished that Eric weren't so tall. He enclosed her into his space, filled it with his warmth, his scent, his heat.

"I'm not sniffing at your door, sweetheart. I'm smelling the goodness of you."

Iona made herself turn and walk away from him. She flipped on the kitchen light because her wildcat wanted too much to melt to him in the darkness.

"I should call the police," she said. "Shifters aren't supposed to harass humans."

Eric looked pointedly at the phone on the wall, all the way across the room. "Why haven't you, then?"

Because the human police would overreact, lock up Eric, maybe go after his family, and who knew what else. Eric didn't scare her . . . exactly. He was a threat, yes—to her secrets and to her sanity.

But . . .

But what? Hell, she was confused every time she got around the man.

"I'm hoping you'll leave me alone without me having to report you," Iona said.

"You won't report me."

"What are you doing, trying to plant suggestions in my head? Not working, sorry."

Eric laughed, a low-throated laugh. He braced himself on the counter.

"You have a sassy mouth," he said. "It tastes even better with chocolate."

Iona's breath caught as she remembered the sensation of his dark kisses, Eric's body caging her against the wall, the strength of his mouth, the fire of his tongue.

"You need to go," she said. *Before I drag you against that counter and start kissing you again.*

"No, I don't." Eric straightened up and put his back to the counter exactly as Iona had been picturing. "I didn't come here to tease you, though that's always fun. I came because I need your help."

"*My* help? With what?" The alpha Shiftertown leader, *I'm such a badass I can keep anyone in line*, was asking for help?

"Long story, but you have to promise me this goes no further than us." Eric's smile was gone, and he looked grim. "I have children to protect. Understand?"

"No, I don't understand, but if you think I'll harm children, you read me wrong."

"I know you won't harm cubs, Iona. That's why I came here."

Iona made a noise of exasperation. "Eric, you do know that you could drive someone insane, don't you?"

"My sister says that. A lot. Come to think of it, my mate always did too."

His mate. Iona had learned when she'd looked up background on Eric Warden that he'd been mated to a woman named Kirsten, who had died a long time ago.

"Your wife," she said.

"No wives for Shifters, love. Only mates. *Wife* is a human term. *Mate* is so much more."

Why did he look at her so intently when he said that? "I'm sorry," Iona said. "About Kirsten."

Eric gave her a slow nod, as though he took her words to heart. "She was a good person." Another nod, compartmentalizing the pain and moving back to the question at hand.

"Five un-Collared Shifter females have come to Shiftertown," he said. "I mate-claimed all of them, and unfortunately, I have to get Collars on them. They're terrified, and I'm doing this under the radar. I'll get them as many painkillers as I can, but . . ."

"And you want me to what? Get pain medications for you?"

"No." Eric fixed her with his alpha Shifter stare. "I want you to let me bring you in. To lead the way, to show them that it's all right. Become their alpha, and let me put a Collar on you first."

CHAPTER TWENTY-FIVE

Iona stared at him, her blue eyes huge. "You want me to *what*?"

Eric knew that this would be easier if Iona weren't so sexy. He watched her confusion and outrage and at the same time couldn't keep himself from studying her body. A tight business skirt hugged her legs, and her blouse was open just enough show a hint of cleavage. Thick black hair framed her face, wisps of it not staying put.

I want you to come home with me, be my mate in all ways. The thoughts wouldn't leave Eric alone.

"They need reassurance," he said. "These females have been living in captivity, held by a feral Ursine, in pretty horrible conditions, Cassidy told me. I'm trying to bring them out of it, and I need to reassure them, especially about the cubs."

"You're going to put Collars on kids too?"

The horror in her eyes made Eric feel so damn guilty. "Cubs don't get Collars until they're seven, and I'll lie like hell and say they're all under seven if anyone asks. They've been underfed, so they look young anyway."

Iona waved her hands in front of her face, which moved her

breasts in an enticing way. Were they fettered under that shirt? Or tucked into a lacy bra that his hands would enjoy opening?

"What did you mean, you need me to become their alpha?"

"Top female of my pride. Humans, in some of their cultures, call it head wife or first wife, but as I told you, mates aren't quite the same as wives."

"Wait, wait. Are you saying that these five women are your *mates*?"

Iona's dismay had him talking fast. "No, I'm saying I mate-claimed them. That means that no other Shifter males can claim them without going through me. I don't want the females worrying about fending off mate-claims on top of everything else they've gone through, until they've found a place in Shiftertown and are ready to live their own lives. It also means that I take responsibility for their cubs, so they're not hurt or taken away from their mothers."

Iona blew out her breath. "I guess that's good. So, what does all this have to do with me?"

"I'll mate-claim you and make you my alpha. They need someone to follow, someone to reassure them until things get settled. Cassidy defeated their alpha, but once I made the mate-claim, she as my sister can no longer have precedence over any of my mates. You as head mate would supersede all. The woman who'd been the Ursine's head mate has given up, and the other females are confused and uncertain. You can help me calm them down, show them that they're all right. Then I'll release them from the mate-claim and give you the choice to reject it as well."

Iona stared at him with a mixture of disbelief, rage, and fear. "Give me the choice? *After* you out me and Collar me? Oh, then I get the *choice* to tell you to kiss my ass?"

"You get the choice to let me make the mating permanent. Or not."

Iona put her hands around her bare neck. It made Eric's heart sing to see her un-Collared, but he feared that humans would discover her, lock her away, slap the Collar on without preparing her. That fear made him want to put her under his arm, whisk her to Shiftertown, and never let her go.

"Eric, from what I understand, putting a Collar on a Shifter causes a hell of a lot of pain. Is that what you want? For me to be rolling around on the ground, screaming, while a Collar I can never take off again infuses itself to my flesh?"

"No, that is *not* what I want."

"Then why are you asking me to do it?"

Eric went to her and cupped her face, unable to keep his hands off her any longer. "To keep you safe. If they find out you've been passing as human—Iona, love, I don't know what they'll do to you."

Iona stared up at him, her eyes enormous. "Then leave me alone. Stop stalking me, and no one will ever know."

"Yes, they will." His fears poured out. "Sweetheart, they'll find you. Some Shifter will scent you and let on what you are, whether he means to or not. Or a human will see you, watch you, figure it out. You're holding your wildness in, but you can't forever. If you suppress the wildcat too long, it will take over." From the fear flooding her face, Eric knew she was already fighting that. "Let me protect you, Iona. Please."

She shook her head, the ends of her hair brushing his fingers. "I can't just give up my life. I have a mother, a sister, a career, a home. I can't walk away from it. It's *mine*. I want it."

"I know." Eric kissed her wet face. "I will try to make everything the best I can for you."

"By putting the Collar on me? To make me go through that pain and make me a slave? You can't. *I* can't."

She broke his heart. "I don't want to, sweetling. The laws are stupid, but someday they won't be. We'll get free of the Collars and do what we want." Eric looked into her eyes, her beautiful eyes that saw past his hard-ass shell to the true man inside. Kirsten had looked at him like that too. "And when that day comes, I want you by my side."

Iona tried to shake him off. "What are you talking about? Shifters are captives. How is that better than letting my wild-cat take over?"

Eric didn't answer, because he didn't have an answer. Shifters were working, in secret, to become stronger, unstoppable. The ones leading the movement wanted Shifters to live in peace, to be well, to raise cubs without fear. Until then, they had to do what they had to do.

But when Eric imagined himself latching the Collar around

Iona's beautiful neck, he balked. The pain would bite deep, as it had done to him, to Cassidy, and to Jace on that awful day. Iona's eyes would flood with tears, and she'd not be able to stop her cries of agony.

Eric couldn't do that to her. Not now. Not ever.

He gathered her close, pressing his cheek to her hair. "I'll find another way, Iona." The scent of her, the nearness of her, drove him wild. "You don't have to be afraid," he whispered. "I promise."

C assidy had something on her mind. Diego knew it by the way she didn't mention it as they rode through the streets on the way to Jobe's.

Beautiful dusk was spreading over the valley. The mountains hid their secrets, becoming a distant wall of blue gray. Against that backdrop sparkled red, blue, green, and gold lights of the heart of Las Vegas, beckoning the unwary.

Diego paralleled the lights of the Strip when he came out of Shiftertown and headed west to where Jobe's widow lived with her teenage sons and daughters. Cassidy looked around with interest as they pulled up in front of the deceptively compact house with its neat cactus garden edged with spring wildflowers.

The front door slammed open as Diego and Cassidy emerged from the car. Jobe's youngest daughter, Christine, thirteen years old, ran out. "Uncle Diego!"

She launched herself at Diego, and he swept her into a hug. He kissed her cheek and set her down again, and Christine turned interested brown eyes to Cassidy. "Who's she? Your girlfriend?"

"Yes," Diego said. Cassidy looked gorgeous tonight in a black sheath dress and shiny black high heels. "This is Cassidy."

Christine tore away and ran back into the house. "Mom! Diego has a girlfriend!"

Jackie Sanderson appeared at the door, the black woman as elegant as ever in pants, silk blouse, and softly clinking gold necklaces. Jobe had always liked to ask: *How did a classy lady like her end up with a lowlife like me?* Diego felt a deep gouge of pain, as he always did when he saw Jackie.

"Christine, stop shouting like that," Jackie said. "You'll have everyone in the neighborhood out wondering what you're yelling about. Diego, get in here. Now I know why you've been hiding yourself away."

Jackie opened her arms, rings glittering in the dying light, a smile of genuine welcome on her face. Diego embraced her, trying not to remember the day he'd come to console her after Jobe died, and how Jackie and her kids had ended up consoling *him*.

Jackie let him go and looked Cassidy up and down, taking in Cassidy's height and her Collar. "All right, Diego, introduce me. Come on."

"This is Cassidy Warden. Cassidy, this is the nicest woman in Las Vegas, Jackie Sanderson."

"Warden?" Jackie said before Cassidy could speak. "Isn't a man named Warden leader of the Shifters?" She leaned to Cassidy. "Honey, I know he's your brother, but if he looks anything like he does in his pictures, he is damn *hot*."

Cassidy grinned. "I'll let him know you think so."

She moved, Shifter-fashion, to embrace Jackie. When Jackie's strong arms closed around Cassidy, Cassidy's expression changed.

"I'm so very sorry," Cassidy said, tightening the embrace. "Your loss, it hurts you."

Jackie looked over Cassidy's shoulder at Diego, her eyes soft. "Yeah, it's bad, having Jobe gone."

"I lost my mate too," Cassidy said, gently pulling away. "And the world changed."

Jackie nodded, clasping Cassidy's hands. "The world changed." She put her arm around Cassidy's waist. "Come on inside, honey. Let's have some wine."

"Can you really turn into a cat?" Christine asked Cassidy after dinner.

Jackie had made her famous lasagna, and Christine and Jackie's oldest son had eaten it with them. The two middle kids, seventeen and eighteen, had been out with friends, and the oldest son left to go out once they were finished eating.

They're growing up and moving on, Diego thought. *Remembering Jobe, but still having a life. Jobe would like that.*

Pictures of Jobe were prominent—on the fireplace mantel, on the piano, on the shelf that held his badge, his official photo, and a flag. But the room wasn't a shrine to the dead. Jobe's big smile filled every picture, as though he listened, benevolent, as they laughed and talked.

They'd retreated here after dinner for coffee. Christine folded herself up on the floor, watching Cassidy with interest.

"I do turn into a cat," Cassidy answered Christine. She'd seated herself very close to Diego on the sofa, unself-consciously resting her arm on Diego's thigh.

"I want to see."

"Christine . . ." Jackie began.

Cassidy smiled. "That's all right. I don't mind." She got up, her hand lingering on Diego's knee until the last minute. "I'll need somewhere to change."

"You can use my room." Christine jumped up, grabbed Cassidy's hand, and started down the hall. Cassidy good-naturedly let Christine take her away.

Diego felt Jackie's keen eyes on him as soon as Christine's bedroom door closed. "So, what's up with you two? Is it hot and heavy?"

Diego picked up his coffee and took a sip. "You could say that."

Jackie laughed. "Look at you blushing. Diego Escobar and a Shifter. What does your mother say?"

"She says I need to settle down and start having kids."

"I agree with her. It wouldn't hurt you. Kids might keep you from tearing off to Mexico, going after gangs, and almost getting yourself killed." Jackie's laugh turned into a glare. "Captain Max told me all about what you did. I suppose you thought you'd come over here tonight and tell me you were some kind of hero."

Diego carefully set down his coffee cup. "I thought you'd be glad. We got the last of the men who did Jobe. Two were dead already, and the final two are in the lockup. That's what I went to Mexico for."

"Glad?" Jackie's voice rose as Jobe kept smiling behind

her. "Did you think I'd be glad if you died running down there playing vigilante? You dying trying to get revenge would have been even worse for me than before. Did you think of that?" Jackie's anger filled the room.

"I wasn't about to die," Diego said. "I went in with backup, which included two other cops—my brother and Lieutenant Reid—and we arrested them."

"Don't shit me, Diego Escobar. There was much more to it than that, and you know it. You don't just stroll into Mexico and come out with everything neatly tied up. I saw on the news that some little town blew up down there. That was you, wasn't it?"

"We didn't blow up the whole town. Just a factory that was already in ruins."

Jackie stared at him, her rage cut by surprise. "What am I going to do with you, Diego?"

"Be happy that I got them?"

"I am happy. I'm damn happy. But I wouldn't have been happy if you'd gotten yourself killed. How would I explain that to my kids? I tell you, Diego, if you ever pull a stunt like that again, I'll . . . I'll tell your mama."

Diego raised his hands in surrender. "I won't. I don't need to. It's over."

A door slammed in the back, and Christine came running down the hall. "Mom! You've got to see *this*."

Cassidy's soft, huffing growl sounded, and then Cassidy as her wildcat strolled slowly out of the back. Her leopard eyes were deep green, and her Collar shone in the lamplight.

Jackie rose to her feet. "Oh, my dear Lord."

Diego remained seated. Cassidy walked to him, very slowly, keeping her claws from snagging the rug or her body from bumping anything.

She reached Diego on the couch and butted her head against his legs. Christine laughed as Diego stroked Cassidy's incredibly soft fur. Cassidy grunted again and then started to purr. Diego never knew that leopards could purr, but Cassidy was doing it.

"She likes it when you scratch under her chin," Diego said. "Come on. She won't hurt you."

Christine came closer. Cassidy remained still, her purrs filling the living room. Christine put a hesitant hand on Cassidy's head. Cassidy didn't move, just let the girl explore. Christine started to pet her.

"Oh, she's soft," Christine crooned. "I didn't think she'd be so soft." Her face glowed in delight.

Cassidy whuffed a little, turning her head to nuzzle Christine. Christine pulled back, but not as nervously as before.

Cassidy kept herself pressed to Diego's knee, Christine tentatively petted, and Jackie watched like a mother bear ready to defend her offspring.

Cassidy was the calmest of all. She let Christine pet and stroke, the girl getting bolder. Finally Christine put her arms all the way around Cassidy and hugged her. Cassidy remained still, making no moves that would startle either Christine or her mother.

Cass is so good with kids. Diego thought of her with Torey, the tigerish Shifter cub who'd lost both parents. Cassidy had dashed back for the cubs and women trapped in the basement of the factory, refusing to go without them. He remembered her grabbing up the last cub and hauling him out of there, making sure none got left behind. She'd raised Jace too after Eric's mate died in childbirth.

She takes care of everyone else's kids. She'd be so happy with her own.

Diego couldn't stop the vision coming to him of Cassidy holding a little boy that looked back at Diego with eyes so like his own.

"Can we keep her?" Christine asked, still hugging Cassidy.

Jackie said, "*Christine!*" and Diego laughed.

"What?" Christine asked, in all innocence. "Geez, Mom, I was only kidding."

After they left Jackie and Christine, Diego drove Cassidy up to his favorite spot, a deserted side street a little way up Sunrise Mountain.

From here, the valley floor spread before them, hotel lights dancing way to the west, calm residential lights to the east, south, and north, a tower light from the air force base blinking not far away. The night was clear, and stars were dense overhead.

Cassidy stretched in the seat next to him. "Thank you for showing me this. It's beautiful."

She was beautiful, with the stars reflected in her eyes. "Jackie really liked you," Diego said.

"Good. I liked her."

"So, what's on your mind?"

Cassidy turned her head on the headrest, looking at him. "Why should something be on my mind?"

"Because I know that when you get very quiet, you're thinking deep thoughts," Diego said. "What's up? And don't say *nothing*. I know that trick."

Cassidy studied the city lights a moment before she spoke. "I heard Jackie yelling at you for going to Mexico. I was thinking that if you'd died, I would have had to face Jackie—and your mother—and tell them what had happened. And how I'd have to confess that I provided the transportation and encouraged you to go."

Diego shook his head. "You couldn't have stopped me, Cass. If you hadn't introduced me to Marlo, I would have found some other way to get down there. I was going, with you or without you. Trust me on this."

"I know but when I heard Jackie, I realized the other side of it, about how fixed *I'd* been about finding whoever had hurt Donovan. What if I'd decided to kill Reid when we caught him, right in front of you, in my living room? Would you have arrested me and taken me in, or let me go? I'd have forced you to make that choice. That wouldn't have been fair to you." She folded her arms and stared fiercely out into the desert. "So stupid, and yet I could only think of grinding my heel in Reid's face."

"We're both idiots," Diego said. "I should have known that Enrique wouldn't give me that information for free, and I should have checked it out better before I rushed in. Enrique ragged me on the phone for hanging out with Shifters, so it must have made him laugh to send me into a nest of them. And I ran right in, Cass. I almost got *you* killed. And my brother. Mamita's not letting me hear the end of that."

Cassidy blew out her breath. "What are we going to do with each other?"

Diego knew what he wanted to do. Had wanted since he'd seen her walk out of her house in that dress and those shoes. "What did you have in mind?" he asked.

Cassidy's glance smoldered when she looked at him, but she didn't say what he wanted her to say. "Help me help Stuart Reid get home?"

Her question took him by surprise. "You mean help him cross back to Faerie?" Diego drummed his fingers on the steering wheel. "Do you have some idea how we can? The physics of it?"

Cassidy shrugged. "I can talk to people, figure things out. Shifters are very resourceful."

"Yeah, so I noticed."

"But really, will you help?" Cassidy took his hand and raised it to her lips. "I don't want Donovan to have died for nothing."

"I get that."

He liked how her breath felt on his fingers. Diego caressed her cheek, his arousal demanding attention.

"This mate-claim thing," he said. "I'm not quite clear on all of it. Explain it to me."

Cassidy released his hand. "It's part of Shifter law, created when we were first free of the Fae, and territory and dominance disputes were common." Cassidy stretched again as she talked, so distracting. She had the sexiest legs in creation. "The mate-claim ensured that a female wasn't just grabbed by any and all males and used until she died. When a female is mate-claimed, that means all other males have to leave her alone. The female either accepts the mate-claim, which means she and the male are joined in the mating ceremonies under the sun and under the full moon. Or, the female can turn down the claim and be free for the next male who wants to claim her. But the mate-claim marks the female as off-limits. If another male wants her, he has to Challenge."

"Tell me about that. The Challenge."

"It's a fight—in the old days, to the death. Now it's just a fight until one male gives up, but they can be pretty dangerous. The winner gets the mate-claim. The female retains the right to reject the claim of the challenger."

Diego rubbed his lip. "So when I said to Miguel, *Consider this a challenge*, he . . . considered it a Challenge."

"Every Shifter within hearing did," Cassidy said.

"But you can reject it, you said. I heard you scream to Miguel that you rejected his claim."

"Yes, a female can reject the claim anytime she wants. She needs to do it in front of witnesses."

"Then why haven't you?"

Cassidy blinked. "What?"

"Apparently, I won the Challenge against Miguel for this mate-claim. You've had plenty of opportunities to reject me. Like when we were standing on the airstrip, and Eric was going on about me Challenging for you, which meant the mate-claim for you was passed to me. We were standing in front of Dylan and Shane and the Shifters we rescued—lots of witnesses. Why didn't you reject the claim then?"

Cassidy reddened. "Maybe I didn't want to."

"No?" Diego let his voice go soft. "But I'm not Shifter."

She moved toward him, her tight dress all kinds of good. "I haven't turned it down, Diego Escobar, because the mating frenzy is driving me crazy, and the mate-claim gives me an excuse to jump your bones."

"Yeah?" Diego smiled in the darkness and slid his arm around her. "Do you want to jump my bones now?"

She growled low in her throat. "You know," she said, kissing his ear, "after I shifted back and got dressed—I didn't bother putting on my underwear."

CHAPTER TWENTY-SIX

Diego went still, and she scented his pheromones sharp on the air.

"*Mi ja*, why do you tell me things like that?" he asked.

Cassidy loved his voice. She lifted herself over him. "To make you want me."

"How could you think I don't want you? But there's not much room in this car. I say we go home. Fast."

"Can't." Cassidy kissed his face, her unfettered breasts pressing his shoulder and chest. "I need you right now. I'm going insane."

She reached around for her zipper and squirmed out of the top half of her dress. Diego's eyes went dark, and he kissed her skin with warm lips.

Somehow he got them into the small backseat. Cassidy yanked open Diego's pants while he laughed, then she scooted up her skirt to prove she really was commando.

"Damn, woman." Diego wrapped his arms around her hips and brought her down to him. "Oh, yeah, there you go. I love how tight you always are."

Cassidy wanted to shout out how good he felt sliding in. "I love how you fill me up," she whispered.

She clenched her fists. She wanted to savor every moment, but her body kept thrusting against his, needing to soothe the burn.

He clenched his fists. "Slow down, sweetheart," he said. "I want this to last."

"I can't." Cassidy pushed herself down on him again. Diego ran his hands over her back, making calming sounds.

Not so much lovemaking, she thought, as frenzied, burning need. He was pressing up inside her, stretching her so wide. He claimed she was tight, but it was him, so big. He reached her secret places and filled them.

Diego murmured to her in his wine-dark voice, hands calming. Diego was her perfect counterpart—matching her wild Shifter frenzy with soothing warmth. A safe harbor for a woman who'd been tossing about in misery.

She loved him.

"*Diego.*"

Cassidy got her mouth on his neck and suckled, hard. Diego groaned. She nipped and licked, sucked and pulled. Diego thrust into her, his touch no longer soothing. He caught her fire, and they both burned.

"Damn you, Cass."

More hot thrusts, and then his release. Cassidy rode him awhile longer, searching for the peak, finding it when he rubbed his thumb over her very wet opening. She screamed out loud, and then she was falling, falling, landing on Diego's strength. He pulled her close and held her, keeping her safe.

Cassidy found Eric the next morning sitting at the kitchen table contemplating six Collars laid out across the dark wood.

Diego had dropped her off last night, saying he wanted to check up on Xavier, who'd gone back to Mamita's. Cassidy kissed him good night, thinking it was just as well. Diego's scent alone was enough to trigger her frenzy, and she feared burning him out. So much complication, falling in love with a human.

Cassidy helped herself to a heaping pile of eggs and bacon that Jace had left on the stove and sat down opposite Eric. "Hey," she said. "You all right?"

Eric leaned his arms on the table, his gaze fixed on the Collars. "I hate this."

One of the Shiftertown leader's duties—assigned by the humans—was to find any un-Collared Shifters in his territory and bring them in. Once Eric had Collared them, they'd be turned over to the humans to be registered and assigned to whatever Shiftertown the human government thought they should go.

"Are you going to report them?" Cassidy asked.

She ate heartily, her brother's distress touching her but unable to dent her mate-frenzied appetite.

"No." Eric lifted his gaze, jade green and empty. "I'll have Neal futz the database and make it look like they've always been here. I don't want those women sent to the ends of the earth, maybe separated from their cubs. They've been through too much already."

Neal Ingram, their Guardian, could access a computer network the Guardians had set up amongst themselves, unknown to humans. They had all kinds of information in their database, sharing across all Shiftertowns. Most Guardians had learned to be expert hackers as well. If anyone could slide the females into the humans' information undetected, it would be Neal.

Eric returned to staring glumly at the Collars.

Cassidy finished her eggs and scraped the plate. Jace had added green chile salsa to the scrambled eggs, the way she liked them.

Eric sighed and pushed the Collars away. "I can't do this, Cass. They thought they'd be safe forever from taking Collars and moving into Shiftertowns. If Miguel had been a better leader, they wouldn't have been wrong."

"Then don't make them wear them."

Eric shook his head, skimming his hand through his short hair. "What happens if someone finds one of the females running around without a Collar? She'd be arrested, interrogated, and the Collar slapped on her anyway. And then they'd come here for the others."

"Then put the Collar on them," Cassidy said.

Eric gave her an aggrieved look. "You're a lot of help, Cass."

"I'm only trying to point out that you don't have much choice. If the females don't take the Collars, they'll have to hide the rest of their lives—or pretend they're human, and I don't think they'll be able to. Peigi's taller than I am, and everything about her screams Shifter. She'd be arrested in a heartbeat. Or hunted down. Do you want that?"

Eric shook his head. "But how do I make them understand why they need to take the pain? Why they should be restricted and monitored?"

Cassidy laid her fork across her empty plate. "Eric, Shifters agreed to take the Collars because we knew that capitulating to the humans was our only chance at survival, remember? The Collars were the price we paid to band together and grow stronger, and besides, they keep us from killing each other. That's all you need to tell them."

"Obviously they didn't buy that argument twenty years ago."

"Maybe not, but look what happened to them. Eric, you know that if those women aren't accepted into a clan or pride or pack soon, they might go feral. Two of them pretty much are already. You didn't do this to them. Miguel did."

Eric clenched his fists on the table, hardening the muscles on his arms. "It's a hell of a thing, Cassidy, to be leader. I hope you never have to do it."

"Stay healthy, brother, and I won't. Besides, if you go, I might have to battle it out with Nell to take over, and even then Shifters might not accept a female leader."

"They'd accept you."

Cassidy warmed at Eric's certainty, but she was skeptical. Shifters were pretty old-fashioned at heart. Females sometimes did take over prides in the wild, but only when necessary, and only until she could find another male to protect her and give her more cubs.

Diego, on the other hand, was good for so much more than protection. He made her laugh, true laughter. He'd made Cassidy think and feel, had torn her out of the numb state in which she'd existed since the night Donovan had slammed out of the house, never to return.

Cassidy left Eric still staring at the Collars and went next door. One of the females, Peigi, was in the backyard, staring listlessly across the green. Peigi turned when she heard Cassidy.

"Stuart told me about the ritual he needs to do to return to Faerie," Peigi said without greeting. "For it, he needs the life-blood of a Shifter. I told him he could have mine."

No one could talk Peigi out of her decision. Not Cassidy, not Eric—who in theory had authority over her—not Reid himself, and not Diego.

Diego arrived with Xavier that evening to find Peigi and Reid at Eric's, Eric and Cassidy trying to dissuade Peigi from offering her life. Diego took one look at Peigi and realized that their arguments weren't penetrating. Peigi's eyes were lifeless.

He knew that look. He'd seen it often enough on junkies so hooked they knew only death would release them. On men and women stuck in terrible situations who had given up hope.

But he realized Peigi's choices weren't great. She'd had to struggle to remain alive with Miguel, and now that she was free of him, she was told she had to put on a Collar and live in captivity the rest of her life.

The other Shifter women seemed resigned, used to doing what they were told. Peigi had a little more spirit. She wanted to act, and she'd decided this would be her act.

"I'll stop you," Reid said, staring her down. "By not doing it. The spell only works at the spring equinox anyway."

"*Around* the equinox, you told me," Peigi said. "It's only a few days past. If you don't try it, you'll be stuck here."

Cassidy broke in. "Not necessarily. Maybe we can find a way to send Reid back without the blood spell. That can't be the only one that will work."

Reid shook his head. "I've searched for nearly fifty years, Cassidy. I've never found another. The *hoch alfar* have locked me out."

"I've been talking to a Fae," Eric said. "Or at least Marlo flew Jace out after breakfast to talk to him, and Jace is keeping me informed."

Diego looked at him in surprise, but Cassidy didn't seem startled. Eric liked to play things close to his chest.

Reid's reaction was electric. "A *hoch alfar*? You've betrayed me to a *hoch alfar*?" He went for where his gun would be if he were wearing it.

"Stand down," Diego said sternly to him. "Eric, what are you talking about?"

"I'm talking about a Fae warrior called Fionn Cillian. I met him a few weeks ago, when he came through a ley line in Austin. He visits there sometimes. I sent Jace to talk to him." Eric looked at Reid. "Have you heard of him?"

"There are many clans of *hoch alfar*. *Dokk alfar* pay them no mind. Why is he *visiting* Shifters?"

Eric didn't answer the question. "Jace tells me that Cillian says that ley lines don't always work for *dokk alfar* because it's high Fae magic, which is completely different from *dokk alfar* magic. Like the difference between electricity and water. Both have force, but in very different ways, and it's tricky to put them together."

"Can't this Fae open a door for Stuart?" Cassidy asked. "If he's a friend?"

"I wouldn't say he was a *friend*. Cillian's kind of a pain in the ass, and he doesn't have much good to say about the *dokk alfar*. But he did say that a strong enough spell on our side near a gate weak enough might work."

Cassidy leaned forward, interested. "Did you ask him about the teleportation? Why it works here but won't get him back?"

"Jace did, but Cillian didn't know," Eric said. "He said that sometimes weaker Fae have latent talent but for various reasons those talents might not manifest inside Faerie. Magic is thinner in the human world, he says, so it's easier for weak Fae to be stronger here. Or something like that."

"Weak Fae?" Reid said with derision.

"His words, not mine," Eric said.

Reid's face was pinched. "Small help he is."

"What was so special about that rock cave?" Diego asked him. "You kept going back there."

"It's on a ley line, and I think there's a gate there."

"Then we should start there," Diego said, getting up. "Maybe we'll find something that you missed."

* * *

Cassidy and Diego rode alone up to the mountain roads that would take them to Reid's rock cave. Cassidy was unusually silent—no laughter, no teasing. Was she that worried about Reid?

The red lights of Xavier's pickup glided solidly in front of Diego's car. Eric's car, containing Peigi and Reid with Eric, rode in front of his. Xavier's front seat was taken up with the bulk of Shane.

"Eric needs to be careful," Diego said. "If he gets caught having Marlo fly your family around everywhere, life will get bad for all of you."

"Eric knows what he's doing."

Cassidy sounded distracted, almost uninterested.

"What's up, *mi ja*? Something worrying you?"

Cassidy turned from the window and looked at him. "Diego Escobar, I reject your mate-claim."

Diego's hands jerked on the steering wheel, then he quickly righted the car. "What?"

"I reject the mate-claim. I'll make it public when we're finished here tonight."

"What the hell are you talking about? I thought you said you didn't want to reject it."

"I didn't. But that was me being selfish." Cassidy folded her arms, closing herself off. "I want you so much, Diego. I love the way you talk and how you move, and the way you don't back down from any Shifter, not even Eric. I love the way you protect your mom and your brother. I want you with every piece of my heart." She stopped, eyes soft. "But you're not Shifter. It's not fair to you."

His chest felt tight. "Does it matter that I don't give a damn?"

"No. The female's decision is final."

"Well, too bad. I'm not ready to accept that decision as final."

Cassidy gave him an exasperated look. "Diego, humans who pair with Shifters are rejected by human society. I've seen it happen; I've lived a long time, and it's always the same. The humans have to live with the Shifters, and they become neither one thing nor the other. Not accepted by humans and not truly accepted by Shifters."

Diego clutched the wheel as Xavier took a hairpin turn in the dark. "You want to let me worry about that?"

"I'm trying to explain that it will be hard on you. Very few humans stay with Shifters, for a good reason."

Diego sucked in a breath as Xavier swung around another corner, revealing a vast dark abyss beyond the road. No lights up here, and no guardrails.

Diego started to sweat. "Can we talk about this later?"

"I wanted to prepare you before I announced it."

"Do me a favor and keep it to yourself awhile. Give me time to convince you to change your mind."

"Diego, I'm not telling you this for the hell of it. I've thought this through. I want you to have your life, not one screwed up by Shifters. I care very much for you. That's why I'm rejecting the claim."

Diego kept his gaze riveted to the road. "You're damn right it's not fair to me. How about the way I feel about you? That it's like all the light leaves the room when you walk out of it? That I wake up every morning just happy I know you?"

Cassidy had tears in her voice. "I mean that I don't want to look at you every day and know that I destroyed your life."

"Destroyed my life. Right." Diego cranked around another bend and pressed his foot to the accelerator to make it up the next hill. "Let's see, you helped me bring down the men who killed my partner after two years of me trying to find them. It was your contacts and resources that got me down to them to finish it. Not to mention, we've had the best sex I've ever had in my life, and I'm happier than I've been in a good long while. How is that destroying my life?"

She gave him an anguished look. "I'm trying to get you to understand. I destroyed Donovan, which is why we're out here tonight. I'm trying to make up for what I did to him, and I don't want to have to do the same for you."

Diego shook his head. "You only get so much guilt, Cass. If you're saying that if you hadn't become his mate, he'd still be alive, I don't agree. You can't know that. Those hunters might have found him anyway, no matter who he was mated to."

"I *can* know that," Cassidy said. "You don't know the whole story of why he was up here that night. He came because we had a fight. Donovan lived for fun. Dangerous fun. He liked to tease humans, test how far he could push his boundaries. He'd go places he wasn't supposed to, talk to people he wasn't supposed to, see how far he could walk the edge."

"A daredevil."

"Exactly. He'd thought I was too, which is why we hooked up in the first place. But he started resenting me being dominant to him, resenting me asking him to be careful. He thought I was too much Eric's second and not enough his mate, and he was probably right."

"So that night, he basically said, *Screw you, Cassidy, I'm going out alone*?"

"The ban on hunting un-Collared Shifters had been lifted. Hunters were going out all excited, wanting to bag a Shifter. Eric and I told Donovan to stop going for his runs up here, that it was too dangerous. I begged him to stop, and when he wouldn't, we commanded him, as his leaders."

"Which I bet did not go over well."

"No. That night, Donovan stormed out. He went out to a bar with some of his friends, and sometime later gave them the slip. I didn't know anything about him not still being at the bar until Eric got a call from the human cops that one of our Shifters had been killed." Cassidy dragged in a breath. "And the kicker was that the cops blamed Eric for letting Donovan run around loose."

Stupid, stupid. Diego had read in the file that Eric had nearly been arrested, though he'd paid no attention to the incident at the time. Shifters hadn't been his department, and he'd been wrapped up in Jobe's death.

He understood Cassidy's guilt, but he'd come to realize that everyone was responsible for what they did. Diego shouldn't have led Jobe into the situation, but Jobe should have waited for backup, even if Diego died.

"You blame yourself," he said. It was natural that she would.

"Donovan wasn't a fool, but I treated him like one," Cassidy said. "I'm a dominant female, which means I have the instinct to protect, even when another doesn't want to be protected."

"Cassidy," Diego said, choosing his words carefully, "what he did wasn't your fault. It was Donovan's fault for being an idiot. I'm sorry, I know you loved him, but why the hell did he go out running around when he knew it was so dangerous? Alone? What, he was thumbing his nose at you? What an asshole."

"Diego."

Her tone held rage. Well, too bad that he pissed her off. Diego wished Donovan Grady was here right now so he could punch him.

"Let me tell you a story," he said. "When I was fifteen, Xavier started running with gangs. Small stuff at first, just being a lookout, then the next thing I know, he has guns in his dresser drawers and he's learning how to make explosives for Enrique. I lit into him, thought I could force him to get out of it by yelling at him. No, Xav keeps on, because he's got a lot of rage about how my dad was killed, and his plan was to go up against the gang whose members shot our dad in the robbery and kill them.

"I went to Enrique and told him to keeps his claws off Xavier, to help me keep him from doing something stupid. Enrique's sister had just run away, and I thought he'd understand my need to protect my brother. But Enrique, he's happy to have Xavier work for him, because he wanted kids all fired up to kill members of other gangs. So, what does he do? Instead of just telling me no, Enrique grabs Xav and holds him hostage. The only way he'll let Xavier go is if I let Xav stay in the gang. If I say no, Enrique will have his goons beat up Xav. These were big men. They'd have killed him."

Cassidy listened, stricken. "What did you do?"

"I told them if they let Xavier go, I'd let Enrique's boys beat me up instead. Enrique was all for it. He hated me. He even let me fight back. I gave pretty good, but I went down. Then they tied me to a chair, tortured me, and tried to get me to beg for my life. In the end, they let me go and Xav too, because they said I had balls. But Xavier hated me for it. He said I'd made him look weak, that I shouldn't have interfered."

"But you couldn't have done nothing."

Diego looked over at her. Her eyes glittered in the darkness.

"I know. What I'm trying to explain is those who need the

most protecting are the ones who resist it the most. Xavier was stupid about it, and so was Donovan. Xav has an excuse—he was thirteen. Donovan was an adult, should have known better."

Cassidy sat up straight. "Should have known better, should he? And who was the fully grown human male who attacked a fortress full of feral Shifters *by himself*?"

"I had Shane and Marlo for backup. *You* deliberately got yourself captured by the ferals so you could protect Xavier."

"You'd have preferred me to stand and watch them drag him away? They'd have killed him."

"I know that. You have the instinct to protect. So do I. If I get myself killed because of it, it has nothing to do with you."

Cassidy glared at him. "This is your argument for why we should stay together?"

"I'm saying you can't break up with me because you think you caused the death of your mate. You didn't. Those hunters did by breaking the law and shooting him. You're not responsible for absolutely every damned thing that goes on in other people's lives."

"I'm Eric's second. Yes, I am."

"Yeah? Then maybe Donovan was right. You're too tied to being second to Eric and not enough to being first to yourself."

Her anger was palpable. "And this is how you plan to convince me that a relationship between us will work?"

"I'm trying to convince you to give me *time* to convince you. Later. We're here."

The dirt road had narrowed. Xavier stopped his truck ahead of them, and Diego pulled in behind. Cassidy didn't say anything or even look at him as they got out of the car.

Diego's heart beat faster as Reid found the path and started leading them to the rock outcropping. Cassidy was pretty stubborn, but like hell Diego was going to let her win. He'd convince her they should be together if he had to argue with her until they were both too hoarse and too tired to talk. Then he'd teach her exactly how he felt about her, in all ways.

Court her, his mother would call it. *Chase her ass* was Xavier's term.

Diego watched Cassidy walking a little ahead of him, her legs slim in jeans, her loose sweatshirt in no way disguising the delectable body beneath. He thought of the way she'd slid onto him in his backseat last night, wearing nothing under her tight dress.

If Cassidy thought this human would run away with his tail between his legs, she didn't know humans. Or at least Latino cops who didn't take shit from anyone.

After twenty minutes of climbing, they came to the clearing and the buildup of rocks within it.

"This is a magical place," Peigi said as she looked around. Cassidy looked around as well, her arms folded hard across her chest.

"How do you know that?" Xav asked.

Peigi touched one of the boulders. "I was raised on the Scottish west coast, where the Fae presence is strong. I learned the feel of it. It's faint here, but Fae magic has touched it."

Diego knew it only as a place where he'd been shot at, and where he'd found Cassidy ready to be butchered by Reid.

Eric walked through the cave with his flashlight, examining walls, floor, ceiling. Shane came behind him, the big bear man sniffing. Diego trained his own light on them but found nothing unusual, only gray and darker gray limestone of the mountains and a coating of dust.

"The gate won't open for me," Reid said. "I've tried."

"What is the ritual?" Peigi asked.

"It involves candles and a big, long knife," Cassidy said.

"And Tasers, apparently," Shane said. "Though I'm thinking they weren't in the original spell."

"A spell I won't try to work again," Reid said. "I don't fit in here, but I won't kill to get back home." Diego heard the dead note in Reid's voice.

Eric pressed his hands on the wall at the end of the shallow cave. "According to my Fae source, the gates on the ley lines go to different places in Faerie. You can walk through two gates right next to each other in the human world and end up thousands of miles apart in Faerie. So this gate might not lead to anywhere near Fionn's territory."

"It might not lead to mine either," Reid said. "But once I knew where I was, I could get home." He touched the wall next to Eric's hand. "I don't know what I'd find, though. My entire clan destroyed by the *hoch alfar*? Or my people restored, and at peace?"

"Moot point if you can't get through," Xavier said.

"He'll get through." Peigi also touched the rock wall. "Maybe only a little Shifter blood will open it enough to assess where it comes out, and what is on the other side. Isn't it worth a try?"

"The spell needs the lifeblood of a Shifter, sacrificed," Reid said. "You're not doing that."

"How about freely given? I sacrifice it for you?"

Reid's face was dark with anger. "Why the hell would you do that?"

Peigi took Reid's hand and wrapped her own around it. "Let's just say I want to see someone get their heart's desire."

Cassidy went to them. "Let her try. It might work."

Reid didn't want to. Peigi jerked her hand from Reid's, turned it palm up, and let her claws come out. As Cassidy had at the club when she'd vouched for Diego, Peigi slashed her own claws across her human hand.

Blood welled up on her palm, and she pressed her hand against the rock wall.

Nothing happened.

Diego kept his eye on Reid as he approached Peigi. Peigi lifted her hand, leaving blood smeared on the rock. Shane tapped the wall. Solid.

"It won't work," Reid said. "It needs more blood. Forget it."

"Spells are tricky," Eric said. "Especially Fae spells. It's not the ingredients that matter, but what they represent. Does the blood stand for life essence? Or a Shifter death?"

His words gave Diego an idea. "If these Fae seriously want to keep you from finding your way back, they won't make the solution one you would like. You hated Shifters, and you were perfectly willing to kill one to open the gate. So maybe spilling Shifter blood really won't work, because you were so eager, even happy, to do it."

"I wasn't *eager*," Reid growled. "Or happy. I don't like killing anything. Except *hoch alfar*."

Diego continued. "What I'm saying is, when you talked to me about Shifters, you despised them. You were ready to make yourself sacrifice one. So do the Fae think it would be harder for you to *kill* a Shifter? Or to *save* one?"

Diego drew his Sig and trained it on Peigi.

Reid snarled in pure rage. He threw himself at Diego, slamming them both into the wall, right over the smear of Peigi's blood. Reid knocked Diego's hand into the rock until the gun fell from Diego's grip.

Diego felt the rocks behind him give. He grabbed Reid and hauled him out of the way, turning to see a gray mist forming where the rock wall had been.

The misty patch expanded until it was about ten feet high and three feet wide. A doorway.

Peigi stared, openmouthed. "What happened?"

Eric gave Diego a thoughtful look. "The sacrifice was Reid saving a hated Shifter. Not killing one. Good perception, Diego."

"Yeah," Shane said. "But what's that stink?"

Wind swirled through the doorway, bringing with it cold and a stench of something rotting.

"Goddess," Cassidy said, waving her hand in front of her nose.

"This isn't right," Reid said. He started forward, but Xavier and Diego grabbed his shoulders and pulled him back.

"Wait," Diego said.

Picking up his gun, Diego moved slowly toward the misty air. As he neared the door, its outline grew more and more clear. The mists rolled back in a sudden burst of cold, to show them a man-shaped figure silhouetted in the doorframe.

The figure turned and brought up a weapon.

"Down!" Diego shouted.

Shifters and cops hit the ground. A bolt pinged a rock in the cave and fell to the dirt, and at the same time, the man fell through the opening.

Not a man. He was tall and strangely lean, like a human who'd been stretched, and he had white blond hair and pointed ears.

He was also dead.

CHAPTER TWENTY-SEVEN

The figure stretched across the floor, his half-putrefying flesh black against his torn clothes.

"What the fuck?" Xavier asked softly.

"Trap." Reid folded his arms over his stomach and looked sick. "They set guards compelled to shoot whoever manages to open the gateway. They're spelled not to leave their post, not even to find food or water. Not even if they die."

"They carry out their mission even if they're *dead*?" Xavier asked. "Why the hell would anyone do that?"

"It's a *hoch alfar* thing," Reid said. "A sick, twisted *hoch alfar* thing. Suicide mission. Their families are handsomely rewarded."

"What's to stop you now, Reid?" Shane asked. "The guard missed, he's dead."

Diego moved back to the opening, around which thick mists had gathered once again. "Careful. There might be more than one."

"Diego, don't you dare," Cassidy said, fury in her voice.

"He aimed at Reid, not me. I'll make sure it's clear, then Reid can go."

"No!"

"Me and Xav," Diego said. He held Cassidy's gaze with his.

"We know how to do this, and we're the best shooters here. We're cops, Cassidy. This is our job."

Xavier drew his Sig and stood at Diego's back. Even though Xavier's left arm was still in a sling, Diego knew Xav could outshoot everyone in this cave, including himself.

"We know what we're doing, Cass," Xav said.

Diego nodded at Reid. "If any other guards are out there, Xav and I will draw their fire and take them out. Then you run through and get the hell home."

"No!" Cassidy snarled.

"Cassidy," Eric said sharply. "They're right. Let them."

Cassidy swung on her brother. "Don't you *dare* treat them like they're expendable."

"I'm not." Eric sounded more alert and focused than Diego had ever heard him. "I'm treating them like part of the team. We each contribute our strengths. Peigi did her part. Let them do theirs. Our part is to back them up. Now stop emoting and start working."

Cassidy gave him a look that didn't bode well for Eric's future, but she subsided.

But the exchange gave Diego a little more insight into Eric. The laid-back Shifter act was just an act. Eric was a watcher, an assessor, who put together pieces while he pretended to laze. And then he struck. Diego decided he'd hate to be on the receiving end of his strike.

"Go," Eric said.

Diego focused his pistol and quickly stepped through the thick mists, his foot landing on solid rock.

There *was* a guard with a crossbow pressed against the wall on the other side of the gate in the dark. Only one.

There didn't need to be more, Diego's mind hummed, because the opening led to a ledge about four feet wide that hung five hundred feet above . . . nothing.

In the split second that Diego saw this, the Fae tried to shoot him. Diego grabbed the Fae's rotting arm and spun him away as the bolt left the crossbow. The dead man crumpled, then he and the crossbow bolt twirled into empty air and fell down, down, down, to a moonlit river far below.

Diego grabbed a dried tree root to steady himself and tried to duck back through the opening to the cave.

And found that he couldn't. The rock had sealed up behind him, leaving Diego standing five hundred feet up a cliff face.

Moonlight flowed like water, lighting the rocks, the thin snake of river below, and a vertical wall that stretched upward above Diego's head. Skeletal, metallic towers leaned over the gorge at intervals, none, of course, conveniently within reach.

Diego recognized where he was, and it wasn't Faerie. He'd been here before, or at least somewhere around here, chasing a crazy suspect with Jobe, long before he'd manifested a watery terror of heights.

He was high above the Colorado River on the tip of the southern Nevada border, a mile or so below the Hoover Dam. And how he'd get down from this perch in the middle of nowhere, he hadn't the faintest fucking idea.

"Holy crap." Xavier jerked back as the rock wall solidified between himself and Diego.

Cassidy threw herself against it. "Diego!"

"What happened?" Reid pounded on the wall as Cassidy dug at it with her claws.

Peigi put her hand on it. "The magic's gone."

"Gone?" Reid demanded. "How can it be gone?"

Eric also touched the wall, too damn calm for Cassidy's taste. "Part of the trap, maybe."

"Why try to close it once someone's inside Faerie?"

"Because it's not Faerie," Eric said. "Smell is wrong, too metallic. Those poor bastards probably died of iron poisoning stuck up there waiting."

"I know where it is," Cassidy said. The fact that Diego hadn't actually been pulled into Faerie didn't stem her panic. "I run up there, sometimes."

"Where?" Xavier demanded.

"The Colorado River gorge. In the cliffs up there. I don't know exactly where Diego is, but that's the area."

"Shit," Xavier said. "Well, let's go get him, then."

Xavier strode out without another word, not looking back to see if any followed him. Cassidy ran after him. She heard Eric calling out for her, but too damn bad. This was Diego. This was her *mate*.

She climbed into Xavier's truck as he started it up. Xavier deftly maneuvered the truck around to go back down the mountain. "I bet you're going to tell me Diego's not in a place that's easily accessible," he said.

"Maybe, if you're a Shifter. Maybe not even then."

"Damn it. I've been in those cliffs. Hell of a trap."

Cassidy clutched the seat as Xavier rocketed the truck down the hill. "They made Reid think he'd found the gateway," she said, thinking it through. "They put guards there to doubly fool him. They put the other side of the 'gate' in so remote a place that humans never see the guards, alive or dead. Probably even mountain goats don't find them. If the guards don't kill Reid when he steps through, he falls to his death. Or gets stuck on a cliff to die of exposure." Cassidy swallowed, thinking of Diego clinging to the side of a cliff face. "Diego doesn't like heights."

"I know he doesn't. Those meth-heads we arrested in Mexico did that to him. Diego was fearless before that." Xavier thumped the steering wheel. "Damn him. He can't stop being everyone's older brother."

Cassidy thought of the story Diego had told her about taking torture so that Xavier would be released by the gang leader. Her heart burned. Diego did that for people, went into danger so they didn't have to.

Maybe that was the reason she loved him so much.

"This is going to take forever." Xavier's jaw clenched as they wound down the track, still a long way from paved roads.

Cassidy said nothing, because there was nothing to be said. They had to drive all the way down the mountain, back through the city, across the desert on the other side, and then to the roads around the dam.

No public roads led to those cliffs along the river. The area was patrolled, but probably not patrolled enough that anyone would notice Diego, in the dark, on the side of a cliff.

As soon as Xavier's truck rocketed onto the highway, he had his cell phone out. He steered down the straight road with the hand of his splinted arm while he punched numbers on his cell with this other thumb.

"Hey, Sheila, this is Escobar. The younger one. Diego's got himself into deep shit, and I need backup."

Cassidy heard the woman on the other side give a startled exclamation.

Xavier went on. "We need to comb every road to either side of Hoover Dam and south of it. Can you get me sheriffs' departments on both sides of the state line? Diego's stuck up on one of the cliffs. We need to get him down in one piece."

I'm on it. Cassidy heard the woman's voice buzz through the phone.

Xavier hung up and called everyone he knew. Eric would be doing the same behind her. Rallying his trackers, Nell, all of Shiftertown if need be.

Cassidy's heart warmed in spite of her frantic worry. They were coming, they were helping, they wouldn't let Diego die.

But only if they got to him in time.

D iego clung to the tree root and refused to look down. Panic poured through him in waves, sometimes receding enough to make him believe he was over the fear, only to have another wave buffet him a second later.

The wind kicked him around as well. The gorge of the Colorado, made deeper by the dam that collected the river upstream, was a giant wind tunnel. The river was nice when you were down on the beaches beside it, when you took a day off to fish or just laze around on a boat. It wasn't its best when you clung to the side of the cliff far above, trying to find handholds.

No way in hell was Diego going to let a gust of wind lift him and send him over the edge. He would climb the hell out of here and call for help. Right?

How the fuck did I get into this?

Helping Reid. Because I felt sorry for him. Teach me to have compassion.

No, this was the fault of whoever had persecuted Reid. Their trap was perfect and cruel. They'd give Reid the hope that he'd found his way home, and then kill him up here.

Two thoughts chased that one: *Sadistic bastards* and *What the hell did Reid do to garner this treatment?*

Maybe nothing. Some people were simply cruel, like Enrique. They practiced brutality because they could. They liked to watch people twisting in the wind, like Diego was now.

A gust blasted Diego, and his toes lost their hold. "Son of a bitch!"

He grabbed for another handhold, his fingers bleeding, toes desperately scrabbling for a crevice. He managed to lodge one foot on a protruding rock. Hanging on to the tree root, he swung the other foot back to the ledge. Scrambling and swearing, Diego got himself on the narrow ledge and wedged his body back against the rock.

The overhang helped with the wind a little, but it trapped him. He couldn't climb out above, and without rappelling gear, he couldn't descend.

He had a cell phone. When Diego was at last able to tug it out and open it, he of course couldn't get a signal. He left it on, though, in case they could find him through the GPS inside it.

It looked like the sky was lightening. Diego didn't remember that much time passing, but the eastern horizon definitely was a little grayer.

No, wait, the sky itself hadn't lightened. Mist shimmered about six feet away from Diego's ledge, right in the middle of empty air. And damned if two more Fae—not dead this time—didn't just raise bows and aim through the mist at him. Not crossbows, longbows, as though Diego had landed in some kind of Renaissance Fair.

Diego brought up his Sig and fired. The Fae ducked aside faster than Diego had ever seen anyone duck, then they stared at him in amazement.

The gun's kick nearly dislodged him, but Diego held on and shouted, "This is steel. That's made from iron. Want a piece?"

More staring. Then the Fae shot. One arrow ripped Diego's cell phone from his hand and sent it spinning away down the cliff. Diego dropped to the ledge, breath snagging in terror as his face looked into nothing.

He felt a sudden, sharp pain and looked down to see an arrow sticking out of his side.

It shocked him more than it hurt, but he knew pain would come. And blood loss, and weakness. Then death when he tumbled over the side from all of that. He brought up his pistol and fired again.

The Fae ducked back but they nocked arrows to their bows again.

"Damn you, I'm not Reid! I sprang the fucking trap by accident."

Didn't look like they cared. *Who the hell guards a gate for fifty years? And why do they hate Reid so much?*

"You're *hoch alfar*, right? I'm human."

They hesitated when he said *hoch alfar*, but obviously they didn't understand any of his other words. Probably wouldn't make any difference if he said it in Spanish. Maybe if he knew Gaelic.

I really should have bought that audio course.

Diego aimed his Sig again. "Stand down or this bullet goes into your chest."

Fire spread through his side. He was going to die up here.

The second Fae nocked another arrow and shot, his fingers a blur. Diego fired at the same time. The Fae he aimed at went over backward, blood on his mail-shirted chest.

So, they could die. But then, so could Diego.

The arrow that had left the bow glanced across Diego's hip, missing because the second Fae had jumped when his colleague went down. Diego aimed again and shot.

The second Fae knew enough to duck aside. The air shimmered and the gate closed.

Diego lowered his aching arm, trying to catch his breath. Would it open again? Would they send more to kill the man who'd just shot one of their own?

His side hurt like hell. He knew an artery hadn't been severed only because he was still alive. Either that or the arrow was holding the blood vessels closed.

Maybe his gunshots had drawn attention. But the wind was hard, blowing sound away. Echoes could come from anywhere. Diego didn't dare keep firing in case the Fae returned and he needed the ammo. He had half a magazine now in his gun and that was it.

Find me, Cassidy.

She had to be crazy, telling him to stay away from her. For his own protection. Right.

Love didn't work that way. That's what *for better or for worse* meant. You didn't run off when times got tough. You worked through it. You helped each other with whatever crazy problems happened and celebrated the good stuff on the other side.

You found your lover when he was stuck on the side of a cliff with an arrow in his side.

Dizziness swirled through him. *Perfect. Just effing perfect.*

He was going to pass out. When he did, there was nothing to say whether he'd lay here quietly or whether the next gust would send him plunging over the side.

The air shimmered again. When the mist cleared, Diego was staring down his gun at five more Fae.

They had rope. They had a grappling hook—not iron. It looked, as it flew toward the ledge and missed, to be hard, carved wood.

They were going to try to pull him into Faerie.

Not a place he wanted to go.

Diego raised his Sig, his hand shaking like holy hell. "Me and my iron," he said. "It comes with me."

Another throw, and this time the hook stuck on a nearby rock. Diego reached over and plucked it out.

The Fae on the other side snarled and started talking in their own language, but not to Diego. A technique to show they had the upper hand. Don't talk directly to the victim or listen when they talked back. Victims were nothing.

The next thing they threw was a net.

Ropes tried to entangle him. Diego fought, pain rippling through him. Finally, he managed to pull the damn thing off him and drop it over the side.

That made the Fae angry. They started shouting among themselves, and then here came the longbows again.

Diego fired at the Fae. They boiled apart, the air shimmered, and the gate closed again.

Diego sighed and slumped to the ledge, waiting for the next round to begin.

Cassidy held on as the truck rocked over the pitted washboard road. Xavier led the way up the hill with a string of sheriffs' cars behind them, lights flashing. Diego's GPS signal had vanished, and Cassidy tried to stem her panic.

The signal had come from a place on the Nevada side of the river, Xavier was told, in a section where no roads led.

They'd drive as close to the cliffs as they could, then they'd have to search on foot.

In the dark, Xavier said glumly, hours from daylight. He hoped Diego could hang on.

Cassidy didn't need roads or light. As soon as Xavier reached the end of the road, Cassidy was out of the truck and tugging off her shirt.

The road was literally at an end; a giant rock wall with boulders strewn at its base rose like a monolith in front of them. Red and blue and yellow lights from the patrol cars and construction trucks swirled across its face.

"Hey, what are you doing?"

One of the sheriff's deputies trained a flashlight on Cassidy as she stood there in her bra, hand on her waistband. Xavier slammed his truck's door and put himself protectively in front of her.

"Leave her alone. Let her do what she's good at."

"Stripping?"

Xavier moved the deputy's flashlight so Cassidy was no longer in its beam. "She can help. Go on, Cass."

Cassidy growled, too far gone to reply. The shift was coming upon her, and she had to get out of these damn clothes.

Cassidy shoved her jeans down and kicked out of her shoes at the same time. She unsnapped her bra as she ran, and flowed out of her underwear as her wildcat took over.

She hit the ground running on all fours. One of the deputies whistled as she bounded up the desert hill. Below her, Xavier started shouting about search patterns and dogs.

Cassidy leapt on up the mountain, trying to get away from the smell of exhaust and the dogs. Rocks slid under her feet as she scrambled to the top.

She couldn't call out in her wildcat form, and she couldn't take the time to shift back to do so. Calling wasn't going to help her. Scent was.

Below, she heard Eric arrive. He'd brought Shane and Brody and his other trackers. Cassidy distanced herself from them, shutting out their scent and focusing on finding Diego's.

She loped to the cliff tops. Below her, far below, the river flowed, released from its confinement by the dam and Lake

Mead. It snaked southward in the moonlight, serenely making its way toward Baja, where what was left of it would empty into the gulf.

Diego could be anywhere along the miles of cliffs. They'd narrowed the search to this side of the river, but that was still a lot of ground to cover.

Cassidy covered it for an hour, which soon became two. Her paws hurt from the gravel and hard ground. Behind her, the deputies, dogs, Xavier, and Eric's trackers fanned out, going over ground she'd already covered.

She smelled it at the end of the second hour. The faint but acrid odor of Faerie.

Cassidy dashed to the next cliff top and looked down. She saw nothing but blackness, but the scent came to her. Mint and smoke—definitely Fae.

Gray mist formed in midair about a quarter mile from her position. The stink of Faerie came to her on the wind.

Galvanized, she dashed along the cliff edge. When she was parallel with the opening, she saw ropes float out of the mist and attach themselves to something on the cliff wall.

She heard Diego's shout, then the boom of his gun, and she smelled the scent of gunpowder. Cassidy frantically looked for a way down to him, finding only a tiny crevice in the cliff that was nearly vertical.

Cassidy picked her way down this as quickly as possible, her wildcat's balance taking over, Cassidy ceasing to think. She leapt the last six feet to land on top of the trussed form of Diego, her mate.

"Shit!" he yelled.

The ropes went taut and yanked Diego off the ledge. Cassidy clung to him, her claws digging deep, Diego clenching his teeth against the pain.

I'm sorry. I'm sorry, my love.

Diego didn't unclench as they swung over empty space and were hauled up onto the muddy ground of Faerie. The misty gate snicked shut, and the dry desert cliffs were gone.

CHAPTER TWENTY-EIGHT

Faerie was muddy and cold. Diego lay flat on his back, tied with ropes that had fastened themselves around him, with a snarling wildcat on his chest. Cassidy splayed herself protectively over Diego, growling at the Fae warriors that ringed them.

They looked like extras in a Knights of the Round Table movie, Diego thought. Shining mail, long braided hair, black surcoats, swords and bows, and hard expressions.

The light was gray like dawn, but Diego saw that the land was bathed in fog. Not a pea-souper, but enough mist to darken the sky and slide between the trees of the dense wood at the bottom of the hill.

One of the warriors, who had the stance of a leader or a general, spoke to Diego. Spoke *at* him. Demands, questions, who knew?

"Do you know what they're saying?" he whispered to Cassidy.

She only growled again and lowered her head to his chest.

The general gave a curt command. Three came at Cassidy, swords drawn.

Diego, who still had his hand around his Sig, pointed it. "No. Back!"

The warriors hesitated. The general snapped something at Diego.

Diego shook his head. *"Lo siento, no comprende."*

The general looked slightly surprised, as much as his granite face let him, then he came back with a halting sentence that sounded Italian. No, not Italian. Latin.

Great.

He wished Cassidy would shift and help him out with the linguistics. At the moment, Cassidy's claws were raking down his chest, raising all kinds of welts, but she wasn't trying to hurt him. She was cutting the ropes.

The general noticed this and motioned his men forward. Diego brought up the Sig.

"You touch her, and I *will* shoot you."

The general snatched a crossbow from the warrior next to him. Diego fired, his sharpshooting skills wrenching the crossbow out of the general's hands. But the bolt had already flown and struck Diego's wrist.

The bolt glanced across his skin instead of embedding itself, but it dug deep enough in passing. Diego yelled, his gun falling from nerveless fingers.

Cassidy attacked. She landed on the general, all four feet on his chest, claws ripping. Her Collar went off, electricity arcing around her neck, but she didn't stop.

She fought for a few seconds more before two of the Fae grabbed her and wrenched her away from the general. Cassidy landed on the ground, shuddering with the Collar's pain, while the Fae collectively laughed at her.

Diego was going to pass out. He didn't want to, but he had an arrow, the end of which had snapped off, stuck into him, and pain was catching up to him. Blood loss, shock. All there.

"Cassidy," he said.

Before he blacked out, he saw Cassidy crawl to him and once more drape herself over him. *At least she's warm* was Diego's last coherent thought for a while.

C assidy didn't speak the languages of the Fae fluently, but she knew a little from the Shifter rituals and Shifter lore. She got the gist of the word *slave*, referring to her, and *fun* for what they wanted to do with Diego. One suggested they make Cassidy hunt Diego herself, but the general said no.

The Shifter female would become a fighting slave for the clan leader, he said, and the human would be put to death for his dealings with the *dokk alfar.*

Cassidy shifted to her human form. "He came through the gate by mistake," she said. "Send him back and leave him alone."

They didn't understand, and Cassidy didn't know enough to find the words in Fae.

"We're friends of the warrior called Fionn Cillian," she said. "Heard of him?"

From their reaction, they had. Also from their reaction, maybe that hadn't been a smart thing to say.

Four of the warriors dragged Cassidy off Diego. She fought, but between the chain mail that protected them and the continuing pain from her Collar, she did little damage. The others cut the ropes from Diego that Cassidy hadn't finished shredding. One kicked Diego's gun away into the mud, then that Fae jerked back his booted foot as though even the small contact burned him.

The warriors staked out the unconscious Diego and got out their knives. Cassidy wrenched herself from her captors and shifted back to wildcat as she leapt onto Diego, shielding him with her body.

"You have mate bond?" a new voice asked.

Another warrior had joined the general. He spoke English with a thick accent and, though he wore silver mail, he wasn't armed.

"He asks me to translate," the new Fae said. "I know some human languages."

Translate this. Cassidy curled her lip into a snarl. She'd spray him if she could.

The general began speaking rapidly without cracking a smile. The translator said for him, "It is known that the Shifters believe they form magical bonds with their mates. That the bond is so great they will die for one another. His lordship wishes to see if this is true."

Oh, I'd die for Diego, all right. Cassidy knew she would, in a heartbeat. *But I'd rather kill you instead.*

Cassidy didn't bother shifting to answer or even acknowledging she was being spoken to. The translator and the general didn't seem to care.

"He will be awakened now."

Two of the warriors strode forward, and one dumped a skin of water on Diego's face. Cassidy ducked in to protect him, taking most of the cold water on her own head. She shook, in the cat way, and the warriors laughed.

Diego stirred beneath her, eyelids fluttering.

No, Diego, stay asleep. Don't feel this.

Stubborn Diego forced his eyes open. He assessed the situation without jerking, without panic, and looked at Cassidy.

The look told her everything she needed to know.

"Human being," the translator said for the general. "You have rutted with this creature?"

Cassidy swallowed bile and forced herself back to her human form. Diego looked past her at the two Fae standing over them.

"Watch your mouth," he said.

"You have formed a mate bond with her?"

"No," Cassidy said quickly. "He hasn't. He barely knows me."

"And yet, you, Shifter woman, rushed to his rescue and did not allow him to enter Faerie without you. And now you protect him like a mother *pukka* with her cubs."

"What's a *pukka*?" Diego whispered.

"Furry, horsy, nasty, ugly thing with claws," Cassidy said. "Another breeding experiment. Some say they were trying to breed more of those and got Shifters instead."

"You don't look that bad," Diego said.

"Thank you."

"Do you have this bond?" the translator said to Diego. "Would you die for her?"

"Yes," Diego said.

"Damn you, Diego," Cassidy whispered frantically. "They're not kidding."

"I know they're not. They're bullies, just like the people I grew up with. Tying me down and sticking arrows into me is easy. Let's see what happens when I get up and fight them instead."

The translator told all this to the general, who shook his head.

"They don't trust you," Cassidy said. "And they don't care what we think of them."

"You understand them?"

"About one word in four."

"Throw yourself on me, Cass," Diego whispered. "And start bawling."

Cassidy did it without asking questions. Diego loved that about her.

"My belt buckle is steel," he said into her ear as she pretended to sob. "Get it off me, use it. Loosen me if you can and help me get my gun. If you can't get me free, just shoot the mo fos."

Cassidy kept on wailing as she unbuckled his belt. She let her hands turn to claws to pop the buckle from the leather.

The general gave orders that the other guy didn't bother translating. Two warriors came forward and dragged Cassidy off Diego again. She managed to snag her fingers and one foot into the bonds on Diego's left wrist and ankle, which came up with her.

Diego rolled over, almost screaming at the pain in his side, jerked his other wrist free, and dove for his pistol.

He got a foot toward it before two Fae, damn strong for their thin builds, grabbed him and flung him facedown, tethered him again, and secured him by driving a bronze knife right through his hand. Diego grunted in pain. The sound was swallowed by a Fae screaming—Cassidy using the belt buckle.

Diego heard bow strings thrum, the whistling release of arrows. *Dios*, they were killing her.

At the same time, the earth began to shake.

The *hoch alfar* didn't like that. Neither did Diego.

Cassidy leapt past Diego, going for the pistol. She brought it up and around, firing at the Fae chasing her. She'd never shot a gun before, obviously. Her aim went wide, but she made the Fae dive for cover.

The earth was erupting. Diego turned his head to see boulders burst upward into the misty sky. Then a strange darkness started seeping from the woods.

Diego blinked, but he wasn't hallucinating. Darkness did emanate from the woods to crawl along the ground, the fog dissipating before it. The Fae warriors were panicking, terrified of it.

Diego wasn't thrilled by it either. "Cass!"

But she was right there, her warm scent on him. "I don't know what it is," she said. "I have to get you free. This is going to hurt."

"Yeah, you think?"

The general was shouting. The translator was no longer bothering with them.

Cassidy used her claws to rip up Diego's T-shirt, then she put one hand on the knife. "Close your eyes and think of something good."

Diego's eyes slid closed. "That's easy."

Cassidy in his shower, her red lips smiling, her hand soothing his body. Leaning her against the wall, warm water pouring over their bodies . . .

White-hot pain shot through him as Cassidy jerked the knife from his hand. The pain dwindled to mere torture while she tightly bound his hand in a cotton strip torn from his shirt. She hated hurting him, he saw, but Cassidy had courage.

The weird darkness flowed up the hill and surrounded Diego and Cassidy, Fae warriors and all. The Fae made a ring, swords and bows out, the translator hiding behind the general in the middle.

The general shouted commands. Diego didn't understand the words, but the man sounded exactly like his sergeant in the Marines.

The darkness disappeared, instantly and without warning. Sunlight shone down on about two hundred warriors dressed in skins and carrying short but mean-looking swords that glittered in the sudden light. They all had dark hair and skin and were tall and wiry like Reid.

Dokk alfar.

Cassidy got Diego to his feet. He stumbled, but she was strong, and they ran, step by excruciating step, as the *dokk alfar* swarmed the Fae and started to fight.

"The gateway should be over there," Diego yelled to Cassidy, pointing. "But I don't know if it will open again, and it's about four hundred feet in the air and six feet away from the cliffs on the other side."

"I could jump it. You can hang on to me."

"I don't think I can hang on to anything. I'd pull you down. Too much weight. Jump it yourself, bring help."

"Like hell I'm leaving you here."

"Cass, remember when they asked if I'd die for you? Well, I would. If that's what the mate bond means—that my world would be all wrong if anything happened to you—then I have the effing mate bond."

"Diego . . ."

"You said you wanted to rescue me. Well, this is you doing it."

They reached the spot. Diego looked for mist, tried to feel a tingle. Collapsed instead.

"Damn it," Cassidy said.

"Come on, Cass. Just go. I *would* die for you, but I'd rather live." He gave a breathless laugh. "Sex with you is fantastic. I want a chance at more of that."

Cassidy had tears in her eyes as she looked at him. "I love you, Diego."

"I love you too, *mi ja*."

She leaned down and kissed him. Diego's pain receded the slightest bit, enough for him to savor the pressure of her lips.

Then she stuck her hand through the mist forming on the other side of the boulder. And shouted in surprise.

Diego tried to haul himself to his feet, but whatever had grabbed Cassidy on the other side of the mist now shoved her back into Diego. A form came through the gate, tall and lean and pissed off.

Reid, carrying an iron crowbar, sprinted toward the fight.

Shane charged in after him, in full bear mode, roaring as he ran past. Then a leopard with a Collar, a smaller bear without one, and finally, Xavier.

"Hey, Diego," Xavier said, grinning, arm in its sling, as he stopped in the middle of the mist. Behind him, morning light shone on dry cliff walls, the Nevada sunshine hard and clear. "This time I'm saving *your* ass."

Reid and Xavier had crossed the gorge on a bridge—a narrow platform seven feet long, drilled and anchored into the cliff walls. Diego learned later that Xavier had made the rescue team build it, using engineers recruited from the fire department plus the best construction workers from the dam.

Xavier held out his good hand. "Come on, *hermano*. Time to get you down off this place."

"Wait."

Reid had joined the fray behind them, incongruous in jeans and T-shirt while the others of his kind wore skins.

More *hoch alfar* were riding in over the open field, on white horses that glowed a little—the cavalry, Diego supposed, coming to rescue their comrades.

"We need to help Reid," Diego said.

"Doesn't look like it's our fight," Xavier said.

"They just saved our butts. I need to do something for them."

Diego held out his left hand for his Sig, and Cassidy reluctantly relinquished it. His right hand, the one the knife had gone through, was pretty much useless, but Diego's left hand was strong, and he was a good marksman with either hand.

"Got a spare clip?" Diego asked his brother.

Xavier wordlessly handed it over. Diego ejected his empty and reloaded. He looked at Cassidy.

He knew he'd waste his breath begging her to run across the bridge to safety. Cassidy was staying, would fight by his side, would haul him off to save him if he fell. As he would for her.

"Nice day for it," Diego said to her.

Cassidy smiled back, her beautiful, loving smile that made his heart beat faster. "I say we go for it."

Diego leaned down and kissed her warm lips. "Love you, Cass."

"Love you back."

Xavier put his arm around Diego's shoulders, his shining chrome Sig dangling from his good hand. "When's the wedding?"

Diego gave him a look and released Cassidy. "Let's go help Reid."

Reid didn't look like he needed a lot of help. During the little time Diego had known him, the man had always been morose and unhappy, lashing out in anger or folding up in misery.

Now Diego saw what Reid must have been before his exile—a fighter. A good and bloodthirsty fighter.

Reid laid into the *hoch alfar* with his crowbar, going up

against those with bows, swords, chain mail—he didn't much care. He swung and brought down a Fae from a horse, smashing the iron bar into the Fae's face. The Fae screamed and then went horribly quiet.

The *dokk alfar* were fighting hard, and the *hoch alfar* were fighting just as hard back. Peigi jumped in, her bear attacking without restraint.

Peigi showed Diego how Shifters were bred to fight—no Collar holding her back. She attacked with the strength and speed of a bear coupled with the cunning of a human. Animals with human intelligence. As dangerous as Reid had once told him.

Peigi fought at Reid's side, keeping the *hoch alfar* from reaching him.

Diego and Cassidy waded in. Xavier stayed at the bridge, guarding the retreat.

Diego knew he wasn't going to be much good for fighting, but he could at least still shoot. Cassidy ran to help Shane, she beating off a *hoch alfar* who had been about to skewer the bear. Diego took aim, ready to shoot if he needed to.

The general broke out of the group and headed for Reid, the target for this whole fight. Pretty elaborate and long-lived trap for one man, Diego thought. Did they consider Reid that dangerous?

A long sword glittered in the general's hand. Reid was unprotected, no vest, no weapon but a crowbar.

Peigi and Reid were fighting, not seeing the danger. Diego held his hurt hands steady, took aim, and shot the sword out of the general's hand.

The general whirled around, and Diego grinned at him. "Hey, remember me?"

The general grabbed a bow out of a passing Fae's hands, his own hands flashing as he drew it. The next moment, the general went down with a wildcat on his back.

Cassidy's Collar went off, but she held the man pinned in place. Diego limped toward them, ignored by most of the fighters. More *hoch alfar* had ridden up, and the tide was going to turn against the *dokk alfar* soon. They were fighting hard, but they'd be crushed by numbers alone.

As Diego reached Cassidy and the general, a weird, piercing

war cry came out of the couple hundred *dokk alfar* throats. It
rang into the mists, scary as hell.

A lone cry answered it. Reid. He held up his iron bar and
shouted one word.

The *hoch alfar* started scrambling away, running in pure
terror. Diego watched over his aimed pistol, not sure what was
going on.

The Fae jumped onto horses, galloping back across the
field for the hills beyond. Those on foot ran like hell. The general, with a surge of strength, got out from under Cassidy, but
instead of turning to fight, he sprinted away like a man trying
to outrun floodwaters.

Reid's iron bar exploded. It morphed from an ordinary
crowbar into a rain of iron shards that flew with the speed of
bullets after the fleeing *hoch alfar*.

Those it struck screamed and fell. A few got up again and
kept running, but now the *dokk alfar* were after them.

The general, at the tail end of his men, shot behind him as
he ran, while iron shards rained down on him like tiny heat-
seeking missiles.

The *dokk alfar* charged after the Fae. The darkness Diego
had first seen coated them like a curtain, and then he could
see nothing but the black cloud.

Reid remained behind, his hands bloody, a defiant look in
his eyes. Peigi landed on all fours beside him, growling a possessive bear growl.

Reid was watching the retreating *hoch alfar*, his usual
arrogance in place. "Weak Fae, my ass," he said.

Cassidy loped back to Diego, with Shane and Eric right
behind her. Eric rose into his human form. "Time to go. No
place for us in a Fae war. Those days are gone forever, thank
the Goddess."

Eric looked lighthearted for the first time in a long time.
He scratched Cassidy's head and strode off—a tall, naked
man with a silver and black Collar, a tatt swirling down his
arm, walking unashamedly past Xavier and through the mists
that led home.

CHAPTER TWENTY-NINE

Diego thought that fighting for his life on a tiny ledge five hundred feet above the ground and then being pulled across empty air in a net of ropes would have cured him of his fear of heights. But, no.

His head spun with dizziness as he limped across the extremely narrow makeshift bridge from the gate to Faerie to the familiar red brown cliffs of home.

Don't look down.

It was so hard not to look down. Diego *had* to look to see where he was putting his feet. Below the slender iron span, the empty air dropped away to reveal the river like a vein of silver at the bottom. The sun had risen by now, so he could see everything in panoramic glory.

The view was beautiful. Upriver the giant span of the dam thrust from the bottom of the gorge, the edifice built nearly a hundred years ago by men braver than Diego. The slab of concrete poured like a sheer cliff from the serene blue lake behind it to the river below. Above it a new bridge spanned from cliff top to cliff top, the sun catching on its arches. Breathtaking.

The beauty of the sights didn't help. Diego was too damned high off the ground.

He clung with one aching hand to Xavier's shoulder and concentrated on putting one foot in front of the other. Cassidy came right behind him.

They won't let me fall, he told himself. *My brother and the love of my life will see me safely across.*

Diego was supposed to have an epiphany. A moment of truth that made him conquer his fear and realize that his love for Cassidy was so much stronger than a ridiculous worry about heights.

No such luck.

Screw this. I'm going back to the counselor.

Diego stepped onto the narrow rock ledge, let the rescue team strap a harness around him, and felt his feet leave the ground as they hauled him straight up the cliff. He thought he was going to puke.

Cassidy smiled at him from below, dressed now in the coverall the rescue guys had brought. She even seated herself on the makeshift bridge and dangled her legs over the side as she waved him on.

Maybe Cass can teach me not to be afraid. That scenario was much more appealing than the one of him sitting in a room droning to a counselor. The rewards would be much better too. Cassidy would smile at Diego, kiss him, show him how much she admired his bravery . . .

By the time he made it to the top, to firm ground, Diego was both sick and dizzy, but picturing Cassidy teaching him not to be afraid of heights helped a lot. Paramedics took over, shoving an oxygen mask on him, unwrapping his hand, taking his blood pressure, generally burying him in modern health care.

Cassidy came into view before they loaded Diego into the ambulance. She leaned down and kissed his forehead. Her face was dirty and scratched, but she looked good for a woman who'd just been in a hell of a fight. *Damn* good.

"You're beautiful, *amada mia*," he said, words muffled by the oxygen mask. Then the paramedics lifted him, slid him into the waiting maw of the ambulance, and slammed the doors.

* * *

Humans wouldn't let Cassidy into the hospital with Diego. She had to fume and rely on Xavier and Diego's mother to tell her what was going on.

Diego's mom was the best resource. She even came to Shiftertown to visit Cassidy that afternoon as the Shifters lay about the Wardens' living room and back patio, recovering from the fight.

"They're keeping him overnight for observation," Juanita said. "Xavier is staying with him. But the doctors are not that worried. My boy is strong."

"And a damn good warrior," Eric said to her.

Eric had fired up the grill again. Nothing for it but to celebrate saving Diego and Reid with a big cookout. Juanita took the invitation to stay for the party to mean she could invade the Wardens' kitchen and put together a meal to die for.

Cassidy enjoyed the carne adobada—meat spiced with chiles—that Juanita turned out, which she served with tortillas and homemade pico de gallo. Cassidy ate it but chafed at having to sit here without Diego. The mate bond pulled at her, making her want to charge to the hospital and demand to see him.

It was hell following human rules.

Juanita leaned down and put her arms around Cassidy as Cassidy sat dejectedly on the edge of the patio. "I know it's hard," Juanita said. "But if you come home with me tonight, you'll be there when he gets back."

"You don't mind?" Cassidy asked.

"Mind what?"

"That I love Diego, and that I'm Shifter."

Juanita sat down next to Cassidy. "Let me tell you a little about Diego, *mi ja*. He thinks he has to take care of everyone but himself. Never himself. He joined the Marines to make some money and give Xavier and me a chance to move and start a better life. He joined the police for the same reason. Then when Jobe died, he lived to hunt down the men who killed him. Diego's never done one single thing for himself. Not ever. He looked after me and after Xavier, and he looked after Jobe and now Jobe's family. That's it. And then he brings you home. *Chiquita*, I have been praying for the day he looked at someone the way he looks at you. He's finally going to let himself be happy."

"But . . ."

"No buts. Don't even think *but*. I want grandchildren before I die. If they can turn into cute little animals, so what? I've always liked cats."

Cassidy stared at Juanita for a stunned instant, then she threw her arms around the smaller woman. The two swayed together for a moment, then Juanita pushed her away and jumped up to go make another batch of meat.

Jace arrived home just as the second helpings were being served. Nell sang out a hello to him and shoved plates of adobada and tortillas at him.

Cassidy cornered her nephew as he was gulping down the meal with great enjoyment. "Spill it, Jace. How did you work it so the *dokk alfar* rushed to our rescue in Faerie?"

Jace looked more interested in the food than the adventure. "I didn't. I talked a little to the Fionn Cillian guy, but he didn't promise anything. Then he comes back right before Marlo and I left, looking proud of himself. He said he found out that the territory Reid is from belongs to a rival of his, so he was happy to alert the *dokk alfar* in the area. He'd use any weapon, he said, to conquer his rival, even *dokk alfar*. From the way Cillian talks, though, any clan he doesn't rule is his rival." Jace shrugged. "He's an arrogant bastard, but then, aren't they all?"

"Well, thank you." Cassidy grabbed the scruff of Jace's neck and planted a kiss on his cheek. "You made your auntie happy. And probably saved her life."

Jace looked surprised, then concerned. "Yeah? What exactly happened?"

Cassidy spent the rest of the cookout filling Jace in on events. He looked sorry he missed them and muttered that it was the last time he ran boring errands for his father. Cassidy tried to mollify him by telling him he'd been key in getting Reid's people in position in time to save Diego and Cassidy.

Before Cassidy packed her overnight bag and got ready to ride back to Diego's mother's house for the night, Reid arrived.

"I owe you a debt," he said to Cassidy as she went out to the backyard to greet him. "I can never repay it. I will never make up for what I've done to you."

Reid looked more confident now, less beaten down, but shame still rested in his eyes.

"You rescued Diego and me from the Fae," Cassidy said. "And did that neat trick with the crowbar. What was that?"

Reid shrugged, as though he'd not done anything spectacular. "I'm an iron master."

"And that means . . . ?"

"I can manipulate iron, make it do anything I want. Only in Faerie. I can't seem to do the same here. Maybe that's why I can teleport in the human world—perhaps my skill is manifesting in a different direction."

"You can make iron do anything you want?" Cassidy asked. "What a great skill to have against people who hate iron. I have the feeling that's one reason the *hoch alfar* wanted you out in the first place."

Reid nodded. "That and they wanted my territory. I was the biggest obstacle in their way, so they destroyed my family and exiled me. And made certain I'd never make it back."

Even if Reid had figured out how to open the gate on the ley line, the Fae had tried to make sure he'd die in the attempt to return home. But Diego had sprung the trap instead.

"So, why are you still here?" Cassidy asked. "You made it back to Faerie. You used your iron trick and scared away the Fae. You were home free."

Reid looked sad again. "I found that my family there is dead and gone, my friends too. The Fae killed them all. I spoke with the new leader for a time and I realized—there's nothing left there for me. I've been gone too long."

The door to Nell's house slammed open, and Reid looked next door. His face changed, softening, the arrogance and anger fading.

Cassidy followed his gaze and saw Peigi emerging from the house, her head high, her long-legged stride taking her toward the cookout and party.

"I see," Cassidy said. "Well, what do you know?"

Reid kept watching Peigi. "I can't explain it. I don't care. She needs me."

"She does." Cassidy put her hand on Reid's shoulder. "And you need her." For the first time, she put her arms around her enemy and drew him close. "Goddess go with you, Stuart Reid." She stepped back and smiled at him. "Now, go get her."

The most beautiful sight in the world was Cassidy's ass bent over the engine of Diego's car in his mother's driveway, her shorts baring her long legs as she stretched to tighten something.

Xavier turned from watching what she was doing and looked up at Diego. "You look terrible," he said. "Should you be out of bed?"

Diego resisted the urge to scratch his arm in its sling, and he was suddenly aware of every abrasion on his body. The deep claw marks he liked, though, because they represented Cassidy trying to free him.

Cassidy looked over her shoulder at Diego. Grease on a nose had never looked so sexy before.

"I heard your engine ticking when I drove your car back here last night," she said. "I thought I'd give you a tune-up."

"She's amazing." Xavier gazed at Cassidy with great respect. "She's working on my truck next."

"Shifters have learned to be good with cars," Cassidy said, bending over the engine again. Diego could watch her all day.

Xavier looked from Diego to Cassidy and back again. He wiped off his good hand and tossed down the rag. "Just remembered, I need to go help Mamita with . . . that thing. You know . . . that thing . . . Right." He turned away and faded into the house.

"He's transparent," Cassidy said. She gave whatever bolt she was turning one last twist and straightened. "Want to start it up?"

Diego slid into the driver's seat, found his keys already in the ignition, and cranked on the engine. The T-Bird purred.

Cassidy gave him a thumbs-up, then slammed the hood closed and snatched up the rag Xavier had dropped. Diego listened to the engine a few more seconds, then shut it off and climbed painfully out of the car.

"You have grease on your nose," Diego said.

"Oh." Cassidy swiped at it.

"You're making it worse. Let me."

Diego took a handkerchief out of his pocket and put it, plus what was wrapped in it, into Cassidy's hand. Cassidy started when she felt the weight on her palm and looked at him in surprise.

"Open it," he said.

Cassidy peeled back the handkerchief, stared at the little velvet box resting in her hand, and then opened it.

The diamonds inside caught on the intense sunshine, throwing little spangles onto Cassidy's fingers. Her eyes widened. "What is this?"

Diego plucked the ring from the box as she held it and started to slide the ring onto her finger.

Cassidy jerked away. "My hands are dirty."

"You won't hurt it." Diego gently took her hand again. "This is the human way, Cass. Instead of mate-claims, mating frenzy, and mate bonds, we say, *Here's a diamond ring. Will you marry me?*"

"Marry." She looked up at him in near panic. "But Shifters can't marry . . ."

Diego slid the ring firmly onto her finger. "I don't give a damn about human rules. We'll do this the Shifter way if we have to. You said you wanted to reject my mate-claim, right? Well, I talked to Eric this morning, and he told me that even if a female rejects a mate-claim, the male can make it again. So I'm making it. I'll keep on making it until you tell me yes."

Cassidy's breath caught. "Diego, I told you why I said no. To protect you. So you won't have to give up your career . . ."

Diego took her hand and held it. "Listen to me. I talked for a long time with your brother, and then with Mamita and Xav. I can still do my job. If my captain gets bent out of shape because I'm with a Shifter and fires me, Eric has offered to let me become one of his trackers. I can help him out when he has to deal with humans. To be honest, I've lost faith in the human system that lets good Shifters be killed and violent drug runners escape without pursuit. Maybe I can do what I'm meant to do, but on the Shifter side instead."

"But there's the age difference," Cassidy said. "I worked the underground in World War Two. Your mom wasn't even born then."

"And I want to hear all those great stories. Jace told me this Fionn Cillian he met can do spells or whatever that lengthen a human life to match a Shifter. Maybe I don't have as many *inches* as Shifters—yeah, I heard about that—but you can have every single one of mine."

Cassidy's look was stunned, as though someone had smacked her between the eyes, and she didn't yet know how to react.

Diego slid his good arm around her shoulders. "This is something you might understand better. Cassidy Warden, second of Shiftertown, I claim you as mate."

Her lips parted, as though to deny him again, and Diego kissed her. "Say yes," he said. "Don't push me away, Cassidy. I'll keep coming back until you give me the answer I want."

Cassidy stared up at him, eyes so deeply green. He loved her eyes, loved her shapely, strong body. All of her.

"Yes," Cassidy whispered.

She still sounded stunned. "Good." Diego licked across her lips, her taste making his need clench. "All kinds of good, *mi ja.*"

Cassidy's eyes flicked to Shifter. "Stop. If I go into mating frenzy right now, we might not come out for days."

"You say that like it's a bad thing."

Cassidy smiled, her face lighting up in her beautiful way. "I wish you could know what it feels like."

"I think I do." Diego leaned closer. "I want you so bad, it's killing me. With you in those shorts, showing me your hot ass, how can I hold it in? I'd take you bent over this car if I didn't know that my mom and brother were watching us from the kitchen window."

Cassidy ran her fingers down his chest. "We need to go somewhere. Now."

"I have a friend with a cabin up on Mount Charleston. I'll see if we can borrow it."

"Hurry."

Diego laughed and kissed her again. He pulled out his cell phone and called a fellow cop who had given Diego the standing invitation to use his cabin whenever. Cassidy chewing on his earlobe while he talked was distracting, but Diego made the arrangements.

It was dusk by the time they arrived at the cabin down an isolated road off the main highway. Diego's friend lent out his cabin a lot, so there was a fire already laid in the fireplace, and Diego only had to light the tinder.

Then he and Cassidy were on the rug, Cassidy on top of Diego because of his hurt arm, their clothes scattered all over the place.

Cassidy loved his warmth under her, the feel of Diego strong beneath her.

Mine. My *mate*. Firelight sparkled on the diamond on her finger, reflecting her happiness.

My mate in all ways.

"Cass." Diego's voice was dark, and so were his eyes as he slid inside her.

Then they were joined. Cassidy ached for him, and at the same time, her body opened and drew him inside her. The mating frenzy began.

Cassidy moved against him, and Diego pushed up into her, both of them touching, kissing, hands everywhere.

"*Mi ja*, I love you," he said.

"I love you, Diego," Cassidy said, but she couldn't keep her voice quiet. "*Querido.*"

Diego's answering smile drove heat through her. Then he started loving her as though he'd never stop.

Their joined voices rang out into the night as mating frenzy played out then wound down into solid love. The mate bond wound around Cassidy's heart, and she opened to it, and let it come.

EPILOGUE

Under the light of the next full moon, Eric blessed Cassidy and Diego as mates in the sight of the Goddess. The sun blessing had happened that afternoon, and the Shifters were still a little drunk from that ceremony.

Now the true partying began. Shifters howled and yowled, roared and shouted. A mating. Another joining, more cubs, Shifters continuing.

The dancing began. Xavier and Lindsay found each other, soon had arms around each other's waists, holding beers and swaying. Nell and Diego's mother were talking loudly together and laughing, probably at all the men present.

The new Shifter cubs ran around screaming with Torey and other Shiftertown cubs, already finding their places. Peigi and Reid sat together on Nell's porch, very close together.

Eric watched Shane lift a beer bottle to Diego and Cassidy, who were kissing. Who had been kissing for about ten minutes now.

"You're lucky I like you, Diego," Shane said. "Take care of her."

Diego looked around at him and grinned, then Cassidy turned Diego's face back to hers for more kissing.

Eric silently saluted them, glad in his heart. Diego had given Cassidy back her life. Eric would love his new brother forever for that.

Only a couple more things left to do tonight. Eric turned from the revelry and approached Peigi, drawing the Collar out of his pocket.

Reid saw him coming and stood up. "No."

"Sorry," Eric said. "It's got to be done. Peigi, if the others see you do it first, and that you aren't afraid, they'll follow you. They need someone to follow."

Peigi nodded. She had guts, Eric gave her that.

Reid got in his face. "You leave her alone. I'm taking her away from here."

"You can't run," Eric said. "You'd be running forever, and the humans will discover her sooner or later. You know that." He looked into Reid's dark Fae eyes. "Someday it won't be like this. We'll win in the end. Understand?"

Reid scowled. "But what about now? What about Peigi?"

"The good news is, this won't hurt a bit. I found a loophole. Peigi? You ready?"

Peigi nodded and stood up. "Stuart. It's all right."

Reid still looked furious, but Peigi gently pushed him aside and faced Eric, head up. "They're watching. Do it now."

Eric sensed the tense gazes of the other Shifter women on them, smelled their fear. He stepped to Peigi, slid the Collar around her neck, and locked it in place.

Peigi tensed, eyes going Shifter white, then she blinked. She touched the Collar, at first hesitantly, then more boldly, and looked at Eric in confusion.

"Looks real, doesn't it?" Eric asked. "I got a nice supply, courtesy of my friends in Austin. Jace brought them back." His smile died. "But you have to help me. The other females have to behave as though the Collar is real, and you'll have to help them adjust here so they can heal from what Miguel did to them. You'll have to keep an eye on them, to make sure they recover and don't go feral. Can you do that?"

Peigi stared at him wordlessly, then she nodded.

Eric embraced her and touched his cheek to hers. "Peigi, I release you from the mate-claim." He let her go and gave Reid a grin. "Now, go party."

He walked away, leaving the two of them staring at each other in shock.

Iona sat on her back porch, enjoying full moonlight on her face, her wildcat itching to come out.

No. The neighbors might see. Hear me. Call the zoo.

She'd just have to content herself with sitting out here to enjoy the feel of the moon. It made her happy somehow.

He came to her in silence, moving through shadows until suddenly he was in front of her, silhouetted against the silver light.

"Damn it, Eric," Iona said after her heart came down from her throat. "Will you stop *doing* that?"

Eric didn't bother to apologize. "You all right?"

"Yes, why wouldn't I be?"

"Good." Eric sat down on the edge of her porch, swaying a little.

"Are you drunk?" she asked.

"My sister is fully mated tonight. Sun and moon. It's a good party. You should come."

"Not hardly."

Eric laughed. A full-throated, deep laugh, one that made Iona's stomach do flips and her blood burn.

Eric got to his feet with liquid grace, pulled Iona up with him, held her face between his hands, and kissed her. His mouth was hot, spicy, lips warm.

He eased back from the kiss, and Iona stopped herself from leaning to him, from silently begging for more.

"I'll bring you in, Iona," Eric said. "And when I do, that will be a good day. A very good day. I'm looking forward to it."

He kissed her again, hands and mouth mastering.

Then Eric flowed away from her, melting into the shadows. The good scent of him lingered an instant before that too vanished, leaving Iona alone in the moonlight, and breathless.

Turn the page for a special preview of the next
Shifters Unbound novel by Jennifer Ashley

MATE CLAIMED

Coming October 2012 from Berkley Sensation!

Iona smelled him long before she saw him—Eric Warden, the alpha Feline who ran the local Shiftertown and who'd decided to make Iona's life hell.

She loped on down the desert canyon, sand grating on her paws. The Nevada night was hot, the sky a riot of stars, the glow of the city far behind. Out here, Iona could be what she was meant to be—a wildcat, a Feline Shifter, running free. Alone, where what she was wouldn't hurt the human mother who'd helped her hide for more than thirty years.

For some reason, Eric wanted to end that.

Catch me if you can, Feline.

Iona ran on, the canyon's rock walls rising around her. She knew by scent how far she was from Area 51, a place no Shifter was stupid enough to run to. The other direction, east and north, was safer.

Last night, Iona had stayed out until dawn, celebrating her sister's engagement with about fifty friends—all human. They'd gone to a human bar, no Shifters allowed, thank God. They'd liberated the bar of plenty of margaritas before limping out in the light of early morning. Iona didn't even remember how she'd gotten home.

The frenzy of that night out followed by the hangover of the day had triggered Iona's need to shift. After work, despite her exhaustion, Iona had driven her red pickup out to her favorite spot in the middle of the desert, off-roading half an hour to get there. She'd barely shed her clothes before her wildcat had taken over.

And now Eric was following her.

He pounded behind her, a powerhouse Shifter Feline, his wildcat more snow leopard than anything else. Sleek, strong, cunning. Feline Shifters had been bred to be a mixture of all wildcats—lion, leopard, jaguar, cheetah, tiger, and others—but most Shifters leaned toward a certain type.

Iona's wildcat tended toward panther, with a black pelt to match the hair she had while human. Her panther was long-legged, sure-footed, and a good jumper. This was her territory, and she'd leave Eric Warden far behind.

Iona dodged across a dry wash, kicking up dust in her wake, and scrambled up into the rocky crevices on the other side of it. She hopped from one sandstone ledge to the next, moving up the canyon wall, her paws scrabbling a little.

In spite of Eric's pursuit, she loved this. The joy of being in wild country nearly impossible for humans to reach was heady. *This is what I'm meant to be.*

Damned if Eric didn't follow right after her, faster than she'd thought possible. Iona crested the ridge at the top of the canyon and kept going.

She ran along a ledge and dropped into another wash that snaked down the other side of the mountain. Before she got to the bottom, she ducked into a shallow cave she knew was there from previous exploration. From the top of the ridge, it would look as though she'd vanished.

But Eric didn't need to see her to find her. He'd scent her. Ever since he'd spotted her in Coolers, one of the few clubs that allowed in Shifters, Eric had tracked her. Not that Iona had gone to the club as a Shifter—no one knew she was Shifter. Her human friends had dragged her there so they could watch Shifters and Shifter groupies, fascinated by the whole scene for some reason.

Eric's scent had triggered something in Iona from the moment he'd sat down next to her in the club's dark corner and told her he knew what Iona was. He'd filled her senses with a spicy scent like cardamom and cloves, and a musk that made everything female in her aware of his maleness. Not that his tall, hard-muscled body and tatt swirling down his arm hadn't dragged at her also.

His scent was stronger now, overlaid with that of his wildcat. He was coming.

Iona ducked into the cave's black shadows, but Eric was at the entrance, his leopard filling the opening, looking straight at her.

Iona faced him, ears flat against her head, fur rising on her neck.

Eric didn't move. Dominants didn't need to show teeth or attack to tell another Shifter who was in charge. They just looked at you.

His wildcat was larger than a normal snow leopard, his head nearly square on heavy shoulders. His pelt was creamy white and branded with the black jagged pattern of a leopard. Eric's eyes, fixed on her, were jade green.

Iona's wildcat was more slender than Eric's but no smaller, though it would be an interesting contest to see whether she matched him in strength. The biggest difference between them, though, was that Eric wore a silver and black Collar, and Iona didn't.

Eric rose on his hind legs until his head nearly touched the roof of the cave, then his fur and cat limbs flowed into human bones and flesh. His face was hard and square, like the leopard's, his chocolate brown hair close-cropped. A black tattoo swirled around his large shoulder and trailed down his arm in a jagged, stylized design. The tattoo wasn't magical— Shifters didn't need tatts. Eric simply liked it.

His green eyes saw everything. There was no escaping his gaze when it fixed on you, even across a packed Las Vegas club. Iona still remembered feeling the burn of his stare across the bar; Eric was the first person in Iona's life besides her mother and sister who'd looked at her and recognized her as Shifter.

Iona's hormones kicked in, even through her worry and anger. Eric was a delectable man. He put to shame all the guys who'd tried to dance with her last night.

What was between Eric's legs would probably put them to shame too. The man was *hung*.

"You can't keep this up," Eric said. His voice, deep and fine, with the barest touch of Scots, had lately started invading her dreams.

Damned hormones. Iona needed to get away from him.

She gave Eric a snarl to let him know he didn't worry her. Which was bullshit. He could take her in a heartbeat and both of them knew it.

"Can you, Iona?" Eric took one step forward.

Iona sprang past him for the mouth of the cave. His leopard she couldn't outrun, but she could outrun him when he was human. She barreled out into the rocks . . .

And found two hundred pounds of leopard pinning her to the ledge. His breath was hot in her face, and she looked straight up into his jade green eyes.

Iona had never been able to shift that fast. Shifting took a while for her, and it could be painful. Eric had flowed into his wildcat so smoothly it made her sick.

Eric's growl became bad-tempered as Iona struggled. He opened his terrifying jaws and locked his teeth around her throat.

Fur protected Iona from the prick of his fangs, but she panicked. He could kill her right now, rip out her throat or slice her belly wide open. Iona couldn't fight him—he was too strong. She couldn't get away—he was too fast. She'd die far from help, never see her mother and sister again.

Iona shifted. She didn't want to, but some instinct took over, told her he wouldn't hurt her if she became a human. She felt her paws sprout fingers and toes, her pelt fade and withdraw to become human flesh.

Eric lifted his mouth from her throat, but he didn't do anything to stop her shifting. He simply waited and watched until Iona was a human woman with a large, soft-furred snow leopard draped across her bare body.

The large, soft-furred snow leopard suddenly became a man. Eric's shift was so smooth it amazed her. Iona quickly ceased being amazed when Eric, the strong human male, pinned her to the ground with shocking strength.

She struggled, but Eric trapped her wrists and held them against the cold ground. He wanted her to look away as he stared her down, but she couldn't look away. Somehow Iona knew that if she did, she'd lose—not just now, but always.

"I told you to call me when you needed to go out running," Eric said.

"So? You followed me anyway. Why should I bother calling?"

Eric's weight held her harder. "I found you tonight because I was on my way to talk to you. I saw you take off, scented you fighting the shift even as you drove away."

Iona struggled again, but it was like trying to budge a large boulder. "Why can't you leave me the hell alone? If anyone finds out I'm Shifter . . ."

She knew exactly what they'd do. The human Shifter bureau would slap a Collar on her without listening to her protests, strip Iona of all her rights, and keep her in quarantine before releasing her to whatever Shifter they designated to keep her under control. Three guesses as to who that Shifter would be.

On the other hand, they might simply kill her. And who the hell knew what they'd do to Iona's mother, who'd kept the fact that Iona was half Shifter quiet all this time?

"I can't leave you alone, because you're in my jurisdiction," Eric said. "And you're losing control, aren't you?"

Iona shivered with more than anger. His long body was hard on hers, muscles gleaming with sweat in the moonlight. Eric's living strength made the wild thing in her want to respond with fire.

"I was hung over," she said. "I'm not like this every day."

Eric lowered his head and inhaled her scent, his nose touching her throat. "You will be soon. How did you survive the Transition?"

"What transition? What are you talking about?"

"From cub to adulthood. You should have done it a few years ago. The Transition is your body telling you it's ready for you to find your place in the pride, to start looking for a mate."

Iona stopped, her heart squeezing. "Is *that* what that was?"

"Tell me what happened."

Eric's breath was warm on her, his hard thigh just fitting

between her legs. It was difficult to think with him on top of
her, difficult even to breathe.

"I wanted to fight everyone, all the time," she said, remembering. She'd thought she was going insane. "I couldn't stop
it. And I hurt all over. Every day."

Iona had tried to stay as far away from her mother and sister—from everyone—as possible. She'd gone up to the family
cabin in the mountains, where she'd let herself shift and run
and run. That had helped, but only a little.

Eric's voice went quiet. "You must be very strong, Iona, to
have made it through alone." He sounded admiring.

"I thought I was going to die."

"You were lucky. I remember what I did during *my* Transition." He chuckled softly, which moved his body on hers
in the best way. "I wanted to fight and challenge anyone—
everyone. My sister kept threatening to hit me with a frying
pan, those big cast-iron ones we had a hundred years ago."

Iona suddenly wanted to meet this sister. "You obviously
got through it."

"Because I had help, had a family and a clan. You have
nothing. You're alone, open for a mate-claim by any male who
chances on you. And your mating need is high, isn't it?"

That need swirled through her, tried to make Iona's body
rise to his. *A male, ready for you, take him now!*

"What I do is none of your business," Iona managed to say.
"Leave me the hell alone, Eric. My life has been fine so far
without you in it."

"But I'm in it now." His voice was deep and rumbling,
almost a purr. The tattoo that wound down his arm kept drawing her gaze, and she so much wanted to touch it . . .

For Eric's part, he was barely holding on to his self-control.
Iona's scent was that of a female Feline who'd recently reached
her fertile years, a little over thirty by human standards, a few
years past cub by Shifter. This female Feline didn't know how
to control her pheromones, didn't realize she was broadcast-
ing her availability to every Shifter male far and wide. She
might as well hold up a flashing sign.

Good thing Eric was so disciplined, still mourning his
mate lost long ago, so uninterested in mating. Right?

Or he'd be hard as a rock, wanting to say, *To hell with it,* and take her. They were in the middle of nowhere, and Eric was within his rights to take whatever stray adult female wandered into his territory.

He didn't necessarily have to mate-claim her. As clan leader as well as pride leader, he could father cubs on an unmated female belonging to no pride or clan if he wanted to. For the good of the clan, for the strength of his pride. So he could claim.

But those had been the rules in the wild. Shifters were tamer, now, civilized. Living together in a community, in harmony. *And all that crap.*

Eric's instincts said, *Screw the rules. She's unmated and unclaimed. By rights, she's fair game, and I found her. That makes her mine.*

Wouldn't that be sweet? Iona Duncan had a face that was pure Celtic, her hair black as the night sky, her eyes the light ice blue of her ancestors. Shifters had been created about the time the Nordic invaders would have been subduing Celts in northern Scotland, and some of that mixture had gotten into Iona.

Now her soft but strong body was under his, and her blue eyes held longing, oceans of it.

"Does it hurt?" Eric asked in a gentler tone.

"Having a big Shifter male resting his weight on my wrists? I'd say yes."

Eric wanted to laugh. He liked the challenge in her, liked that she wasn't cringing, timid, and submissive. Untrained, yes; terrified, no.

"I mean the mating need," Eric said. "It's rising in you, and you can't stop it. That's why you're out here, why you've been running around out here like a crazy thing. You want to be wild, to taste the wind. To hunt. To feel the fear in you flow to the innocent creatures out there, to make them fear *you*."

Iona stopped squirming, her gaze fixing, pupils widening, spreading black through the blue. Eric read the hunger in her, the need to find a male, to mate in wild frenzy for days. Iona wasn't stopped by a Collar. Her instincts would flow like fire. Untamed.

Eric's own need rose in response. He wanted to kiss that fire, to taste the freedom in her that was now only a memory to him.

He leaned to nuzzle the line of her hair, already knowing her scent, already familiar with it.

"I'll take care of you, Iona," he said. "You'll become part of my clan, and I'll look after you. Me and my sister and my son. We'll take care of you from now on."

Iona's glare returned. "I don't *want* to be part of your pride, damn you. They'd put that Collar on me." Her frenzied gaze went to the chain fused to Eric's neck, the Celtic knot resting on his throat. "It's painful, isn't it? When the Collar goes on?"

"Yes." Eric couldn't lie. He remembered the agony when the Collar had locked around his neck, every second of it, though it had been twenty years ago now. The Collars hurt anew whenever a Shifter's violent nature rose within him— the Collar shocked so hard it knocked said Shifter flat on his ass for a while.

"Why would you want me to experience that?" Iona asked. "You say you want to take care of me, but you want me to go through taking the Collar?"

"No, I don't." And if Eric did things right, she wouldn't have to wear a Collar, ever.

The urge to take Iona far away, to hide her somewhere from prying eyes, to protect her from all was making him crazy. *Protect the mate* was the instinct that drove all males.

He controlled himself with effort. "But if you don't acknowledge the Shifter, if you don't figure out how to control what's going on inside you, you're going to go feral."

"What the hell does that mean?"

"It means what it sounds like. The beast in you will take over, and you'll forget what it is to be human, even in your human form. You'll live only to kill and to mate. You'll start resenting your family for trying to keep you home. You'll try to get away from them. You might even hurt them."

Iona looked stunned. "I'd never do that."

"You won't mean to, but you will. You can keep them safe if you learn to be Shifter and live with Shifters. I won't let humans know anything about you until the Collar is on you and you're ready."

Iona struggled again. "My point is that humans should never have to *know* I'm Shifter. No one has ever suspected, but they will if an asshole Shifter keeps following me around."

Eric held her hard, at the end of his patience. "Iona, if you go feral, they might not bother Collaring you. They'll just shoot you like an animal, and your mother might go to prison for not reporting your existence. Is that what you want?"

He felt her fear reaction, but Iona kept up her glare. "I'm half human. Won't that keep me from going feral?"

Eric shook his head. "Sometimes that happens. Sometimes it doesn't."

"I am not going to meekly give up my whole life to live with you in a ghetto because you say I *might* go crazy. I'll risk it."

Eric tightened his hold. "I can't let you go on living without protection."

"The hell you can't. How do you plan to protect me? Abduct me and lock me in your house? What would the human police say to that?"

Taking her home and keeping her there was exactly what Eric wanted to do.

At any other time, he'd simply do it. Iona was nearly out of control, and she needed help. But Shiftertown might not be the safest place for her at the moment, now that the idiot human government had decided to shut down a northern Nevada Shiftertown and relocate all those Shifters to Eric's. The humans, in their ignorance, had decided that the new Shifters would simply be absorbed under Eric's leadership.

What the humans didn't understand—despite Eric talking himself blue to explain—was that Shifters of both Shiftertowns were used to a certain hierarchy and couldn't change it overnight. The other Shiftertown leader was being forced to step down a few rungs under Eric, which wasn't going over well, especially since that leader was a Feline-hating Lupine.

Eric had at least persuaded the humans to let him meet the other leader, Graham McNeil, face-to-face. Eric had found McNeil to be a disgruntled, old-fashioned Shifter, furious that the humans were forcing him to submit to Eric's rule.

Graham McNeil was going to be trouble. He already had been, demanding more meetings with humans without Eric, insisting that Eric's Shifters got turned out of their houses and crammed in with others so McNeil's Shifters wouldn't have to wait for the new housing to be built. McNeil was going to challenge for leadership—Eric had known that before the man had opened his mouth. McNeil's Shiftertown had been all Lupine, and his Lupines were less than thrilled to learn that they had to adapt to living with bears and Felines.

And in the middle of all this, a young, fertile female with the rising need to mate was running around loose and unprotected.

Iona struggled to sit up again. It went against Eric's every instinct to lift himself from the cushion of her sensual body, but he did it.

Iona leaned against the rock wall and scraped her hair back from her face. Goddess, she was lovely, bare-breasted in the moonlight, lifting midnight hair from her sharp-boned face. Naked and beautiful, filling Eric's brain with wanting. *And* if he did this right, she might provide the answer to some of his Shiftertown problems.

"I was coming to see you tonight for a reason," Eric said. "Not just to track you down. I came to ask you to have Duncan Construction bid on the housing project to expand Shiftertown."

Iona stared at him in shock, letting go of the hair she'd been smoothing. "Why on earth would I want to do that?"

"Because the truth is, Iona, I need someone I can trust to build these houses. Shifter houses aren't just places for Shifters to live. I need them constructed in a way that's best for Shifters. It's important."

Iona looked curious, in spite of her caution. "What do you mean, in a way that's best for Shifters?"

Eric couldn't explain—yet. He'd have to wait before he revealed to her that Shifter houses didn't simply hold Shifter families. They held secrets that humans could never know about. Even McNeil would need to protect the secrets of his clan, probably why the man wanted the Shifter houses already there. Eric had planned to modify the new houses the same way he and his Shifters had modified the old houses over time, but using Iona's company and guiding her through the process could help both her and Shiftertown—if he was canny.

"I can't tell you until you win the contract." Eric said. He met her gaze, not disguising anything in his. "Please."

"Are you saying you need my help, Eric Warden?"

"Yes." He said it simply, no shame attached.

"And what do I get in return? You leave me alone?"

Eric felt a grin spread across his face. "I can't leave you alone, Iona, love. You're unmated and unclaimed, in my territory. I need to look after you. But I think we can come up with some kind of agreement."

"Oh, really? Why should I trust you? The moment I enter your Shiftertown, all the Shifters there will know what I am. This has to be another ploy to out me."

Eric shook his head. "Your sister or your mother can be the on-site manager. You never have to leave your office if you don't want to."

Iona wrapped her arms around her knees, gathering herself in. Her naked limbs exuded beauty. "Never leave my office? Never go to Shiftertown? Seriously?"

"Seriously. I'd come to you."

Iona looked annoyed that Eric didn't mean she'd never have to see him. "I'll think about it."

Eric moved to her side again but kept himself from touching her. "I really do need you, Iona. And you need me. Think of it as an opportunity to better understand your Shifter side."

"I'm not sure I want to understand my Shifter side."

"Yes, you do. You're going wild, and you need to learn how to contain it."

Iona shivered, looking away, and Eric's protective need came to life again. He wanted to fold her in his arms, take her home, keep her safe.

When Iona looked up again, her fear was raw. "What do I do?"

Eric nuzzled her, inhaling her ripe, sensual scent. "I'll help you through this. But you have to trust me."

Iona went still, but he sensed her body reacting to his. She wanted him, and everything in Eric knew it, and responded.

"You have to give me reason to trust you," she said.

"No, sweetheart. *Trust* means believing in me even when you don't understand."

Eric nuzzled her again, and Iona let him, not pulling away. He'd scent-marked her the first night he'd met her so that any Shifter who did come across her would smell Eric on her. A scent marking was not the same as a mate-claim—Eric could

scent-mark his children, his siblings, and anyone else he needed
to—but it did mean that Iona was under Eric's protection. Any
Shifter finding her would know he'd need to deal with Eric
if he messed with Iona. Even Graham McNeil would understand that, though whether Graham would leave her alone was
another question.

Eric breathed his scent on her again as he brushed the line
of her neck, renewing the mark. Goddess, she was sweet. She
smelled clean like a mountain meadow, but her underlying
scent was warm with wanting.

Eric made himself sit up and push away from her, rising in
one move. Before Iona could scramble to her feet herself, he
reached down and hauled her up next to him.

Eric cupped her shoulders. His human side was fully aware
of her nudity and the petal-soft feel of her skin. Her breasts
were full, the tips dusky, and the twist of hair between her legs
as black as that on her head. Beautiful.

"You need me, Iona," Eric said.

Iona took a step back, breaking the contact. "You need *me*,
you mean."

"In theory."

"Chew on this theory, Eric. I'm not one of your mate-
claimed females, or whatever you call them. I'll give you what
you need to build your Shiftertown houses, and you'll leave
me the hell alone. Bargain?" She stuck out her hand.

Eric looked at the hand, offering a handshake in the human
way. He didn't bother to take it. "No bargains, Iona. We do
what's necessary."

Iona was gorgeous when she was fired up, blue eyes hot,
her stance challenging. Eric's reaction to her was obvious,
even in the dark.

Iona's gaze dropped down his body, stopping at his very
erect . . . erection. She put one hand on her bare hip and kept
her voice light. "So, what is that? An extension of your tail?"

Eric shrugged, unembarrassed. "I'm a male Shifter at the
prime of life, and you're a female entering her hottest mating
years. What do you think it is?"

Iona's eyes flickered, her need strong. Her pheromones
filled the air until Eric swore he could taste them. "Damn it,"
she whispered.

She shifted to her wildcat. She couldn't shift as swiftly as Eric could, and Eric saw that it was painful for her. His hard-on faded as he watched her struggle, but his wanting for her didn't die. Iona was beautiful, and wild, and he wanted her to be free. And safe.

Iona bounded past him. Her wildcat was sure-footed and fast, her pelt beautifully dark, her eyes as ice blue as her human eyes.

Eric watched in pure enjoyment before he fluidly shifted and ran after her.

Graham McNeil watched the humans shrink back in a satisfying way when he walked into the meeting room at the courthouse. The waiting humans tried not to react to him, pretending they had all the power, but Graham knew he'd soon rule this room.

The only person who didn't look intimidated was Eric Warden, the leader of the Vegas Shiftertown. Not leader for long, if Graham had anything to say about it.

The humans didn't like Graham's buzz of black hair, the fiery tatts down his arms, and his motorcycle vest. Eric had a tatt as well, jagged lines down one arm that started somewhere under his short-sleeved black T-shirt.

Graham wasn't an idiot, though. Eric was going to be a problem. Warden was a strong alpha and had been leader of his Shiftertown for a long time. As soon as Graham walked in, Eric's jade green eyes fixed on Graham's and stayed there.

The shithead wanted Graham to look away. To acknowledge that Graham was going to be second, maybe way less than that. Pussy.

Graham wasn't about to look away. Neither was Eric. Graham felt his hackles rise, the wolf in him ready to shift. Eric's eyes flicked to his cat's, slitted and very light green.

They'd have stared each other down for hours if a clueless human male, having no idea that a dominance fight was in progress, hadn't walked between them.

"Mr. McNeil," the man said. "Sit down, please."

"Graham's fine." He'd rather remain standing, a better position for facing an enemy, but humans had a thing for chairs.

They wanted Graham to sit next to Eric. Idiots. Eric proved he wasn't stupid by walking to the other end of the table and planting himself in a chair, leaving Graham to sit at the opposite end.

What did the humans expect Graham to do? Shake Eric's hand, give him a big hug, wait for Eric to say, *Welcome to my territory; let's be friends?*

They did by the look of things. Amazing.

Graham's Shiftertown had been tucked inside a mountain range south of Elko, a long way from anywhere, and he and his people had done pretty much what they wanted. A liaison with a check sheet came around every once in a while to make sure Shifters were behaving themselves and not eating people or whatever they thought Shifters would do, and then he'd go.

In this effing city, there were humans everywhere. They smelled like shit. Even Eric smelled wrong.

Graham had seen, on the way to this meeting, a sign on the top of a taxi advertising Shifter women dancing nude in clubs just off the Strip. Females, taking off their clothes for human males. That had to stop.

He felt Eric's eyes on him again, and Graham shot him a hard look.

It's begun, Graham's gaze promised. *You're going down.*

The trouble was, he was getting the same message back from Eric. This was going to be a long, bloody fight. The humans in this room had no idea what they'd just started.